But a
Walking
Shadow

But a
Walking
Shadow

Jacquee Storozynski-Toll

authorHOUSE®

AuthorHouse™ UK Ltd.
500 Avebury Boulevard
Central Milton Keynes, MK9 2BE
www.authorhouse.co.uk
Phone: 08001974150

First published by AuthorHouse 4/19/2011

ISBN: 978-1-4567-7726-5 (sc)
ISBN: 978-1-4567-7727-2 (dj)

With grateful thanks to my husband Malcolm Toll, Martyn Waites and Heather Myers for their support and encouragement.

CHAPTER ONE

'O mother; mother! What have you done? Behold, the heavens do ope, the gods look down, and this unnatural scene they laugh at.'
                                                    Coriolanus Act 5 Sc 3

It came again. That horror. How could I have thought that it had gone forever? Desperately I resisted and struggled, a crushing weight on my chest grinding into me as I tried to cry out,

'Help me! Help me!'

The words crackled from my lips as bony fingers tightened on my throat, choking my breath from me. My eyelids seemed glued together, and no amount of effort could prise them apart. I was paralysed, and unable to move. My whole body trapped by some unknown suffocating presence. Hysteria rising and rigid with fear, I clenched my teeth, agonisingly struggling for my life. Over and over I tried to convince myself that it was only that familiar childhood nightmare, only now there were no words of comfort and reassurance from a caring mother.

At last I prised my eyes open and saw what I most dreaded. That grotesque figure's demented bloodshot eyes staring into mine. The hideous thing cackling at me, laughing insanely. A monstrous gargoyle, crouching, grinning and salivating in the gloom. The slime dripping down in globules from his cavernous mouth. I screamed out loud and as I did so the skeletonal fingers released their grip and the monster faded into a transparent shade, the weight lifted and I was free.

Shaken I leapt from the bed and frantically looked around but there was no one there. I was alone in an unfamiliar half furnished cold and dirty room. Shivering with cold I caught sight of my white face in the mirror, a phantom in the dawn's early light. Beads of perspiration trickled down my face and I scrubbed them frantically away, leaving salty traces on my lips. I brushed away the damp hair that clung to my face, only to find that the strands were imaginary wisps and I desperately tried to rub away the invisible hair that stuck to my wet skin. Shuddering and gasping, I realised that the nightmare that had haunted my dreams in childhood had just been laying dormant, waiting to return.

Confused I looked around at the unfamiliar surroundings, trying to make sense of it all. Then I remembered. This was Stoneleigh. I had passed an anxious night in a room in my dead sister's home. The glorious, ornate building full of riches, where she had lived after her marriage to Roland Fitzroy. The grand, castellated building that I left only five years ago, which last night had greeted me with horror and decay?

The torn pieces of the letter lay on the floor and as I reached out for them a stabbing pain shot through my arm. A deep bloody scratch showed through the ripped folds of my sleeve where I had caught it on the tangled branches, as I had made my way in the moonlight. Instead of the welcome I expected, I had to find my way through the overhanging branches that obscured the path that led down to the entrance. Tripping and ducking through the bushes of the landscaped garden that was now so unrecognisable, the area so run down that if it was not for the turrets in the distance I would have thought I was in the wrong place.

Although still in my outdoor clothes I shivered with cold. What had possessed me, Aphra Devereaux, to have travelled here from Paris? My frozen fingers toyed with the pieces of the unsigned letter that had led me to this place of dread. Who was that large woman in the bright pink dress that had opened the door? Why had Roland greeted me with such fury and shoved us both with such force that this woman and myself fell in a crumpled heap on the marble steps? I could make no sense of it. What had happened to change everything? The picture of him cursing me so vehemently was imprinted in my brain. Why had my dead sister's husband been so frightening and unrecognisable?

I tried to warm myself, rubbing my shoulders, ignoring the pain in my arm as I recalled how Roland had greeted me, screaming at me insanely. The man I remembered was now so different. His face had been puffy and swollen and he appeared so thin and stooped, as he loomed over me. The unknown, large woman had pulled herself to her feet, screaming back at him and had forced herself in between us to protect me. Forlornly trying to

2

suppress the tears, I desperately wanted to leave the place that had held such promise and where I had known such happiness. My first thoughts were only to run away, but I had nowhere to run to.

Now sad and alone in this dirty, dust covered bedroom, I was endlessly going over the events of the night before. Why had my brother in law been so angry at my arrival? I had tried to explain about the letter, but he wrenched it from my hand and tore it into pieces, throwing the bits in the air. He had grabbed me as I scrabbled in the dark to pick them up, and shaken me so violently that my head spun. The force ripped my hat from my head and my unruly hair had tumbled down. In an instant he let out a terrible animalistic howl that sent a shudder through me. Yanking my hair so hard it jolted my head back, he hit his own head violently against the door frame. All the time screaming obscenities in a strangulated voice.

'What do you want? Who told you to come? Leave me alone!'

Then he manhandled us both off the step and slamming his fist into the door, he stormed away. The woman and I had stared at each other, unable to speak, as she helped me and we both gave an involuntary start at the sound of an interior door crashing shut.

I did not understand what was happening. I had been excitedly looking forward to staying in my dead sister's home. The place I had spent so many happy hours with the Fitzroy family after she married Roland, but now his behaviour seemed insane. The woman had smiled at me and tidying her greying, blonde hair had asked in a London East End accent,

'What yer doing 'ere miss?'

I had tried to explain about the letter, now in shreds, but the words stuck in my throat. Instead I mumbled incoherently as she placed an oil lamp close to my face and said,

You're 'er wot died's sister ain't yer? Yes, I can see it now. Same red 'air.' As she spoke I tried to cram the curls back under my hat as she handed me the light and pointed the way up a grim staircase where I wandered along dark corridors until I found a cold, damp room to spend the night. There I had spent a miserable time clutching my cloak around me trying to keep warm. All the while feeling terrified of noise and shadows, in case it was Roland coming to berate me again.

At last I had fallen into an exhausted sleep only to be awoken this morning by my childhood night terrors. During my sister's time this house had been so grand, yet now it seemed dark and threatening. I tiptoed to the door and peered down the long corridor. Everywhere was still and I could see that all the paintings and ornaments had disappeared. Stoneleigh was not the place I remembered. I sat down on the hard, bed in despair, uncertain what to do, as I did so I heard the door creak open to reveal the lady from the previous night, still dressed in her pink finery. She was perspiring and out of breath from climbing the stairs and clung on to the door frame for support.

'God all mighty! I ain't managed all them stairs for years. It's me 'eart,' she exclaimed gasping for air, 'She smiled at me as I waved the pieces of letter at her.

'Did you send me the letter?' I asked.

'Not me! I ain't got no learning.'

'Well someone did.' I replied. I came all the way from France because I thought I would be welcome. I thought that Roland would be pleased to see me.'

She smiled forlornly, folding her arms across a well padded breast.

'E ain't well.'

'Are you the housekeeper?'

'Lord no. There ain't no money for no servants.'

Miserably, I murmured,

'I shouldn't have come.'

' No. What was yer thinking of?'

I looked around at the dirty room devoid of all luxury with only bare floorboards and sighing said,

'I do not know. I thought...' I did not continue. There was nothing to say. It did not matter. My hopes of a new life after my father's death were as nothing. It was all a mistake. I sighed heavily and picked up my travelling bag. I had no change of clothes as my trunk had been sent separately and I mournfully picked at my torn, bloodied sleeve, trying to repair it.

The woman came over for a closer inspection.

'You've 'urt yer arm. I spect yer did it on them blooming bushes. They're a death trap, but there ain't no one to look after 'em now. I'll fetch yer some water and yer can bathe it.'

'Thank you, but please do not bother. I can see the stairs are too much for you. It is quite dry now and I have no other clothes to change.' She nodded and we both stood in embarrassed silence. All my hopes had been placed on an expected welcome from Freya's husband. The least I expected was that I could stay happily in my sister's house. Standing up, my bones stiff with cold, I wrapped the stained bed cover around me and tried to warm my frozen hands by blowing on them. She observed me in silence as with my breath turning to steam in the cold air, I tried to rub some of the smears off the dirty windows and look out. In the distance of the early morning light I could see the remains of the roman folly. It had been a place where Freya and I had spent so many happy hours talking and laughing, wandering amongst the classical statues that decorated the landscaping that led down to the lake. Now everywhere was overgrown and unrecognisable, yet it had previously been maintained by legions of staff. Sadly I asked,

'What happened? Stoneleigh was such a wonderful place, with parties and balls, now it looks deserted. Everywhere is so unkempt. Where are the carpets? Where are all the paintings? There used to be a crystal chandelier on the stairway. Where has it all gone?

'No money left,' she said in a matter of fact tone and sat down heavily on the bed.

'How can it be? The family has the estate. Surely Edmund must be aware of the situation? What is he doing about it?'

At the mention of Edmund's name her eyes brightened but she did not reply. I continued trying to obtain answers. Five years ago, the day before I left for Paris my sister had held a grand county ball in a place that in those few years had become unrecognisable. Shaking my head in disbelief I sighed,

'Edmund and I danced the night away. Now the place seems like a house of shadows.'

'You must have been no more than a child then?' She smiled in a motherly fashion.

'I was sixteen.' Forlornly I toyed with the pieces of paper and replaced them in their rightful order and read the words out loud.

'Come to Stoneleigh. Your sister's child needs you.'

As I did so, I sensed a change in the woman's expression and seizing the moment I quickly asked,

'Do you know about this child? My sister died in child birth, didn't she? Did the child live?'

The woman squirmed uncomfortably and whispered,

'I don't know nothing 'bout anyfing.'

'But you are the housekeeper. You must know what happens here.'

Affronted she stood up and pulled herself into a majestic pose, tottering slightly as she did so, 'I told yer before, I ain't no housekeeper. Me name is Rosie. I'm a friend of the family.'

I stared in amazement, this woman was much too lower class to be a family friend? I could not believe that she was not one of the servants.

'A friend?' I tried to keep the astonishment I felt out of my voice. Her expression now one of resentment she tossed her head disdainfully and began walking grandly around the room.

'If it weren't for me, where would 'e be? That is what I'd like to know. I have cared for 'im when everyone else 'as abandoned him.'

'I don't understand.' I said weakly.

'I told yer. You shouldn't ave come.' She said in an affronted manner and indignantly left the room, grandly holding up the edges of her frayed, pink silk dress. I heard her heavy breathing as she made her way downstairs. It was all most strange if this woman wasn't the housekeeper what was she doing there?

Disconsolately I sought to wash my face but when I picked up a nearby china ewer I hastily put it down. It was full of dead insects floating in greenish liquid. The water had obviously been standing for some time and with disgust I struggled to open a cracked window and threw out its contents. As I did so, I heard the doorknob rattle and I quickly slammed the window shut and held up the jug as a weapon, in case it was Roland. Heart pounding I watched as the door edged open but to my surprise it revealed a small child in the doorway. She was dirty with lank, greasy hair and was clutching a piece of material that could possibly once have been silk, but was now unrecognisable, wrapped around a dirty rag doll. Thin and undernourished, she stared at me with large eyes that seemed too big for her white face. Relieved it wasn't Roland I smiled at her, but she did not speak and continued to stare at me. She was clad in a thin cotton shift, but did not seem to be aware of the cold. The small figure stood there frozen like a little statue.

'Come in,' I smiled, 'you will catch cold; let me put my cloak round you and keep you warm.'

I moved towards her, but she quickly scampered out of the room. I ran behind her but she disappeared down the endless corridor. For a moment I thought I was dreaming again, but then I noticed the scatter of footprints in the disturbed dust on the landing. Slowly I followed them as they led up staircase after staircase, but still there was no sign of her. At last I had reached the attic area, and still hadn't found the child.

The footprints suddenly ended but did not seem to lead anywhere. I shuddered and felt as if someone had walked over my grave. A thought suddenly struck me. Could this child be an apparition, or a ghost? I was beginning to let my imagination run away with me because the house was so dank and depressing. Losing my nerve, I began to run back down the stairs. As I did so the sun began to shine through a large picture window, lighting up the area, highlighting the dust that floated around but it made me pause for thought. Feeling foolish, I recovered myself and taking hold of the banister to return to my room, I recoiled with disgust, as my hands slipped on the greasy wood and became covered in thick grime.

Trying to rub them clean, I noticed that there was a large faded square on the wallpaper, where a painting had once held prime position. I tried to recall what had hung there, and then I remembered it was where Freya's portrait had been. The one that had been specially commissioned for her wedding day, when she had looked so beautiful in her green silk gown. Her glorious mane of red hair had been draped and pinned with pearls and she had been wearing the Fitzroy diamonds. Surely that exquisite jewellery must be locked away somewhere as it had been in the family for generations. I felt so confused and overwhelmed that I sat down on the stairs and leaned against the greasy banister feeling abandoned and alone..

After a few moments I pushed the maudlin thoughts aside and began to wonder about the child again. I had been so overwrought after the night's events that perhaps she did not exist, but had been the product of an overactive imagination. Was that waif the real reason why Rosie had not escorted me up the stairs? Could there be a ghost of a child haunting the place? I had never heard of such a rumour but then the house went back generations. Surely every mansion has a ghost?

As I looked around again I noticed a covered frame propped against the wall, and thinking it was the one of Freya I pulled back the cover. Instead it revealed Major Edmund Fitzroy, Roland's brother, It was a relief to see a familiar face staring back at me, he was younger than I remembered, but his blue eyes that had always been so distinctive seem to follow me around. He looked so lifelike that I began talking to him for reassurance. The picture gave me courage and made me pull myself together. The child could not be a ghost. Ghosts do not leave footprints

Making my way back up to where I had last seen her, I called out, but there was no answer. Then as I returned to the attic landing, I saw there was a door that was very slightly ajar. I walked along and gently pushed it open more widely and found the little girl cowering behind it. However, as I did so I instantly recoiled at the stench that emanated from that room. It was so powerful that it took my breath away, the smell of ammonia, stung my eyes and tears blurred my vision. I placed a handkerchief over my nose and mouth and trying not to inhale too deeply, I entered the disgusting room, calling out to the girl as I did so,

'Come out of here immediately.'

My voice sounded strange and echoing in the empty room.

The child swung round startled, at the sound of my voice, even though she had known I was there, her eyes rolling with terror. Then seeing me her expression changed. Seemingly unaffected by the overpowering atmosphere, she began to chant to her doll as she wrapped and unwrapped it in the shabby piece of silk that she had been holding and began talking in a strange high pitched fashion.

'Don't yer worry Annie, it ain't 'im. 'E ain't going to 'urt yer.'

Her accent was the same as the woman called Rosie and assuming it was her child I tried to persuade her to leave the room.

'Is your doll called Annie?'

The child still ignored me, still cooing quietly to the doll.

'Annie is all right. Yer can sleep now. The man ain't 'ere today.'

I was puzzled, why wouldn't this poor little waif answer me? Why was there such a dreadful smell in the dingy room? I took her arm and gasped as her skin was like ice. She seemed oblivious to my touch as I took off my cloak and wrapped it round her thin body. As my arms went round her shoulders she instantly reacted. Her body stiffened and making strange animal noises she backed against the wall.

The atmosphere was now becoming unbearable, but she wouldn't move and was rigid and unyielding. Not knowing what else to do, I staggered out of the room, the smell making my head swim. Leaving her, I ran down the many staircases, until I was back in the reception hallway. Ahead of me I could see through an open door, into the dining room. Like my bedroom it was empty of furniture and had no carpet. All that remained in the room was a naked marble statue of a woman holding a lamp and a black granite bust of Beethoven on the mantelpiece and a damaged table. The ornate gold framed mirror that had once hung above the fireplace had also been removed.

As the sun shone through the high windows, permeating the house, I was beginning to feel a little warmer. I strode purposefully along the oak panelled corridors, trying all the doors but most of them were locked. It was a strange sensation, making me feel as if I was still dreaming as I wandered down the endless corridors. Occasionally I found a room open, but it would only contain odd items of furniture. Everywhere was devoid of any objects or items of value. Unable to find anyone I sat down on a chair padded in well worn red velvet, only to be enveloped in clouds of dust making me cough and the sound broke the silence. Everywhere was still and I was uncertain whether I was alone or whether Roland was in the house.

'I can't stay here,' I said to myself. I still had friends in London, and surely they would help me? However, until arrangements could be made, there was nothing that could be done. I would have to remain at Stoneleigh, if my brother in law would permit it. Since my father's death there was certainly nothing for me in Paris. After the reception on my arrival I was uncertain what my future would be. I tried to console myself that in the cold light of day Roland would be in a more affable frame of mind. He had looked so gaunt and ill. I wondered if he was still grief stricken over my sister's death but it had been four years. He had been such a kind, loving husband and brother in law, it was not possible that he could have changed that much.

I found the study door, and looked into the room. The heavy drapes were closed and there was no natural light. However, in the gloom I could see that the shelves were still covered in books but there were papers untidily littered around and there slumped over the desk was Roland. There was also a strong medicinal smell pervading the air which I recognised from my father's sick room. It was the smell of chloral that emanated from the brown, ribbed medicine bottles that were lying around. I stood for a moment looking at the wasted figure, snoring loudly. He was dirty and unkempt, his eyes were shut and his face, which was slightly turned toward me had an unhealthy, purple tinge.

Spilt on the floor were the remnants of a jug of ale, now seeping into a pool of congealed stickiness on the floor. The heavy snoring informed me that he was at least alive. As I turned to leave, a movement caught my eye and I suddenly realised that there was another figure stirring in the shadows. Rosie was sitting quietly on a wooden chair in a dark corner of the room. She held her finger to her lips, silently gesturing to me not to speak. Then standing up stiffly, she led me quietly out of the room and gently closed the door.

'Don't wake 'im miss, 'e has been up all night.'

I answered with annoyance that Roland needed to be woken. I wanted to speak to him, believing that he was not ill but sleeping off the effects of his drinking. Rosie sighed and sat down awkwardly on a carved wooden settle by the parlour door. She looked as though she had the cares of the world upon her shoulders. However, now in the sunlight I was amazed by her appearance. She appeared to be about forty years old and her lined, pallid face was heavily rouged; making an odd and grotesque appearance on, what I could tell, had once been a pretty face. She leaned forward and put her head in her hands.

'You don't know 'ow 'ard it 'as been Miss. I've tried my 'ardest but it is no good.'

I was nonplussed,

'Yes! It must be very hard trying to run the house, but the place is filthy.'

A look of anger flashed over her strained face, and she assumed a more refined accent that was destroyed by the lack of grammar in her speech.

'What can I do about it? I told yer, I ain't no 'ousekeeper, I'm only 'ere as a friend. Why, it is only 'cos of 'ow good 'e and Edmund 'as been to me that I keep coming. 'Ow can there be any servants when we ain't got no tin. I've sold everything I can fink of and it still ain't enough!'

'You sold everything,' I responded with irritation. How dare this woman sell things belonging to my sister?

Rosie immediately adopted the lofty tone that she had used earlier as she retorted,

'I was merely trying to 'elp.'

'What about my sister's jewellery?'

'They went first,' She continued.

'Then there must be money. Why are there no servants?' I asked

'They won't stay, we can't pay 'em, and they are all frightened of 'im Miss.'

'But when my sister was alive, this place was full of servants!'

'Your sister, it was 'er fault, 'e should never 'ave, married 'er, 'e was never.....'

Shocked at her tone I interrupted her,

'I would ask you not to speak of your master's dead wife in that way.'

Rosie bristled,

''E ain't my master.'

'I don't understand all this,' I said becoming impatient.

The woman shrugged,

'I shouldn't speak ill of the dead, but 'e ain't been the same man since.'

I looked at her intently and realised that despite the rouge she looked very tired. Realising that there was nothing to be gained by losing my patience I softened my reply.

'I suppose it has been difficult for Roland after my sister's death. I had no idea about any of this. We received no letters after Freya died, apart from the one I showed you. It is very good of you to try to help. However, surely you should take your child home. It is not appropriate to bring your child here. She is quite blue with cold.'

Rosie smiled wearily,

'My child? I ain't got no child. Whatever gave you that idea?'

' Surely she is yours. That tiny child who is hiding in a room at the top of the house.'

Rosie looked puzzled,

'A child upstairs? Then her expression changed, 'Oh no, she ain't 'ere is she?'

Disconcerted I answered,

'Yes that little girl who won't come out of that foul room.'

'What?' She responded with surprise. 'Oh Lord miss, that must be Annie. She is your sister's girl. I never knew she was 'ere. Roland said that she 'ad gone away to school'

Astounded at this information my knees buckled and I sat down weakly by her side.

'My sister's child! That half starved girl upstairs is my niece?

Rosie looked distracted.

'He said she'd gone. Gone for to be learned.'

She stood up and slowly walked to the staircase, placing her hands in the small of her back as if in pain and begun calling up the stairs. Hearing nothing she began to climb the stairs but slowed down after the first few steps, leaning over the banister to catch her breath. She began to call again.

'Annie, come down. It's me. Rosie!'

It was obvious that she found it too difficult to climb the stairs, so I offered my arm in support and the two of us began to slowly ascend the staircases until we reached the attic landing. I pointed out the door where I had left the child, warning Rosie about the terrible atmosphere in the room.

She tried to open the door, but something was caught behind it. Finally Rosie used her shoulder to force it open to reveal the little girl tightly curled up asleep. She was wedged behind the door, wrapped in the cloak that I dropped when I left the room. The noise awoke her but she didn't move but continued to lay there staring at us. The big eyes registered nothing, but the thin fingers idly picked at raw weeping scabs that covered her arms and legs.

Nothing could make me enter that room as the smell made me nauseous, but Rosie, who also gasped at the stench, picked up the child. This time the girl allowed herself to be carried unresistingly out of the room, whilst Rosie gently asked,

'Annie, my love, what you doing 'ere?'

Through the gloom I could see layers of dead flies glued to the window ledge and squashed in a bloody mass against the filth smeared windows. I looked around the room in disgust. There were lumps of green, mouldy bread littered about. On the floor was some maggot ridden meat and a large cracked jug was lying on the floor stuck in the congealed mess that had once been milk. There were cobwebs and spiders dangling in every corner.

Still holding the handkerchief over my nose and mouth, I held the door open to allow Rosie to edge past and as I did so I brushed against the wall. Immediately I realised the cause of the smell. The whole of one wall was smeared with excrement. Some hard and encrusted, embedded into the paper and some still greasy and wet. I felt the gorge rise in my throat and I had to run from the room to stop myself from being sick, the nausea overwhelming me, slamming the door as I did so. Rosie, stood on the landing still holding on to the child and wailed,

'I never knowed she were 'ere. She must have stayed up 'ere. I never come up the top of the 'ouse cos I can't walk up them stairs now. It's too 'ard.'

'When was it that you last saw her?'

'I dunno. 'E said that she was going to go away to a school, I fought she'd gone and it was the best fing for 'er. I could see 'e weren't looking after 'er.'

'So she must have been there for some time. How could Roland have been so cruel as to neglect his own child?'

'It ain't 'is fault. 'E is ill.'

'So you keep saying. That is no excuse. The house is a ruin, his child half starved. Yet it is not his fault. Surely his brother must have known what was happening here?'

Rosie sat dispiritedly on the nearest step, still clutching Annie.

'The Major don't know. We ain't seen 'im. I 'spect 'e is with 'is regiment and not even in the country.' Then addressing the child who was still looking blankly at her she cooed gently,

'You'll be alright now Annie.'

As she did so the strange, high pitched, voice suddenly broke the silence,

'We don't talk to no peoples do we. We stay 'ere. You keep quiet you bitch. Shut your mouth or I'll shut it for you,' and she began to nod her head up and down and rock to and fro.

Shocked at what I was hearing I gasped,

'Is there something wrong with her? Is there something not right in her mind? Has she been shut away because Roland is ashamed of her?'

Rosie looked angrily at me.

'No she ain't no lunatic. Don't you dare say such fings? She weren't like this afore. She used to be so lovely, smiling all the time, but Roland never wanted ...' she stopped in her tracks.

'Roland never wanted what?'

'Oh Lord, 'e hasn't been the same, since yer sister went. 'E blamed the child, but 'e wouldn't'ave 'urt 'er. I don't know what's 'appened.'

Stunned, I watched as she carried the child downstairs gasping and wheezing with the effort as I followed my mind in turmoil.

'Is there any food in the house?'

'No, I ain't brung any.'

This was the final straw and I became so angry that I stormed off in the direction of the study. Rosie struggled behind me nervous and agitated.

'What are you going to do miss?' Rosie called out nearly dropping the quiescent child.

'I am going to demand that something is done. This cannot continue. Look at the start of the child. Surely her name is not Annie.' I raged.

Rosie looked stricken, and leaning against the wall for breath said,

'It is Annabelle, but don't wake 'im miss. 'E gets angry if he wakes afore 'is time. It's the medicine. I stays 'ere until 'e wakes. I am the only one who can deal with 'im miss. Let me speak to 'im. I'll go to the village and get some food if you've got any money. Don't disturb 'im please...'

She seemed so anguished that my courage failed and I paused at the door and turning I took the child from her arms and made my way back to the room I had slept in. I placed her on my bed and wrapped her in the coverlet and searched in my bag for some money. Then I sent Rosie down to the village to fetch some provisions. The child just lay looking at me with her little, pinched white face, her cheek bones so sharp and pointed with malnourishment that I could not stop the tears. Whether I was crying for Freya's child or myself I did not know.

CHAPTER TWO

'Thou art a soul in bliss; but I am bound upon a wheel of
fire, that mine own tears do scold like molten lead'

King Lear Act 4 Sc. 7

For some time I sat in silence, overwhelmed by my situation. Then at
last forcing myself to stir, I tiptoed down to the kitchen. My heart
was pounding as I filled a jug with water and nervously looked around in
case Roland heard me. Returning to the upstairs room, I ran past the closed
study door, and dashed up to the next floor. Tearing a piece of cloth from my
petticoat, I began to wash the filth encrusted on the face of the poor child.
Some of it was stuck fast to her skin and I was shocked when I realised that
what I had thought was dirt around her mouth, was in fact dried faeces. Her
condition was something beyond my comprehension. I knew in some areas of
London, people lived in filthy conditions and ran around in rags. However,
I never could have imagined that any child of my sister's would be living in
the stinking conditions this child survived in.

As I cleaned her face, her hollow eyes opened and stared at me but she
did not resist. Gently I bathed the sores and scabs that covered her arms
and legs, all the time reassuring her as I did so. Searching in my bag I found
some balm and covered the weeping, broken skin with it, hoping it would
help it to heal. Passively, Annabelle let me wash her. However, when I tried
to remove the filthy cloth she wore as a dress, she screamed hysterically and
struggled with me so violently that I had to admit defeat and the ragged shift
stayed put.

As I gently washed away the grime and excreta that was welded to her
skin, I could see that there was not one part of her that was not covered in

14

festering sores or yellowing bruises. Dried muck and encrusted faeces were ingrained in the material that hung from the thin shoulders. Additionally, there were dark reddish brown stains that looked like blood. I wrapped my cloak around her again, to keep her warm. As I did so she resumed the mindless picking of the sores on her arms. Although all the time I was talking to her, I had a sense that she was listening, there was no response. She had not uttered one word.

When we had finished the bathing, she sat quietly by the window as I continued to talk to her. I told her about her mother and my life in Paris, really to console myself as I knew it would mean nothing to her. On hearing the door open downstairs, I anxiously peered over the banister. It was only Rosie, carrying a bag of provisions and she tiptoed apprehensively past the study door as I joined her, both desperately trying not to make any noise as we headed for the kitchen. She immediately began bustling about cutting bread and cheese, putting the items down on a table that was none too clean. However, it was obvious that this room had been superficially cleaned, which was more than any of the others that I had seen so far. I went back upstairs to fetch the child but she refused to move. Each time I took her firmly by the hand, she promptly sat back down on the threadbare carpet and groaned and moaned so loudly that I was afraid that it would awake her father.

Now that I had time to think, my initial courage had failed. I was not sure that I was strong enough to deal with a demented man screaming at me. I couldn't stay in this house, but I couldn't leave the child. Suddenly to my surprise, I heard a tiny voice whisper,

'We don't go down there, do we Annie? We don't want to see the man, 'e 'ides in the day, we like that don't we Annie?'

Overjoyed that she had spoken I hugged her to me, but her body stiffened and became rigid and her face was blank. Giving up the struggle I crept downstairs to obtain some of the food and took it back to her. As soon as she saw it, Annabelle fell upon it like a starving animal. Cramming large portions into her mouth and spitting out crumbs. It was a shocking sight to see. I was appalled and horrified that this child had been brought so low. Unable to bear watching her eat I went back to the kitchen where Rosie was tidying the remains of the food and I heard her singing. She seemed to be in a happier frame of mind and seeing me she smiled,

'I've been finking, we'll 'ave to send for 'is brother.'

'Edmund?'

'Yes, 'e'll help. It was 'im that told Roland that the girl should be in a school. Of course that was afore 'e 'ad the argument with him.'

'Did he use to come here before?'

'Yes, after your sister died. 'E often came when he was on leave from 'is Regiment, but there was an argument over money or somefin and 'e never came any more.'

'Something needs to be done for Annabelle. Yet I can't just take her away, she is Roland's child after all. Do you know where Edmund is? Can we get a letter to him?'

'No she can't and I'll trust you to keep your nose out of my affairs.'

A cracked voice hoarsely interrupted our conversation. Startled I swung round and I let out an involuntary scream as Roland loomed up behind me, his face dark with fury. He was so tall he towered over me as I backed away; bracing myself in case he struck me. I was frightened of him but I refused to be bowed and I stared him out, defying him to do his worse, yet all the while trembling inside. There were bruises on his face and his eyes were yellowed and bloodshot.

I tried to speak, but the words stuck in my throat as he glared at me, clenching and unclenching his fists, as if trying to control himself.

Finding my voice I croaked,

'You should be ashamed of yourself. My sister's child is upstairs, starving and neglected!'

Rosie gasped that I had been so bold and tried to hush me as Roland's expression turned into a sneer. Muttering something under his breath he turned and walked away and I watched the stooping body disappear down the hallway and there was a crash as the front door was slammed shut.

'Blimey you was lucky,' Rosie said in amazement. 'I fought he was going to strike yer dead.'

'What is to be done Rosie?' I felt tears sting my eyes. Having stood my ground, my nerves now failed as I realised the enormity of my situation. I was completely friendless. No one could help me. Rosie sat down wearily and I could see that underneath the bright, expression she looked care worn. This poor woman had taken on the burden of life at Stoneleigh. She could not help me. I was going to have to resolve the situation myself. There was no one else I could rely on. In despair I sat in silence, blankly chewing on a stale piece of bread.

At last sighing I decided that there was nothing to be gained by sitting with maudlin thoughts, I stood up and rinsed my plate,

'You are right! We must send for Edmund Fitzroy. Do you have an address where he can be reached?'

'No miss, I ain't. I told you, I don't know words.' Her face crumpled and I thought she was going to cry. Then her face lit up.

'I knows where Roland keeps 'is letters and fings. Perhaps it will be there!' She slowly stood up and walked breathlessly towards the study. Then as if a thought had suddenly struck her she called out,

'You can read can't you miss?'

'Of course I can.'

I quickly followed her.

'What happens if Roland finds us searching in this room, I don't think I can face his anger again?' I asked.

'Don't worry, 'e won't be back yet. 'E will have gone to drown his sorrows. I knows 'is movements like clockwork. I calls in every night and sits wiv 'im until 'e wakes. 'E doesn't like to be alone at night. Then in the morning 'e goes out.'

'But why do you this?'

'Cos 'e needs me!'

I didn't pursue that response. I could not believe that Rosie, good hearted as she appeared to be, could be someone that Roland Fitzroy would need to depend on. It was all very strange.

Disappearing behind the study door, she pulled open drawers and began rummaging through letters and parchment papers. On top of the oak desk, with the red leather inlay, there were stacks of papers. Some were crammed on a vicious looking spike and some were littered around. Most seemed to be bills with threatening words scrawled across them. With one sweep of her strong arm she hurled the papers from the desk, setting up a cloud of dust as she did so.

She bent down to pick up some of the medicine bottles and placed one in her pocket without comment. Rosie hardly looked at the papers that she was throwing aside whilst I watched in silence. Then with a cry of glee she cried out

'These is letters and fings.' and triumphantly laid them carefully out on the desk.

I sat down and rifled through them. Amongst them I recognised my own handwriting on letters that were unopened. I now realised why I had never had any reply to my letters. Roland had not read them. I looked through the pile; some were legal documents that had been scrawled over in a heavy hand, with black ink. Others were correspondence from various sources. Some names I recognised, invitations to card evenings or London gatherings. Some were more threatening in tone and I put them to one side. As Rosie could not read I wondered what she was seeking as she continued to rummage. Disappointingly there was nothing to throw any light on Edmund Fitzroy's whereabouts.

'I wonder,' I said, almost to myself, ' whether we should write to some of these people and ask if they know of Edmund's whereabouts if we can't find anything here?'

Rosie nodded, but didn't answer. She seemed in awe of me sitting at the desk reading the documents. Papers for her were like a foreign language. Having ploughed through everything we could find, there was still nothing that would help us. Fed up with searching, I wandered out of the study and noticed Annabelle sitting on the top stair, still talking to the rag doll. Her reedy voice had an unearthly quality to it and it made me feel uneasy.

'It is all right now Annie, the bad man 'as gone. We can come down now.'

I felt a shiver run over me, was this the normal routine for this child? Spending days in hiding, waiting for Roland to leave the house before she ventured out of her room. I wondered if the mouldy scraps of food that were in her bedroom had been taken from the kitchen, when she was left alone to wander the house. My heart sank, surely there was somewhere that I could stay and get away from this awful place.

'I have some money. Is there somewhere nearby that I could stay, an inn or lodging house?'

'No miss, you wouldn't want to stay at any inn near 'ere. My alehouse is the only place but it ain't no place for a lady.'

'What! You own a business?'

Rosie flushed and looked uncomfortable, 'Yes, its mine. Well me an me 'usband.'

I was even more surprised, 'You are married?'

'Yes of course!'

'Yet your husband lets you come here every day and tend to Roland?'

Her face darkened, and she ran her fingers through her hair.

'E don't care what I do, if it weren't for Roland we wouldn't 'ave the alehouse...' she tailed off, still looking uncomfortable. I realised that the situation between Rosie and Roland was something that I did not want to venture into. I wondered if this lady had been around when my sister had been alive. I could not imagine that my sister would have accommodated her presence. I was certain that she had not been at Stoneleigh on my visits. However, I thought it best not to pry and changing the subject asked,

'What can I do? Until we have contacted Edmund it will be impossible to stay here. I couldn't leave the child.'

'It will be alright miss. You stay, if you've got some tin, I could bring food everyday in the morning and we'll make up a fire in the front room and your bedroom.'

'What about Roland?'

"'E ain't always like you've seen him miss. 'E loses his temper but sometimes 'e can be nice. Just stay out of 'is way. 'E won't 'urt you. 'E ain't like that. Sometimes, I don't see 'im for days, I don't know where 'e goes but when 'e comes in at night, 'e takes 'is medicine and I sit wiv 'im while 'e sleeps. Then I leave in the morning, I just look after him, I 'as to..'

'But what about the child? She needs medical attention. She is filthy dirty, and needs care and proper food. Something has got to be done.'

'She looks cleaner now.'

'Yes I have washed her but she can't remain in that awful foul smelling room.'

'No miss, can't she stay in your room with you?'

'I suppose that is the only answer if I am to stay here. However, I have no experience with children and this child seems seriously unwell.'

'No, she just needs a bit of love Miss. She'll be alright, give her some proper food and she'll be like she used to be, when she was living with me.'

'Maybe, it would be best if she came to live with you again, until something can be arranged through Edmund.'

Rosie looked uncomfortable.

'Me 'usband wouldn't like it!'

Having finished our bread and cheese which Rosie ate almost as enthusiastically as Annabelle, we went back upstairs to try and persuade the child to come down.

'No one else is here,' I said gently, 'only Rosie, and me.'

However, it was to no avail. Each time we tried to take her firmly downstairs, each of us holding one thin arm, her cries were pitiful. Her thin voice screeched like a wounded animal and the pain of it stabbed through my heart like a knife.

Rosie went along the musty landing that seemed to stretch endlessly into the west wing and disappeared into the darkness. Her large figure, vanishing in the distance as if she had merged into the shadows. After a short time she returned carrying a pale blue dress. It was a child's dress and although too short for Annabelle it was much too big in the body. Ignoring the demented screams, we managed to relieve the child of the dirt encrusted shift and dress her in the blue dress. Some of the material had welded into the scabs on her body and we had to repeatedly soak it off. I didn't know where Rosie had gone to find the dress and after the awful shock of the attic room, nothing would possess me to venture anywhere near any of the upper floors again.

As we finished dressing Annabelle I noticed that Rosie was becoming increasingly nervous and anxious. Finally I asked her what was the matter? She announced that she had to return to her husband. That she had been away too long. I realised that she was worried about the reception she would receive at her home. I told her to leave and soon Annabelle and I were sitting by the fire in my bedroom, where at last she was clean and warm.

Annabelle resumed her rocking and talking in whispered tones to the doll whilst I found some writing paper and began to write a letter to Edmund. Although I had no address for him, it made me feel as if I was doing something positive to relieve my situation. As I heard the front door close and Rosie walk off down the path my heart sank. I was once more alone. As I was writing I suddenly became aware that Annabelle's conversation had become more intelligible and I heard her say,

'Nice lady 'as come 'ere Annie. We like 'er don't we. See the pretty dress, mother loves it doesn't she?

Again I tried to engage her in conversation, but she continued addressing the doll, as if unaware of my presence. It was so cosy and warm in the room, that I became drowsy and for a few moments must have fallen asleep, when I was jolted awake by the sound of the front door being slammed shut. Heart pounding, I listened to the sound of footsteps running up the staircase as Annabelle, leapt to her feet and threw the doll on the floor,

'Bad girl, you won't do what I say. You'll be sorry, sorry, sorry, sorry.' She kept repeating the words, all the time striking the doll around the head. I ran to shut the open bedroom door just as Roland arrived outside. This time he seemed cold and disinterested but at least his anger seemed to have subsided. Bravely, I said,

'I need to talk to you, Roland.' He looked at me with distaste but replied in a restrained fashion.

'I do not believe Madam that I have anything to say to you.'

'Why was I not informed that Freya had a child? Why has she been neglected in such a fashion? The house is in an awful condition. Why have you allowed this to happen?'

I heard my voice as if it did not belong to me saying over and over, 'Why! Why! Why?'

For a moment his face began to darken again but a set look drifted over his mouth as if he was trying to control himself. Then to my surprise his whole demeanour changed and he began to whine and whimper,

'You don't know what it has been like. I can't trust anyone now. They are all against me. They'll try to beat me down but they won't succeed. She does it. She thinks I don't know!'

I was appalled at the change. His demeanour was now that of a wheedling child, self pitying and whining about how there were spies everywhere.

'I don't understand what you mean. I wish to write to your brother, can you tell me where he can be contacted?'

I regretted the words almost as soon as they left my mouth. His manner changed again and he became threatening. Advancing towards me he exclaimed,

'Edmund! He is not wanted here. You've come from him, haven't you? He's sent you to spy on me, like all the others. Leave me alone.'

He raised his fist and I steeled myself, expecting a blow. However, his hand glanced by my face and hit the wall just by my head, as I screamed. Then with a cry of disgust, he turned away and ran back down the staircase, to what was obviously his bolt hole. He crashed the study door with such fury that the house shook. With an adrenaline rush, I ran down the staircase behind him. I reached the closed door and I could hear him violently tearing through drawers and cupboards. As I listened suddenly, the door was flung open and Roland reappeared. Raging, he shouted,

'Where is it? Where is it? You've hidden it you bitch? Give it to me or I'll kill you?'

He pushed me up against the wood panelling with such force that I crashed my head against it and everything spun around me. Purple with rage, his bloodshot eyes, glared into my face. Breathlessly, I managed to gasp,

'I don't know what you're talking about.'

'I'll find it. I'll find it.'

With those words, he threw me violently aside and retreated into the room. Papers were everywhere, as he furiously tipped out drawers. I could see him through the doorway, scrabbling around on his hands and knees. The bony fingers picking up the medicine bottles that were strewn around and tipping out the last dregs of the liquid that had once been in them.

Then I understood, what was happening. Roland was looking for bottles of chloral. The smell that had reminded me so much of my father's sick room. This was the reason that he had become so paranoid and foul tempered; he was addicted to this medication. I watched through the half open door with pity and disgust. At the sight of me observing him, he returned to the whining and wheedling tone,

'Don't be cruel to me Freya, just give me the bottle. I won't be angry.'

'Freya?' Did he think that I was his wife?

'I am not Freya. I am Aphra,' I said coldly. Again he pleaded and begged, crawling around at my feet like a lunatic. He clung to the hem of my dress in a demented fashion whilst I held onto the doorframe for support, scared and disgusted. I tried to shake him from me, but he clung on tightly until I was surprised by a voice behind me.

'Leave it to me Miss. I 'ave what 'e wants.' Rosie was standing there holding some brown bottles. Prising Roland's hand from my dress, she ushered me outside and closed the study door. I tried to listen as raised voices could be heard but I could not catch what was being said. After a few minutes, Rosie reappeared,

'Did 'e hurt you miss?'

'No! I am all right,' I answered. rubbing the lump that was emerging on my forehead. My ears were still ringing from his curses.

'What has happened to him?'

'I don't know miss. It started a long time ago, after your sister died. The doctor gave 'im some medicine to help 'im sleep and now he can't seem to live without it. Sometimes, I 'ave tried to get 'im off it. I watered it down and 'e was getting better. However, one day 'e found me doing it and 'e was so angry, I have never dared do it again.'

'He needs to see a physician.'

'I know miss, but 'e won't see no doctor. Everyday 'e goes to the inn and drinks and gambles. There always fights over money that is where it has all gone. All 'is so called friends 'ave taken 'im for every penny. Then 'e comes 'ome and sleeps. Sometimes, 'e walks about all night and sleeps all day. Sometimes when I leave 'im at night 'e is asleep and 'e is still asleep when I gets 'ere in the morning.'

I was at a loss. There was nothing in my previous life of order and sanity that could prepare me for this situation. I had nursed my father for several years and never seen anything like the behaviour that I had witnessed today.

'He seemed to think I was his wife.'

'I expect it was the colour of your 'air. 'E gets confused.'

We both stood in the hallway in silence, lost for words. Then Rosie said quietly,

'I've 'ad a piece of luck. Look what I've found.'

She waved an envelope at me,

'It's from Edmund.'

'How do you know?'

'Look it's got 'is regiment's picture on the front.'

Looking at the paper, I noticed that there was an embossed regimental crest on the outside. I unfolded the letter and saw that there was an address care of an agent's office in London. Edmund had obviously realised that his regiment would be moved from place to place and used the lawyer as a postal address. The letter was quite recent and very short. It read,

> *'I shall shortly be stationed abroad with the regiment, as the situation with the Russians does not look very good. As you are my only relative, should I not return, I have named you as next of kin. However, as a result of your ruinous gambling debts, be made aware that I have protected the family estate which will be held in trust by nominated guardians. The lawyer at the above address will contact you in the eventuality of my death. I realise that we did not part on the best of terms and hope that can be put behind us.*
> *I remain your brother.'*

It was signed by Edmund and I almost fainted with relief. Now at least I had someone else that I could contact to help me. Although I had intended to write to my friends in London, I was in great difficulty. How could I tell them what level Sir Roland Fitzroy had descended to? There would be such a scandal that would ruin the family name. I could not take the responsibility for that. At least Edmund was a family member and would know what to do. My joy was short lived when I realised that if his regiment was on the move, he may have already left the country. There was no time to lose and a letter needed to be despatched to the lawyer immediately.

Rosie went into the kitchen and began singing loudly some song about a bird in a cage. The noise only ceased when she called out to let us know that she was busy making a stew. She had bought some scrag end of lamb and saw herself now as the cook.

'What about your husband?'

'E's all right. It don't matter. I 'ad to bring Roland's medicine.'

I frowned and she added,

'It's for the best miss.' She began singing softly and I thought to myself how childlike she seemed. As far as she was concerned everything was all right now. Edmund Fitzroy would ride in on a white charger to save us all. If only it were that simple. I sat in my bedroom, finishing the letter whilst Annabelle watched me from a corner in the room. Her large eyes watching every move, the doll still clutched to her chest.

'Rosie is making us something to eat later,' I said quietly. ' That is kind of her isn't it? You must be hungry, would you like something nice.'

Annabelle studied me quietly for a moment and then addressing the doll said,

'Cake! Annie wants cake!' It was the first time that the child had answered a question that I had addressed to her. Even though she still talked of herself in the third person through the rag doll, I was so pleased that she had responded that I threw my arms around her again. However, just as before she stood there in my arms, stiff and unyielding, her skin as cold as a block of marble.

'If you will come downstairs, we'll find you cake.'

I saw her eyes flicker and she wriggled out of my grasp. She seemed to be struggling with herself and was having difficulty in forcing herself to go outside. Firmly I took her hand and managed to steer her out of the room and we hesitantly we made our way down to the kitchen. Rosie greeted our arrival,

'My, don't you look pretty in your blue dress.'

'She wants some cake and I promised we would find some. Have we any?'

Rosie went back to stirring a cauldron of stew and looked thoughtful,

'Well I have some buns, would you like that Annie....'

Seeing my look of disapproval at the child being called Annie, she quickly corrected herself,

' I mean, Annabelle.'

Then rummaging in a bag she pulled out a bun wrapped in newspaper.

Annabelle ran to the food and there was a repeat of the food being forced into her mouth.

'You must eat slowly Annabelle, or you will be ill.' I remonstrated but she paid no attention.

'I can't understand it miss, she weren't like this before. She is so thin, all covered in scabs and bruises. It reminds me of when I was a kid and we lived at Blackfriars. I had ten brothers and sisters. We had no money; if we got a meal we fought we were in paradise.'

'Where have the bruises come from? Do you think that Roland beats her? She seems too terrified to come downstairs.'

'What, you think Roland..., no! He wouldn't hurt that tiny girl. I know 'e flies into rages but 'e wouldn't beat her. Not 'is own daughter.'

'He doesn't seem to have any fatherly affection for her. How could he have? If he did he would not have left her in this neglected state.'

'But that is because 'e is ill. Roland don't know what 'e is doing, but I know 'e wouldn't deliberately 'urt her.'

I realised that it was pointless debating with Rosie. She had no understanding of the situation and I did not have the answers myself. In her eyes Roland could do no wrong.

Leaving me tending to the stew on the stove, she set off back to the alehouse. I had given her the letter to take to the post and the large figure had gone off clutching it to her well padded bosom.

Although it was winter, the sun was shining brightly and I decided to put on my cloak and escape from the gloomy house for a while. Try as I may, Annabelle could not be persuaded to go outside and taking her back to my bedroom, I left her there. Wandering outside, it made me sad to see how neglected everything was. There were tall oak trees waving in the breeze, their leafless boughs gnarled and twisted that gave an air of death around me. The green of the leafy rhododendron bushes gave me a feeling of hope and edging my way past prickly bushes and low hanging trees I headed for the Roman temple folly. I was so happy to see it. I had spent so many hours sitting there in the past, just watching the birds and the wildlife. However, it was now run down and full of dead leaves and insects, with cobwebs dangling from the cornices. I went inside and sat on the wooden seating and surveyed the unkempt gardens.

The Tudor walled garden, which had been so neatly laid out with small bushes of evergreen Box, was now just a jungle of tangled weeds and plants. The large stone birdbath had crumbled into the dust. The basin upended on the ground. The garden had a forsaken beauty about it and I sat remembering the times I had with my sister. We often sat by the fountain dropping stones into the water, watching the small whirlpools fanning out. We would laugh and talk about our plans for the future. Discussing love and romance but it ended all too soon for Freya.

After a while the sun withdrew behind a cloud and the air became chill and I sadly returned to the house. Annabelle was in my room with her doll, rocking from side to side. However, the fresh air had cleared my thoughts. I would have to stay at Stoneleigh until I heard something from Edmund. The child was not able to socialise and I was not about to leave her. In the meantime, I would write to my friend Leticia and let her know that I was in England. I would reveal nothing of my situation. Then when proper arrangements had been made for Annabelle, I would leave Roland to his fate. He was responsible for his own decline and there was nothing that I could do to help him. Anyone that could have neglected his own daughter as he had done was not worthy of consideration.

CHAPTER THREE

'What is your substance, whereof are you made, that
millions of strange shadows on you tend?'   *Sonnet 53*

I returned to my room feeling much more confident with regard to my future. I knew that my friend Leticia and her mother Lady Westerham would help me. Excitedly I began writing to them furiously, but not enlightening them as to what had happened. I was sure that they had no knowledge of Stoneleigh after Freya's death. When my father and I received letters from them, they had made no mention of Roland's situation at all.

As I sat busily writing, I felt the large eyes in that wan face staring at me. Annabelle sat transfixed, her thin bruised legs hugged tightly to her chest and her body constantly rocking back and forth. When at last I had finished my letters, I noticed that Annabelle had fallen asleep and gently picking her up so as not to wake her, I laid her on the bed that now had clean linen and covered her with my shawl.

In a large oak chest, I had found sheets, pillowcases, shawls and various other items of linen and silk. The sheets had an old musty smell, but they had seemed clean, although the folds had yellowed with age and the cotton was rough to the touch. I put dabs of my lavender water on the material to try to remove the odour and remade the bed. Now as Annabelle slept, I spent a long time polishing and cleaning my room, even though I was unused to such labour. My father's household in Paris had always maintained servants to do such tasks. In a strange way I enjoyed the work as it took my mind off things. I washed the floor and cleaned the leaded windows until my hands were sore and red from the lye. It stopped me from drifting through the day waiting and watching. Finally exhausted, I too joined the child on the bed and fell into a restless sleep.

It was some hours later that I was awakened by a sound outside my door. The light had faded and I became aware of someone coming up the staircase, the footsteps echoing loudly on the wooden floor. Annabelle slept on unaware of the world around her as I held my breath and strained to listen. My whole being was on edge. As the footsteps reached the door, I tensed, too frightened to make a sound, uncertain what to do. It could only be Roland as I knew that there was no one else in the house.

As the footsteps passed my room and ventured along the landing, my nerve failed me and heart pounding, I quickly leapt from my bed and drew the bolt across the door. Taking no chances, I heaved a chair against it and wedged it under the door knob. I heard the door next to my room also being rattled, and I knew that it was locked. I had taken the key when I had found the sheets. I heard Roland muttering to himself, but I could not make out what was being said.

Leaning against my door, holding my breath, I listened intently. Then I heaved a sigh of relief as I heard the footsteps return along the landing. I was uncertain whether Roland had passed by, or was still outside until with a start I saw my door handle began to shake furiously,

'Let me in, let me in,' he raged. Roland shouted so loudly that Annabelle sat bolt upright in the bed in terror. Her eyes almost leapt from her head and her teeth were clench so tightly that I could see the muscles of her neck straining.

'Go away!' I cried.

There was an intake of breath outside and then the voice took on a wheedling tone,

'Please Freya, let me in. You know I love you. Why are you doing this to me?'

My blood ran cold; he thought he was talking to his wife. Surely he was not re-enacting his life with my sister? The man had lost his senses. Had he forgotten that his wife was dead? Despite my fear and loathing I could not help but pity him. Gently I whispered,

'Freya is dead Roland. I am Aphra. It is late I think you must be tired. Go to bed and we will talk in the morning.'

'Please, please,' his voice broke into a sob as he pleaded through the door. I was horrified at the sound of a grown man crying and whining through my bedroom door. Anxiously I stood leaning against the wood, willing him to leave. At last, getting no response, he thumped the door with his fist; hitting it with such force that I thought it would break open. Terrified, I clung to Annabelle, petrified that we were at the mercy of his violent attack.

Even more enraged Roland began to kick the door furiously and the wood splintered, but held fast, as he screamed oaths through the fractures. Obscenities gushed from his mouth. They were words I had never heard in my life. Panicking I held the door shut even though it was bolted and the realisation dawned that Roland must really be insane. This was not the man that my sister had married. He had always been such a gentleman and now he was shouting disgusting things through the door in the belief that he was talking to his wife. I was shocked and appalled and turning back to the frightened waif beside me, I became so angry that I screamed back at him. How dare this man subject his child to such behaviour? I shouted out that he had lost all right to live in a civilised society and he began to snivel and whine again.

Then just as quickly as the screaming had begun there was silence. As I listened with my ear against the door, I heard his footsteps walking away and with relief I sat trembling. If Roland was mad it was too dangerous to stay. I would have to leave this house as soon as possible and take the child with me, but where could I go?

Trying to comfort Annabelle I pulled the unyielding body to me and tried to reassure her. However, I was trying to reassure myself at the same time. I was uncertain whether either of us was safe in the company of this deranged man. A man who had been feted by the best of society and was now brought so low as to be screaming abuse at a woman and a child through a door. I clung to the small child, until darkness descended, and I lay in my clothes, fitfully sleeping, waking at every little sound. I was terrified that I would have a repeat performance and that this time my door would not withstand the beating. How could I escape? What could I do? My nerves were at breaking point and it had only been one day.

Little was I to know that this same performance would take place every night that I stayed at Stoneleigh. Every week, night after night, I went through the same routine of ensuring my door was firmly locked. After a few days of stress, I had pulled a heavy cupboard in front of the door before retiring. My body ached with the effort of moving the furniture each day and night. In the morning Roland would be slumped in the study, where I had first spied him, in a stupour. Comatose all day, he'd walk the house all night and cry and plead at my door, night after night.

The whining and pleading only stopped when Rosie arrived and I would hear her voice pacifying him and persuading him to return with her to the study. He would walk back down the stairs still pleading and crying and then everywhere would be still.

I repeatedly asked Rosie to get help, to make him see a doctor but she and I knew that he was beyond persuading.

Every day was an eternity of watching and waiting. Each minute passed like an hour, day after day. Although it had only been three weeks since my arrival I felt as though I had aged ten years, starting at every noise and frightened of shadows. Each morning, I would venture quietly down the stairs, knowing he was unconscious in his study. Sometimes Rosie would emerge looking careworn. Other days I did not see her at all. I could not understand why her husband permitted his wife to nurse a lunatic. Annabelle still addressed me through her doll, but she now seemed reassured enough to come downstairs with me and clutching my hand tightly and if the weather was not too cold we would walk outside. I tried to play games with her to develop her speech and bring her out of herself. I hoped that I could help her to come back to the real world that she had left when abandoned with Roland for company.

Everyday on our walks I would chant over and over the names of all the family members but she would just look blankly at me and walk on. I wanted her to learn her history. If the sun was out, I persuaded her to walk with me down to the lake which was now clogged with green weed. Sometimes she came with me to the ruins of the temple. However, she would only follow the same tried and tested path we had mapped out. Everyday we sat there and I encouraged Annabelle to draw, but sometimes she would snatch up the finished picture and crush and stamp on it laughing in a demented fashion as she destroyed it beneath her feet.

I tried to encourage her to draw pleasant objects. However, she would just sit and look at the blank paper in silence. Staring at the whiteness as if willing something to come to life. She was only happy when she was drawing dark silhouettes of people in grotesque, twisted shapes. Over and over she drew huge staring eyes that stood out in frightening fashion. They unnerved me so much that I took the materials away, and she did not protest at their removal. From then on we passed the time indoors or out with me sitting quietly, reading to her. She would appear to be listening but did not respond, it was a one way conversation.

Everywhere I went, Annabelle would just follow me around, always watching me with her large, unnaturally bright eyes. She was totally inscrutable; I had no idea what she was thinking. Now her hair was washed and combed the family resemblance was marked. Her hair had the same unruly curls as my own, the brilliant red handed down from the Devereaux family. Roland always seemed enraged at seeing my hair as the night of my arrival bore witness. Rosie had suggested that I wore an unbecoming black snood when in the house, in case I was caught unawares by him. On the odd occasion when he stirred and saw me as I fled out of the front door, he did not react at all. I understood now why he had disliked the child that had been the means of killing her mother. She was too much like her, as was I.

Each morning I eagerly awaited a reply to my letters. The semblance of normality that I had made for myself in the day time during the long weeks became a nightmare every night. Roland would continue to bang and scratch at my bedroom door, screaming and cursing in a demented fashion. Annabelle would stiffen with fear and I would comfort her until she slept, whilst I lay awake in fear and trepidation. Rosie had helped me to nail a bar across the door frame which I lowered every night and it gave me a little sense of security.

It was several weeks before the longed for letter arrived. Disappointedly I saw that it was from Edmund's agent's office. Eagerly, I opened it, but my heart sank when I read that my letter had been received and passed on to Major Edmund Fitzroy. He would no doubt contact me in due course. It did not even inform me whether Edmund was still in the country. I had been relying on hearing something more positive and could not help weeping helplessly with dismay. If I did not hear anything soon, I did not know what I would do. I was frightened of staying too much longer. However, a young woman and a child with no friends or relatives would not fare well in the outside world. I had avoided Roland as much as possible, but my luck would not last out forever. However, where could I go?

Some days I left Rosie with the child and walked down the long country lanes to the village at the bottom. I noticed that there were some cottages on the estate and I made enquiries to see if one could be rented but to no avail. As people soon began to know that I was staying at the 'big house' as they called it, I became a subject of interest.

One day the curate from the church called on me to ask why I had not attended church. When he commented that I was not looking well, I used that as my excuse for non-attendance. I said nothing of my predicament. I was surprised that what had happened at the house was not common knowledge as I was sure that the people who frequented the alehouse, knew of Roland's behaviour. How could they not? I asked if the curate knew of somewhere that I could stay with the child and he had merely enquired as to when she would be returning from school? He obviously had no idea that she had been at Stoneleigh all this time. How could I tell him in what condition she had been living? He promised to seek me out a suitable property but seemed puzzled as to why I could not remain at Stoneleigh. I felt trapped. My other concern was what to do about Annabelle? If my friends invited me to stay, how could I take her with me? This neglected child did not behave like a child of society people. I was desperate for Edmund to come and save me and the child. I could not bear to think of the possibility that he could be serving abroad and we would be left on our own even longer.

Everything was all taking too long. Each night, when Roland had stopped screaming and cursing through the door, I prayed, not to God but to Edmund. Wherever he was, I hoped he would be my saviour. For a couple of days respite came as Rosie informed me that Roland was not at home. I decided to go to the upper floors for the first time and to my joy found on the fifth floor another bedroom with some furniture. Rosie could not manage to walk up the stairs as her heavy build made it difficult for her. I moved my belongings to the upper bedroom, which luckily had a lock and for the first time in three weeks, I was able to sleep. Roland wouldn't know where I was and I believed that he would not think of looking at the upper storeys. However, I still had to judge my time carefully during the day. Waiting until he was asleep before tip toeing out of the house or staying by the fire in the bedroom. There was a servants' bell system in the house which worked and Rosie would pull the bell from the kitchen that ran to my room to let me know when he was asleep or had left home.

Annabelle had still never spoken to me or even looked at me directly. I asked Rosie if she knew of a physician in the locality, who would be able to treat the child? However, she seemed unable to understand the problem. She merely brought me back some medicines from the apothecary and always said the same thing,

'Annabelle is all right now miss. She just needed feeding up.'

However, I knew that Annabelle was not 'all right'. Something much deeper was wrong with this small thin child. Although the bruises on her poor little body had now faded, she still shook with fear as we descended the staircase. Even though everyday, I would bath her and put healing balm on the sores that covered her body I could not prevent the constant picking and scratching of them that continued night and day. The sores around her mouth had healed and her face, although still wan and pinched, was beginning to look healthier. A month had now passed and she had ceased grabbing her food and forcing it into her mouth with such greed that she would make herself sick.

Some nights she cried out in terror and I rocked her to sleep whilst I was exhausted and felt nervous and strained. If I did not leave soon, I felt I was on the verge of a nervous collapse. I was clear to me now that the violent blasphemies and cursing with which Annabelle reprimanded her doll were a re-enactment of the words her father screamed through my bedroom door.

I spent as much time as possible outside of the dark and dank house. I had more clothes now as my trunk had arrived after the first week. However, most of my dresses were too grand for my stay in this mausoleum. They had been my finery for the soirees in Paris. There were only two plain dresses and these I alternated until I was sick to death of them.

Many a day passed with only Annabelle for company but sometimes, Rosie would stay and talk to me. I tried to ascertain what had happened to bring Roland to such a state. However she could not or would not answer me. Just on one occasion I had caught her off guard and she had commented,

'I wasn't 'ere then. I never came to the 'ouse; I only came back 'ere when I saw the state of 'im as 'e 'ad always been so good to me. I 'ad to 'elp 'im.'

When I had pointed out that Roland was not her responsibility, especially as she had a husband and an alehouse to run, she just smiled ruefully. Each day she would dutifully turn up at Stoneleigh bringing the provisions for me, wearing the same frayed silk dress, but the hem of it was torn and dirty from walking through the country lanes. I realised that she was wearing her best dress for my sake. Her hair frizzed and her cheeks and lips rouged so brightly that the effect was startling. I knew that she was the kind of person that I would never have associated with in any form of society. However, she was my only friend and I depended on her.

On one occasion returning from my walk, I found some local men banging loudly on the front door, demanding payment for bills. As I arrived, they harangued me in a threatening manner. However, I stood my ground and ascertaining what sum was owed duly paid it. Their attitude changed immediately and they went off tipping their hats and thanking me for my understanding. I was worried that my funds were getting low and I realised that if I did not hear something soon, I would be in dire straits. I would need to arrange for my father's money to be transferred from Paris and for that I needed to consult a bank. That would mean travelling to London.

One night, just as Roland had stopped berating me through my bedroom door, another commotion started under my window. Looking out over the courtyard, I saw a thick set man, with dark curly hair, staggering along the pathway, and it was obvious that he had taken too much liquor. He appeared to be calling for someone but I could not make out whom, as his speech was slurred. Suddenly I heard the courtyard door open and Rosie appeared and began to remonstrate with the drunken man. He waved his fist at her and pushed her roughly, but she managed to pacify him. Taking his arm she walked off with him, her large bulk supporting him as he staggered drunkenly against her.

Looking back she spied me at the window, her face looked stricken and I felt an overwhelming feeling of sadness emulate from her, which made me unsettled and depressed. The next morning when I enquired what had happened, she merely told me that it was her husband so I thought it was best not to pursue the matter.

On occasions, when I knew Roland was out and the weather was inclement I wandered around the house. It comforted me remembering how it used to be. There were now no objects of value in any of the rooms. Some of them were still locked and those that were open had layers of dust on the remaining furniture. To pass the time I began to clean the open rooms. However, I was so exhausted with the lack of sleep that I found the role of housekeeper to much for me. After a while I gave up the task as being to onerous and just about managed to maintain my room and the kitchen. I asked Rosie to see if she could find a girl to help me, but she told me that everyone was frightened of Roland and nobody would come.

Occasionally, I would find myself almost collapsing with exhaustion onto the wooden settle in the hallway. Listening to the grandfather clock chiming the hour, I would realise that I had sat in a trance-like state for several hours. Meanwhile Annabelle would fall asleep at my feet.

One day I ventured out of my room, having heard the front door slam, when to my dismay, I saw I had been mistaken and Roland was still in the hallway. He had obviously tricked me into believing that he had left the house. I shook with fright on seeing him, and I was about to run back to my room, when he caught me by the arm. I screamed involuntarily but to my surprise he said calmly,

'It was a mistake you know! You shouldn't have come.'

I stopped in my tracks. I was so relieved at his calm manner that I stammered,

'I had to come. I received a letter that said that my sister had a child. I had no idea. She is all that is left of my family.'

He nodded and peered at me, his eyes boring into my face as if trying to read my thoughts. Then towering over me as I shrunk back uncertain what was happening he said quietly,

'I sent the letter.'

His fingers eased their pressure and releasing me he strode away and disappeared out of the front door. Un-nerved I peered out behind him and saw he was headed towards the stable. Soon I heard the sound of horse's hooves on the stony path as he galloped away in the direction of the village. The moment having passed, my legs gave way and I clung onto the banister rail trying to calm my nerves. This man who was so obviously deranged at night had been the one who sent the letter. I did not understand why he had sent it when I was obviously so unwelcome. I realised that somewhere deep in the dark recesses of his insanity, the man that had been my sister's husband had emerged for a moment. However, I did not let his appearance of normality make me relax my guard and I still waited every morning for confirmation that he was in a drugged stupour before I ventured out.

If I heard him moving around downstairs, Annabelle and I sat in my bedroom, until it was safe. I spent many hours just willing the time away. This seemed second nature to Annabelle as she merely sat passively, as I read to her. I even tried to give her some tuition but it was extremely difficult, as she did not acknowledge that I had spoken to her. Only once, was there a glimmer of hope when on my calling her name several times, she said to her doll,

'Tell the lady Annie, that my name ain't Annabelle. The man don't like it.'

'Do you want to be called Annie?' I asked.

'It is our secret, don't tell anyone, or you will be punished. Daddy will punish you. Don't worry, I won't let the man hurt you,' she chanted in an ethereal voice that sent shivers down my spine. It was the same tone that Roland used as he pleaded and whined at my bedroom door.

What was the secret that Roland did not want told? The child was terrified of him I knew that. Pulling her to me as I always did, I held her tight and she stood rigidly within my arms. Then for the first time she looked me straight in the eye. The look was deep and penetrating as if she was trying to read my mind. Surprised, I whispered her name and she immediately looked away and returning to the bundle of rags that was her doll, started to sing eerily,

'Go to sleep Annie. You ain't got no mummy. I'll be your mummy now.' I wondered if this was what Rosie used to croon to her for the short time she stayed with her at the alehouse.

I had still heard nothing from my friends. In desperation, when I could, I sat out on a tree stump waiting for the expected mail coach. All the while hoping that a letter would come. I must have looked particularly despondent each time there was no letter, as the coachman used to call out to me,

'Nothing today miss. You want to go inside. You will catch your death. You don't look well!'

I knew that I did not look well. I spent a lot of time looking in the mirror to see a pale, strained face staring back with a cloud of red, unruly hair, stuffed in an ungainly fashion in a black snood. I also noticed that I had diminished in size. Although I had never been a very large person, I had lost weight and my clothes were beginning to look too big for me. I disguised my body with the shawls from the linen chest, and I was chilled through to the bone most of the time, even with a roaring fire in my room. The house's musky smell and damp seemed to permeate my clothes and my senses.

I found some material and made some warmer things to wear, but neither of us looked the height of fashion. In fact we looked like the poor people from the village in our plain woollen clothes. The most colourful person was Rosie, still in her faded dress. I knew she was not respectable, but I did not care. Her cheerful nature was the one bright part of the day. I would eagerly look out for her arrival. However, although she would still sit through the night she did not come so often in the day. When I asked her about it she told me that her husband would not permit it as he did not consider that Stoneleigh was a safe place. I could only agree, not a day passed without anxiety about Roland's state of mind.

One day she came in smiling that Roland had gone away and immediately a relaxed atmosphere descended and she sat and talked freely. She had bought some provisions and putting down the items she leaned back in the chair sighing.

'When I first knew 'im miss, 'e was so kind and 'andsome, 'im and 'is brother. We used to go to Vauxhall Gardens and had such a wonderful time. Roland used to buy me such trinkets......' she stopped suddenly, seeing the scandalised look on my face.

'You are shocked miss. I shouldn't 'ave said nuffing. You're a lady, you don't know about gentlemen. Why should you?'

'Are you telling me that you and Roland socialised together?' I was astounded.

'Them's all the same miss. They fink they're gentlemen but they ain't. Them's all the same. Roland always treated me so kind though, giving me money for me brothers and sisters. I knew nuffing could come of it. 'E was young then, just a lad sowing 'is wild oats. I knew one day 'he'd find someone and it would be goodbye to old Rosie, but 'e always saw me right. It's no good though. I've got to say it. That poor man should never 'ave married yer sister?'

'What on earth do you mean? They loved each other.'

'Yes, 'e idolised her, but she was always mooning around, reading them books. She was always ill. Roland used to come to me and cry about how much 'e loved 'er and 'ow she 'ad withdrawn 'erself from 'im.'

'Withdrawn herself?' I asked, not understanding. 'If she was ill he surely could understand that she did not want to socialise and entertain.'

'No miss, you don't understand. 'E was a man with men's needs you know, miss, a wife's duties...'

Scandalised I interrupted,

'Stop! I think you are forgetting yourself. Please don't tell me any more. Yes my sister was delicate and artistic but I don't understand any of this. When I last saw her she was happy and in love. How dare you speak like that to me '

'I'm sorry miss, I have upset you, please don't be angry. I wanted you to understand but you are young, you don't know about such things.'

'Please! I am not a child!'

'There are all kinds of love miss. I don't think you understand men. You 'ave 'ardly experienced life. I can't describe to you what it is like to be dragged up in a dirty 'ovel, with ten brothers and sisters and 'ow you have to beg to stop yourself starving. 'Ow grateful you are when, a decent, respectable man offers you 'is protection......'

Shocked as I was I felt ashamed at my outburst. No I did not understand the poverty and degradation that life had brought her. I had always been well looked after in a family that loved me. Taking her hand which was rough and cracked I said,

'Don't let's talk about it anymore. I am sorry that I was angry. I know that I can't imagine how it must have been for you. All I know is that I am grateful for your help. We must not disagree; I need you to help me. Without you I can't imagine what I would have done. I rely on you to allow me to stay at Stoneleigh in relative safety.'

'It's the medicine miss. It's driving 'im insane.' I noticed that tears were beginning to roll down her cheeks and sniffing loudly, she wiped them away with her crusty and reddened hands. There was so much I wanted and needed to know, but Rosie couldn't help me. My dear sister had married with such hopes and happiness and had died within two years. She left a husband and child who both seemed on the verge of insanity. I knew I had to leave Stoneleigh before I suffered the same fate as my sister. There was nothing for it, if I didn't hear soon I would have to take action myself and take the coach to London and visit the lawyer and see if he could help me.

The two of us sat together, consoling each other. Every few minutes Rosie would sniff loudly and I offered her my lace handkerchief, which she took with a sigh. She wiped her rouged face, now streaked with tears and blew her nose loudly. The noise attracted the child and she suddenly peered into Rosie's face. It was a completely different expression to the blank lost look that was usually on her face. Then a voice so shrill, ethereal that it startled me asked,

'Why is she crying?'

Annabelle's little fingers then rubbed at Rosie's tearstained face, making dirty marks on the fat cheeks. Rosie rubbed her face again with the now grubby handkerchief.

'Old Rosie is all right love. Don't you worry!'

Annabelle took the piece of rag that she held and scrubbed at her own face, then looked surprised that her own cheeks were not wet. I too began to cry, only this time with happiness. For the first time, Annabelle had actually become involved in what had been happening around her. Hugging her tightly, I kissed the little face but she struggled free. The moment had passed. Not looking at either of us, she began rocking and murmuring to her doll again. However, there was hope; we had actually broken through the communication barrier at last.

CHAPTER FOUR

'I am giddy, expectation whirls me round. The imaginary relish is so sweet that it enchants my sense.'

Troilus and Cressida Act 3, Sc 2

It was several days later as I took up my usual position waiting for the mail coach, when the driver called out to me that he had a letter for me. Excitedly, I took it from him and sat down on my tree stump to read it. I recognised the writing; it was from my good friend Leticia. It rambled on in her usual disconnected fashion. Full of grand balls, dinners and the latest gossip, until finally, there it was, what I had most hoped for, tacked on as a P.S. It was an invitation to come and stay in London for as long as I needed. It was as if a great burden had been lifted from me. I could leave Stoneleigh now and go to Holland Park immediately. Happily I made my way back, the castellated building even beginning to look less gloomy after my news. Joyfully I began wandering passed the lake and down the overgrown paths, singing to myself in the winter sunshine. Then just as quickly as my joy arrived a cold dagger stabbed my heart. I would not be able to take Annabelle with me and I could not leave her at Stoneleigh. It was no use. The child was too strange to be accepted by such a difficult woman as Leticia's mother. Lady Westerham, was an unmitigating snob. She would never permit a child who spoke like the worst kind of guttersnipe, to live in her household. What is more Annabelle, did not behave like a normal child. I could see her ladyship now, her tall angular figure pacing the floor. The stern features contorted with disgust, bellowing,

'Oh the shame! The disgrace!'

What is more, when she became aware of Roland's decline, it would become public knowledge in a few days. I was in despair. What could I do? If I left Annabelle with no arrangements made for her welfare, I would never forgive myself. Sadly, I folded the letter and headed back to the house. The skies turned overcast and it seemed as if the heavens had decided to match my mood and soon sheets of rain began to fall as I hurried inside. I felt as if I was being drawn back to a prison. It was too cold and wet to sit in the folly, so I returned to my bedroom and my little companion. There had been no repetition of her engaging with me. Annabelle still addressed everything through the rag doll, which was absolutely filthy and torn, and still wearing the dirty silk. I had once tried to remove it, so that it could be washed, but Annabelle had become hysterical at the prospect and so I left it alone. As we sat in the bedroom, the house seemed eerily silent; I was quite relaxed as I knew that Roland was in his drugged sleep in his study. On my way in I had peered through the crack in the door, to check that we were safe and seeing him slumped over the desk as usual, I knew that he would be there for some hours.

I was tired of being trapped in my room and taking Annabelle with me I wandered forlornly around the house. I looked again into the dining room, where there was a large wooden table and a dresser that had been full of crystal glassware and was now empty and covered with dust. I idly drew pictures in the dust, on the dining table and Annabelle copied me silently. I walked along the corridor trying the other doors, even though I knew they were always locked. I remembered that there had once been a large grand piano in the music room but it was not in any of the rooms that I could gain access to. I used to love to play the piano when I lived in Paris. Sometimes my father would hold evening soirees and my friends and I would entertain the guests with our playing. I felt sad that, I could not even pass a few hours playing for comfort.

I entered the library and sat on the window seat, looking out at the grey day. Sighing, I looked for a book to read and I noticed that there was the edge of a gold leaf picture frame poking out from the side of a bookcase. I wedged my fingers into the gap between the wall and the bookcase and gently eased out the frame, scraping my fingers as I did so. The frame was quite tightly wedged and it took some effort to manoeuvre it out of its storage place. The picture had been bound in sackcloth, which became caught on a splinter from the bookcase as I pulled it out from the gap. It took a great deal of force to heave it out, when the cloth suddenly ripped and the picture was free, nearly knocking me over as it was released. I removed what remained of the cloth, sneezing amidst the clouds of dust. Thinking it was probably another Fitzroy ancestor, I turned it over and with shock I saw Freya's wedding portrait. The one that had been missing from the staircase.

I shivered just as though someone had walked over my grave. There she was just as I remembered her. The Devereaux red hair, beautifully dressed and interlaced with pearls. Tears welled in my eyes as I looked at the exquisite heart shaped face, the malachite eyes, staring out at me from the painting. She was wearing an emerald green satin dress and around her neck were the Fitzroy diamonds. The artist had captured her perfectly. Those green eyes watched me thoughtfully, as I stared back. It was an expression I knew so well. She was forever 21 years old, the age that I was now. Had she experienced the same trauma in the two years that they were married that I had experienced in the weeks I had lived in her home? I hoped not, surely their life together had not been one of fear and hatred. I hoped that the Roland I knew now was not the Roland that she had married.

Sadly, I draped the sacking over the portrait but I could not bear to leave it, unloved and unwanted. Hidden away as if it was something no one should see. With Annabelle trailing behind, I struggled up the stairs with it and stood it on my bedside chair where I could see it everyday. Annabelle looked at me watchfully, and several times I saw her stand in front of the portrait as if studying it. I knew that she had no idea who the beautiful woman in the painting was. However, she seemed interested in just looking at it. I stood behind the child and told her how beautiful her mother was and what a loving kind person my sister had been. The child did not seem to understand but I wanted her to know who her mother was. I wanted her to feel that Freya watched over her. Just saying those words made a feeling of calm descend over me and I felt instinctively that I was speaking the truth, and that Freya wanted me to know it. The sense of her radiated from the portrait. After that day, Annabelle repeatedly stood in front of the painting, tracing the outline of my sister on the glass. Occasionally she went up to the glass and pressed her face against Freya's and then I heard her shrill little voice,

'No, 'e watches!'

'Who?' I asked

'The man. This pretty lady, don't come, 'e comes. Quiet Annie, go to sleep Annie, shut up you bitch or you'll be sorry. 'urts Annie.'

Scandalised by her language I gasped,

'What man? Was it your father? Did he hurt you?'

She didn't answer but returned to stare at the painting. As I looked over her shoulder with a start, I saw my reflection in the glass. My face had blended with Freya and I realised that I was looking at a mirror image of myself. I had become relaxed about the unbecoming black snood and my long curling hair was unrestrained for a change. I had forgotten what I looked like. It had been a long time since I had looked in a mirror. Although my eyes were grey not green like my sister, and due to my weight loss my face was thinner, we looked the same. Now like her and at the same age, I was in the same situation, living in her house. Only now it was a house of tears ruled by a lunatic. The only difference was that I could escape. I asked Annabelle again about 'the man' but she did not reply, instead she gazed at the painting in wonder, chewing on the dirty rag doll.

Suddenly, my heart stopped as I heard the sound of the door opening downstairs and the sound of footsteps in the entrance hall. My nerves were on edge as I peered round the bedroom door; ready to slam it shut and bolt it quickly, if I should see him there. Instead of the stooping figure I saw someone else. It was a taller man than Roland; his back was toward me, as he took off his rain soaked cloak and threw his gloves onto the table. I watched in silence, unsure whether to speak. As I anxiously looked on, the floor board creaked noisily and I darted back. The man turned and overjoyed I recognised Edmund. In my relief I began to run excitedly down the stairs, and for a moment he looked startled, and then his sun burned face broke into a smile,

'Why its Miss Sparky, forgive me for a moment, I didn't recognise you. I thought it was...'

'Miss Sparky! A feeling of joy ran through me, I had quite forgotten that name. It was a long time since I had been called by it. My brother in law had christened me that the first time we met, when he said that I made him laugh. He held out his arms in a brotherly welcome and I desperately wanted to run into them. However, I suddenly remembered Roland in the study and I merely hovered uncertainly on the stairs.

'My goodness you took me by surprise. You look so much like your sister. Of course it was a trick of the light.' He smiled broadly, 'I came as soon as I received your letter.'

I raised my finger to my lips, to warn him to be silent. Whispering I said,

'Edmund, things are so awful here. Roland is insane, there is a child. I can't stay here and yet I have no where to go!' The words came tumbling out and I collapsed into a pool of tears. My nerves at breaking point.

Edmund looked concerned,

'My dear girl,' he said taking my arm in kindly fashion and sitting me down on the wooden settle. 'Sit down and we will talk properly.' As he did so I realised that we were talking loudly near the study door and I shuddered with fear and quickly stood up. 'We can't talk here. Your brother is in the study. If we wake him, we will be subjected to another violent outburst. Please come to my room upstairs. Annabelle and I spend all the day there when it is cold outside. Edmund looked puzzled.

'Annabelle?'

'Yes, I found her here. A sad and neglected child, starving and cold. She does not seem to be able to communicate with anyone. Something is seriously wrong and I do not know what to do.'

'Where are the servants?'

'Servants! There are no servants, I have been here several weeks and have had to struggle on alone, just so that I could protect the child. It has become a nightmare.'

'I don't understand. Why is my niece here? I thought that the child was away at school.'

'No, she is here,' I said quietly. 'Come with me!'

He paused on the bottom step,

'I don't think I should......'

'What does propriety matter now?' I shouted as I raced up the stairs and angrily opened the door to reveal Annabelle sitting on the floor rocking back and forth, clutching her doll.

'She looks so strange,' he murmured.

'Annabelle is terrified of her father. Most of the time she is too traumatised even to speak. If it wasn't for Rosie I do not know what I would have done.'

'Rosie!' A flicker of annoyance appeared on his face, 'Is she here?'

'She comes everyday. Without her Roland would behave even more like a lunatic.'

Edmund's eyebrows rose with disapproval and it irritated me; he had no understanding of what was happening. Looking closely at him, I noticed that he seemed older. There were deep creases around his eyes leaving white marks that contrasted with his brown face. However, the blue eyes were still just as intense as in the young portrait that I had spoken to on the attic landing. His face softened,

'Forgive me! It is just that the thought of Rosie looking after anyone, interests me. The only one Rosie looks after, is Rosie!'

'No! She has been a good friend to me. Without her we would not have survived. Just come with me and I will show you the room where this child has spent the last six months. It is right at the top of the house.'

We climbed the endless staircase together, the sound of his boots ringing on the wooden floor. Reaching the door I put the key in the lock and it would not turn. My hands were numb with cold and Edmund took the key from me and with a quick flick opened the door. He immediately recoiled at the revolting stench that emanated from the room as my eyes stung.

'Good heavens, what on earth is in there?'

'Filth! It has been Annabelle's living quarters for months. It is filled with mouldy food, dead flies and excrement......'

'What on earth has been going on here?' He slammed the door angrily, making me jump at the sound. He steadied me but looked distracted,

'Goodness your nerves are disturbed. I will arrange for someone to come and fumigate the place immediately.'

'Do you know that Rosie comes everyday to check that Roland is all right. She sits up all night with him.'

'I didn't even know she was here. I have known Rosie for many years, but I know what and who she is. She is not to be trusted, especially with money. I suggest you lock any valuables out of temptation's way.'

I laughed scornfully,

'What valuables? There aren't any.'

He frowned,

'I knew that things were pretty bad with my brother but I had no idea about the child. I thought she was away at school. The last time I saw him he was making the arrangements'

'What can I do Edmund? Where can I take the child, please help me to take her away. Somebody must do something.'

'Don't worry, Miss Sparky, leave it to me. I can see you are not well. It has obviously been a stressful time for you. I will make all the necessary arrangements. This is not your responsibility, I am only sorry that you have become involved. I should have returned and looked into the situation before. However, my brother and I have never been close and after the last time I left him to his own devices, besides I have been away with the regiment.'

We walked down in silence and we reached my room he asked,

'Have you any friends with which you can stay?'

'Of course, but how can I with Annabelle?'

As I went to enter my room he took my arm,

'Propriety or not, I do not think that it would be appropriate for me to enter your bedroom. Come downstairs and we will see what we can do.'

I nodded,

'But first I must tidy my hair.'

'Leave it. That is how I remember you with that crowning glory,' he smiled.

'No I cannot,' I sighed. I wear a snood as the sight of my hair seems to anger Roland. I cannot bear more arguments.' Edmund walked on ahead as I ran inside and crammed my hair into the snood, just in case I met up with Roland.

'Not vanity then? ' he smiled. I didn't answer he did not know what life had been like here. As I rejoined him he asked,

'What on earth possessed you to come here?'

'I had a letter telling me that Freya had a child. I didn't know. Apparently Roland sent it, but since I have been here I have been unable to speak to him. When he sees me he becomes so angry, especially as my hair disturbs him. I have spent the last few weeks hiding from him.' I thought it politic not to mention the nights of pleading at the bedroom door.

Edmund expression changed into one of annoyance,

'Do not worry, Aphra. I will talk to him and try to resolve the situation.'

I leaned forlornly against the wall.

'I noticed that you have removed Freya's portrait?'

'I didn't. I found it hidden away in the library.'

'I see!' He sat, deep in thought then continued, I do not know what has happened but Roland must have become even more degenerate than he appeared when I last saw him.' Then standing he added, 'Still that is my problem.'

Weakly I asked, 'Was it my sister's death that has brought him to this? What happened to her?'

'I do not know. I hardly ever saw her. I must admit on the last few occasions that I visited, she seemed very tired and listless. She had not long had the child and I assumed she was recovering. Whenever I saw her she was usually lying on the couch in the salon. I believe the family physician diagnosed low spirits.'

'Were you here when she died?'

'No I was abroad.'

'What about her child? I suppose a wet nurse was arranged after the birth.'

'I wouldn't know. As far as I am aware, Freya looked after Annabelle herself.'

'But how could she? She died when she was born.'

'No, when the child was about six months old.'

'What!' I gasped. 'That can't be true!'

Edmund's brow wrinkled and he looked puzzled,

'But surely you know that she took her own life!'

'No!' My head spun and I visibly swayed at the awful news, and Edmund steadied me.

'Come and sit down. You look ill yourself, all this must have been a terrible ordeal for you.' He ushered me into the library.

'How?' I asked weakly.

'I believe she took an overdose of laudanum. There was a note.'

I was unable to speak. I felt as if there was a lump that was so large in my throat that I could not swallow. After a few minutes I asked,

'What did it say?'

'I never saw it. I believe it was destroyed before the funeral, I do not think Roland wanted anyone to know what she had done. The way she died was kept as quiet as possible. It was not long after your sister's death that Roland and I quarrelled and I have not seen him since.'

I felt sick at the news. My sister had been in such despair that she had ended her life, leaving her child. Was there nothing in this house except sadness and grief?

'How could she have done such a thing and left her baby?'

'You are asking the wrong person. She did not confide in me. I heard that she had no interest in the child from birth. I only gleaned that information from the servants afterwards, Roland did not usually confide in me. I became concerned about the state of the finances as there were rumours of enormous gambling debts and notes being given all over London. I was trying to buy them up but it could not continue and when I challenged him about his mismanagement of the estate, we argued. I decided that if he wanted to squander his inheritance, then he was a grown man and responsible for his own actions. I had enough responsibility with my mother's estate at

Threshingham Park. I left with my regiment shortly afterwards and have not had any contact with him since.'

I must have looked totally shocked as I could not speak, my thoughts in a muddle at the news of Freya's suicide. Edmund put his arm about my shoulders and said softly,

'I am sorry. I suppose the news about Freya must have been a shock to you.'

'Since I came to Stoneleigh, life has been nothing but shocks.' I sniffed now trying to stop the tears.

'Don't let this place make you lose your sparkle.' Edmund said quietly. 'We want Miss Sparky back. You look tired. Leave everything to me. I will arrange things. I think it best that you and the child come with me to Threshingham Park, you can't continue to stay here. As it is your reputation will be in ruins, if it is spread abroad that you have stayed here alone. What will people think about a young woman being here with someone of Roland's character?'

'I was not alone. I had a chaperone, Rosie.' Edmund shook his head in disbelief and absentmindedly brushed his thick blonde hair out of his eyes,

'Where is Roland now?'

'In the study!'

'You stay here. I am going to speak to him.'

'No! Please do not. He'll be angry if you disturb him.'

'To hell with him! I am the one who is angry. If I'd known that the child was here I ....' he didn't finish, on seeing my stricken face.

'Please excuse my outburst but this situation is intolerable!'

'Rosie thinks that he is ill. He is completely paranoid. He thinks that everyone is spying on him. I don't want to witness another incident of his rage, besides it upsets Annabelle. Wait until Rosie comes. She is the only person he seems to listen to.'

'Ah, yes Rosie!' He stopped for a moment as if thinking about his next step and then continued,

'I am going to finish stabling my horse and then I shall return. You take the child and go into the garden. The rain has stopped now, wrap up warmly and wait until I call you. I will speak to my brother and obtain some answers. Whether he likes it or not, this situation will be resolved once and for all. However, I think it will be better if you don't hear what I am going to say.'

I was so relieved and glad that someone else was making the decisions for me that I ran up the staircase to fetch Annabelle. As I did so I could not help but look anxiously at the study door as I whispered,

'Thank you for coming. What would I have done if you had not?'

He replied,

'I was finalising my affairs, before the regiment goes abroad. It was it was a piece of luck that I was on leave and called into my agent's office. He had not yet forwarded the letter and I was able to read it. I came as quickly as I could. I owe it to my family name if nothing else to try to improve matters. Already people are beginning to enquire why nothing is seen of Roland in London. His voice sounded so reassuring and I was so overwrought that I burst into tears again. Putting his arm around me he said softly,

'Don't worry! I will sort out this mess.'

Leaving the house Annabelle and I made our way to the Roman temple. The sun was trying to peep out from behind a cloud and it seemed a good omen. I was so happy that I decided to run down to village, to tell Rosie, that our saviour had arrived. Annabelle resisted walking out of the area she was familiar with, but at last for the first time gave in and we walked down the lane to the village. For once I had lightness in my step.

As we passed the tied cottages, the sky darkened again, but luckily the rain held off and I soon found myself outside the rundown alehouse. I knocked loudly on the red front door, which was splintered and rotten. It seemed an eternity before the door opened and a thick-necked man, with curly hair, who I recognised as the man I had seen from the window previously, asked aggressively what I wanted.

'Is Rosie here?'

'No,' he barked and shut the door.

I could hear the sound of raised voices and then the sound of a scuffle and the door opened again. This time Rosie appeared in the doorway, she looked upset and I noticed that there was a red mark on her cheek. Her eyes looked red from crying.

'What has happened Rosie?'

Before she could reply the man pushed her aside and bellowed,

'I gave it to her and she'll get another if she don't watch out. She ain't running off to the big 'ouse, pandering to the likes of you. You want a servant, then you pay wages likes yer should. Getting 'er to cook and clean for nothing. She can do that 'ere.'

I was surprised at the vehemence of his speech, but I refused to be intimated. I had been indoctrinated by a master. The man was quite burly, but not very tall. Glaring at him I retorted,

'How dare you speak to me in that fashion? I came to speak to Rosie. I have no wish to discuss anything with you!'

'Oh don't you my lady upstart. Well I'm 'er 'usband and I says she ain't talking to you.'

Realising that it was no use remonstrating with this rude, uncouth man, my only thought was that I should offer him money. I knew that was the only thing that a person like him would be interested in.

'I will give you one guinea, if you will let Rosie come with me.'

I saw his eyes light up and his manner changed and he became more acquiescent,

'Well that puts a different complexion on it,' and he greedily grabbed the money from my hand. All this time Annabelle had been standing there watching him in silence until she clung to my skirt and shouted loudly,

'Man 'urts Rosie. Man 'urts Annie.'

Surprised I protectively put my arm around her shoulders as Rosie's husband sneered,

'Take that lunatic child away from 'ere!' The pushing Rosie out of the doorway, he aggressively called out,

'Well go on then, clear off to the big 'ouse. That's what you want ain't it?'

Rosie miserably walked along beside me,

'I am sorry about me 'usband miss.' I didn't reply as Rosie addressed Annabelle.

'So you decided to speak to us today, Annie....,' then instantly correcting herself added, 'Sorry, Annabelle?'

Annabelle responded with a strange chilling smile. There was a knowing look on her face which disturbed me. After we had walked a little way I asked,

'Does your husband hit you often?'

'No, only when 'e gets angry.'

'I thought you said he was worried about you coming to the house.'

'I lied. 'E is angry cos there is no money. Roland was always generous. He brought me the alehouse but now everything has changed. We ain't got no tin. The ale house don't pay its way and we owe money to everyone.'

'Rosie I have some good news for a change' I said excitedly. 'Edmund has arrived.'

Rosie beamed, revealing that one of her teeth was broken. Noticing my stare she quickly put her hand over her mouth and mumbled,

'I knew 'e would come. Didn't I tell you miss. I knew 'e wouldn't leave Annie.'

As we walked along suddenly Annabelle began shaking her doll and in a complete imitation of Rosie's husband screeched.

'Rosie get your fat arse out of 'ere and take that brat with yer. Get some tin out of 'im or don't come back.'

Rosie gasped and flushed a dramatic scarlet. Shocked, I realised that Annabelle was repeating parrot fashion, words she had heard during the time she had stayed with Rosie. Returning to the ale house had triggered her memories. Rosie turned away in embarrassment but I squeezed her hand reassuringly.

'It is all right Rosie. It doesn't matter.' I was sorry for her. The poor woman had tried to look after one deranged man, whilst living with another. How could I be judgemental about a woman living an existence that I could only imagine?

'You should not 'ave given 'im that money miss, 'e will drink or gamble it away.'

I shrugged.

'I would have thought that he has enough ale in the alehouse, without buying any?'

'No! I told you, the ale house don't pay. We can't get stocks cos we owe too much money to the suppliers.'

As she spoke I realised that we were very near the house and thought it better that we did not return as Edmund had requested.

'Edmund is trying to resolve things with Roland. I suggest that we go and sit in the folly for a while.'

Rosie looked puzzled, as she didn't understand what I was referring to but just followed me and we sat inside just passing the time until we saw Edmund walking along the overgrown pathway looking for me. His expression was one of irritation and seeing that I was with Rosie he looked furious. I could only assume his discussion with Roland had not been fruitful. Rosie spied him in the distance and squealing like a child ran out to him excitedly,

'It's the Major! It's the Major,' she almost shrieked and Edmund stopped in his tracks at the excitement in her voice. She took his arm and almost danced up the path with him whilst he tried to extricate himself. I remained apprehensively in the background as he disentangled himself, and ignoring her addressed me,

'I have tried to reason with Roland but I feel that he is beyond reasoning. I had no idea that things had deteriorated so far. I think that he is in need of medical treatment. In his present condition he will not listen to any sensible suggestions. I will have to consult my lawyer and make the necessary arrangements to prevent Stoneleigh from being sold from under our feet.'

'What about Annabelle?'

'I do not think that he even acknowledges her existence. He didn't seem to recognise her name. As you stated he is completely paranoid. I could hardly convince him that I was his brother. He seemed to think that I was someone sent by the authorities to spy on him. I think that your arriving at Stoneleigh has caused even more turmoil. In his insanity he believes that you are Freya.'

Rosie had been quiet whilst he was talking, but she suddenly broke into the conversation at the word insanity.

'It ain't true that 'e is insane. Oh Edmund, you can't 'ave im locked away. What will I do?' and she began to wail loudly. I saw his expression change at hearing Rosie address him as Edmund as he said coldly,

'I thought that you were worried about Roland. I should have known that you were more interested in your own welfare,'

'Please, don't be unkind.' I said. 'This is not helping matters.'

He replied brusquely,

'I will have to stay a couple of days and make the arrangements.' He then bent down to pick up Annabelle. As he did so the little girl reacted with terror and began to fight and scream, kicking Edmund violently, her teeth sinking into his hand. As he pulled his hand away, she became stiff with fear, her eyes rolling in her head. . Having been lulled into a false sense of security, by her seeming to be unaware of Edmund's presence, I was taken aback.

'What on earth is the matter with the child? She has seen me before,' he urged

'Annabelle! Annabelle! It is all right, it is your Uncle Edmund. He loves you, he would not hurt you.' It was all to no avail as she continued to scream, her teeth fixed together and her eyes rolling upwards so only the white could be seen. Shaken Edmund hastily placed her back on the ground.

'I think I had better return to the house. I will speak to you when the child is not present.'

'No, it is all right, Rosie will take her on ahead and we can talk on our way back.' Rosie pacified the child and as the child calmed down, Edmund shook his head,

'I think the child will need to be taken to London to see some medical people. They will decide what to do with her. She looked like she was having an epileptic fit. I had no idea that she suffered from that condition.'

'No!' I said firmly. 'I will not permit her to be examined and pulled about and then locked away. She has already suffered terribly. The poor child has been sorely used and mistreated. You know what they will do! She needs to be helped and loved, not locked away in some dreadful institution. She does not have epilepsy. No, she is Freya's daughter and I will look after her myself.'

'That is impossible. How can you look after this child? You have a rightful place in society with your London friends, Annabelle can't be a part of that in her present condition.'

Dispiritedly, I had no idea how to reply. He was right. Then Edmund said kindly,

'I know it is difficult for you, but you must understand the predicament that you find yourself in. You are a woman alone. You are in need of protection.'

'Like the protection you gave Rosie.' I retorted angrily. Edmund looked stunned,

'I think that you are confusing me with my brother. I will ignore that comment as you are upset and we will not refer to it again. I am trying to help you and resolve the situation. However, I am a bachelor, I am a serving soldier, and my regiment is due to embark for Varna in two weeks, besides at present I live in rooms in the Albany. There are no women allowed there. If you keep the child, what are the alternatives? Staying at Stoneleigh? I don't think that recommends itself at all.'

My heart sunk and I murmured an apology, adding,

'Perhaps, we can hire some servants, and a nurse for the child?'

'And what of Roland, you yourself said that you have to hide away, for fear of his rages. That is no way to live and it will be an impossibility.'

'I think his problems stem from the medicine that he seems to be addicted to. Perhaps, we could water it down and try to wean him off it. If he did not rely on it so much, perhaps he will be his normal self again.'

'What medicine?'

'I think he is addicted to chloral.'

'Good heavens! What does a young woman like you know of such matters?'

'I recognised the smell of the medicine from my father's sick room.'

'I see!' The expression on his face hardened.

Rosie said that she tried before, perhaps we could try again......'

Edmund interrupted,

'If the cause of his decline is due to chloral, that explains his paranoia. I believe that Roland is seriously beyond any help that you can offer. I knew that he was facing ruin from his gambling debts but this situation is beyond even my understanding.'

'What can we do?'

Edmund didn't reply as we reached a tangled rose arbour and stood for a moment, and pulled a rosebud from the bush and handed it to me.

'Please don't look so sad. I remember your beautiful smile and I want to see it again. The first thing we must do is to arrange somewhere for you to stay. Perhaps I can find you a place to stay nearby. My brother's situation is another matter. I can stay for a few days so I will arrange for the child to be seen by a physician and then perhaps he can advise what is to be done. Meanwhile, we will see if we can persuade a few of the people from the village to help us open the house up again.'

'Rosie said that they were frightened of Roland.'

'Until I make the necessary arrangements, Roland will be away. It has been agreed that I will pay off some of his debts on condition he leaves Stoneleigh for a short time.

I nodded forlornly, but as I edged through the arbour my hair caught on the branches. Edmund tried to free me, as I squirmed and wriggled to escape from the thorny prickles. He bent over me and gently teased the snood free, as he did so, my hair tumbled down to my waist in its usual unruly fashion. His expression became unreadable and a look passed between us until I, embarrassed by his proximity, felt my cheeks burning and turned away. Feeling foolish, I tried to force my hair back into the snood at the back of my neck as Edmund gently pulled my hair free. An awkward silence followed until he laughed, his eyes twinkling merrily adding,

'The hair! I remember it well. The Devereaux sisters with the clouds of beautiful red hair were always the belles of the ball.'

'I think those days are gone.' I said sadly.

'They will come again,' he reassured. I didn't answer. It felt strange talking to Edmund in this way. Although we were relatives by marriage, we hardly knew each other. The intervening years had made him almost a stranger and I had been so young when we last met. Ignoring my silence he continued,

'Do you remember the engagement ball? How beautiful the two of you looked, all the other young ladies were quite jealous? The young blades were filling up your dance card and I had a long wait for you to find me a spare dance before the end of the ball.'

I smiled, wanly,

'Yes that was when you first called me Miss Sparky and said that I would break many a man's heart. I was just a silly young girl. I have had to grow up a lot since then.'

He laughed,

'Nothings changed. It is unfortunate that you have been thrust into this situation, but I promise you, that I will always be there to help you. Please allow me to do so.'

'Thank you Edmund. You do not know how relieved I am to have you here. I suddenly became aware for the first time that he was wearing his hat and cloak again.

'You are not leaving?' My voice rose in panic at the thought.

'I must go to Lemington, but I shall return as soon as possible.'

I knew Lemington was a village about 5 miles away and the prospect of being alone in the house again, was terrible for me,

'But what about Roland? Is he still at Stoneleigh now? Is he angry because you wakened him?'

He laughed, showing his white teeth,

'Please don't concern your pretty head any more. I can deal with my brother. He has already left very grudgingly I might add. In the next few days, I will arrange for some staff from my household to come to Stoneleigh and start putting it back in order. I assume most of the valuables have been stolen and sold, especially if Rosie is around.'

I could say nothing he knew Rosie much more than I did. He then continued,

'You and the child must come to Threshingham Park'

'Will Roland permit Annabelle to do that?'

'He has no choice. If he wants me to cover his debts and make him an allowance, then he will do as he is bid.'

'Perhaps Rosie can stay with us in the house, until we leave?'

Edmund looked displeased,

'I do not think that is possible. I don't think that you understand the kind of person, Rosie is. What kind of a life she has led. She came from the sewers and left to her own devices would soon return to it.'

Astonished that he should speak to me as if I were a child I stopped in my tracks and angrily replied,

'Edmund, I realise that my life has been sheltered and you are right. I have no understanding of her life, but she has been my sole support for weeks. No one else from the village would stay. How could they understand the situation, we have found ourselves in. Whilst Roland acts as he does it will be pointless for a servant to come. They will leave within a few days.'

As we reached the entrance to the house Edmund thought for a moment.

'I did not mean to upset you. I realise how hard it has been and I suppose there is some truth in what you say. Perhaps it would be better for there to be a woman with you for the immediate future, until something can be arranged. I will call in on the alehouse and suggest to Rosie's husband, that she stays with you until you leave. It will take a few days anyway for me to make the arrangements. I know this man he will not argue, if I pay him enough.'

I stood on the steps watching as Edmund disappeared around the back of the building and returned leading his dappled grey horse. As he mounted, he called out,

'I shall return as soon as I can.' In despair, I watched as my knight in shining armour disappeared into the distance. Although he had told me that Roland was not at home, it was still with a sense of foreboding that I entered Stoneleigh.

CHAPTER FIVE

'Finish good lady; the bright day is done, and we are for
the dark'   *Antony and Cleopatra Act 5, Sc. 2*

All was silent as I entered the house and I made my way to the kitchen
where Rosie was preparing a meal. Annabelle was patiently waiting for
the food to be prepared, secure in the knowledge that this would not be her
only chance of a meal. However, I had not been able to restrain her from
stealing and hiding food, when we were not looking. Each time I cleaned
the room, I would find food concealed in nooks and crannies. One of the
favourite places being inside the pillowcase and it stayed there mouldering
until found.

We finished our meal, passing the time with Rosie excitedly talking
about how everything would change now that Edmund had arrived. We were
so engrossed that I did not hear the front door; it was only when I heard
the footsteps and thinking Edmund had returned I ventured out into the
hallway. With shock I realised it was Roland who leered at me in such a way
that it sent a chill through me. Wrenching my arm behind as I struggled to
free myself he hissed,

'This is all your fault. Who asked you to come here and spy on me? It's
you I have to thank for bringing my conniving brother here.'

'Edmund is trying to help you,' I gasped.

'Help me! I don't think so, he's come to wheedle his way into my life,
snooping and prying.' With each word his gripped tightened and he twisted
my arm making me cry out with pain. 'You will suffer for this. Don't think
I haven't seen you, sneaking about the house.'

'I have not,' I managed to gasp out indignantly. 'I have only been looking after the child.'

'Child!' his eyes glittered and he flung me aside just as Rosie and Annabelle came out of the kitchen to see what was happening. Annabelle began to scream, her body once again rigid with fear. Her eyes rolling crazily and even Rosie looked horrified at the child's re-action to her father.

'Man! Man!' Annabelle screamed.

Ignoring her, Roland's eyes fixed on the large woman behind me,

'So even you are joining them against me. I thought at least you were the only one I could trust' He was incandescent with rage, his drawn face flushing purple as he cursed us vehemently.

Rosie whispered platitudes trying to pacify him, speaking to him as a mother would to a child but it was to no avail. I stood back in astonishment, as this violent man screamed at us. I tried to remonstrate with him, but he violently pushed me aside and strode off as Rosie ran behind him with Annabelle hanging from her skirts as she tried to explain.

'Roland, what's a matter? I ain't betrayed no one.'

She got ahead of him and barred his way. Being of a bigger build, Roland could not easily push her out of the way. Instead he picked up the terrified child, and threw her against the wood panelling and I desperately I threw myself between the wall and the child to cushion the blow and we both crumpled to the floor with a sickening thud. I skinned my knees and elbows as I hit the skirting board and my ears rung with the impact of my head on wood. The child did not cry out, but went limp and I held her to me as Roland rampaged back into the kitchen. Immediately there was the sound of china being smashed as we cowered in the hall.

Taking the opportunity of his distraction, I managed to get to my feet and picking up Annabelle staggered to the stairs. Although she was thin and small she seemed to suddenly become very heavy. As I did so I heard Edmund's deep voice in the hallway. I laid the limp child on the bed and returned to the top of the stairs, where I saw Edmund take Roland by his collar and physically throw him out of the house. Roland caught his face on the tangled bushes, and screamed and cursed as the thorns drew blood. Trying to stand, he grabbed them, tearing his hands but he seemed impervious to it and he fell again, looking like an ungainly crane fly, his thin legs sprawled in the dirt.

Rosie screamed,

'Don't 'urt 'im!' as she tried to help him to his feet. However, he pushed her rudely aside and ranted and raged at us all, cursing us to hell.

Edmund's face was white with anger as he raced up the staircase, two steps at a time, to reach me. I was still trembling with shock at the top.

'Has he hurt you?'

'No, I am just shaken. I grazed my elbows but I am perfectly all right. You promised he had left,' I cried. ' Oh Edmund the child is terrified, she is so afraid of him. I have to take her away from here as quickly as possible. How can she ever recover from this nightmare? Every time she sees him, he is so cruel.'

Annabelle did not seem injured but there was a stricken expression on her face that now wore a greenish hue. She curled up in the foetal position and rocked back and forth on the bed, whilst Edmund thumped the door with his fist so vehemently that he frightened me. The fury on his face reminded of the nights with Roland. I sat down weakly as he continued,

'I passed Roland on my way to Lemington. I saw that he was making his way back to Stoneleigh so I returned. I am glad that I did.'

'We can't stay here Edmund, we can't.' I gasped, trying to control my hysteria. Edmund looked as if for a moment he had forgotten I was there and then he said,

'Wait here, I'll ensure that Roland stays away until we have everything arranged,' and he ran downstairs and I could hear raised voices as Roland's demented voice screamed,

'How dare you throw me out of my own house? I'll kill you.'

I sat forlornly in my room until everything went quiet and then looking out of the window I saw Rosie walking into the distance. She was supporting Roland's thin stooping body on her plump arm. They made an incongruous sight, she round and bulky in that well worn, blush pink dress and Roland thin and skeletonal towering over her.

Edmund returned looking strained but not wanting to upset me further, managed a smile.

'I have persuaded Roland that if he wants to see the colour of my money he must stay at the alehouse. If he does not I will arrange for a visit by the magistrate. He has seen sense. Rosie's husband will not make any trouble, my money has seen to that.'

'What about Rosie?'

'She will make sure that Roland stays there. I will delay my return to London until I have made arrangements for you and the child. News of

Roland's behaviour is becoming known. Already I am certain that half the village knows what has been happening here. The name of Fitzroy is already a black one in this area. His tenants are starving and the servants are still owed wages. If you are to return to your friends in London, it is essential we protect your name.'

My head was thumping. I was too tired to care whether there was a scandal if it became common knowledge. What did I care what people thought? I had enough troubles to last a life time. If only I had stayed in Paris. My reputation was of little consequence to me at the present moment, I just want this nightmare to end. Almost as if he had read my mind, Edmund added,

'There is an inn at Lemington. It is quite respectable, but five miles is too far to walk there. I will ride over and make the arrangements for you both to stay there. I do not want to compromise you any more than you have been already. There is also a physician at Lemington and I can arrange for the child to be examined. I also think you should see a doctor as you are looking most unwell.'

'I am just shaken. Won't questions be asked about Annabelle's strange behaviour?'

'My dear girl, if the child is the only strange person that has ever stayed at an inn, it will be a miracle.' He laughed and patted my cheek, his hands rough and large. I smiled wanly.

'That's better. It is nice to see that smile again. I thought I had quite lost my Miss Sparky. Don't worry, I will make the necessary arrangements and all this will be forgotten when you are amongst friends in London.'

'I hope so,' I said.

Just before he left I suddenly remembered the pianoforte.

'There used to be a pianoforte in this house,' I said. 'I played on it, whenever I came to stay. There was a music room but I can't remember which one it was. . Some of the doors are locked and there doesn't appear to be any keys. Do you suppose that it still here?'

'I am afraid I do not know, but it is the easiest thing in the world to open the rooms, I have some keys. This was always the family home in the past. After my mother died, I acquired Threshingham Park through her brother, Lord Ashcroft, but my boyhood was spent at Stoneleigh'

'Could you see if the pianoforte is there please? It would be such a pleasure to be able to play again?'

'Anything if it brings the smile back,' he laughed and going to a leather bound bag that he had left on the hall table he felt among its pockets and produced some keys. Taking them in hand he walked quickly to the locked door that I had often tried and in a trice the door was open. The room was very dusty and smelt of must, but this room still possessed quite a lot of furniture. There were chairs and tables stacked in piles, covered in white dust sheets. There in prime position was the pianoforte that I had such a yearning to play.

I was so glad to see it that I quickly pulled off the covers and lifting the lid, ran my hands along the keys. Pulling out the piano stool, I patted out clouds of dust from the maroon velvet and sitting down, ran my fingers softly over the keys as I did so. It had been some time since I had last played and my fingers felt stiff and inflexible but soon my hands began to play as if they had memories of their own. For a moment I was transported back to the musical evenings in Paris, with my father and his friends. All the cares and woes of life in Stoneleigh for that moment in time disappeared and I was lost in the beauty of the music. Suddenly I realised that Edmund had sat down and was looking at me in amusement and I stopped,

'Sorry, I became carried away.'

'No, please continue. It is nice to hear music again. You looked as though you had been transported to heaven!'

'Forgive me, but I was so pleased to be able to play again.'

'You certainly play very well. I am afraid that as far as music is concerned, it is a skill that I have never mastered.'

'It will be so wonderful now to be able to pass the hours playing some music. It will be like a medicine. If you are sure that Roland is not here I can come down with Annabelle. Perhaps music will have a healing effect on the child. I have heard that music can be soothing to the mind.'

Edmund stood up,

'I am afraid that it will take more than the music of a pianoforte, no matter how beautifully played, to help that child. I blame myself for not realising what was happening. However, I am forgetting myself, I was on my way round the estate. I need to find out what provisions are needed for the workers. I will return when I have made the arrangements for you to travel to the inn, and tomorrow I'll take you both there. I have some business to resolve first so that will probably take me some time. However, you have no need to worry. Roland will be busy at the alehouse, drinking and gambling away the money that I have supplied him with. I have promised more if he stays away.'

'How could this have happened to him?' I asked.

'I have no answer. We were never close. Perhaps he has a sickness of the brain. Who knows? I only know that if arrangements are not put in hand very soon, Stoneleigh will be bankrupt.'

'When he married my sister, he was such a wonderful person. How could he have changed in only a few years?'

'I don't know. My father always had concerns about him when we were young. He was always a spendthrift, mixing with the wrong people. He had a violent temper even as a child. Let's not talk about him. Soon you will be away from this and it will all be a distant memory.'

'I think that will be an impossibility.'

He disappeared into the study and began rifling through the papers and then I watched as he rode away. I went back to check on Annabelle, who was not injured. It was my body that had taken most of the impact. Annabelle's injury was mostly shock. She had uncurled herself and was once more talking quietly to her doll. I tried to read, but I had a splitting headache. I tried to rest but my mind was a whirl so I began to engage with her again.

'Well Annabelle, Uncle Edmund has come to take us away from this horrid place and he will find someone who will make you better.'

She turned and smiled at me. The corners of her mouth turned up but the smile did not reach her eyes. There was oddness about it. Then turning away from me she began repeating the words that I had used, over and over. It was un-nerving, as though she was mimicking me. Even her pronunciation sounded like mine. I found it strange and un-nerving.

Unable to bear the constant repetition I left her alone and headed back to the piano which I had an overwhelming desire to play again. I had enjoyed it so much. Edmund had left the door unlocked so that I could use it. I nervously made my way there, still unsure if Roland would suddenly appear. Having reassured myself, I made myself comfortable and in a few moments I was lost in the reverie of the music that I loved and knew so well. I found some music sheets in the piano stool and played those. Some were simple songs and I found myself singing along to them. I felt like I was newly born. My heart soaring with pleasure at the sound that emanated from the instrument.

Soon the light began to fade and as there were only small lozenged shaped windows, and it was a grey day, the room became dim. I began to find my eyes were becoming strained reading the music. I regretfully closed the lid of the instrument, but as I did so I became aware that I was not alone in the room. Someone was standing in the shadows, quietly listening and thinking it was Edmund, I laughed,

'Edmund, you startled me. Did you forget something?'

'It is not Edmund!' The voice was not the deep, melodic tone that I was expecting to hear. It was a snarl, that I was all too familiar with.

'Roland, I....' There was nothing more I could think to say, my heart was beating so fast.

Sneering, he came and stood by the piano

'You think you can conspire with my brother and turn me out of my own house,'

'No, I am leaving Stoneleigh. Edmund is making arrangements for us to stay in Lemington.'

'Us? Us who?' His voice was cold but calm and I began to relax a little, at least he was not in a rage.

'Well, if you will excuse me. It is becoming dark and I was about to fetch an oil lamp.' I tried to walk passed him but he barred my way.

'What are you doing in this room? Who said you could sneak in here?'

' Edmund unlocked it for me,' I quivered as I anxiously tried to pass whilst he again barred my way. He began to pace the room shaking his head like a trapped animal,

'Edmund! Edmund! Is there no escape from him? Everywhere I go that is all I hear. We will tell Edmund. Edmund will make the arrangements. Why isn't Roland more like his brother? Everywhere I go, people spying and sneaking about. Well it will stop. It will end.' He towered over me threateningly and I could smell alcohol on his breath. I took a deep breath and said as bravely as I could,

'Can you let me pass please?' As I went to edge past him he gripped my arm, his bony fingers digging into my flesh.

'Nobody asked you here. Why are you here? Get out of my life. I've seen you sneaking in and out of the shadows. Spying! Don't think I don't know what you are up to! Conniving with that fat cow. Hiding it! Interfering! Snooping in my papers and running whining to Edmund.'

I was terrified. He looked so nasty and brutish, his face purple and mottled. I tried to speak calmly.

'I don't know what you are talking about. I haven't hidden anything. I told you I am leaving as soon as the arrangements are made.'

His voice became harsher and he gripped me even more tightly

'You're a liar! Just like her! Just like her, but she soon learned didn't she. You'll learn the same.'

'You are hurting my arm Roland,' I said.

He began to repeat my words in a wheedling tone,

'You're hurting my arm Roland. You're hurting my arm.'

'Please let me go? Edmund will be back soon.'

At the mention of his brother's name, his eyes flashed and he became even more enraged.

'Edmund again! Will I never stop hearing that name?'

Furiously he shook me until my teeth rattled as I squirmed in his grasp. I dug my nails into his hand and bit it with such force that he cried out and released me. Taking advantage of my freedom I ran out of the room, desperate to reach the safety of my bedroom and lock the door. Roland ran after me and in my haste I trod on my dress and stumbled on the staircase. Reaching out he caught me by the hem of my dress and as I tried to flee, he held on and material ripped from the waist. Momentarily caught off balance, he fell backwards as the dress tore away. With a scream, I gathered my petticoats, and shaking with fear, I quickly escaped again. For an instant, Roland was caught off guard and to prevent himself falling down the staircase, he caught hold of the banister, throwing aside the blue silk material that ripped from my dress. He steadied himself and then pursued me up the staircase. His legs being longer than mine he ran up several steps at a time and we both arrived at the top together. Roland managed to get to my door, before I did and again barred my way.

I tried to run back but he pushed me into the room. I tried to shut him out, but I could not close the door as he was holding it. He was much too strong for me and I was hurled backwards as he forced the door open. As I stumbled, his hands encircled my throat. He began to curse me in terms that were almost satanic. I could feel his hot breath on my face and his yellowing, blood shot eyes swam before me. My head began to pound and lights danced before my eyes as I tried to force his fingers open. I scratched and bit his hands but to no avail. I couldn't breathe. It felt as if my head would explode, as I croaked and gasped as his fingers tightened, strangling me. The room began to swim around me as I twisted and turned trying to escape.

'Try and shut me out will you? Well you tried that before didn't you but I soon settled that. Didn't I? Didn't I? As he spoke he shook me like a rag doll, my body being swung around by the hands that were gripping my throat.

I couldn't answer, I did not know what he was talking about, I tried to plead but no words could escape from the pressure on my throat. Around me I could hear the sound of Annabelle howling pitifully and the more I struggled the angrier Roland became,

'Gave me that bitch didn't you? Well this time I'll have a son.'

My whole body was on fire with fear and loathing and desperation to escape. I believed that he was going to kill me and there was nothing I could do about it. All I could think as I struggled was that poor Annabelle had been conceived by an act of violence. Had my sister suffered as I was now suffering? I wanted to be sick, the gorge rising in my throat. Was that why she had preferred death? I did not want to die. I kicked him hard with my booted foot. I sank my teeth into his hand again and tasted blood. I felt for the china jug that stood on the side cupboard and hit him on the head with all the force I could muster but it had no effect. All my attempts to hurt him were feeble; he had the strength of ten men. Nothing seemed to affect him no matter how hard I tried to injure him to make him release the pressure on my throat. My hands were gripping his hands around my neck, scratching and pulling at them, trying my hardest to prevent this man from being the cause of my death. All the time I was trying to scream but no sound could escape from my swollen lips.

Then without warning, his hands relaxed and I was able to breathe again. I staggered back against the chair, which fell over and I collapsed on the bed where the child was. She began screaming and ran and locked herself in the wardrobe, the noise of her sobs echoing around me. I bent over, struggling to breathe, shuddering with the exertion of getting air back into my lungs. I tried to speak, but my throat was hoarse and my lips parched and dry. As I tried to gather my wits, he began to whine pitifully,

'Freya! Why are you doing this to me? You know I love you.' He crawled around the hem of my petticoats as I sat trying to breathe and he clutched the white linen to his face, burying it amongst the lace and ribbons. Frightened I tried to shake him off, but this time he took me by the shoulders and bent my arm behind me, pushing me back on the bed holding me down.

'This time you won't escape, Freya.'

'Please Roland, don't hurt me. I'm not Freya,' I gasped, but it was no use. He pulled my head towards him and ripped off the snood and with that my hair came tumbling out around my shoulders. Gripping it he wound it around his hand and dragged me towards him by my hair. His lips brutally sought out my mouth, and his teeth grated against mine. He pushed me onto the bed, still twisting my hair and yanking my head around as he climbed

64

onto me. His weight was holding me down whilst his mouth slobbered over me. The smell of stale liquor and body odour sickened me.

As I struggled to rise from under him, my head was jerked back, trapped by my hair. His free hand pawed and ripped at my clothes as he tore the cotton and ripped away my bodice. Somewhere far away I heard screaming and did not realize that it came from me. I tried to cover my breasts, but he clamped his mouth to them, biting me savagely. I was in agony. I could taste blood on my lips as they cracked and split with the force of his mouth upon mine. I clamped my teeth as hard as I could to prevent his tongue from entering my mouth. However, he forced my lips apart as he kissed me forcefully, biting my already torn lips, filling me with disgust. The weight of his body crushed me and I tried to roll to one side with my knees pulled up to my stomach, to prevent his access to my body, but he wedged his thin bony knees between mine and pinched the flesh on my thigh with his bones. The pain was excruciating and there was no escape. His hands were round my throat, and all around me was becoming black. All I could think was that he would kill me as I gasped and struggled. The tears began rolling down my face and mixing with the blood. I felt for something, anything that I could use against him. Finding a brooch on the side table, I raked his face with it, and he howled with rage but did not let me go.

All the time his fingers were prodding and ripping me, his demented eyes glaring at me as he forced his mouth upon every part of me. As I fought against him, I remembered the nightmare. The vision of the wild eyes staring at me, and the heavy weight upon my chest that prevented me from breathing. The fingers around my throat crushing the life out of me. The nightmare had become a reality. The monster that I had dreamed sitting on my chest, choking the breath from me, had been a premonition of the violence that I was now suffering.

I thought I would die as he bit and clawed at me and I struggled to free myself but he was too strong for me. My arms flailed uselessly, trying to prise him from me. The blood from his scratched face dripped into my eyes and blurred my sight. I felt nauseous and despairing as I tried to rub the blood from my face and push him away from me. All the while he cursed and spat at me, his bones dug into my flesh and burned me like hot irons. I wanted to vomit with revulsion as his legs pinned my own apart and pinched and hurt me. My whole body was in agony as my underclothes were ripped away and my deepest self was violated.

I struggled in desperation, still screaming as I felt him feel for the clasp on his breeches. Ripping them off he entered me with such force that my body lifted from the bed. I felt my bones crack with the force of him as I begged and pleaded. The feeling of him inside me was loathsome and terrible to me. The pain ripped me apart and I truly felt my life was over and I was about to die and I just wanted it to end. I was used by him not as a man uses a woman but as if I was a thing to be abused and degraded. I prayed and prayed.

'Please God, make it end. Let me die!'

I could not escape his brutality and I was certain he would kill me. I tried to block it out. I tried to persuade myself that it didn't matter. He could ravage my body but he could not take my soul. Over and over in my mind I repeated poems that I had learned, trying to blank out what was happening to me. Into my head came some words, from a poem by Byron.

'I'll go no more a roving, so late into the night'

I chanted the words, going from the first to last verse and round and round again, and somehow it seemed as if I was outside myself watching what was happening. As though it was happening to someone else. I was brought back to reality when with a roar he heaved himself up from my body and then collapsed on me sated with the effort. My torture was over! There was a silence for a moment as I lay there, my body still pinned beneath him. His head upon my breasts. I could still hear the demented screaming but I did not realise that it was coming from me. My life was at an end. If he had killed me at that moment I would have thanked him. What was there left for me now? I was nothing but a used up thing. No better than the 'unfortunates' that no one in polite society would ever recognise.

Then suddenly the crushing weight was lifted and I almost levitated from the bed with the release. Scrambling up, I tried to pull my clothes around as I backed against the wall still screaming hysterically. Through my hysteria, I became aware of someone else. Roland's satiated body was dragged from the bed as Edmund smashed his fist into his brother's face. With a sickening crunch, Roland crumpled to the floor and lay in the gloom, blood pouring from his mouth and nose. Edmund ignored him and offered his hand to me, to help me down as I screamed like one insane,

'Don't touch me! Don't touch me!' I tried to retreat away even further, trying to escape through the wall. I couldn't understand why I couldn't. I was invisible, without shape or form and yet I was still there. Edmund trying to help me draped the bed cover around my naked, battered body. However, not knowing what I was doing, I fought against him, trying to strike him.

He gently tried to pacify me, telling me that he was helping me but I was in another place. I had descended into hell.

I stared around wildly, seeing and not seeing, for a moment I did not even know who he was. At last I could resist no more and exhausted I collapsed. I felt someone gently brushing my tangled hair out of my eyes and bathing my face. I was numb, cold and sick with disgust and shame. I could not stop shivering. I had no idea what he was saying to me, it was as if I had become deaf and dumb. My throat was scratched and sore but I could hear nothing, I could feel nothing. I was dead to all.

He took some more water from a jug, and looking at the sprawled figure of his brother, kicked him with fury. There was a sickening thud as Roland groaned and clutching his stomach rolled around the floor. Edmund spat out with disgust,

'You are an animal, to think that someone of my blood could behave......'

Roland began to sob and plead,

'She shouldn't have shut me out. She is my wife. Don't hurt me! Don't hurt me. I haven't done anything.'

Edmund looked at him coldly,

'Your wife is dead.'

CHAPTER SIX

'My only love sprung from my only hate! Too early seen
unknown, and known too late'

Romeo and Juliet Act 1 Sc 5

As he tried to help me, I curled myself up into a ball on the bed, traumatized, I was unable to speak or think. I felt as if I was locked inside a bubble from which I could not escape. From somewhere far off I could hear Edmund's voice but it seemed to be so distant and I could not react to anything around me. I lay unfeeling and unthinking, numb with grief and desperation, my eyes fixed on a torn piece of gold embossed wallpaper by my head. I heard the door of the wardrobe creaking open and in the distance a child's high pitched screaming as Edmund shouted,

'No!

But I did not care what was happening around me as I heard someone say with disgust,

'Dear God! What next?'

I didn't know who it was and I didn't care. It did not matter, nothing mattered. Nothing else that could happen to me would ever matter again. I lay there fixed, unable to move, wrapped tightly in the bed cover, stiff and cold, as slowly the gloom changed into night. I was sure there was someone else there and I heard an unfamiliar voice whisper,

'This is a bad business Edmund.'

Then there was a hum of voices around me and I drowned them out and didn't move but just continued to look at my torn piece of wallpaper which somehow seemed to comfort me. At last it was too dark to see it, but I knew it was there. Someone had lit a candle and the flame flickered making shadows around me but I didn't stir. All I cared for was my place on the wallpaper. In my mind I could still hear Roland whining and pleading and that drowned out everything. Suddenly a hand stroked my hair and I shuddered with fear as someone said,

'I am a physician my dear. Let me help you.'

I didn't respond. I was not interested in this person. All I wanted was to stare at the torn piece of wall paper. If I sat up this man would see me and be disgusted. He would look at me and know my shame but I knew I would be safe if I still looked at my wallpaper.

I became aware that someone was bathing my face and a solitary tear squeezed itself out of my eye as I lay unresisting. A glass of white liquid was held to my split lips, but I could not swallow the contents. They ran from the corners of my dry mouth, burning and stinging.

'It is a sleeping draught,' the voice said. 'It will help you.'

As the liquid began to seep into my throat, I felt the pain and anguish begin to fade into a floating blur. Then suddenly to my intense pleasure I saw my father. He looked plump and happy and was standing by an open door, gesturing to me to go in. Freya was with him wearing the same green dress as in the painting. If this was a dream I was overjoyed. The relief at seeing them overwhelmed me and I was sure that I was standing up to go with them but when I looked back I could see myself still curled up like a foetus on the bed.

Suddenly, I was brought back to reality and realised that the sun was shining brightly through my bedroom window. Overwhelmed with relief that my agony had only been the familiar nightmare I went to sit up and immediately began to retch and vomit and cried out as my body was racked with pain. Horror and disgust washed over me like a toxic sludge and I was drowning in the mire. I was alive but I wished I was dead. Over and over I moaned that Roland should have killed me. Now I would have to live with the shame. My body felt battered and bruised, and my mouth dry and swollen. In my grief I became aware of a shadowy figure by my bed and I screamed thinking it was Roland returned but I heard Rosie call out as she bent to clean up the mess on the floor.

'It is all right! Thank goodness you are awake. You have been asleep for two days. How are you feeling? Do not try to move. I will run and fetch the Major. He has been so worried about you.'

'No! Do not fetch him,' I croaked, my voice sounding strange as if it belonged to someone else.

'But I must, 'e will be angry. The Major asked me to come and get 'im as soon as you woke up.'

'Don't leave me.' I pleaded. 'He will come back again.'

'I must. The Major said so.' She sobbed

'Don't let him in. Don't let him in.' I cried, clinging to her dress as she tried to stand and free herself.

'The Major won't hurt you,' she sighed trying to free herself.

'Not him, the other one.' I screamed terrified that Roland would come for me Rosie began to set up a loud wailing as she cried,

'Roland won't come any more. My poor boy is dead.'

I too began to sob with relief and distress only managing to croak

'How! Did Edmund.....?' It was too horrible to think about.

'Roland took a pistol from the desk and shot 'is brains out. Why couldn't 'e love me? Why couldn't 'e love me? I would have looked after him. He was everything to me and now 'e's gone' she continued to wail pitifully.

'I don't understand!' I whispered hoarsely.

'My old Roland wouldn't 'ave done it miss. 'E was ill, 'E was ill.' She kept on repeating the words over and over. 'Even 'is own child tried to kill 'im, oh miss!' Her voice tailed off and she stood up still snivelling, wiping her nose and eyes on the lace trim of her dress. I lay back on the pillows and stared at her. I had been brutally attacked and she was crying for my attacker. I was appalled.

'It will be all right miss. You will be all right, you. You will forget all this. The Major will help you. You will get better soon.'

'Nothing will make it better!'

'Don't upset yourself. It will be all right. You are a lady. You 'ave money. You 'ave the Major. You 'ave everything, nothing will change that. Not like me I 'ad nothing.' She started to cry again as dazed and sickened I heard an inherent rambling. 'Me mother sent me out to be a friend to gentlemen, when I was twelve years old. It weren't 'ard. Sometimes they was kind to me, I would bring back food for me brothers and sisters. Some times, if I didn't find a friend, I would go 'ome, and my mother would beat me and send me out again. I met 'im when I was seventeen, I was walking out in Vauxhall Gardens and 'e was there with 'is toff friends. I called out something cheeky to 'im and 'e came and talked to me.' Her eyes shone with the memory of it as she relived the moment and I felt sick to my stomach, my body drenched in perspiration as I tried to prevent the vomit that was rising.

I could hear her, saying how kind Roland was, her common voice grating on my nerves. On and on she droned. I didn't want to hear it. I hated and despised him. I was glad he was dead! I hoped he suffered as I had. He had made my life a living torment.

I lay against the pillow and clamped my eyes together trying to shut everything out. Still she continued,

'When 'e came to London 'e would visit me and take me out. When I got married 'e bought me the alehouse to help me make a living. 'E weren't too 'appy about the man I married. 'E said 'e was a drunk and 'e was right, but you don't know what it's like. You 'ave to 'ave an 'usband. 'Ow can you survive? I didn't want to go to the workhouse. I don't care what 'appens. I ain't going to the workhouse. Do you know when you die there, they chop your body up and sell it to doctors for experiments.'

I turned my face away and found my piece of wallpaper. She wasn't expecting a reply; she was lost in her reverie.

'I never saw 'im when 'e married 'er. 'Only after the baby was born, 'e started coming to the alehouse. Just to talk to me. That is all 'e wanted to do. Roland said she didn't love him. That she wouldn't give 'im a son. I would 'ave given 'im children. I loved 'im. I would 'ave done anything for him.'

Rosie's grating voice began to reverberate through me until I could stand it no longer,

'Shut up! Shut up!' I screamed. My throat hurt with the effort as I rolled in the bed trying to stop my ears from hearing about Roland's sordid life with this woman of the street. She looked startled, but her expression changed to one of extreme sadness.

'You don't understand. Why should you. You ain't got no understanding of men.'

I forced myself to sit up and grabbed her by the sleeve, ripping it from her shoulder as I hissed,

'If he is dead, I am glad. May he rot in hell! I do not want to listen to the foulness of your life and his. I hate him and this place. Leave me alone! Leave me alone!' I began to cough and choke with the violence of my shouting.

Rosie looked as if she had been struck. She opened her mouth to speak and then closed it again, just as Edmund appeared in the room. His face flushed with anger,

'I told you to come and call me if she woke. Why are you bothering her with your stupidity?'

Rosie began to stammer nervously,

'I was going...'

'Get out,' he snapped. Stung at his tone she walked out miserably her head hung down in sadness. Her broad shoulders slumped as if she had the cares of the world upon them.

I turned away from him, unable to bear looking at him, my whole battered body diffused with shame. He waited for me to speak but as I did not he said gently,

'There is nothing I can do or say that will change any of this!'

'What is to become of me? I whispered, more to myself than him. I am degraded and ashamed! Where can I go? What can I do? Who will want me now?' I rocked back and forth not expecting an answer.

'I will!'

The sound of his voice shook me back to reality,

'Look at me,' he said quietly, and wiped the perspiration from my face.

'Don't! Don't!' I begged. Ignoring my pleas he took my face in his hands and gently turned it towards him. I couldn't bear to look at him and screwed my eyes tightly shut. I thought if I could not see him, he would be unable to see my disgrace.

'Open your eyes and look at me,' he whispered and he brushed my wet hair away from my forehead. I did as I was told and saw him looking at me with concern. His face looked tired and strained, but he smiled.

'Any man would be honoured to have you for his wife. I can't change what happened but I can put it right. I am asking you to marry me.'

I miserably once again turned to my place on the wallpaper. He continued,

'Aphra, such a long time seems to have passed since I saw you that day at the top of the stairs. Yet it was only a few days ago. The moment I saw you, I knew that it was meant to be.'

Miserably I replied,

'When you mistook me for my sister.'

'No, you chose to believe that. It was something else that happened. I couldn't stop looking at you. It was destiny. We are bound together. Please let me make amends for the way the Fitzroy family have treated you. Let me look after you.'

'You can't help me!'

'I want to marry you Aphra, to care for you. I want to help you and Annabelle.' At the mention of her name I suddenly remembered her pitiful cries from her hiding place.

'Where is she?' I tried to struggle up again, gasping with pain, my swollen mouth making it difficult to speak.

'The child is safe. However, the doctor believes that she is suffering from a severe disorder of the nerves from which she may never recover. I am afraid that what happened last night has caused her untold damage. The physician has removed her for the safety of herself and others. She attacked her father with a pair of sewing shears. It is a sad affair but I am afraid that she is beyond help.

'He is dead and I am glad.. I hope he suffered a terrible, painful death' I cried bitterly.

'Yes he is dead.' There was sadness in his voice as I tried to climb out of the bed.

'I must go to the child. She needs me!'

Trying to pacify me he responded,

'There is nothing you can do for her now. The child is half crazed. She kicked and bit the doctor with such force that he will need medical treatment himself. I think he may have a broken rib. I am afraid she had to be taken away in a constraint. Her screams could still be heard on the estate as they left. Neither Rosie nor I could do anything with her. She needs special care.'

'You have not placed her in a foul asylum!' I asked, my voice rising hysterically.

'Of course not. The doctor has taken her. There are people there who know how to deal with disorders of the mind. She will get the best treatment that money can buy.'

'But she is a child. She needs love and care.' I whispered forlornly.

'Aphra, she was like a caged wild animal and something had to be done. It took three men to get her into the carriage. That child has suffered more in her short life than any human being should. I fear that she has become insane.'

Too weak to argue, I lay back on the pillows and Edmund picked up my hand and raised it to his lips,

'You have not answered me.'

'The answer is no!' I replied coldly still unable to look at him.

'I know you have suffered terribly. Surely I can repay that suffering by making you my wife?'

'I cannot be your wife!' I am not fit. I am a dirty and disgusting.' As the words left my split lips I turned to the security of my wallpaper and idly picked at it. I heard the door open and Rosie's voice asking if she could come in as the Major had requested some food. Edmund audibly sighed and stood up.

'Let Rosie help you to eat something and we will talk later. I have to return to London in two days. I have sent someone with a note to your friends. Hopefully, there will be a reply that enables me to take you to stay for your recuperation. You will be with friends who will support and love you.'

'No,' I shrieked, dementedly waving my arms, begging and pleading. 'I do not want them to know. Please say nothing....'

'Calm yourself.' He put an arm around me in comfort but I tensed. Audibly sighing he removed it and added,

'Do not worry, I have informed them that you have been ill and in need of convalescence. Nothing of what has passed will ever be referred to again.'

He tucked my hand under the bed cover and frowned as he saw the scratched and bruised knuckles. Shaking his head in despair he walked out of the room, calling out that I should rest, but he sounded weary.

Rosie stood uncertainly by the bed. I felt sorry I had shouted and gestured to her with a weak wave of my hand. My body seemed fixed and unable to move. However, the wave gave her the signal she wanted and she sat down and tried to help me to sit up. Holding a spoon to my lips, she tried to get me to eat but I pushed her hand away. My throat was too scratched and raw. She sat in a depressed state as I quietly observed her care-worn face that seemed to have aged overnight.

'What will you do now Rosie?' I rasped.

'I don't know miss. I have no money. What little profit we made with the alehouse has all been drunk away. I'll go back to London, I still have family there.'

'To the old life?'

Rosie flushed and said bitterly, 'What does a young woman like you know of my life?'

I didn't reply.

'Marry him miss.'

'What?'

'I heard 'im ask you. It will be for the best, a woman alone in this world is worse than nothing. I should know.'

'How can I?'

'When you feel better, all this will be behind you. The bruises will fade and so will the memory. Believe me it will fade. Would you like me to brush your beautiful 'air for you?'

'If you like. I don't care.' She picked up my silver backed brush from the side table and gently began brushing. She was humming to herself like a mother detangling the hair of her child. I realised that everything that she had valued in life had been tied up with Roland. What would happen to her now? I was not the first woman to have been degraded and abused in this fashion. It was true for me it was not the end but this woman had nothing. I would recover, it was only my body that was lost, but my mind was still my own. As I looked at my bruises, my skin covered in purple marks and deep bloody scratches, I became aware that I was wearing a linen night shift,

'Where is my dress?' I asked.

'I burnt it. I thought when you awoke you would not want to see that dress as a reminder.

'I'm sorry I abused you.' I said full of remorse.

'Don't you worry. Old Rosie said too much she should 'ave known better. You rest now and everything will be all right, you'll see!'

I nodded meekly and settled back in the bed. My whole being was exhausted, my eyes would not stay open and I began to drift off into a fitful sleep, the sleeping draught still doing its work.

The next day I felt a little stronger, and decided that I did not want to stay in bed. I asked Rosie to find me a dress as I wished to go downstairs. Protesting at first she found me a pale silk dress but I threw it aside. I would not be dressing in finery again. She gently helped my stiff and painful body into it. As she did so I suddenly became aware that she was not wearing her familiar pink dress, but was dressed in black. I assumed she was in mourning for her lost Roland and a look of scorn came over my face but I did not comment. As she helped me she chattered incessantly,

'The Major 'as heard from your friends. A carriage has been arranged to take you to London the day after tomorrow. There is business to tend to today and so 'e will not be back until this evening.'

'Are you to stay with me?' I whispered struggling with the fastenings.

'Yes. The Major 'as spoken to me 'usband and settled some money on him, so that I can stay and nurse you until you leave for London.'

Suddenly I caught sight of the open brooch, bent and crushed on the floor. I felt a wave of revulsion wash over me as I remembered how its jagged edge had ripped into Roland's flesh. I began to weep silently as I picked it up. I turned it over in my hand but dropped it quickly on seeing traces of dried blood congealed around it. Rosie looked puzzled and bent to pick it up for me.

'Leave it!'

Rosie reacted with a start and dropped the brooch as if it was hot coals as I struggled into my shoes and I ground it into the dust. As I did so the room began to spin around me, and I almost fell. Rosie steadied me and she bid me lean on her as she helped me to go downstairs.

'Can you help me to the library?'

She led the way and we staggered along with me leaning on her for support. I saw the door to the salon was open and I almost fainted at the memories the sight of the piano caused me.

'Please shut the door to the salon.' She looked at me uncomprehendingly, but did as she was asked and then settled me on the sofa. She placed a book by my side and I idly thumbed through it. However, I could not concentrate and after a while, I had no knowledge of what I had been reading.

Annabelle came back into my thoughts and I became nervous and anxious. Edmund had said that she was now in the care of someone that was used to treating extreme nervous disorders. Where had she gone? I needed to know that she was being well cared for. It was essential that I saw her and I needed to visit her to reassure myself that she was safe. In my anxiety, I repeatedly asked Rosie when Edmund would return but she also seemed nervous and kept replying that he would be back soon. I felt suspicious as I recognized the signs of Rosie not being honest.

Unable to wait any longer, I began to pace painfully around. I suddenly caught sight of myself in a mirror and saw with shock a person that I did not recognise. I stared with horror at the face reflected there. My eyes were bloodshot, with purple weals beneath and my mouth was swollen and split. On my cheek a dark bruise was yellowing. How could I go to stay with my friends in this condition? It was impossible. I would have to prepare a story. They would not accept that I had merely been ill. Perhaps I would concoct a tale that I had fainted when I had been suffering from a debilitating illness and hurt my face. It had only been a few days, the bruises had not had time to disappear. Would they believe me? I hoped they would. Of course, they would never imagine anything as awful as the real cause.

I managed to stand by the window as Rosie suddenly announced that she had an appointment and would be gone for a short while. She looked awkward and embarrassed but I was not interested enough to enquire where she was going. She left me alone with my thoughts and sometime later, when she returned, she found me exactly as she had left me, staring motionless into space.

'It's done miss!'

'What's done?' I looked up and I noticed that tears began to roll down her face,

'I've been to Roland's funeral. The Major told me not to tell you, but I 'ave to say something. It was so cold and grey and only me and 'im were there. Roland was a Fitzroy, 'e should 'ave been buried with all 'is friends there. I know what 'e did can't be forgiven, but it was so awful. The parson said a few words and then we left.'

'Is he buried with my sister?' I asked my voice rising in panic. The thought that even in death she had not escaped him was abhorrent to me.

'No miss!' Rosie sniffed, blowing her nose loudly into a grubby handkerchief.

As she did so, I looked outside at the grey day. The rain drops trickling down the glass leaving smudgy streaks that mirrored Rosie's sad, tear stained face. As I stared out my sister came into my thoughts. Then with an overwhelming feeling of guilt I realised that I had no idea where she had been laid to rest. Why had I never thought about it? All the times I had wandered around the estate and never once thought to ask. Shame flooded through me. I had been so wrapped up with myself I had never even laid a single flower on grave.

'Rosie, is my sister in the family vault?'

'No!' She began to look uncomfortable.

'Where is she?'

'Down by the churchyard?'

'What do you mean by the churchyard? Is she not in the churchyard?'

'No! They wouldn't let her. She died by her own hand. The old reverend would not permit it.'

'What!' I exclaimed. 'My sister is buried in unconsecrated ground. Take me to the place!' Finding hidden reserves I walked forcefully to the door. However, as I did so I doubled up in pain, screaming as a searing agony ripping through my stomach. Rosie rushed to help me,

'You can't go anywhere. You must wait until you are better.'

'I am going. I wish to see where she is buried. If you do not take me, I will find it myself.'

'I know a short cut through the avenue of trees. Don't you think we should wait for the Major?'

'I am going now, with or without your help!' I cried.

Realising that I would not listen to her protests, Rosie brought my cloak and helped me to set off down the pathway. I leaned on her heavily as every step was painful for me. I pulled my hood around my face for fear of meeting anyone and I staggered along in great discomfort. My legs were as weak as cotton wool. The rain had started again and was now a fine drizzle, but it was not cold, and the shelter of the avenue of trees kept us dry. I could see the church tower in the distance, but on all the occasions that I had walked the mile to the village, I had not known that there was a shorter way.

At last we came to a clearing and there were the remains of a tree trunk that had been struck by lightening lying across our path. I took the opportunity to sit on it and gather my breath, clutching my stomach tightly, trying to dull the pain.

'Is it far now?'

'No, it is just ahead!' I sat quietly until we became aware of someone walking towards us. Pulling my hood even tighter about my face to avoid this man, I tried not to engage him in conversation but he was determined to address me. He asked what I was doing in the area and mentioned that he was the Verger. He ignored Rosie when she tried to speak to him. I could see by his manner that he did not look on her favourably. He then asked if I was unwell but I informed him that I had been ill and hurt my face when I became giddy and fell. The man, who was elderly, looked at me more intently and I hastily pulled my hood even more tightly around my face, and turned away. He adopted a sympathetic air, saying how sad he was to hear of Roland's untimely death and asked what would happen to Stoneleigh now? I had no idea what tale he had heard and I ignored him. Not to be swayed he continued asking if Stoneleigh would be closed as the Major would probably be embarking for foreign climes? His voice seemed to drone on for eternity until unable to bear it any longer I rudely interrupted asking,

'Where is Lady Freya Fitzroy's resting place?'

The Verger's expression changed to one of embarrassment and he wrung his hands as if trying to form a reply. I asked again and after a few seconds he stood back and gestured to me to follow and led the way past the churchyard. Around us were the grey gravestones of generations of villagers. At last we arrived at a small thicket. To my horror I saw a few markers in rows in a separate area of ground apart from the village graveyard.

'Why are we here?' I asked

'This is where Freya Fitzroy was laid to rest,' he said gently.

'But there are no headstones.'

'As your sister took her own life, she is buried in unconsecrated ground. She cannot be laid to rest in holy ground.'

'What?' I gasped, 'My sister does not even have a gravestone, just a marker. How can that be?'

The Verger fidgeted, and coughed with embarrassment.

'There is nothing that anyone could do. The reverend was adamant that she took her own life and that is a sin. She is lucky to be so near the church. Not many years ago she would have been buried at the crossroads.'

'How dare you? I screamed. 'We are all sinners! Where is this reverend? Consecrated ground or not, she at least deserves to have her life marked with more than her name on a stick.'

'He was the old reverend. He died last year. We have the curate now.' He looked downcast, unable to look me in the face.

'I will speak to the curate. I want my sister buried in a decent fashion. I will not tolerate it.'

Shocked by my tone, the elderly man muttered a few words, and advised me that he would speak to the curate and perhaps something could be arranged. All this time Rosie had stood meekly by, as if she had no right to be in his presence. The anger that I felt about my sister made me stronger and I walked along the row markers, oblivious to the pain in my lower body. Some of the plots had numbers on and some had names and dates. They seemed to be mainly babies who had only lived a few hours before leaving this world. The only indication that they had ever lived was a stick in the ground. Then I found what I had been looking for. There was an unmarked grave, bearing a wooden stick which merely said 'Freya Fitzroy.'

Despite my agony I began almost dancing with rage, as I looked around for some spare twigs. Finding them I twisted a cross shape and placed it on the grave. I then picked a few berries and holly from the bushes around about. The Verger watched for a moment and then came to my side.

'Come away. It doesn't do any good to stay here. Besides the rain is getting heavier and you look unwell and should be resting.'

Turning I gasped,

'What about these poor babies? Did they ask to be born? Are they sinners?' Taken aback he shook his head and started to walk a way. Suddenly he turned and called out sharply,

'I think that I should warn you. If you wish to live in this area, you will not do your reputation any good, if you continue to associate yourself with that lady,' and he gestured in the direction of Rosie.

Stung by his words I leapt to her defence.

'That lady,' I croaked, 'has more human kindness in her soul than your so called Christian reverend. I hardly think that my reputation is of any consequence, when a lady of my sister's status is treated in this awful fashion.'

The Verger stomped away angrily battling against the wind leaving two lone women standing mournfully amid the mud and dirt of a bare field containing nothing but rows of sticks.

There was nothing more to be done and taking Rosie's arm, we began our slow journey back, my face stung by the sharp blasts of the cold wind, that made my eyes water. In all this time Rosie had not spoken. Now neither of us spoke as my thoughts were in turmoil and I was in such a rage with life. To think that my sister, who had been married into a family of landed gentry like the Fitzroys, should have been buried like a pauper was unthinkable. I silently argued with myself all the way back, submerged in a black cloud of hate and disgust. As I hobbled painfully through the avenue of trees, I leaned heavily on my companion. I was exhausted but I would not give in. Suddenly Rosie began to mumble.

'I told yer you shouldn't have come. It doesn't help to upset yourself so. You will make yourself even more unwell. '

Unable to restrain the sobs that rose in my throat I cried,

'She is in that awful, dreary place with those poor little babies.'

Rosie rubbed her eyes and sighed,

'I know. That marker in the corner was my baby.'

I turned to her in dismay,

'Rosie, you had a child?'

'It doesn't matter .It was a long time ago. It was a boy. He only lived a few hours. I never 'ad any more.'

'When I speak to the curate I will insist that both your child and my sister have the ceremony and headstone that is due to them.'

'He won't agree. The curate doesn't like me anyway. He might listen to you about your sister but he won't do anything for me!'

'We'll see!' I gasped staggering with pain and exhausted with the effort I found a mile stone and sat down trying to stop the ache. I wanted to throw myself on the ground and die in the cold. I was struggling to continue but I just wanted to lie on the cold ground and let death wash over me. Rosie pulled my cloak tightly around me to shut out the cold and after a few moments urged me to go on. I struggled to my feet as she said,

'Can I tell you something?' she asked.

'Of course you can. 'I sighed, not really listening. My whole body now on fire with the effort of walking.

'You won't think badly of me will you, if I tell you.'

'No!' Was the only reply I could muster.

'My poor dead baby was Roland's son.'

Unable to believe my ears, I stopped in my tracks and looked at Rosie whose face flushed and she walked on saying,

'I loved 'im, but I was nothing to 'im. I knew that, but it didn't matter. I wanted nothing from 'im but I loved 'im. No one could 'ave loved 'im like I did. I knew 'e'd get married to some rich lady one day but I wanted 'is child.'

'You were lovers?'

'No! Roland was too grand for the likes of me, but 'e liked my company when 'e was in London. I told you. I made 'im laugh. No, it was later, after yer sister died and 'e was at Stoneleigh. When 'e was out of his 'ead with the drink. He didn't remember. I tricked 'im. I was so happy when I found out I was carrying 'is child, but I didn't tell 'im.'

'But the baby?'

'He never knew about my condition, he didn't know it was his child. I told 'im it was Davey Barnes' child.'

'Your husband?'

'Yes, only 'e weren't me 'usband then. Roland bought me the alehouse, and paid me 'usband to make an honest woman of me. I 'ad known Davey since I was a child, 'e was always 'anging round. He kept saying 'e loved me, but I didn't want 'im. Once I knew about me condition, I had to do something. It didn't take long for 'im to be persuaded, especially with the alehouse. I then found meself tied to a violent drunk and it was all for nothing. The baby only lived a few hours and me 'usband drank away all the earnings from the alehouse. We only kept it going, with Roland's help. After Roland lost all his money, we 'ad to try and keep it going, but its no use. Me 'usband is in prison most of the time. Now there will be nothing.'

I put my arm round her thick waist and leaned my head against her.

'I am so sorry, Rosie.' I could think of nothing else to say. As we stood in mute sympathy I suddenly saw Edmund angrily striding through the clearing.

'What on earth are you thinking of,' he blazed to Rosie glaring at her furiously. He was hatless and his thick blonde hair was wet from the rain. Taking off his cloak he wrapped it around me. As he did so, all the strength went out of me and my knees buckled. As I collapsed, he caught me and swept me up into his arms carrying me home. How safe and secure I felt held against his chest. I felt like a small child again as I felt the buttons from his jacket pressing against my skin. He marched angrily along, striding quickly through the avenue of trees.

'Please do not be angry with Rosie. She didn't want me to go. I made her take me. I wanted to see the place where my sister is buried. Did you know Edmund, that she is not buried in the churchyard?'

He looked grim, his mouth set as he replied,

'No, I did not know. I did not attend the funeral. I was not even in the country, when she died. I expect she is in the family vault!'

'No! She is in a grave with a marker, in unconsecrated ground.'

'I had no idea?' He looked surprised and staring up at him I stated,

'I want her moved.'

He nodded, still carrying me in his arms.

'You can put me down, I can walk now, but we must do something for Freya.'

Edmund didn't argue.

'Whatever you wish. I am sure something can be arranged. I suppose it was remiss of me, but I never thought to enquire where she was buried.'

'What if the curate refuses?'

'I am sure we can come to some arrangement. The curate's living is provided by the Fitzroy family so I do not think there will be any argument. Do you want her to be laid to rest in the family vault in the chapel?'

'Not with Roland,' I shouted the effort causing me to cough dramatically. 'Do you think I want her buried next to that foul man who has been the cause of our misery?'

Edmund looked at Rosie with irritation, realising that she had told me of the funeral.

'Yes, Rosie told me that Roland was buried today. Don't be angry with her.'

'I am not angry, I did not want you to be upset, that is all. However I will speak to the curate before I leave for London. Where do you want her re-interred?'

'I want her to have her own tomb, with all the title and rights due to her as Lady Fitzroy.'

He thought for a moment, and then as we arrived at the portico he said,

'There is an empty tomb that is reserved for me and any future family I may have. However, I think with my choice of career there will be little chance of me dying in my bed and being laid to rest there. Besides, I have left instructions that should I die I want to be buried at Threshingham Park next to my mother. Your sister can be placed in my empty one with all due ceremony.'

'Thank you!' I cried with relief.

'Now go upstairs and rest. You look very ill. I do not want you to catch a chill on top of everything else.'

'Yes, I will, but before I do I have another wish.' I said as I leaned on his arm to climb the steps. 'There is a baby buried in that same desolate spot as my sister. I wish him to be moved into the chapel?'

At this request, Edmund looked puzzled,

'A baby, whose.......?' Then seeing me glance towards Rosie he stopped and a dark flush permeated across his face and he seemed to be struggling for words. Then with a set look he said,

'Whatever you wish.'

CHAPTER SEVEN

'So shaken as we are, so wan with care....'

Henry IV, Pt 1 Act 1 Sc 1

ack in my room once more, I managed to eat some of the broth that Rosie brought but I was unable to finish it. Exhausted I slept soundly and the next day I dressed with difficulty and sat my bruised and aching body in the library where I could sit in silence, only to be disturbed by voices outside. On opening the door I found the curate standing there. He was a thin young man, with receding fair hair and a pince nez fixed firmly on his nose,

'Ah Miss Devereaux, I am glad that I find you up and about, only my Verger, Mr Figgins told me you looked unwell yesterday.'

He looked at me intently, his eyes roaming my face as if trying to search out something from my expression. I turned away, unable to meet his gaze, conscious of my damaged face. He continued,

'I understand that you are unhappy about your sister's resting place. When Mr Figgins told me of your conversation yesterday, I felt duty bound to come and explain the situation.'

He nervously took my hand and shook it limply, his eyes looking pale and watery behind the glasses. As he did so, Rosie appeared in the doorway and looking even more discomforted he added, 'Perhaps, if you could dismiss the er...lady, we can talk in private.'

'No, Rosie is quite welcome to stay,' I replied and I gestured to her to come in and sit down, which she did.

'My dear lady, I hardly think....,' he tailed off as he saw my look of disapproval. He sat down and mopped his face with his handkerchief and there was an awkward silence. I stood up and looking out of the window said firmly,

'My sister is to be moved from the unconsecrated ground that she has been placed in, and given the burial that is fitting with her status.'

'I am afraid that is not possible. I know that all this has been very upsetting for you, but my hands are tied. It is the rules of the church as she took her own life.'

'All that is irrelevant to me. She is to be moved and placed in the family vault in the Stoneleigh family chapel.'

'That cannot be. We will need an order from the magistrate. We can not remove people from graves just like that!'

'She can be moved and she will! What do I care for magistrates? You will arrange for her to be buried in the family vault and it will be soon.'

'This is most irregular. I shall have to speak to Major Fitzroy. I have the deepest sympathy for your grief but.....'

'Sympathy? I do not think that you understand anything of my grief. My sister, a gentleman's daughter, the wife of Sir Roland Fitzroy has not even been granted the respect of a headstone.'

'I know how sad this is for you, but in God's eyes she is a sinner. She took her own life.'

'Are we not told that God is a forgiving God? My sister was ill. She did something that she would never have done if she had been well. Could the church not show any mercy? Is she to be punished for it in death to add to her suffering in life?'

The curate looked even more discomforted and he began to pace around the library with nervous tension obviously un-nerved by confrontation. I did not care, with all that had passed I was angry and beside myself. I glared at him in fury as he stood awkwardly trying to think of something to say. At last he said,

'It is not possible. Even if, the church would permit her to be placed in the chapel, papers for the exhumation would take weeks. In any case approval would probably not be given.'

'I am not waiting for approval. She will be moved.'

The curate again mopped his brow,

'I think young woman that you should remember to whom you are speaking. You do not understand such things.'

'I understand very well! Your living is granted at the behest of the Fitzroy family. I rasped. 'If you wish to continue as curate of this parish, you will do as you are told.'

A look of astonishment passed over his face.

'That is impossible.'

'You will do as requested.' Edmund's voice came from the doorway and the curate looked at us both in astonishment, as if desperately seeking a way to end his predicament but he was lost for words.

'I want my brother's wife buried in the family vault. It will take place tomorrow and any expenses incurred will be covered by me.'

'But it is not that simple,' the curate gasped, his face now flushed.

'It is very simple. You will arrange matters today and in the morning the coffin will be brought to the chapel!'

'But I...' The curate adjusted his collar as though it had suddenly become too tight for him and it was cutting off his breath.

'You will do as I ask.' Edmund commented in a tone that meant the discussion was at an end. Wearily I sat down, drained by the effort and Edmund came and stood by my chair adding,

'Well?' The curate struggled with himself for a moment and then sighing loudly he accepted defeat.

'Yes, I will make the necessary arrangements, I will return tomorrow.' Mopping his forehead again, he walked out of the room in an agitated manner. As he reached the hallway Edmund added,

'There is also a child there. A boy, it too will be moved, Rosie will show you which one.'

'Rosie!' I heard him gasp, 'but surely......' Seeing the look on Edmund's face his cheeks quivered and then he turned on his heel.

I was exhilarated. The battle was won, but I was weak and exhausted from the struggle. Edmund watched the man walking off from the library window and commented,

'Well you certainly put the fear of God into that poor man!'

'No I think it was the fear of losing the Fitzroy money.'

'Well that poor curate must rue the day that he tried to win an argument with you.' Despite myself, I allowed a smile to flicker around my lips and Edmund returned it.

'That's better. At last you are beginning to look more like your old self. Doesn't she Rosie?'

Rosie visibly brightened at being spoken to and brushed down her grubby black dress, straightened her hair and beamed a broken toothed smile at him, delighted to have his attention. Then Edmund addressed her in the most kindly tone I had ever heard him use when speaking to her.

'Now run along, and instruct the curate as to the correct grave for the baby.'

Then turning to me said,

'I must leave shortly to finalise some more Stoneleigh business. After the re-interment I will arrange for you to be taken to Lady Westerham's. Your friends are expecting you. I was going to wait a few more days until you were stronger, but for the sake of your well-being I think the sooner you are amongst your friends the better. This building is just full of gloom; you need to be in society once more. I myself must be in London by the end of the week at the latest. The regiment's orders are due shortly and I believe in a few weeks we will be embarking for Varna.'

'Varna?'

'Yes in Bulgaria. The situation with the Russians and the Turks is very unsettled. I believe we shall shortly be at war.'

'Oh Edmund, with everything that has happened I have forgotten what a dangerous life you lead.'

Edmund smiled and took my hand in his.

'Do not worry. I am too fond of my life to lose it yet awhile. Now you sit and rest and recover you health.' He looked at the bruises on my face and I wilted under his gaze again feeling sick with embarrassment. However, he did not comment on them but I wondered what the curate had made of them.

Later in the day the physician called and was very surprised to see me up and about and he insisted on my returning to my bedroom to rest. As he was about to leave I enquired after Annabelle. The doctor seemed taken aback that I should have mentioned her and then seeing that I was intent on having an answer, replied,

'The child has a severe disorder of the nerves. I have arranged for her to be given the appropriate care. Major Fitzroy has been more than generous with the financial arrangements.'

'When will she be well enough to come back and live with me?'

'Live with you.....' he looked puzzled, 'I am afraid that she will never live a normal life.'

'But surely, with good food and love and care, she will recover.'

'Major Fitzroy knows the situation, I am afraid that I cannot discuss Annabelle's medical condition with you young woman. There are certain things that are not for a lady's ears.'

'What do you mean?' I asked shocked at his response, 'I am her aunt. I want to know the truth about her medical condition.'

'You are tired and suffered a great deal. You need to rest and recuperate. It is better to forget all about the child. She is in good hands. You must concentrate on getting well yourself.'

'Forget? I will never forget!' I retorted.

'I see that you are becoming agitated and it is not good for your nerves. Do not upset yourself. She is being well cared for. Think of your own health!' As he spoke he took out a small bottle and began to pour some liquid in a glass. Angrily I knocked it away and shouted,

'Please do not try to drug me into a stupour. That will not change my mind about my niece.'

Startled he started to mop up the mess as the sound of footsteps were heard outside and there was a loud knocking on my bedroom door.

'Come in,' I shouted angrily.

Edmund entered looking extremely harassed and the physician quickly seized him by the arm and ushered him out of the room, closing the door as he did so. As they left I heard the doctor and Edmund standing on the landing whispering. The voices were muffled. I climbed out of the bed and tiptoed to the door and tried to listen, but the voices were indistinguishable. Then I gently opened the door allowing a small gap to peer through and my blood ran cold as I heard the physician talking.

'I am very concerned about this young woman. She is upsetting herself over the child and should be resting. Miss Devereaux has suffered an appalling outrage. Something that no one should have to endure. Yet within two days she is up and about as though nothing has happened. She has pushed it all to the back of her consciousness and that is extremely worrying. Women always are a martyr to their nerves and it is essential that she recover properly. If she tries to go on as normal she may suffer a complete breakdown of health. There has to be quiet and rest. There should be no upsetting conversations as she needs time to mend. Already she is becoming hysterical. I have seen cases like this before, the body heals but the mind does not. How can I tell that young woman, what outrages that child has suffered under the hands of her father? It is too horrible to contemplate.'

I didn't understand what he meant and disturbed stepped back from the doorway. As I did so I caught sight of the wardrobe and then a dramatic scene re-enacted in my head and the room spun and I nearly fell. That dreadful night of horror, I had heard Annabelle, screaming dementedly as she ran to hide in the cupboard. Slamming the door and then whimpering inside, sounding like a pitiful, distressed animal.

Shuddering at the memory, I steadied myself and opened the wardrobe door and peered inside. As I did so, I noticed a bag concealed in a dark corner. Interested in ascertaining its contents, I removed it and untied the string that was keeping it sealed. As the bag opened, the room was filled with a disgusting smell reminiscent of that awful odour that had pervaded Annabelle's old bedroom.

Now holding my hand over my mouth hardly able to breathe at the smell, I looked inside and became aware of green and mouldy food, including maggot ridden meat. It was all squashed and compressed in this linen bag. Annabelle must have been hiding food in the wardrobe. When I had thought she was no longer starving, she had been secretly storing away food that she had stolen during the day, leaving it to rot and decay. Quickly I tied up the bag and threw it on the fire. Perhaps the doctor was right. My niece would never recover from the damage inflicted on her. As I watched the bag burn, the smell was even more overpowering as the foodstuffs crackled in the flames. Forlornly I stared at the shapes and pictures the fire made as it burned just as Edmund returned frowning.

'What on earth is that awful smell?'

'I found this mouldering food stored in the wardrobe. Annabelle must have been so used to starving that even when she was well fed, she hid food away, in case she would starve again.'

'Poor child. How she must have suffered, here alone!'

'What did the doctor mean about the outrages that Annabelle experienced?'

Edmund taken aback sighed,

'You heard that. I am sorry that you did. I can not discuss it. It is best you do not concern yourself with it. There is nothing to be done now. It is not a suitable subject for a young woman.'

'Or a child?'

'It is finished. We are doing all that we can for her. I cannot undo what has happened.'

I bent down and lost my balance as I tried to poke the fire to rid it of the horrible package. Edmund steadied me and taking the poker from me did the deed. As I insisted,

'I want to know what is wrong with her'

'She has a disorder of the mind. The physician thinks she will never be well again.'

'I want to look after her. She was getting better I know she was. I want her to live with me.'

'It is too late for that. We will have her assessed by the best doctor's in their field but it is not hopeful.' Tears welled in my eyes and I bit my lip trying to suppress the sobs that were rising in my throat.

'Aphra, you must think of yourself. Come. Rest. The doctor is very concerned, that you are not looking after yourself. You must rest more. He was aghast when I told him that you had walked to the church yesterday.'

However, I was not listening. I could hear his refined voice talking in the background but I heard nothing of what was said. My body was on fire and could stand no longer as I felt so weary and exhausted. Annabelle, Freya, Roland, all of their faces seemed to swirl around me and I just wanted to sleep and never wake up. I sank down on the bed in despair.

Edmund looked at me with concern.

'I will leave you to rest,' he said. 'Tomorrow we will conduct a service for Freya and we will deliver you to your friends in the afternoon. Are your clothes packed?'

I smiled forlornly,

'I only have one trunk, as most of my clothes remain in Paris, '

'Well you will need more clothes in London, especially if you are staying with Lady Westerham. She is a renowned party giver.'

Weakly I replied,

'Yes she is. I believe Leticia attends at least one party or soiree a week and she never wears the same dress twice.'

Edmund replied,

'Yes I have attended some of them and it is always no expense spared. You will have to ask Leticia the name of her dressmaker. Send all the bills for my attention.'

'I am able to pay for my own dresses,' I retorted with pride.

'Please Aphra, let me help you? That is all I ask. Let me do something for you. It is the least I can do.'

'Please do not think that I am ungrateful, but I do not wish to be beholden to you.'

'Beholden, what on earth do you mean? Your life has been shattered by events here. Not just yours but also your sister and her child, and you do not want to feel beholden to me. Nothing that I do for you could ever repay the debt that I owe to you. I want you to regain a place in society with your friends, and have the status you deserve. If that can be achieved by purchasing a few dresses, than that is the least I can do.'

'What is the point of wearing expensive dresses? 'The tears now starting to fall. 'That life is behind me now. I am worthless. I will be staying with friends that I am unable to confide in for fear of scandal and shame. Frightened that no one will see me for anything other than I am. The bruises will fade but the scars remain and I am unworthy. What I have become cannot be disguised with pretty dresses.'

Edmund sighed,

'Please do not talk in that way. It is nonsense. You are the same person that you were before you came to Stoneleigh.'

'No I am not. All my hopes and plans are now as nothing. I will stay for a short while with Leticia and then I shall return to Paris. No one there will know of this, and I will become a governess or a teacher of English. '

'You will not! How could you even think of becoming a governess? How could I sleep at nights knowing that you have been brought so low, when the family estate could support you in a lifestyle that many rich families would envy?'

'I have no call on the family estate, besides I understood that Roland had destroyed the family's wealth. I know that my sister's marriage portion has all been frittered away and the bills and debts that I saw in the study were only a small amount of the debts of this estate.'

'Why are you so stubborn? Why won't you let me help you? I have my own fortune through my mother's family. When I have settled all Roland's debts I will close Stoneleigh until I have a need for it. I will arrange for it to be restored to its original condition and leave some staff here to manage it. Whilst I am away I shall instruct my lawyers to oversee the complete refurbishment of the property and gardens.'

I sat with my head down unable to look at him. He sat down next to me and taking my hand said quietly,

'Please let me be of service to you.'

'You cannot!' I said

'Why? He asked.

'Because, I do not want to be another Rosie.'

'Do not be so ridiculous, how can you be like Rosie?'

'I would be a woman with a protector.'

Edmund stood up angrily as if lost for words and then in a voice full of irritation he said,

'Then let me make an honest woman of you? Marry me.'

I began to shake and tears stung my eyes. There was nothing I could say. Everything was muddled in my head. I kept trying to make sense of what he was saying but all that flashed through my mind was that any involvement with me would only bring shame and disgrace on him. He waited patiently as I struggled with myself trying to form some words. However, it was as if my brain would not engage with my mouth. Somewhere in the distance I heard his voice like an echo ask again for an answer. He did not seem to understand that I was unable to think straight. I tried hard to say something until at last words came but they did not seem to belong to me. It was as if someone else was speaking as the voice sounded strange, yet it was my voice.

'I cannot. In time you would be sorry that you had tied yourself to a woman that you did not love out of a sense of duty. A woman who has been degraded and ruined and is worse than any foul creature.'

Edmund sat down and brushed a stray lock of hair away from his forehead and said gently,

'What can I say to convince you? This is all nonsense. I admire you more than any woman I have ever met. More than that. I love you. Do you think that I could bother with the silly girls that are foisted on me at balls and parties?'

'I was one of those silly young girls at the balls.'

'No you were Miss Sparky, the one who breaks hearts and now you are breaking mine.'

'Please don't continue I beg of you.'

Ignoring my plea he continued,

'From the moment I saw you at the top of the staircase my fate was sealed. Nothing has changed.' He gazed at me his face full of admiration but I had to turn away.

'Yes it has. You don't love me. You are just being kind because you feel a sense of duty after the actions of your brother. That woman who arrived from Paris does not exist any more. It is not me, this is a dream and I am merely her shade!' I sobbed.

'So it is still no!'

'Yes! You will thank me in the end.'

Edmund stood up and stared moodily out of the window, and then kicking the edge of the skirting board waved his hands with resignation and left. I didn't want to talk anymore I just wanted to be alone. My whole being just wanted to sleep and forget everything and lying down in my clothes, I fell asleep exhausted with nervous tension. However, I was not to escape as my subconscious filled my sleep with terrible dreams that woke me leaving me breathless and fearful. When I next awoke it was dark and I felt for that liquid the doctor had poured but I remembered that is was spilt. I drifted off and then that old dream came again, the hands tight around my throat. Only now it was based on a reality and I woke up screaming. When I realized that is was only a dream I was too afraid to sleep again and lay awake until morning.

The next morning three sad individuals stood in the Fitzroy family chapel as the two coffins were re-interred. The curate having arranged for them to be removed under cover of darkness. Rosie, Edmund and I stood in silent worship as the curate read the burial service over one large and one very small coffin. As I stood there, I suddenly had the overwhelming urge for my sister's coffin to be opened and to have one last look at her in death. Walking to the coffin, which now stood, on a metal support, waiting to be slid into the empty vault in the wall, I said quietly but firmly,

'Please open the coffin.'

The curate looked astounded and began to look to Edmund for advice on what to do.

'I do not think that would be appropriate. Your sister has been dead four years.'

I did not listen to his arguments. I looked desperately around and noticed that there were some gardeners' tools that had been left against the outside wall. Taking a rusty hoe in desperation, I tried to lever the lid from the wooden casket as Edmund tried to restrain me. As I struggled with him I shouted,

'Don't you see? I have to say goodbye. She died alone I must give her my blessing.'

Edmund took the hoe from my hand and brushed the rust from my clothes.

'Are you sure this is what you want?' he asked.

I pulled my cloak around me feeling shivery and cold,

'Yes, I wish to see her.'

'What if she is not as you remember? Would it not be best to think of her as she was?'

'I don't care. I must see her!' I stood my ground as Rosie cowered against the chapel wall as if frightened that the devil would appear and she would be struck down.

The curate stood in shock as Edmund gently prised off the lid of the coffin, and gestured to me to look. I was ready for the shock of seeing a decaying body but not for what was revealed. My sister was there just as I remembered like a Sleeping Beauty. There was a gasp from Rosie at the sight. Freya's body had not decayed, and she was exactly as she had always been. Her beautiful red hair hanging around her shoulders, framed the waxen face that looked strangely peaceful. Her long eyelashes still curling against the whiteness of her skin, it was hard to believe that she was no longer alive. Frey looked as if she was asleep dressed in the green dress she had worn in the portrait. I leaned over and kissed her pale dead face, happy that I had seen her. As I did so, Edmund looked over my shoulder and I heard him too gasp in surprise.

'Oh Edmund, she looks beautiful!' I laughed almost hysterically.

'Yes, she does. You could almost believe that she is still living. Have you seen enough? Shall I close the coffin now?'

'Yes! I am at peace. I have seen what I wanted.'

The curate came over to assist as Edmund resealed the coffin, and I heard him whisper, 'I have seen this kind of thing before. It is the laudanum, it preserves the body.' Resealed, the coffin was placed in the empty place in the vault, as the curate read his words over her. The coffin for Rosie's baby was placed in a separate alcove and Edmund left instructions with the curate for a suitable plaque to be engraved.

It seemed that in no time at all we were back in the house and I gathered my meagre belongings in preparation for leaving. I was desperately hoping never to see Stoneleigh again. I kissed Rosie goodbye, and Edmund and I were soon seated in the carriage and heading for London. The driver had to change the horses at 15 miles and we drove off with my battered body tucked up in a warm blanket. He settled next to me and we sat lost in our thoughts as we trotted through the countryside, passed the lake and the village and headed on the London road. We had a basket of refreshments for the journey, but I could not think of eating. I felt sick and numb, my mind still unable to function.

Each country lane we passed became a blur of trees and fields and all I could think of was what would happen when I reached Lady Westerham's house in Holland Park. I felt that I had a label attached to my forehead that identified me as a fallen woman. I knew I was being foolish. Nothing of what had passed would be known. However, the thoughts whirled around and around in my head so that I was completely oblivious to my surroundings. My face was still bruised but the story was that I had fainted whilst ill and hurt myself.

The carriage stopped to change horses and the driver asked if we wished to descend from the carriage and take the opportunity of stretching our legs. Edmund did so but I retreated into the dark corner. I had no wish to see people or be seen. The driver seemed a kindly man, but the sight of his face peering at me through the window had taken me by surprise and frightened me. I realised that my nerves were getting the better of me. I felt sad and alone, even with Edmund for support.

On our way again, it was becoming dark and I at last noticed that the country lanes had changed into city dwellings. It was a sign that we were almost at our destination. As we passed through the slum areas of Whitechapel and Southwark, the hustle and bustle of daily life deafened us with the noise of the carriages and carts. The streets thronged with dark shapes and listening to the cacophony of sound of the cries of the street vendors and the barking of dogs I began to think of Rosie. This was where she had lived, this noise and dirt was her daily life. How could she have spent her childhood here? It must have been a life of filth and squalor trying to survive in this foggy and overcrowded place

At last we came out into the open and I breathed a sigh of relief when I saw the rows and rows of trees just beginning to bud, lining the roadsides as we approached Holland Park. The driver stopped the carriage at the steps of a large grey stone house and opening the carriage door went to take my arm to help me down. Immediately I was filled with fear and stiffened at his touch. Edmund seeing my distress reached in to help me down but I shrank away. I didn't want to do so but I was anxious and couldn't help myself. Why had I come? No one cared at Stoneleigh but now I had to face people it was too much. At last Edmund managed to persuade me to descend the carriage and I waited fitfully on the steps.

The door was opened by a servant who bobbed a curtsey and bade us wait whilst she fetched her Ladyship. I stood there feeling like a stranger, sick with nerves. This house that I had spent so many hours of happiness in as a child now seemed threatening to me. I hoped my face did not reveal that I was now unworthy to be here. Having sat in the carriage so long my body was stiff and cold. As I walked, I lost my balance slightly and Edmund steadied me and I immediately stiffened. Edmund sighed and shook his head but did not comment. I knew he meant me no harm but I could not control my feelings.

As we waited a plump figure came racing down the staircase, and Leticia threw herself into my arms, almost knocking my slight figure down the steps. She was so happy to see me her dark curls tumbling around her bright, rosy face.

'She's here. She's here!' she called out, and then standing back looked at me more intently and added,

'Oh poor Aphra! You look so pale and tired. Have you been very ill?'

Before I could reply, Edmund stated quietly,

'She needs rest and care, but she will soon be well!'

Leticia laughed in her usual way,

'We will look after her. She will soon be like the Christmas goose fattened up.'

Edmund smiled at her, his blue eyes twinkling merrily at her words. She was a bright, lively girl, her face always wreathed in smiles as she chattered excitedly.

'Are you staying Major? You know how we always like to have a handsome man around the house.'

'Leticia!' A voice boomed as Lady Westerham appeared. Her tall stately figure bustled along the open hall way with a looking of disgust on her face at the lack of dignity shown by her daughter.

'Please behave yourself! She ordered as Leticia visibly wilted. 'I am sorry about my daughter's lack of propriety. However, despite this ridiculous performance we are delighted to see you.' The large features flushed with annoyance and she peered intently at me, as if trying to decide whether I met her approval by my appearance. Then continued,

'Well young lady I have seen you appear to better effect.' I didn't answer as Edmund said formally,

'I am afraid I have business in London, I just took the opportunity of escorting Miss Devereaux to your house. I will have to leave. I shall be staying at the Albany.'

I found it strange that he referred to me as Miss Devereaux as I had always been Aphra when he had addressed me at Stoneleigh. Lady Westerham nodded and pursed her lips, a glitter in her eyes as she peered at me again and I quailed under her gaze.

'That is a shame. We could do with you making up the number at cards.'

Edmund laughed. 'You know I always cheat Lady Westerham.'

'Yes I know m' boy, but then so do I!' she guffawed loudly. 'Still enough of this. If you must be off, we shall have to look after this young gel here. I must say she presents a sorry sight.' As she spoke she looked me up and down disdainfully.

'My goodness child, there is nothing of you. You are all bones and salt cellars.'

With that remark she marched back inside and there was an overwhelming smell of lavender pervading the air as her deep voice boomed out again calling for the servants. Instantaneously, there was a flurry of people as my cloak and baggage were removed. Edmund followed her to speak privately and I was ushered into the waiting area. Miserably I looked at the gilded mirrors and the marble statues. It all seemed so cold and unfriendly. Just as Stoneleigh had seemed so dark and threatening on my arrival, this house, bright and light as it was, made me shiver with cold. Soon Edmund returned and once more I was subjected to the critical eye of her Ladyship. I was uncertain whether Edmund had revealed anything of my circumstances but she did not look at all perturbed as she continued,

'What on earth have they been doing to you at Stoneleigh?'

I felt tears well up but I bit them back.

'I have been ill!' I replied meekly.

Edmund added,

'Her Ladyship knows that you have been unwell. She is ensuring that you will have the best of care. However, I must take my leave now. I will be in touch nearer the time of my embarkation.' He seemed so different to the Edmund at Stoneleigh that I was unsure how to respond as he nodded to me and immediately ran down the portico steps and jumped into the carriage. There was a clatter of horse hooves and he disappeared into the distance.

Leticia took my arm and excitedly showed me to my room and then leaving me to settle, disappeared back down the staircase, bouncing along like a puppy. Sadly I watched her go. She was always so full of life. Sunny natured and happy, it was a sensation that I wondered if I should ever feel again. Alone, I stood forlornly in my room and looked at my one lone bag. I was too tired to even think of asking the maid to unpack my things. Why had I come? I should have gone away from everyone. I had no right to be in respectable society. If my secret was revealed my friends would ostracize me, and yet for them not to know was to be in their home under false pretences.

As I stood there Leticia reappeared in my room, chivvying me to hurry and change, as she was desperate for my news. The maid came and started unpacking as I sat forlornly disinterested and uninvolved. Leticia watched wide eyed, becoming more and more astonished.

'Aphra where are all your lovely clothes? There is hardly anything here.'

'I left most of it in Paris. I just bought the one trunk and that is left at Stoneleigh.'

Picking up my brown cretonne dress and fingering it with distain she added,

'Never mind, we shall have such fun buying new ones. We will go shopping tomorrow and have such a wonderful time. We shall look at the catalogues today and there is a wonderful dressmaker in Chelsea. She will make you some beautiful gowns.'

I did not reply. I felt distracted and hardly heard anything that she was saying. I couldn't help but stare at her, as she chattered on. Her face was so wholesome, round and rosy, with large dark eyes that flashed with enjoyment.

'Oh Aphra, you look so sad. What has happened?'

I sat down wearily on the bucket seat by the door and she continued.

'Why do you stare at me so?'

'No reason,' I replied, 'I am just so pleased to see you. It has been a long time, you look so pretty.'

'Aphra, why didn't you come here when you first arrived in England? Then you wouldn't have caught that horrible illness, whatever it was. We could have had so much fun? You are like a sister to me. I have been so excited waiting for you but you look so different. I have never seen you look so pale and thin.' Throwing herself on the bed she added, 'You should have come straight to us. Not that horrid Stoneleigh I can't imagine why Freya lived there I never liked it.'

'I had things to do when I first arrived.'

'I know. I know. It's all to do with that Roland Fitzroy. How your sister could have married him I don't know. Do you know that we have heard that he has lost nearly all his fortune, gambling and drinking?'

I started at the mention of his name.

'He is dead,' I murmured.

Leticia put her arms around me as though to comfort me,

'Poor Aphra, no wonder you are so upset. First your sister, then your dear Papa and now that horrid Roland it is too bad. You are quite alone in the world. Never mind, we will look after you until you are well. You know how much we all love you.' As she spoke her big eyes widened and her face assumed a sad expression, but she soon shrugged it aside.

'Thank you Leticia, it is very good of your mother to permit me to stay here.'

'Nonsense! Mother thinks of you as another daughter, only a more sensible one than the one she has. I know I am silly and love all the superficial things, like parties and dinners, but what is life for other than to enjoy oneself. Anyway, you are a sly boots. When did you catch our handsome Major?'

'Catch him! Nonsense, he just escorted me from Stoneleigh!'

'Rubbish! He could have got a servant to do that. He is besotted with you. It was written all over his handsome face.'

'No Leticia, you are wrong. He was merely being kind. That is all.'

'If you say so.' She laughed and tapped her nose as if she was sharing a secret. However, I knew she was wrong; everything he did for me was out of a sense of duty. Why would someone fine like Edmund be interested in a woman who had been degraded by his brother?

CHAPTER EIGHT

'For I will wear my heart upon my sleeve for daws to peck
at: I am not what I am.'   *Othello Act 1 Sc 1*

My stay at Westerham House was strange to me. I had spent so long with my own company that I could not bear to be with the family. I started at shadows. The noise of Leticia's brother and sister gave me a headache. I awoke in the mornings exhausted and all I longed for was to return to sleep. The house seemed so cold and bright after the darkness of Stoneleigh, but the marbled hallway and staircase, with its gold decoration and statues that towered over me, made me fearful. To walk them felt like a trip through an ice palace.

Lady Westerham was kindness itself, trying to keep the younger children out of my way so that I could rest. I spent a lot of time in my beautiful bedroom with the ornate bed tapestries and blue and white walls. However, the room was full of mirrors and I could not bear to see myself in them. Each time I caught a glimpse by accident I had to duck my head down and try to blot out the image. There seemed to be something strange about my face and it frightened me. The tray of food that the maid bought would stay untouched as I had no appetite. The family cosseted me, treating me like a recovering invalid and I felt guilty because I was so much trouble and yet could not enjoy their company.

Leticia would sit with me and offer to read. However, I just wanted to be left alone with my thoughts. I felt as though Lady Westerham was watching me. It was as if she was trying to seek out something from my inner soul and at any moment would catch me out. I tried to tell myself that I was imagining things, but I became even more anxious and fearful than I had been on my arrival. When the family persuaded me to sit with them, I felt they were staring at me. I crept about the house feeling as if I was being watched and judged. I had a strong feeling they were looking for proof of my shame. Everywhere there seemed to be eyes staring at me, I was sure the staff and the family were always behind me at my shoulder. I know they were there because I sensed their presence and caught their reflections in the glass as I passed. I could never prove it though because when I turned quickly they disappeared. However, they couldn't fool me. I started to lie in wait for them but I couldn't catch them. When I entered a room I would see the servants deep in conversation with her Ladyship and when they saw me the servants would scuttle away. I tried to ask Leticia but she did not understand me and said that as I had been ill I was imagining things. I didn't believe her.

Occasionally, Lady Westerham insisted that I joined Leticia and her brother and sister Imogen and Freddie at cards. She would ignore my protests and insisted I would recover more quickly with some relaxing company. However, she persuaded Leticia that I was not well enough to go on the shopping sprees that her daughter was looking forward to. Leticia kept remarking how much my looks had improved but I didn't believe her. I was a bag of nerves, starting at every noise. When anyone addressed me unexpectedly, I was taken by surprise and tears would well up, whether I wanted them to or not.

The bruises on my body had faded, but I always wore what became my uniform of the brown cretonne dress that covered my body up to my neck. I was terrified of revealing anything of my skin in case the fading marks would be noticed. Two weeks passed in the same way and every day, Leticia asked if I had heard anything from my handsome major, winking and nodding as if party to some secret. I explained that I did not expect to hear from him but she did not believe me and his name was raised in every conversation. I did not want to discuss him and began to avoid my dear friend and would return to my bed and try to sleep my life away.

I had been there four weeks when Leticia insisted that I join her on a trip to leave her visiting cards at her friend's houses. I begged to be excused but she would not listen to my excuses. Lady Westerham insisted that I needed fresh air and had hidden away too long. Wearily I dressed in my outdoor clothes and dragged myself down that cold, unwelcoming staircase, all the time keeping my head down so that the blank eyes of the statues could not see me. There was a statue of a huge blackamoor at the bottom that always seemed to stare right through me with his gold painted eyes. As

I stood waiting in the entrance Leticia arrived dressed in red velvet and with irritation said,

'When are you going to stop wearing that dreadful brown thing? You look like a governess.'

Taken aback by her rudeness as she had always been so kind to me, I whispered,

'I told you, I left most of my things in France.'

Leticia's voice changed as she took my arm as I reached the bottom,

'Oh Aphra, you are so different now. The spark of life has gone out of you. You were always so bright and cheerful and such good company.'

Under my breath I breathed,

'Miss Sparky?'

'What do you mean?' she sighed loudly as if I was boring her.

'Nothing!' What could I say? I could not tell her that there was nothing left of Miss Sparky now. She shrugged and tapped her foot with annoyance but didn't say anything further.

It was a bright spring day and to my surprise the fresh air did make me feel a little better. Leticia waved away the carriage and insisted that the walk would do us both good. We toured around her friends in Holland Park leaving the cards. Leticia thought it was essential that people knew that I was in London so that we could receive invitations to attend gatherings together. However, as soon as we arrived at the houses my heart would pound so loudly I felt sick. I thought everyone could hear the noise of it and I broke out in a cold sweat at seeing the people around us. I made excuses to return home but Leticia would not listen and brushed my protests away in a brusque manner. My legs were like soft cotton and I kept holding on to the nearby railings for support as I feared I would fall. At last I persuaded her to let me sit down for a moment and we found a seat in the gardens. After a short while Leticia made it clear that she was impatient to walk again and was hovering around waiting for me.

It was obvious that her patience was wearing thin and I forced myself to continue the walk. As it was warm, I became aware that the tree lined streets were beginning to bloom. There was cherry blossom and apple blossom in pink and white and it all looked so beautiful that despite myself I found that the sight quite lifted my spirits. The imaginary cobwebs that I felt constantly irritating my face and which I tried to constantly rub away suddenly stopped and by the time we returned home they had completely disappeared. As the maid helped me remove my cloak I suddenly saw my reflection and I saw my cheeks were now pink and I was surprised and pleased and the feeling of dread at my image faded away.

Although I had not heard from Edmund, all the newspapers were full of the troubles concerning Russia and Turkey. It appeared that England would soon be at war. I knew that Edmund had mentioned that he would be embarking for Bulgaria in the near future and I wondered if he had already done so. I was under no illusions that he would come and say farewell before he left. He had done the noble deed in taking me to the care of my friends and I would see him no more.

It was over a month since my arrival and I now came downstairs much more often and even joined the family in the dining room. The thin waif that had arrived was now a little plumper, or so everyone kept telling me. One day, Leticia came rushing headlong into my room, laughing excitedly and waving a white card.

'There's a ball, at Brougham Hall, and we are all invited. Do say that you will attend? I won't go without you and you wouldn't let me miss the biggest society event of the year, would you? You look so much better now. Please come.'

I smiled at her childish enthusiasm saying,

'I could not possibly attend a ball, even if I wanted to. You know I have nothing to wear.'

'Don't be silly, we will have new dresses. Mother will arrange for the dressmaker to come and fit us. We will have such fun visiting the haberdashery and choosing materials. We are all attending, even Imogen and my dreadful brother. That is if Freddie can be persuaded to behave himself. I need you there to help me pass an evening under sufferance with his company.' With that she danced around the room excitedly holding dresses against herself and admiring her reflection in the mirrors.

I wanted to attend a ball. I did feel better since our daily walks and I was desperate to be Aphra again. The girl who had enjoyed parties and fun and wore beautiful dresses. However, as much as I longed to, I was still nervous about being with people but Lady Westerham would brook no arguments. One day when she was resting in the Salon she sent for me. I meekly went to see her as she lay out on her chaise wearing her black lace day gown. She told me to sit down and then launched into a tirade. That for my own good I had to be amongst people. My illness had long past and I was becoming neurotic. I was shocked by her tone as she stood up and paced the room. She would hear nothing of my excuses, stating that I was in danger of becoming a permanent invalid and she owed it to my father to prevent it. Angrily she continued that there was too much pandering to young ladies and if not shaken out of it, they had a life of misery drooping around the house like an invalid. She had seen it so often and whether I wanted to or not I was going to the ball. When she had finished, she peered at me through her glasses an added,

'Do we understand each other?'

I was much stronger now and her sharpness did not upset me as it would have done a few weeks before. She was right about being amongst people and in my heart of hearts I wanted to go. Back amongst the mirrors I took a good look at myself and decided that whatever happened I would go. That night I went to bed with my head full of memories of parties and balls and the days followed in a whirl of excitement. Surprisingly, I found myself carried along with Leticia's enjoyment. I almost enjoyed poring over dress catalogues and picking out materials. The dressmaker arrived and we spent hours being measured and fitted with more trips to the stores to choose trims and ribbons and despite myself, I began to be lost in the activities.

At last the day arrived and the carriage waited outside Westerham House to take us to Brougham Hall in Knightsbridge. Leticia began impatiently standing in the hallway, stamping her foot at the inconvenience of having to wait for the horses to be fitted by the ostler. The dress that she had chosen was a beautiful oyster silk that showed off her exquisite shoulders, and rosy colouring. Her long dark hair had been lightly coiled and interlaced with diamond pins. She looked so beautiful, her eyes sparkling with happiness, that it quite brought a lump into my throat at the innocence she presented.

So used to wearing the brown cretonne, I was unable to choose material for a new gown. I felt I had no right to be dressed in finery and chose the plainest styles. Ignoring my protests, the choice was made for me and I was dressed in a heliotrope velvet dress, inset with lace leaving my shoulders bare. Lady Westerham lent me a pearl choker, whilst Leticia's personal maid had dressed and plaited my unruly hair. To keep it in place she had fixed pearl pins. The poor young girl had been perspiring profusely at the effort required in restraining my thick unruly locks. However, when I looked in the mirror I was startled at the transformation. When I had dressed and joined the party in the salon there were gasps and everyone commented on how beautiful I looked. I felt embarrassed at the attention and this fed my anxiety. Lady Westerham in a black and gold gown came up close to me and murmured admiringly,

'The Devereaux girls were always beauties. I thought that you had quite lost your looks but you have been hiding your light under a bushel. My young ladies are certainly going to cut a swathe amongst the young men tonight!'

Freddie and Imogen were settled into the carriage, with Freddie under the threat of dire consequences if he did not behave himself. It was the first time he had been allowed to attend a ball, but it was felt at fourteen years, he was of an age to do so. Imogen being eighteen years was quite as beautifully dressed as her elder sister in blue silk. Her hair was a much lighter colour than Leticia's and the blue contrasted nicely. When we were all settled in the carriage we set off for Brougham Hall and as it was not far from Holland Park, we arrived within a short time.

Soon everyone disappeared into the melee whilst I looked around for somewhere inconspicuous to sit down. I was still lacking in the confidence to join the crowd. I soon spied a large, potted fern by an ornate column and seated myself behind it in the desperate hope that I would be left alone and could fade into insignificance. As I watched the activity in the ballroom, to my dismay several young men found me and asked for dances to place on my card. I shook my head and they drifted away, but their presence made me uneasy and I wished I had not come.

The old familiar feelings welled up again and I felt that all eyes were on me, judging and criticising. Even in my secret hiding place people would find me and stop to speak. Each time someone approached me, I retreated further and further behind the fern. Meanwhile I saw Leticia whirling around on the dance floor, with one young man after another. I even saw her dancing with Lord Brougham who was at least sixty years old. Meanwhile, I sat with eyes downcast for fear of catching someone's eye and drawing attention to myself.

Miserably I wished that I had not been persuaded to come. Suddenly I sensed a presence behind me and became aware that someone was there. I nervously turned to decline another offer of a dance only to be taken aback to fine Edmund standing there. He was in full dress uniform, his gold, buttons and braid coiling along the dark blue jacket. His blonde hair was longer than I remembered and it shone from the reflection of light from the crystal chandeliers above. A huge wave of embarrassment flushed over me. I began awkwardly searching in my reticule for some imaginary item so that I did not have to look directly at him.

'I wondered if I would find you here?' he laughed, bending low over my chair, his arm resting on my shoulder. I recoiled at his touch as his hand felt like a hot iron burning my skin. Part of me was overjoyed to see him and the other part felt only shame and disgust at the memories he provoked. I felt there was a great barrier between us and I was so overwhelmed that I wanted to run out of the room. However, my feet seemed to be rooted to the spot. Instead I gazed disconsolately at the floor.

'You are looking quite beautiful,' he continued, pulling a nearby chair closer to me. 'Staying with Lady Westerham obviously suits you.'

'Yes!' I replied, trying to edge myself away. 'They have been very kind.'

'Is your card full yet? Would you grant me the favour of the next dance and not make me suffer the wait as you did all those years ago?' he smiled, his eyes crinkling and his full mouth turning up at the corners. He stood up and made a formal bow and laughed. I stammered and stuttered that I was not intending to dance, but my objections were brushed aside.

As the music started for the quadrille, he took my hand and led me onto the door floor. I felt foolish as we paraded the ballroom; the interest I sparked made me even more self-conscious and ill at ease. Edmund seemed unaware of my dismay. I would occasionally observe him with a sideways glance and was struck at how handsome he was. Then I became more aware of the glances from other ladies in the room and heads bending to gossip.

At last, to my relief, the music ended, and Edmund escorted me to my seat, to hide by the ferns and palms. As he sat me down he took my hand in his and gently kissed it. I hastily pulled it away, blushing with embarrassment but as I turned away I could not resist a smile at the feelings it evoked. Then as I did so those emotions faded as an image of Roland flashed into my mind and I felt tired and ill and I began to shake and panic, desperately looking around for a means of escape. Everything was beginning to be a cacophony of heat and noise, but Edmund was oblivious to it. Strange faces loomed up all around me, staring and talking. There was rush of whispers getting louder and louder and I was sure it was not my imagination as people were definitely looking my way. I was struggling to breathe as I heard him say,

'I wanted to talk to you,' he said formally. 'I wasn't sure whether to call on you at Lady Westerham's house. I thought that it would mean you became the subject of un-necessary talk. I have made arrangements for Annabelle, she is well cared for.'

'Thank you.' I mumbled, not even sure what he was saying. I heard him continue,

'I didn't think her Ladyship would take too kindly to her beautiful young guest having an un-invited gentleman caller.'

I didn't answer but stared at the floor, which seemed to be rising and falling in time with my breathing. My heart was thumping so loudly I thought everyone could hear it. I tried to control my rising panic and spluttered,

'Everyone is looking at me!'

Edmund patted my hand reassuringly as everything swirled around me and I heard him say,

'Of course they are. You look quite beautiful! Don't be anxious. Most women here would be only to glad of any attention. They did not spend all this money on new gowns to go unnoticed.'

The room seemed to become more and more crowded and I felt as though I was suffocating with the heat that burned me.

'Please go!' I almost begged, 'I do not want to be stared at.'

Edmund, unaware that I was becoming distressed laughed,

'Of course they are. You look so beautiful. It would be strange if they were not.' As he spoke I struggled out of my chair just as the room spun around me and everything became a blur of colour and noise. Desperately I gripped Edmund's jacket to steady myself as my legs buckled.

When I next became aware of my surroundings, I was lying on a sofa in the library. I hastily sat up and to my surprise saw Edmund sitting in an armchair looking at me thoughtfully. Seeing I had begun to recover, he quickly came to my side,

'How are you? It must have been too hot in the ballroom for you. Perhaps you are not yet strong enough to attend such functions. Whatever were the Westerhams thinking of permitting it?'

'I wanted to come.'

'Well, I am glad that you did, for it gave me the chance to talk to you. Do you think that you would feel a little better if you take the air outside?'

He helped me from the sofa and led me out onto the verandah. It was a cool spring evening, and the air felt refreshing on my face as I tried to flap away the imaginary cobwebs that had returned again. We stood by the balustrade, over looking the Italian garden with the large stone urns and marbled stairways and patio. The night air was so cool and as the music drifted from the open windows of the ballroom it was so peaceful. For a few moments we stood in silence, drinking in the atmosphere until finally Edmund said,

'You must have read in the newspapers that war has been declared in the Crimea. Well we are making preparations to leave. I can't tell you very much except that our first port of call will be Varna in Bulgaria. It is where we will disembark, after that who knows. If the trouble with the Russians continues at some point we will head for Turkey.'

Listening to him my heart felt heavy.

'Oh please take care. I can't bear to think that you will be in such a dangerous place.'

Edmund laughed, and took my hand which felt cold and damp.

'Don't worry. Rumour has it that the Russians are very poor fighters. It will all be over before we know it. However, I shall try to write.'

'Yes, please do, I shall worry about you so much.' As I spoke I shivered and he put his arm round my bare shoulders.

'You are cold.'

'No! I am so worried about you going to fight.'

'Don't worry about me. We Fitzroys are made of sturdy stock. I shall look after my own skin. I like it too much to have it damaged. However, it is a strange thought for me to have someone in England who is interested in my welfare.'

'Don't, please!' I whispered, 'I can't bear to think that your life will be at risk. Supposing something happens to you....' I couldn't continue as he gently placed a finger on my lips to silence me.

'Nothing will happen!' He smiled and for a moment he gazed at me intently, his eyes searching my face but I couldn't bear it and turned away. However, he stroked my cheek and turning my face towards him whispered,

'Whenever you want or need me, I will be there.' As he did so he bent his head and his lips brushed mine. Trembling, just for a moment I wanted to cry out how much I loved him and rest in his arms but I pushed him away and cried,

'Stop it please! Everything is different now. Can't you see that?'

'What on earth do you mean?'

'You know what I mean. A fallen woman has nothing to look forward to but despair and degradation?'

A stunned expression flickered across Edmund's face and then shaking his head he said,

'What has happened can't be undone, but I have tried to make reparation. I have offered you a status in society as my wife. I have offered you my protection, what more can I do?'

'How can we marry? If the world at large should discover that I am degraded, it will be a scandal. No polite society would accept me and it would ruin your life, just as mine has been ruined.'

'Do you think I care for society? You are forgetting my fortune would always allow me into society, whatever anyone thinks!'

'Yes it is different for a man,' I said angrily, 'I would be deemed a sinful creature and no woman would want me as a friend. How can I marry you?'

Edmund turned away and despondently gazed out at the garden and said quietly,

'Because I love you.'

'No! You pity me!' I said shaking my head, 'You feel that you owe me a great debt. That you must make amends for the behaviour of your brother. Allow me some pride? I do not want to be the subject of pity. I shall go away and make of my life what I can. I will live somewhere away from London. There I will live a solitary life, where nobody knows me. Perhaps I can set up a small school for poor children; I do have some money of my own.'

'Why won't you let me love you?'

'Because you do not!'

I gazed at his beautiful face with its high cheek bones, trying to read his thoughts, but only saw his blue eyes darken with irritation. Sadly turning away, I suddenly became aware that Leticia was hovering nervously in the doorway. Unsure whether she had heard our conversation I asked her if anything was the matter. Edmund who had not noticed her turned on hearing my voice and his expression of annoyance became more intense as she said awkwardly,

'Mother has sent me to fetch you. She thought you were ill. You are behaving improperly, standing out here on the veranda. Mother says you are making yourself the subject of gossip, and people are talking about your impropriety!'

'Too hell with people,' Edmund raged and struck the balustrade with his boot as he strode angrily back into the ballroom. Leticia and I were both startled by his outburst and gazed at each other in amazement.

'What has happened?' she enquired, putting her arm around my shoulders as I shivered in the cold air.

'Nothing! I was unwell and Edmund suggested taking the air. He was advising me that he is leaving England in the next few days. There will be a war with Russia.'

'Edmund, is it? You sly old thing! I thought you were just friends.'

'Don't be silly, Leticia, Major Fitzroy is my brother in law!' I re-emphasised his formal title as we returned to the crowded ballroom. As we did so, young Freddie ran to greet us,

'Mother has sent for the carriage to take us home as it is quite late enough. She has instructed me to tell you that she wishes to speak to you.'

I made my way to the punch table where Lady Westerham was ladling a drink into a glass. She informed me that I would also be leaving and I was disapprovingly informed that as I had behaved inappropriately, she would speak to me in the morning.

Once home, my mind was so full of feelings and emotions that I was unable to think. My cheeks were burning with shame at the memories Edmund had resurrected. Once amongst the mirrors I gazed at my reflection in the expensive dress and the tears began to flow. Was I crying for myself, for Annabelle or for the danger that Edmund would be facing in the Crimea? I knew I loved him but I had turned down him down because I could not allow him to be tied to someone who would be ostracised by society. He could not love me. Edmund could marry any young woman of his class, and there were many who were far more beautiful than I, that would be a help to him and not a hindrance. It could only be out of a sense of duty that he offered his hand to a soiled and unclean woman. All the pretty heliotrope velvet ball gowns in the world would not wash away the dirt that covered me. I lay on the bed tormenting myself with my feelings of degradation and disgust, remembering the look on Edmund's face as he left the ball, until at last I fell into a fitful sleep. The night passed as if an eternity, my dreams full of grotesque images and memories, as I relived each moment of my time in Stoneleigh and mentally walked its gloomy corridors over and over again. I awoke feeling exhausted.

Later, when I was called down to breakfast Lady Westerham fixed me with a critical eye, as she helped herself to some kedgeree from the side table. The waft of lavender that always surrounded her, making me feel queasy.

'Well, young woman, what have you to say for yourself?'

I was uncertain how to respond, but assumed she was referring to my fainting fit of the previous evening.

'Yes I am sorry to have caused such concern. There were so many people and the room was so hot that I was overcome.'

'Yes, indeed! That could happen to anyone. Although it has been known for young women to feign a faint to attract the attention of an admirer.' Taken aback I was about to refute the suggestion when she continued.

'Enough of that! I am referring to your lack of propriety in disappearing outside with a gentleman.'

My face reddened at her comment and I began protesting strongly,

'I have done nothing wrong. Major Fitzroy is my brother in law. He helped me as I became ill. When I had recovered he suggested that the night air would be beneficial. Surely there is no harm in that?'

Lady Westerham softened her tone slightly and she peered at me knowingly and added,

'No harm at all. That is if the young man in question is not the most eligible bachelor in the room. You come along, a stranger to most of them and succeed in gaining his sole attention within a few minutes of arriving at the ball. I congratulate you.'

'He merely wanted to advise me of his imminent departure with the regiment,' I protested.

'Was that before or after the dance that drew everyone's interest? The Major hardly ever dances and having achieved that accolade you promptly faint. No wonder people are thinking that you are a young woman who can use feminine wiles to her best advantage.'

This comment angered me and I replied with indignation.

'How can people be so cruel? I felt unwell and the Major helped me. When I first arrived at Stoneleigh from Paris, there was no one to help and support me. Major Fitzroy has been kindness himself unlike my sister's husband...' I did not finish the sentence as I was in danger of letting my emotions run away with me.

The older woman stood up and brushed down the black lace she was once again wearing and continued,

'I have no doubt that you found it difficult. A young girl alone and you had obviously been unwell, that much was true. We could see that for ourselves when you first arrived here. Why I thought that you had quite lost your looks, but yesterday has shown that not to be the case. However, it is wise not to cause yourself to be the subject of gossip. A certain lady Venetia Wentworth, is making sure that everyone knows that Major Fitzroy was spending a lot of time in your company. I believe at one time there was talk that she was herself a subject of his interest.' She stopped for a moment as if thinking and then continued. 'Well enough of that. To disappear outside on the verandah alone with him was quite inappropriate. It will cause a scandal.'

'Surely Major Fitzroy is permitted to speak to whomsoever he wishes?' I asked meekly.

'Of course. Miss Wentworth is not important, especially as she had hopes in that direction herself. However, as there are several young ladies who are living in the hope of being his wife, it does not take long for tongues to start wagging. After all he has a large fortune and several estates.'

Before I could stop myself I blurted out,

'They have no need to worry. Major Fitzroy's wife can be any one of these girls, should he or they desire it. I have already refused his hand in marriage.'

There was a deathly hush as Lady Westerham visibly paled. Leticia, who had just entered the room, opened her mouth to speak but a frosty look from her mother silenced her.

'Leticia, please leave.' she barked and her daughter, surprised and discomfited at being spoken to so sharply, ran from the room. The silence that descended left me nervously standing by the table like a schoolgirl about to be reprimanded by her tutor.

'Do I understand correctly? That you, a young woman without family, have refused an offer of marriage from Major Fitzroy?' Her face took on a look of astonishment and her chin began to tremble with fury.

I stammered a response, only for it to be brushed aside as she boomed,

'Have you lost your senses girl? Do you realise that he is now the sole heir to the Fitzroys? The Major is not only the owner of the estates at Stoneleigh, but Threshingham Park in Hertfordshire. Why he is worth a fortune.'

'What is that to me?' I answered and crashed a plate down on the servery.

'What is that to you?' I thought the domineering woman would explode as her angular body quivered with rage, 'You have nothing. How will you manage in the world? Your poor father is dead. What fate awaits you, other than that of a governess? You have turned down a fortune.'

Taking a deep breath I refused to be bowed down by her and responded,

'I have my own money. I intend to find a small cottage somewhere and look after myself.'

The stately figure seemed to crumple and she sank into a nearby chair, a diminished body in ribbons and lace.

'Don't be ridiculous girl.' She sighed, her tone somewhat softer, the moment of rage having passed. 'Do you know what it is like for a woman on her own? Of course you don't how could you. A young, slip of a girl, you know nothing of the world'

I didn't reply and she waved a heavily ringed hand at me as a signal to be seated and continued,

'You have been a very foolish and insolent girl. You have thrown away an opportunity to settle yourself for life and now you will always be reliant on the help of friends.'

As I sat down I answered defiantly,

'I can maintain my own household.'

To my surprise I noticed that this grand lady now wore an expression of despair as she leaned forward and said,

'Please accept the advice from someone older and wiser than you. The only help for a young woman in your circumstances is to make a good marriage. You have thrown away the chance of not only a good marriage, but an excellent one. This opportunity is never likely to come again for a young woman without a fortune.'

I merely sat at the table idly toying with the cutlery feeling silent rage. I knew I had thrown away a good marriage, I did not need reminding. Suddenly she stood up and said brightly,

'Won't Lady Bonham and Mrs Cranleigh be outraged when I tell them that you have achieved in a short while, what they had hoped for Felicity and Vanessa for years not to mention poor old Venetia?'

I was shocked; this was not what I wanted at all. I leapt from my seat imploringly,

'Please, do not tell anyone. I would rather that it was kept to ourselves.'

Lady Westerham stopped in her tracks and her expression changed.

'Why, are you not telling me the truth?'

I began to stammer again,

'Of course I am. I understand that you think that I have been foolish, but I am not someone who makes up stories to make themselves more interesting.'

Lady Westerham looked down her nose at me and rang the bell for the servant. As she did so she scrutinised me again.

'Or faint? Very well! Perhaps all is not lost. Your refusal may make him all the more keen. Sometimes it does not do to acquiesce too easily. Too many young girls have set their cap at him for that. How was the situation left? People observed that he was not at all happy when he returned to the ballroom and I believe he left shortly afterwards. Did you make him angry?'

'No!,' I cried. 'He was not angry with me. He was angry that people in the room were talking about us. The Major merely promised me his support as a family member. His proposal was not genuinely meant, he was just offering to help me.'

'Well then, we must make sure that you are seen in circles where he is likely to be. If he is still interested in you, your refusal may encourage him even more'

'Please?' I pleaded. ' I do not want to encourage him. Besides he told me that he is embarking for Varna with his regiment.'

The woman's gimlet eyes lit up with excitement,

'Then we can make arrangements for you to take the ship. I believe quite a few wives and family members are boarding ship with the regiment. Why some ladies that I know are taking nearly all their household, not to mention their best horses. We will find someone you can attend with as a companion.'

'I will not!' I cried, my voice sounding harsh to my ears. 'The Major has my answer. I have told him that I am going to live quietly somewhere. He has given me the name of his lawyer who can help me with the arrangements.'

Lady Westerham studied me silently.

'This all seems most strange. You are certainly a beautiful young woman, but perhaps in danger of losing your looks after your illness. There are so many young women in London. I wonder what it is about you that has sparked this interest.'

I could stand it no longer. Affronted I stood up and she towered above me as I said firmly, trying to keep my temper,

'When I arrived at Stoneleigh, Roland was ill and so was his child. If it had not been for the Major helping us, I do not know what would have happened. I believe now that he feels only pity and to help provide for me has offered marriage as the gentlemanly thing to do.' She looked startled and did not appear to have listened to my outburst as she frowned,

'Roland's child! What child?'

I suddenly realised that I had said too much. Lady Westerham obviously did not know of Annabelle's existence.

'My sister had a child?'

'Yes, she died in childbirth. Everyone knows that.' She folded her arms against her chest and huffed with impatience.

I paced the room nervously as I replied,

'The child survived.'

'Where is this child now?'

'I am afraid that she has been unwell. Major Fitzroy has made arrangements for her to be cared for until she is well.'

'Seems to me that Stoneleigh is a very unhealthy place. I do not know what has been happening. You yourself looked like a ghost when you arrived.' She sniffed huffily as she waved the serving girl away.

'Yes, we have all been ill. However, you see the Major wants to help me.'

'Rubbish and fiddlesticks!' she snorted. 'I will ignore your impertinence as it appears that you have indeed had difficulties but whatever that young man feels for you can not be pity. He wouldn't offer the family estates to someone he felt sorry for. You do not understand men my dear. Why, that young man must have fallen in love with you.'

I felt the heat rise to my cheeks at her words and the difficulty I had in making her understand,

'No I am sure you are wrong.'

'Well!' she continued, still wearing the haughty expression. 'Time will tell. In the meantime, I owe it to your father that you take your place in society.'

Now almost in tears, all argument wasted, I sobbed,

'I have no wish for society. I have been away too long to value it. My sister married into the aristocracy and did not lead a happy life. I just want to live quietly with her child.'

Lady Westerham studied me carefully and then said sharply,

'Why will you not listen to someone who has only your best interest at heart? You do not understand the difficulties that lie ahead. A young woman with no fortune can't support herself and her sister's child. She is Roland's heir, the niece of Major Edmund Fitzroy. That child has a rightful place in society on her own account. She can't be living in poverty with you. Yes you have a small income but how will that enable you to pay for her medical care, and run a household?'

'Major Fitzroy has made arrangements.'

'And if, God forbid, something should happen to him?'

I felt sick and ill again at the thought of what lay ahead for him with his regiment. Then having looked at me with such piercing eyes that they seemed to bore right through me, she strode from the room. I sat down weakly and gasped as the cold shock of the leather against my skin cut through my back like the pain in my heart.

CHAPTER NINE

'Eternity was in our lips and eyes, bliss in our brows bent'
Antony and Cleopatra Act 1 Sc 3

The morning passed with an awkward atmosphere having descended over the household. Not wishing to have to face any more questions, I retreated to my room and sat quietly reading. Some time later the maid came with a note advising me that I was not to attend dinner that day until I had taken time to think about my actions and would be sent for to discuss my change of heart. This was too much. I felt that I was beginning to outstay my welcome. Lord Westerham had been a good friend of my father and his widow had continued that friendship. In the past Leticia and I had been as close as sisters but now I felt that we had drifted apart. She seemed so much younger than I but we were the same age.

My experiences had left me so despondent that the few days of happiness had been spoiled and had sapped my spirit once again. I would have to make arrangements to lead my life independently. To have to constantly answer for my actions made me feel like a prisoner. The house was so light and bright with its marble, glass and gold but to live there was as oppressive to me as the dark, dank of Stoneleigh had been but for different reasons.

Later that morning, despite having been told that she was not to come to my room until her mother had given me the promised audience, Leticia bounded noisily into my room, her brown hair in disarray and her rosy face shining.

'You have a visitor,' she laughed.

'Who?' I asked not looking up from my book.

'Come and see you sly old thing.' This phrase seemed to be constantly on her lips now. I placed my book down and tidied my hair and made my way downstairs. As I did so, I heard Lady Westerham's voice ring out and my heart sank. I hoped it was not more questions.

'We are in here child.'

I peered anxiously around the door and saw to my shock and amazement, Edmund sitting comfortably in a large armchair.

'Our friend the Major has come to say his farewells to us all,' she smiled.

I stood frozen in the doorway, as Lady Westerham brushed past me with a satisfied grin on her face.

'I have just remembered that I have to see the servants about some small matter. Please wait here until my return Major. ' She could not have made it more obvious that she was taking an opportunity to leave the two of us alone. Mortified at her behaviour I felt awkward and embarrassed.

Edmund and I stood in silence, until the door closed behind her and gestured to me to be seated.

'I could not leave without saying goodbye,' he smiled.

I tried to remain calm.

'I am glad that you did. We parted in such a strange way last night.'

He appeared to be in a good humour as he laughed.

'Yes, I was angry at your stubbornness. However, let us forget that. I want to reassure you that all arrangements have been made for Annabelle should I not return. The doctors have advised me that she is quite a sick child, it will be sometime before she is well again.' He paused for a moment then added thoughtfully, 'It was remiss of me not to know sooner, how things were.' Then he brightened. 'However, she is in good hands, and I have ensured that no expense is to be spared for her treatment. Should anything happen to me, then appropriate arrangements have been made. I have arranged for a private nurse to attend to her every need and she is in the care of the physicians.'

I watched as he glanced around the room and then pulling up a chair he sat near to me and added,

'I will write directly to my agent's office regarding any business matters that may occur whilst I am away. I shall also send letters for you care of that address. Then should you decide to move away from here, my letters will not go astray!' Then his eyes creased in laughter and he smiled, 'That is if you wish to receive letters from me.'

'Oh Edmund of course I do.' I said vehemently. 'I must know you are safe.'

He leaned over and took my hand brushing his lips against it and I willed myself not to shudder or pull my hand away. Although I had tried not to be cold with him as I loved him so much, he obviously felt the resistance. He stood up and leaned against the mantelpiece of the Adam fireplace. There was a silence until not looking at me he said calmly,

'If only things had been different?' Then turning to me he asked, 'Do you think Aphra that one day your feelings may change?'

'Feelings?' I shifted in my chair, trying to look anywhere but at him.

'Can you at least give me hope that you may one day love me as I love you?'

I was at a loss. I had to let him know how I felt. He was going to fight and who knows what would happen. God forbid he should die without me letting him know how I felt. My heart almost bursting I cried out,

'Oh Edmund, I do love you, how could I not, but can't you see that it is hopeless.' He rushed to my side and I quickly stood and he pulled me into his arms but his closeness overwhelmed me and I struggled involuntarily and he released me. I could see he was in a quandary about my behaviour but I could not help it. Quietly he stated,

'Nothing is hopeless if it is truly meant.'

I knew if this meeting continued I would have difficulty in preventing myself from breaking down. I seemed to always be in tears and yet there was a time I would have been much too strong for tears. I bit them back.

'You deserve someone better than I.'

'Will you stop this self pity,' he said his face set and angry as he gripped my shoulders and shook me. Realising that he had gone too far, he quickly released me and putting his arm around me, apologised.

'I am sorry! Please forgive me? I was forgetting myself, but why do you persist in this? Why are you doing this to yourself? Forget what has passed. It will never be mentioned again. I love you. That is all that matters. Who do you want me to marry that you insist deserves me more than you? Those scatterbrained society girls, all dresses and parties? You are the one I love and want. Your strength of spirit in the face of adversity has made me respect and admire you even more. Why won't you believe me?'

I looked up at him, as his blue eyes searched my face for some kind of response. Unable to fight off his arguments any longer I wearily sank down into the chair and words tumbled out of my mouth that I had no control over.

'Yes Edmund, I will marry you. When you return, if you still feel the same way, we shall be husband and wife. However, I do not wish it to be made known, until you have had time to consider. Then should you decide that you have changed your mind, I shall not hold you to any promise.'

Edmund looked ecstatic and he gathered me into his arms. Again I felt my body stiffen and sensing it he gently released me. I wanted nothing more than to be in his arms but my body constantly resisted it.

'Foolish girl, I will never change my mind! This war will be over in no time and we can marry as soon as I am back in England. I have something for you.' He felt in his pocket and produced a small box. Handing it to me, he took my hand and was surprised at its coldness.

'Why you are cold. What is her ladyship thinking of not having a fire in this room. You will catch a chill.' He rubbed my hand to warm it as he continued,

'I want you to have this and wear it for me.' Opening the lid the box revealed an amethyst and pearl ring set in yellow gold.

'It was my mother's ring. It is now yours. Whatever happens, I want you to keep it and think of me.'

I nodded; I did not need a ring to think of him.

'Edmund, whatever happens I will always think of you. I love you more than I can say. I think deep down I have always loved you from the time I first met you all those years ago. When I found your portrait, you were my only comfort at Stoneleigh. I do not need something to help me remember...' he put arm round my shoulders and taking my hand gently placed the ring on my betrothal finger.

'It will be our secret until I return.'

As he said those final words, the door opened and Lady Westerham re-appeared and I had the sense that she had been listening at the door. I searched her face for displeasure but found none.

'Would you like some refreshment young man?' she enquired looking inquisitively from Edmund to me as if trying, by telepathy, to know what had passed between us.

'No thank you. I must be on my way.' He bowed politely and making his farewells, he handed me some papers from his attaché case and was gone taking my heart with him. Left only with the uncertainty of whether I would I ever see him again. He was a soldier. Who knew what would happen when he was with his regiment?

Lady Westerham looked very pleased and sat down merrily, her beady eyes now twinkling with pleasure.

'Well child, all is not lost. It seems the Major is still interested even after your refusal. As I said before, sometimes it is necessary to make a young man work harder to win your affection.'

'Perhaps!' I did not wish to enter a discussion, but I foolishly looked down at the ring on my hand and this drew her attention to it.

'Good heavens, child, is that Major Fitzroy's ring. You have agreed to marry him?'

She gripped my hand with her bony fingers and stared at the ring admiringly. All the time I felt as if I was on a treadmill that was going faster and faster, my life spinning out of control.

'Yes, on his return. I am wearing his mother's ring as a token but there is to be no formal announcement. I have agreed to marry him on the condition that he still wishes it when the war is over and he is back in England.'

She was triumphant,

'No announcement! That is nonsense, we must have a dinner party and invite our friends, and everyone will be so surprised....'

'No' I said firmly, 'Nothing is confirmed. Nothing must be spread abroad to anyone. It is purely an arrangement between Major Fitzroy and myself. When he returns he will have had time to think and may have changed his mind. I have made him understand that he is free to do so, should he wish it.'

'What a strange child you are. Why would he change his mind? Do you know the value of that ring you are wearing? I recognise it as the Cavendish ring. It has been in his family for years, his mother was the daughter of Lord Cavendish. That ring belonged to the Cavendish family for generations. He would never have given you such a priceless object, if he had not decided irrevocably that you were the woman he wanted for his wife. If your father were alive he would be so pleased that you are to marry into such a family.'

'You forget, Lady Westerham, that one of my father's daughters did already marry into the Fitzroy family and it brought her no happiness and an early death.'

'Yes, it was unfortunate, that Freya should have died in childbirth like that. Unfortunately that is a woman's lot in life. However, why do you say she was unhappy? Roland Fitzroy was a wonderful husband and so rich. In fact I believe that it was because he was so grief stricken at her death that it led to his decline.'

I was too weary to argue. Whatever society felt about my sister and her life with Roland, I did not want to enlighten them. Lady Westerham continued to crow with pleasure at the thought of the wealth and status of the Fitzroy family which had killed my sister.

She arranged herself in a stately fashion on the sofa and continued,

'Edmund is a different case entirely. He has his mother's genes, much more cultured and artistic, although he has the Fitzroy blue eyes. It was a shame that he was the second son, it would have been much better for him to inherit Stoneleigh and Roland to buy a commission in the army. Still what will be will be. However, he does also have that magnificent estate at Threshingham Park. Roland's mother was of Italian origins I believe. After she died, Lord Fitzroy married again to Edmund's mother who came from a wealthy Dutch family.'

She looked expectantly at me to confirm her words but I didn't reply as she continued,

'Well child, surely you can look a little more excited on your betrothal. Regarding that other matter consider it at an end you may join us for dinner.'

'Thank you.' I replied. 'May I go back to my room?' She waved me away with irritation. Leticia came running in a few minutes later to hear more of the news. Despite my insistence that nobody should know, her Ladyship had obviously announced it. Leticia excitedly came to congratulate me and could not understand why I looked so forlorn. Believing it to be because my lover would be sailing off to war she persuaded me to join her in a jaunt to St James Park in an effort to cheer me up. It was a warm day and the flowers were in bloom, with many tulips and daffodils blowing gently in the spring breeze. A dazzling display of colour that normally I would have enjoyed but this day I could not. As we walked she constantly questioned me about what Edmund had said and if he had romantically gone down on one knee. I brushed her questions aside. Leticia then revealed that the real reason we had ventured to the park was that she was hoping that a young man from the ball would be riding there.

I swore her to silence about my engagement but immediately her conversation turned to wedding lists and plans for the celebration. She was astounded that I was not shouting from the rooftops that I was to be married to Major Fitzroy. However, I silenced her by telling her of my plan to find a small cottage in the country and live alone. At this news a look of absolute horror passed over her face and she snapped at me in a way that was completely out of character.

'What on earth is the matter with you? I thought it would be so nice having you here and yet all you do is shut yourself away. If only you had not gone to Stoneleigh when first arriving from Paris, all would have been different.' All the time she walked on ahead, stomping her feet like a child. Pulling the petals off a tulip that had broken from its stem. I felt sick at heart and could not but agree with her. My life was full of 'onlys.' If only I had not gone to Stoneleigh from Paris. If only Edmund and I had met again when I was still his Miss Sparky and not the sad creature that I had turned into. A woman terrified that scandal would befall her at every turn. If only I believed he truly loved me, how excited I would be. However, no matter how many times he insisted he did, I would never believe he felt anything but pity. It ate up at me like a tumour, gnawing away. All my inner confidence that had steadied me through life had vanished

As we returned, having seen no sight of her young man, I informed her that it would be best if I should leave. Leticia begged me not to, saying she was sorry she had been unkind. Explaining that she just wanted to see me well and happy like I used to be. I advised her that I could not leave immediately anyway as I needed to speak to Edmund's lawyer about finding a home. At the earliest opportunity, I went to Lincoln's Inn to see the lawyer.

Mr Stebbeds' offices were down a narrow cobbled street, which was too narrow for the carriage to negotiate. The building was set back from a large expanse of grass that seemed an oasis of calm from the dark and dingy streets. Mr Stebbeds was an elderly gentleman who was so small he seemed to disappear behind the rows of dusty deed boxes that piled up in his office. He had a nervous habit of pulling at his moustache whilst distractedly searching through papers. However, I was surprised to discover that in addition to the small annuity I had from my father, Edmund had settled an allowance on me. This meant that I would be able to live quite comfortably. At first I argued with the lawyer that I could not accept Edmund's kind offer but I was advised that everything was arranged. Even if I refused, the money would still be forthcoming to use or not. Whether I chose to use the money was in my control but the allowance was not.

Back at Holland Park I wrote out my plans for the future. I had hopes of starting a small school and each day the family tried to talk me out of it. I was still spending a lot of time in my mirrored room and although I had put on weight I was definitely feeling unwell. Several mornings I had hardly been able to arise from my bed as I felt so sick and ill. As yet I had not made my appointment with the doctor and I could see that the family were becoming concerned for my welfare. I was too busy with my arrangements to waste time with seeing a doctor. I stopped coming down to breakfast because I would feel unwell in the morning and when the servants brought my breakfast on a tray, I could not bear to eat it.

Once a week I would take a drive in the carriage to the offices of Stebbeds and Partners to see if they had any success with finding me a property, but really I wanted to ascertain if there was any news of Edmund. Each day I scanned the newspapers for reports of the situation in the Crimea. It was reported in the newspapers that some of our soldiers had reached Scutari in Turkey and I had wondered if Edmund was with them.

Mr Stebbeds advised me that it was not necessary to come to the office as he would send a messenger to Lady Westerham if there was any news, but I insisted on my visits. At first Leticia came with me but as she found the offices dreary and the outing boring and soon left me to visit unaccompanied. She was much taken up with Garrick Henby-Smythe who was her admirer. He was the young man from the ball that she had hoped to see on our outing. I did not see her very often now as my listlessness and lack of participation in the things that interested her was becoming tiresome to her.

One particular morning, it had been raining but a hazy sun was beginning to work its way through the clouds. I made my regular visit to Lincoln's Inn and rang the bell of the offices and the clerk, a strange young man with a pronounced stoop opened the door. He seemed too tall for his weight and had to bend quite low to address me as he ushered me into a waiting office. Soon Mr Stebbeds, stroking his moustache, a white lace collar frothing out of his black coat, came hurrying out.

'My dear, how glad I am that you have visited us today, we have some good news.'

I could only think that he had found me a suitable cottage. I had more or less given up hope of hearing anything from Edmund. He ushered me into his office, which was piled high with papers and dusty files.

'A letter has arrived. A messenger brought it this morning.' He handed me a rolled vellum parchment, and continued, 'It was in a document bag of instructions that was delivered by the ministry this morning. It is addressed to you care of this address.'

I was so excited to receive a letter that I nearly fainted with pleasure. The elderly man looked concerned,

'My dear young lady, please sit down. You do not look at all well. I hope that you are being taken care of. It would never do for our young man to return and find you have wasted away.'

He poured me some water and I sat down gathering my thoughts.

'I am perfectly well, I assure you. However, I have been worried about Edmund's safety. If the newspapers are to be believed, the situation in the Crimea is very dangerous.'

Mr Stebbeds nodded in agreement,

'I expect you are worried. It is certainly a terrible thing that our young man is away preparing to fight. I am sure he will do his duty but you must look after yourself. Why there is nothing of you, if there was a draught in here it would blow you quite away.'

I did not reply, desperate to read the news but unsure whether to open it or nor as a sudden thought hurtled through me like a thunderbolt. This letter had arrived from the Ministry. Perhaps it was not from Edmund at all and it was bad news.

'My dear young lady, what is the matter?' The lawyer asked not sure why I had not opened it excitedly, having waited so long. I explained that I was too frightened to do so for fear of what it contained.

The lawyer reassured me and sitting at his dusty desk took the letter from me and held it up.

'Look at the writing. It is a letter from Major Fitzroy. It came with other despatches regarding instructions concerning his property. That is why it came via their offices. He is quite well. Well,' he continued thoughtfully, 'as anyone could be under the circumstances. I believe that the situation out there is appalling. The usual army mismanagement of affairs. Still enough of that. I think dear girl that you should consult a physician. You have been coming six weeks now and all that time I have seen you become paler and thinner. Your eyes are like saucers and I believe that your nerves are quite shredded with worry.'

I shrugged with disinterest and asked,

'Have you had any success in finding me a property?' All the while clutching the unopened letter.

'I am afraid that I must own up to a little deception on my part dear girl. I have not been looking.' He blew dust from a pile of parchments stuck on a spike on his desk as he spoke.

'Why not?' I retorted in horror. 'I must find somewhere soon. I cannot impinge on Lady Westerham's good will much longer and I need to start my own life. I want to start a school. I have to find somewhere soon. Already I have stayed too long.'

'Nonsense. The reason I have not looked is that I am under instructions from Major Fitzroy. He wants you to live at Threshingham Park.'

'I cannot do that. I do not know anyone there. Besides it is not a suitable thing for an unmarried woman to do. People will talk. They will think I am a kept woman that I am his mistress and he is my protector.'

Mr Stebbeds looked shocked that I had used such words,

'What do you know of such things? There is no scandal involved in a gentleman's fiancée awaiting his return in the family home. The household staff will see to your needs.'

'You know that I am his fiancée. That he intends to marry me?' It was now my turn to be shocked.

'Of course, my dear, I am his lawyer, all his arrangements and legal situations have to be arranged through me. Major Fitzroy is a very organised and thorough person. He could not go off to the unknown without settling his affairs at home.'

'It is not publicly known. I wish Edmund to be free until his return. If I live at Threshingham Park it will be a commitment. At least people will look at it as such. Besides, as I understand it, there is only a housekeeper and servants there. I will be an interloper and a nuisance to them. It is best I find my own property, I have the means as you know.'

The small man smiled and patted my hand,

'The future wife of Major Fitzroy cannot run a school. It will not do.'

The words stung me and I retorted,

'I have been independent all my life. If I wish to manage a school I will. When Edmund returns, we will have to discuss the situation. However, until then, I cannot continue to live at the mercy of friends and I refuse to live in a strange household with only servants for company.'

Mr Stebbeds looked concerned as he tidied some of the papers on his desk.

'Calm down, my dear. I see that Edmund understands you very well. When we made the arrangements, he was quite firm in his instructions that you should be unaware that I was not seeking a property. I should not have told you. He wanted me to act on your wishes but I persuaded him otherwise. He knew you would not agree to go to Threshingham Park. If you do not wish to go to a strange house, then it is better that you stay with friends. It is very hard for a young woman alone, even one with such an independent spirit.'

'I have stayed too long. I am becoming a burden. I am grateful to my friends, but I must make arrangements to live elsewhere. My father always said that a guest was like a fish, after three days it starts smelling and I have been there for at least two months.'

'You will be part of the Fitzroy family on the Major's return. Surely that is enough. The household of Threshingham awaits you. Surely to go a little sooner is not a problem.'

'My sister was a part of the Fitzroy family, it only bought her unhappiness.'

The old man's eyebrows raised and he bit his lip with concern.

'I know nothing of that my dear. The young woman is dead that is all I know but I must emphasise, Major Fitzroy is not his brother.'

I was sorry for my outburst and pulled my cloak around me, still feeling the cold even though it was a warm day.

'I must ensure that when Edmund returns he can be free to marry where he chooses. I do not want him beholden to me. I have his ring, but should he wish for the engagement to be broken I will understand. However, for my own self respect, I do not wish all of London to know that we are engaged, should he change his mind.'

'I think that is very unlikely. Major Fitzroy is a man of firm judgements. He has made his decision and he must have been very sure that it was the correct one. He does not give his heart lightly.'

'That is my concern,' I added. 'He wants to help me because he feels sorry for my situation. He is my brother in law and has a natural concern for my well being. Should I become his wife out of a sense of duty on his part, he will come to despise me. Then our marriage will be like a prison sentence. I could not bear to live such a life.'

'What on earth can you mean?' Mr Stebbeds gasped, mopping his face with his handkerchief. 'You are a beautiful young woman, with great charm and a gentleman's daughter with your own income. Any young man would consider he had won a fortune should you consent to be his wife.'

'Nevertheless, I have to be sure that Edmund does not marry me out of a sense of duty. We have not had enough time together for him to know whether what he feels is love or pity and until that is resolved I want him to retain his freedom.'

Mr Stebbeds pursed his lips and frowned.

'I see I cannot change your mind, but if I find you a cottage somewhere, it will be against Major Fitzroy's instructions. I persuaded him and he agreed that you could not be allowed to live alone. I cannot go against the instructions. I will have to write to him and ask for his permission to change what we agreed.'

'I want a small home, where I can live with my niece.'

'Your niece! I don't think that is possible,' the old man stammered, a frown wrinkling his face. 'I believe that she is in the care of the medical profession and has quite lost her senses. She is beyond being able to be cared for by a young woman. The poor child needs nursing and constant care.'

'I believe with loving care and attention she will be well. I wish to visit her as soon as possible and when the physicians decide that she is well enough, I will make the necessary arrangements. Do you have the address where she is being cared for?'

Ignoring my request the lawyer said firmly,

'I do not think it would be advisable for a young woman to visit the child. In any event the physicians will not discuss her condition with you. It is not proper.'

Standing to leave I asserted,

'I am her aunt. Surely blood is everything.'

The elderly man walked with me to the door and continued,

'Blood relationships mean nothing, my dear. Major Fitzroy is her guardian and he has made the arrangements for her. I must re-emphasise that her carers will not discuss her situation with you.'

'I mean to visit her.'

The old man sighed at my implacability,

'Yes of course. That is your right. However, you may find it upsetting.'

'Nothing that I find there can be anymore upsetting than the condition I found her in on my arrival at Stoneleigh. I assume that she is getting the best care that money can provide. Edmund assured me of that.'

'Yes, she has her own nurse. He took a piece of paper from the desk and scribbled on it. He then handed it to me.

'This is the address of the physician. I suggest that you write to him and make an appointment.'

'Yes, I will do, and will you still look for my cottage, whilst you wait for the Major's instructions?'

'Yes of course my dear.' He smiled and in a fatherly fashion patted my face. 'Meanwhile, you take care of yourself. You look pale and unwell.'

'I will tell Lady Westerham that I will leave at the end of the month. If nothing is found for me by then, I will return to Paris with my niece.'

'I don't think I can...' He tailed off, seeing the determination on my face and shrugged, knowing to argue was pointless.

'Thank you very much for your help,' I smiled. He was such a kindly old man that I was sorry that I had disturbed him with my requests. Still clutching the sealed letter, I made my way back to the waiting carriage and eagerly opened the long awaited news.

I recognised the large scrawling handwriting and smiled to myself. Even under the adverse conditions that he was no doubt experiencing, I was so happy that he had managed to write to me. The letter started off very formally, asking if I was well and hoping that I was enjoying my stay with Lady Westerham. It then detailed the appalling conditions, explaining that he had delayed in writing because many of his unit had been struck down with dysentery and cholera. The regiment was on its way to Scutari in Turkey, but supplies were not arriving and some of the officers had to sleep outside on the damp ground in their coats. They had idled away their time at Varna and had finally left without a bullet fired, when the Turks had routed the Russians.

Having worried me to death outlining the situation he then advised me not to worry as he was made of hardy stock and so far was quite well. The problems in the Crimea were becoming common knowledge now as there had been details in the newspapers, so he explained that he wanted to put my mind at rest and reassure me that although things were bad, they were managing the situation.

It was a strange letter; it was cold and formal and left me feeling a little bereft at its coolness. I did not know what I had been expecting. However, there was an overwhelming sense of relief, knowing he was safe. I folded the letter and then unfolded it over and over until suddenly I noticed that there was a tiny piece of paper that had been rolled into a tight little cone, stuck under the seal. I scratched at it until it was free. At first I thought it was just a waste piece of paper but as I unrolled it I saw the words,

'Remember, I love you!'

Edmund must have been concerned that the letter would be opened and read by someone else. This way, he was able to let me know that he was thinking of me. A surge of joy swept over me and I sat back in the carriage feeling absolute happiness for the first time in weeks. Just those few words, gave me such hope and I was filled with such longing to see him again. Perhaps he did have feelings for me more than pity.

As I gazed out of the window, I caught sight of my reflection in the glass of the carriage window and saw a small pale face peering back. Then as if by some miracle I was sure that I saw Edmund's face peering over my shoulder, merging with my own reflection. It was a good omen. That whatever happened we would always be united and I felt comforted and at peace.

When I arrived back at Holland Park, an excited Leticia greeted me. Lady Westerham was going to give a small card party that evening and she had agreed that Garrick Henby -Smythe and his sister Sidonie could be invited together with their mother. Leticia had been waiting for the carriage to return so that the driver could be sent on the errand of delivering the invitations as the party had been arranged at short notice. I informed the family that I had received a letter from Edmund and they expressed concern at the conditions that the troops were experiencing. However, the card party seemed much more important to them and the day passed in a swirl of activity. Leticia spent the day running in and out of her dressing room trying to decide whether to wear the cream silk, the blush rose or the lavender dress and having her hair curled and dressed. As usual I did not really want to be part of a social activity in the evening but felt it would be churlish to retire to my room again when there was company. Leticia was desperate for me to see Garrick and give her my opinion on meeting him formally.

Every now and then I could see that Lady Westerham was scrutinising me as we bustled here and there. She spent a lot of time giving imperious instructions for the preparations of the cold buffet for the guests and overseeing the organisation of the games room. About an hour before everyone arrived she took me to one side and looking at me with concern asked if I was feeling quite well. I merely replied that I was a little tired.

'It is probably the excitement of the day and the receipt of the letter from your fiancé.'

I started at the word 'fiancé' but I did not rise to it and merely agreed.

'I must admit,' she continued, 'that we have been quite concerned for you. You look very frail and not at all well. I spoke to you before about spending too much time alone. I think it is more than that and I insist you see the physician.'

'Yes, I think I shall. I was going to make an appointment. I do not feel quite myself.' I knew that my nerves were still not recovered but now I felt as if I was sickening for something.

'Of course, I will send for Dr Robertson tomorrow. We do not want you wasting away, pining until your love returns. Am I to see the letter?'

I agreed to her request, 'Of course, I will fetch it immediately.'

I returned a few moments later and handed her the vellum parchment and she sat down on the sofa feeling in her pocket for her glasses to read the document. I could sense that she was a little disappointed at its contents and she handed it back to me, with a disdainful look.

'Well, whatever you might say about our Major, he is hardly one for declarations of undying love in his correspondence.'

I smiled to myself knowing that she had not seen the little slip of paper. That was my secret. I smiled proudly,

'He is a soldier first and foremost. It is only natural that he writes what he knows.'

'Yes, I suppose so. Anyway at least he is safe. If the newspapers are anything to go by, the regiments are finding things very difficult and that is without even facing the enemy. Why I believe large numbers of horses have had to be shot as they became quite disturbed and unmanageable after the sea journey. Colonel Tavistock's wife took her best mare with her and it was lost. I have heard through friends that she is quite distraught.' I didn't reply, but the thought of Colonel Tavistock's wife being distraught over her horse, when according to Edmund's letter the men were experiencing death and disease was, I thought, rather ridiculous.

The guests soon arrived for the card evening, and were seated at the tables. Not being a good card player myself, I sat and read a book quietly until protesting, I was ushered over to make up the number on Leticia's table. When she thought Garrick was not looking she peered at him from behind her hand of cards and flushed red as a beetroot should he catch her eye. Lady Westerham had placed him with his sister and mother out of harm's way. He looked very young with a round pleasant face and dark brown long hair. Sidonie was a pale faced blonde with a retrousee nose and something doll like about her. She was very giggly and every time Leticia was spied looking towards their table she would giggle excitedly and elbow her brother. He would flush like Leticia and try to ignore his sister who would be silenced by a glare from her mother. Mrs Henby –Smythe was very plump and breathed very loudly every time she put down her hand of cards.

After a few hours the gentlemen retired to the smoking room and the ladies sat around amusing themselves, Leticia insisted on a walk around the room whilst she asked me eagerly what I had thought of the young man.

'Of course,' she said airily, 'I know he is not like your Major, but he is heir to an estate in Buckinghamshire.

'He seems very pleasant,' I responded and squeezed her arm. 'If you like him, he must be a fine person. After all my dear friend would not like anyone who wasn't.'

'Oh, Aphra,' she laughed, 'you make him sound so boring. Isn't he just the most divine person you have ever seen? He has wonderful brown eyes, they are like dark pools.'

Despite myself I joined in with the laughter but we were interrupted by Lady Westerham announcing loudly that,

'Miss Devereaux will entertain the ladies by playing the piano, whilst Sidonie will sing.' It seemed we had no choice in the matter. I remonstrated with her and tried to persuade someone else to play, for I was sure that there were others who could play much better. However, she would have none of it and soon I was seated at the piano playing accompaniments whilst Sidonie sang in a trilling childlike voice.

I felt nervous at finding myself seated once more at the piano. I had not played since that last dreadful day at Stoneleigh, but I steadied myself and ran my fingers over the keys. However, soon I found accompanying the singing a pleasure, forgetting about myself for a few moments. I laughed at the fuss of the girls all trying to outdo each other with their singing. At last Lady Westerham tired of hearing voices singing out of tune, suggested I play some Handel or Purcell for them. I did not wish to play and be found wanting by the assembled company. However, as usual after initially protesting, I was coerced into it and soon the music was taking me out of myself and I began playing with all my heart. Some of the men from the party drifted back having heard the music wafting down the hall and I soon found myself the centre of attention.

At last, beginning to feel anxious at all eyes on me I suggested that someone else should play. Resisting their importuning I stood up and went to close the lid. Just as I did so, a tall, dark man quickly rushed to my side. Putting his hand forcefully on mine, he prevented me from closing the piano lid,

'We will not hear of it.' he smiled, 'You play so beautifully. Why I have not heard such a polished performance in years,'

The closeness of him and the smell of alcohol on his breath made my head swim and for an instance I was back at Stoneleigh. The images in my head were so vivid that I thought Roland had returned. I couldn't breathe and I struggled to push the man aside. The room became a rush of colour and I felt a tight pressure on my chest as I tried to breathe, but no air could pass through my lungs. There was a pounding in my ears and I tried to hold on to the piano but I crashed to the floor, knocking the piano stool over as I did so. Through the blur around me I heard a voice echoing as if far away.

'I say! I didn't mean any harm. I only wanted her to play again.'

CHAPTER TEN

'When in disgrace with fortune and men's eyes I all alone beweep my outcast state'   *Sonnet 29*

O nce more in my room I weakly tried to sit up on my bed and immediately the room began to swim around me. My stomach churned and I began to vomit profusely, ashamed and embarrassed that Leticia who held a basin to my face, should see me. As I lay back in exhaustion, she placed a cold compress on my forehead trying to reassure me.

'Mama has sent for the physician, she thinks that you are quite unwell. This is not the first time that you have fainted. Poor Lionel was quite disconcerted when you swooned away at his touch. I hope he doesn't have that effect on all the ladies he meets.' I gasped as the vomiting eased and I lay back on the pillows, feeling wretched.

'Could I have a glass of water?' I asked, my throat feeling raw.

Leticia picked up the jug from the side table and poured out the liquid and held it to my lips and I sipped it. As I did so the waves of nausea began to rise again and I brushed it away.

Leticia looked concerned.

'Mama says that you need plenty of iron. She is insisting that the kitchen makes you a glass of porter and you must drink it every day. She says that your blood is too thin, that is why you are always cold.'

'Porter!' I winced. 'That is a foul drink.'

'Never mind, it will build up your strength. You have never been the same Aphra since you came here from that horrid Stoneleigh place.' I felt too weak to reply, lying meekly on the pillow unable to lift my head.

Leticia busied herself around the room, making light conversation.

'You must hurry and get well. You have to look beautiful for the handsome one when he returns. Everyone is so jealous that he is paying court to you.'

'Everyone?' I started at the word and struggled to sit up. 'I asked that no one should know. Oh Leticia, I trusted you.'

She blushed profusely and murmured something that I did not catch and then added,

'I haven't told anyone you are betrothed to him, but when they were talking of the ball and how the Major paid you so much attention, I could not help saying that he called and ...' she began to be lost for words and nervously plumped up my pillows. As she did so I waved her away and in that moment the amethyst and pearl ring on my finger, slipped off and fell onto the floor.

'Your ring!' She exclaimed, quickly picking it up. 'What are you doing? That is a bad omen. You must keep it on and never take it off.' She handed it to me and I gazed at it, the stones shining like a beacon. For a moment a wonderful feeling of hope washed over me. Everything would be fine, Edmund did love me. Soon he would return from the Crimea and we would be married. All the horror of Stoneleigh would be behind me and I would regain my rightful place in society. Smiling I hugged Leticia tightly,

'I do wear it. I shall wear it on chain around my neck and never take it off again.'

'But it should be on your finger.'

'I have lost so much weight that it is too big for me. I am frightened I will lose it.'

The next morning the doctor arrived to check on my health. He was large and red faced with wispy grey receding hair and a large hooked nose. His hands were gnarled and freckled, but his manner was easy and friendly. As he examined me, he questioned me about my fainting fits and general health. After a few minutes, his manner became more brusque and sharp. Finally, he curtly informed me that the examination was terminated. I was at a loss to understand why he was being as cold towards me as he closed his bag and without speaking left the room.

I was dressing, when the tall figure of Lady Westerham swept in, her eyes blazing furiously.

'Well, madam and what have you got to say for yourself?'

Shocked by her tone, I stammered,

'I don't understand!'

'No, I am sure that you do not,' she continued, striding around the room, tapping loudly on any available piece of furniture that she passed.

'I wondered how a young slip of a thing like you could have drawn in someone like Major Edmund Fitzroy. Now the truth is out'

'Truth? What truth?' I replied with incomprehension, not having the slightest idea what Lady Westerham meant by her attitude. She threw herself heavily into the carver chair by the bed and drummed furiously on its wooden arm, her knuckles white. For a moment she did not speak as I waited for an explanation of her manner. Then she exploded.

'You, madam, are expecting a child. What a scandal! How can I face my friends, knowing that I have a harlot in my house? What effect will that have on my daughter's place in society? Oh the shame! How will we live it down?'

Shocked, I could not speak. I felt a large lump lodge itself in my throat and a heat washed over me as if I was drowning in a pitch of boiling tar. Everything in the room blurred around me, all I could hear was her high pitched voice screaming at me, the words all merging into one. It didn't matter what she said, it was my own thoughts that hurtled through my head.

'I am expecting a child? It can't be true' my voice parched and dry. Distressed I looked down at my thin, white body. My stomach looked flat and I gasped,

'It's a lie,' and the words seemed to burn in my brain.

Lady Westerham caught me by the arm her ringed fingers digging into my flesh, 'Come my girl! Isn't that how you trapped Major Fitzroy?'

Despite my stunned disbelief, her accusation enraged me and finding some energy from deep within I shouted,

'I did not! I did not!' Lady Westerham staggered back, shocked by my vehemence.

'If you remember,' I raged, 'I turned down his offer of marriage. How dare you speak to me in that fashion? I have done nothing but suffer at the hands of Roland Fitzroy and now my degradation is complete.' I stood up as proudly as I could, trying to stop the floor from moving beneath my feet whilst she glared at me open mouthed.

If, as you say, I am with child, the child is that of Edmund's brother who forced himself on me in a drunken state. I was sick and ill and Edmund tried to make amends for the ill done to me, by marriage. How could I do anything but refuse? What am I to do?' I wailed loudly, and my courage failed as I began vomiting again. Sick with dread and shock!

Lady Westerham gazed down her nose with disgust and as I weakly sat on the edge of the bed, handed me the basin again. She waited until the nausea had passed and then as if nothing had intervened continued.

'What are you to do? That is a very good question. I am sure you believe what you are saying, but I do not. If the child is indeed that of Roland Fitzroy, then it was because of your own wicked nature. To think that your father's child could be such a wanton. Heaven knows what sinful behaviour has been perpetrated in that house. A young woman alone with two men! If you were a decent woman, you would not have compromised yourself by staying. This rubbish about being attacked can't fool me.'

She towered over me whilst all I could think of was the child that was growing inside me. It was like some monster feeding off me and I could not escape it. I sat down forlornly as she continued to berate me.

'Why, everyone knows that a lady cannot be with child as the result of being forced by a man. The act has to be reciprocal! It is your own evil nature that has been your undoing. I have it on good authority from the physician that it is an impossibility to conceive from a violent act.' Then storming about the room she flung open my wardrobe that contained my few dresses inside and her face purple with anger shouted,

'I will not have you in this house as a corrupting influence on my daughter.' As her voice rose, she flung my dresses in a pile on the bedroom floor.

This act snapped me out of my trance as I looked at the pile I controlled myself and speaking disdainfully said,

'I have been the victim of an outrage and you call me a corrupting influence. It was who you would call a gentleman who was the corruption. He was a degenerate who ruined his own life, that of his child, my sister and now my own. However, he is someone to be envied in society, whilst I through no fault of my own will become an outcast.' Pushing the woman aside, I bent down and picked up my dresses, and began to crush them into an empty trunk which had been left standing under the windowsill. As I did so I sighed,

'Do not worry Lady Westerham, I will leave today. I will cause you no scandal.' As the words left my lips, the mirrors reflected the early morning sun and dazzled me, causing me to stagger. Despite the sun everything seemed cold and I shuddered violently and she said in a thick, strangulated voice.

'You ungrateful wretch!' She then slammed the lid shut on the trunk catching the silks in the closing mechanism.

'Ungrateful?' I said quietly. 'I am not ungrateful.' Opening the trunk again and packing the dresses properly. Then standing with as much dignity as I could muster I said,

It is with gratitude that I thank you for permitting me to stay. However, should I be grateful to be maligned so. I shall leave immediately. It is my intention to start a small school.'

The woman looked at me with scorn and then laughed in a derisive manner,

'Don't be ridiculous child, no parent would send a child to be tutored by a scandalous woman with a bastard.'

The sound of that ugly word rang in my ears and I felt tears swell again, but I refused to let her see how she had wounded me and I blinked them away. How short my feelings of happiness had lasted. Was I to be spared nothing?

'Well, Lady Westerham, should my income not be enough, I can always sell my ring.' I retorted. She continued to look contemptuously at me as she said slightingly,

'Dress yourself girl.' I did not reply, but pulled a shawl around to protect myself from the cold, the sickness rising again. She rang the bell for the maid and standing by the door stated majestically,

'I am sorry for you, but you have acted very foolishly. I will bid you goodbye and say that I am only glad that your father is not alive today to see your shame. I will tell Leticia that she is to no longer have any contact with you. From this day on you are considered dead to us.'

I shivered at the cruel words but replied coldly.

'As you wish. I see that I have been judged and found guilty. Do not concern yourself. Major Fitzroy's lawyer will find me some lodgings. I hope I can leave my belongings here until I can arrange for them to be forwarded to my new address.'

She nodded stiffly.

'They will be placed in storage. The arrangements for their removal shall be made between our lawyers. When you are dressed you will leave this house and all contact between us is at an end.' With these words we parted and she swept out of the room. I was now really alone. What could I do? I had foolishly thought that after what happened at Stoneleigh my degradation was complete. However, now it seemed life had even more shame in store for me. Who could I turn to? Where could I go? I felt so ill, how could I travel? There would be a child of someone I hated and despised and there would be no one to help and support me.

With force of will I pulled on my brown cretonne dress and, draping my cloak around me, packed a small travelling bag. The maid arrived to see why the bell had been rung. She did not speak at seeing my tears but tried to help me with the clothes. However, I could not bear her presence and sent her away, insisting on clearing up the mess I had made myself. I crammed in the clothes without any thought for their preservation, until finally I pulled out the velvet ball dress. This I laid out on the bed. This I would leave behind. It had been paid for by the Westerham's and I would have no use for it. It belonged to a different life. I then walked down that friendless marble staircase and out of the house with only a few things in a carpet bag.

Outside the sunshine brightly shone putting a spring in the feet of the passersby. Meanwhile I walked soullessly along the street, every footstep heavy with care. There was a gnawing pain of anxiety in my chest at the prospects that awaited me. I knew there was a cab stand not far from the house and I headed towards it and hired a driver to take me to Lincolns Inn. Sitting forlornly in the vehicle listening to the clip clop of the horses hooves I brooded on what had happened. I had no friend in this world except Edmund, and he was too far away to offer support. In any case his opinion of me would change if he knew that I was carrying his brother's child. I knew that no decent person would admit as their friend a woman with an illegitimate child. I knew that everything had changed. To marry me now would be an impossibility with the child always there as a constant reminder of Roland.

I could not believe what was happening to me. I could not bear to accept it as a reality. Perhaps if I blotted it out it would cease to exist. It could not grow if my body willed it away. It was a forlorn hope but I made a decision in an instant. The thought that Roland's child was growing inside me was so abhorrent to me that I cursed it. My only hope was that it would die and me with it. If I thought about it secretly waiting to take over my life it would drive me to the edge of insanity. Therefore, I would not admit its existence. I would find somewhere to hide away and all my troubles would disappear.

As we turned the corner of a dank alleyway, I caught sight of a large blonde woman standing in a doorway. Her clothes were ragged and dirty and for a moment she reminded me of Rosie. At that moment a thought struck me. Rosie, who had lived a life in a world that I knew nothing of, would not be disgusted by my condition. I knew she would help me. Rosie was the only one I could turn to. I would seek her out and hire her to become my companion. I would have to make arrangements to return to Stoneleigh. Much as I dreaded the place I could live there quietly out of sight until Edmund returned. However, before I sought out Rosie, there was one thing that I wanted to do and that was to visit Annabelle.

Preoccupied with my thoughts I did not notice that we had arrived outside Mr Stebbeds offices. We had stopped for several minutes until the driver becoming irritated called out to me that we were at our destination and startled me by banging loudly on the roof. I hastily climbed out and entering the lawyer's premises, I was ushered into a room by the stooped clerk. As I made my way inside, Mr Stebbeds came hurrying out, mopping his brow with a large handkerchief, expressing his surprise to see me. Saying nothing of what had befallen me, I stated firmly that I wished to return to Stoneleigh and asked him to make the arrangements necessary for me to do so. Mr Stebbeds tried to dissuade me, telling me that the refurbishment had not yet begun, that there were no servants there. Explaining that I would be unable to manage a household alone, but I brushed these arguments aside.

He suggested that arrangements could be made for some of the staff from Threshingham Park to be transferred for a short while but I turned down the offer. I wanted as few people as possible to be aware of my condition. When he finally realized that I was intent on going to Stoneleigh he finally gave way. Then I asked him to arrange some transport to take me to visit Annabelle. The poor man looked absolutely shocked and stammered worriedly,

'Surely you cannot be thinking of visiting the child alone?'

'Yes, I am thinking just that. If I am to leave London shortly it will be more difficult for me to visit and I have to take advantage of this opportunity. I have a desperate longing to find out for myself what improvements have been made to her health, now that she is having the best care and the best physicians.'

'I can quite see that,' he replied, 'but when she was first taken into their care, she was a very sick little girl. I am afraid that she has been moved to an asylum. Her doctors will not allow a young woman to arrive unannounced. I did warn you of this before.'

'An asylum? I was promised she would be well cared for. Edmund would not permit it. How dare she be moved without my knowledge, I am her aunt. Asylums are for lunatics not a child.' I was outraged at the news.

'I know! I know, but unfortunately her condition deteriorated. As I have the power of attorney to handle Edmund's affairs, the physician advised me it was the best thing. The Major is her guardian and I have to make decisions for her welfare in his absence. I had no choice.'

A black rage descended upon me,

'Does a blood relative have no say in the matter? How dare this happen without even discussing it with me?'

The elderly man looked uncomfortable and sank into his chair.

'Please do not distress yourself. I was trying to do what was best. Edmund said that you had been ill and you were not to be worried with anything. In any case the physicians would only make decisions through the law firm.'

'I want to see Annabelle.' I said firmly, 'With or without anyone's permission.'

He shrugged as if thinking, uncertain what to do. He looked at me closely,

'Are you sure that you are well enough? Would it not be better to wait until you have your strength, you look paler than when I last saw you. Sit down and I will send for some cordial.' He opened the door and sent his clerk for the drink. On his return he said, 'Now where were we?'

He seemed genuinely concerned and picking up a sheet of paper sat at his desk and began to write. There was a look of intense concentration on his face as he scratched urgently with ink and pen. Finally blotting the ink and folding the paper he rang for the clerk who came in and was given instructions to deliver the letter. Turning to me he said,

'I have notified the asylum that we will be attending in the morning. I shall accompany you. Please in the meantime return to your friends until tomorrow.'

'I do not wish to return. I want to see Annabelle today.'

The lawyer frowned,

'But my dear that is impossible. I am making the arrangements but it is unreasonable to think that we can attend today. Return home and I will send a carriage tomorrow.' Then for the first time he became aware of my carpet bag by the chair and surprised his expression changed.

'Has something happened?'

'I have decided to leave Holland Park and will need some accommodation

BUT A WALKING SHADOW

until I find the property that you are supposed to be seeking.' He smiled ruefully,

'Yes, indeed! I am seeking something rest assured. However, that does not solve the immediate problem. If you do not wish to return to Lady Westerham then I suggest that you stay in the nearby rooms that I keep for my clients. A meal will be provided and you can rest overnight. You have distressed yourself and look extremely tired. I would be failing in my duty if I let you make yourself ill. I will collect you in the morning and take you to see Annabelle.' He took my arm and escorted me to the outer office and left me for a moment whilst he collected his coat.

The rooms were only a short walk away and I was led in to a clean lodging house where a motherly figure fetched me some linen and soon I was left alone to gather my thoughts. I slept for a while until there was a knock on the door and a meal arrived. I passed the time writing letters to some friends in France and reading waiting impatiently for the next day to arrive.

The next day the carriage arrived and we soon left the green field of Lincoln's Inn and trotted along the cobblestone streets by the embankment. I looked out of the window and watched small scarecrow children picking up flotsam and jetsam amongst the mud on the foreshore. We continued over the bridge and as we crossed the river I wished with all my heart I had never come to England on that packet boat from France.

It had started to rain and the rhythm of the horse's hooves on the cobblestones seemed to be in unison with the sound of the raindrops on the side of the cab. After a few moments the old man leaned forward and took my hand in a gentle fashion,

'I cannot repeat enough how sorry I am that my actions have been so upsetting for you. However, I hope that what we find will not be too shocking to you.'

'Why, should it be? I do not think that you realise just what a poor condition Annabelle was living in at Stoneleigh the past four years of her life. Nothing is shocking to me now. I am afraid the naïve young woman that arrived at Stoneleigh has become unshockable.'

'I hope that you are right, my dear, but sometimes, these nervous illnesses of the mind, can never be made well.'

'When it is an adult that has been affected by the traumas of life, I believe that could be the case. However, a child has strengths to overcome anything as she grows. It will one day just be a dim memory. I shall remove her from the asylum and take her with me.'

He patted my hand and released it,

'I do not think that you are being realistic, besides it will be very difficult for a young woman to gain admittance, relative or not. My letter I hope will gain us admittance but even then I am not sure.'

The carriage soon came out into the wider streets and after only a short time, we pulled up outside a large Palladian building, its tall marbled pillars placed at intervals around the exterior. Imposing, it stood back from a tree lined road, its courtyard surrounded by iron railings and a large rusting, padlocked gate. A porter sat in the gatehouse and Mr Stebbeds went ahead and exchanged a few words with him. The iron gate clanked open and we walked up to the colonnaded entrance.

The building looked grim and I shivered as the lawyer rang the bell rope. The skies had turned grey and it seemed to me that the weather looked as threatening as the building. At last the door opened and a stern, thin faced man asked us to wait in the vestibule. I looked around at the décor and it filled me with dread. The ceiling was very high with an ornate wooden coving of embossed gargoyles and monsters. There were dark oak pews arranged in rows in the side rooms, with elaborate wooden carvings on the arm and head rests. Solemn and oppressive, the place rekindled the feelings I used to have as a child, when I went to church.

We stood patiently waiting as now and again a door would open and a man would hurry through but would take absolutely no notice of Mr Stebbeds and myself standing there. It was as if we had become invisible. At last Mr Stebbeds suggested that we sat down on one of the oak pews and as we did so, a tall distinguished man rushed passed. However, this time the lawyer leapt up quickly and caught him by the arm. The man who was wearing a crumpled frock coat looked surprised at being stopped and almost as if seeing us for the first time, surveyed us coolly.

'And what pray, do you want?' he asked in a booming north country voice, his expression one of irritation at being interrupted.

'We have come to speak to the Principal.' Mr Stebbeds stated firmly not intimidated at all by the man's imperious manner.

'Have you an appointment?'

'No, but a letter was forwarded advising of our visit today.'

'Well I'll bid you good day,' the man retorted and brushing Mr Stebbeds hand from his sleeve he made as if to walk away. However, Mr Stebbeds, small as he was, could not be so easily pushed aside. He stated firmly, raising his voice,

'I think when he knows that we are here on business for Major Edmund Fitzroy, he will see us.'

The rude man stopped in his tracks. His manner changed immediately and he became very obsequious,

'I see. I am sorry, I am the Principal, and my name is Fanshawe. We receive so many callers. One has to have appointments only otherwise, no work would be done at all.'

'Quite! Quite!' Mr Stebbeds said, 'My companion here is Miss Aphra Devereaux, the aunt of the child Annabelle Fitzroy that is in your care.'

The Principal glanced my way for a second, but I was immediately dismissed as being of no consequence as Mr Fanshawe's gaze returned to the old gentleman.

'Come into my office,' he said, 'it is much more comfortable there.' He stood back to allow the lawyer to pass, but ignoring him, Mr Stebbeds came back to my side and assisting me in rising from the pew said,

'Come along my dear, we will go with this gentleman.'

The other man's eyes opened wide with astonishment,

'I don't think that we can discuss business matters with this young woman present. I..'

Before he could finish I interrupted,'

'I am afraid that you will have to do so.'

The Principal looked to the lawyer for affirmation but as he did not speak continued,

'This is most irregular. There are medical matters involved. Things that might be unsuitable for a young lady's ears. It would not be at all proper.'

'There is nothing that you could say about my niece that I do not have the right to hear.' I said firmly taking off my gloves and waving them at him.

The Principal glared at me and then at Mr Stebbeds, who confirmed that we would attend together. Mr Fanshawe shrugged.

'Very well, then, but whom do I have the pleasure of addressing?'

Mr Stebbeds handed the man his card. He then informed him that he was Major Fitzroy's legal representative and as the Major was out of the country, had full authority for his finances and business arrangements.

The Principal led the way into an office, which was much more comfortably furnished than the exterior. . There were heavy velvet hangings and a silver tray of decanters on a rosewood dresser, filled with various coloured liquids. We were told to sit down and wait. That he would be with us shortly but had some business to attend to. After a few minutes, he returned looking harassed and annoyed. We waited for him to make himself comfortable at his desk and then after what seemed an eternity he asked why we were here.

'I want to see Annabelle Fitzroy.'

'Impossible, Miss...?' He looked at me as if waiting for me to state my name, pretending that he had forgotten it. Then as if we were wasting his time he pulled out a fob watch from his waistcoat pocket and with a supercilious manner looked at it and frowned.

'Devereaux,' I answered. Angry at the way he was making it so obvious that he did not want to waste his time talking to us.

'Yes, yes of course.'

Insistent I asked, 'Why has my niece been locked up in an asylum? She is only four years old.'

Mr Fanshawe looked, clicked his teeth loudly, his face beginning to flush with exasperation.

'My dear Madam, please do not alarm yourself. We have come a long way from the days of people being locked up in lunatic asylums. We are an enlightened hospital. I cannot remember the exact circumstances of your niece's condition, but she has been placed in the best of places for all medical assistance. If you wait a moment, I will consult the files and ascertain the exact situation.'

He stood up and rang a bell loudly and soon a little wizened man entered from a side room.

'Fetch me the file for Annabelle ... what was it?'

'Fitzroy,' replied Mr Stebbeds his eyes glittering.

The wizened man with long side-whiskers disappeared and within a few minutes returned with a large file and placed it on the Principal's desk. As he did so, there was such a cacophony of screaming from outside that I quite started from my seat. The Principal ignored the noise and said firmly,

'Shut the door behind you, Smeeton. How many times have I told you, when we have visitors.'

'Sorry sir,' the man said hoarsely as he shuffled out of the office closing the door.

'I must apologise for my clerk. He will simply forget his instructions.'

'But what was all that screaming? Surely, Annabelle is not subjected to that noise day after day.'

'What! Oh, good heavens no. Annabelle has the best of care.' He flicked through the papers and continued without looking up.

'According to the file here, I see that she is in one of the exterior buildings in the private wing.'

What does that mean?' I asked.

'Well, she is not in the communal building, but is isolated with her own private nurse who minds her night and day. The physician's visit her regularly and all medication is administered as prescribed.......'

I stood up, impatient with his procrastination and said loudly,

'I wish to see her.'

'I have already told you that it is not possible. Do you realise that the child is very sick?'

'No matter I shall be taking her with me.' I said and stared at him defying him to argue. The man looked horror struck. He seemed to be waiting for the lawyer to speak. Mr Stebbeds who had been waiting patiently now reinforced my request.

'As I am responsible for the payment of the treatment received here, I insist that you do as Miss Devereaux requests.'

The Principal's eyes bulged at being addressed in that fashion.

'I do not think this can be arranged, I shall have to consult with the child's physicians I....' He tailed off.

'If, I am forbidden from seeing my niece,' I interrupted, 'then we will inform Major Fitzroy to cancel all financial arrangements.'

Mr Fanshawe looked as if he was about to have a fit of apoplexy, as his flushed face began to redden to a deep shade of purple and he tried to loosen his necktie. He gestured imploringly to the lawyer as if expecting him to remonstrate with me. The lawyer looked on impassively having no intention of intervening. The Principal anxiously continued,

'Mr Stebbeds, I think you should explain to the lady, this is an asylum. People here are suffering from all kinds of disorders of the mind. It would not be appropriate for a young woman to go visiting one of its inmates.'

'Why?' asked Mr Stebbeds. 'If as you say she is in a private wing, I can not see there is a problem.'

The Principal, stood up and came round the desk to stand at the lawyer's side and catching him by the elbow, whispered just loud enough for me to hear.

'There are things about this child's condition that are not to be mentioned in polite company.'

'Please do not whisper in my presence,' I angrily intervened. 'Nothing about Annabelle's condition is to be kept secret from me. I insist on seeing my niece, which I am quite at liberty to do. Even prisoners in the debtor's prison are allowed visitors.'

Seeing that there was no recourse but to go with my wishes, the Principal admitted defeat. Taking a large bunch of keys from a hook on the wall, he showed us out into the grounds of the asylum and we headed towards another grey building, again surrounded by huge iron railings. He opened the rusting gate, which swung back towards us and we had to leap back out of its way. He then knocked on a small side door just inside the entrance. An oblong spy hole, pulled back in the doorway and an eye appeared. After a few seconds the door slowly creaked open.

We entered a narrow passageway and the owner of the eye bowed dutifully at Mr Fanshawe, who signed in a ledger on a side table. He then muttered something to the man who bid us follow him. The Principal announced that he would wait for us in the waiting area. We watched him make his way into a sparsely furnished room whilst we followed the man who had opened the gate. He was short and fat with a large belly and he found it difficult to walk as he slowly edged along in front of us. We walked along the dark grey corridors behind him in appalled silence and I felt a shudder run through me at its musky smell and dankness.

At last we came to a battered door, chained with a large rusty padlock. The man produced a key and with difficulty, turned it in the lock. The door opened to reveal an empty room with no furniture apart from a broken, wooden chair. At the sound of the door opening a small thin woman appeared and quickly began brushing down her apron and straightening her dress to tidy herself.

'I'm sorry, I weren't expecting no wisitors.' She walked forward smiling, showing a mouth full of broken and decayed teeth, and bobbed a curtsy to us and waited quietly for instructions.

'The Principal has asked us to let the visitors see the patient,' the fat man said coughing loudly into a dirty handkerchief.

'Patient? What patient?' the woman asked looking at us with a puzzled expression. The man nodded sideways in silence as if to make her see that he was referring to someone behind the closed door at the end of the room.

Light suddenly dawning, the woman began to cackle loudly,

'Oh the young 'un, Gawd almighty, she may be many fings but she ain't no patient.'

146

I pushed forward, but a gentle restraining hand was placed on my arm.

'We have come to see the child,' Mr Stebbeds said. 'Will you please open the door?'

'Course yer worship,' the woman laughed, bowing and nodding and then coming close to me, she asked,

'You a relative are yer?'

The fat man barked

'Mind yer manners,' to the woman who shrugged and blew her nose noisily. I could not believe the impertinence and insolent manner of this awful woman. The fumes of alcohol that emanated from her were so strong they made me recoil in disgust.

The man still coughing took a key from his belt put it into the lock and opened the door at the far end. Nothing could have prepared me for the sight that greeted us on that door being opened. The room was small; no more that 10ft by 10ft, the walls were all padded and on the floor was a soiled flock mattress. Sitting in a corner, with a manacle securing her leg to the wall, was Annabelle. If I had believed that she was so ill used when I first saw her at Stoneleigh, it was nothing to the condition that I found her in now. Her head was completely shaved and her thin body was once more covered in weeping scabs. By her side was a stinking slop bucket and an enamel water bowl like a dog would have when it is chained to the kennel outside. Unprepared for the sight, I cried out in horror and the thin woman started with surprise.

'What's a matter?' she asked, 'Why you quite made me nearly lose me wits. You could 'ave made me end up in the asylum instead of just nursing them lunatics.'

'This isn't nursing.' I exclaimed angrily. 'What has happened to her? Why is her head shaved?'

The woman grinned, 'To get rid of them lice.'

'Who gave you permission to cut off the girl's hair?' Mr Stebbeds asked firmly.

Taken aback the woman replied indignantly,

'Permission? I don't need no permission. I looks after 'er. I tend to 'er needs, it is up to me.'

The fat man began to look nervous and his flabby face began to bead with sweat. Trying to speak with authority he said,

'Of course it is not your decision. You have overstepped your position here, and the Principal will be informed of this.'

'Informed? He knows. I told 'im. Mr Fanshawe I says, that girl wots lost 'er wits, 'er 'ead is full of them crawlies and I can't get near 'er to comb 'em out. She won't sit still, and screams and shouts and so 'e says, cut orf 'er air and get one of them men to fix up the chain.'

I could stand no more and began to shout,

'How dare you treat this child in that cruel fashion? Even an animal would be better cared for than that. We understood that Annabelle was having medical care and attention. Major Fitzroy has paid for a nurse not some drunken hag.'

It was the woman's turn to look offended and she drew her thin body up haughtily.

"Ere who you calling a hag? So wot if I has a bit of gin? You would too if yer 'ad to sit 'ere day after day wiv a lunatic.'

At her words I burst into tears at the sorry prospect sitting before me. Annabelle's hollow eyes looked accusingly at me as if I was to blame for her predicament. I felt so guilty that I had not checked on her before now. I tried to wrestle with the chain that tied her to the wall and for a moment, I felt there was a flicker of recognition but the moment passed.

'Please! Please!' I implored Mr Stebbeds, 'Please remove her? We must take her away. I cannot tolerate her treated in this fashion. Cut that dreadful chain and free her.'

The old man tried to help me but the chain was too fixed and could not be moved. The crone was sitting slovenly on the broken chair, tipped against the wall whilst the fat man stared at the floor nervously.

'Get someone to cut this chain, he ordered. The fat man then snarled at the woman to find the key and free the child. The woman didn't move.

'I ain't doing it. I still 'ave bruises from them other times...' I didn't wait to listen to the rest of her excuses and snatched the keys. As I did so a hacking cough echoed around the cell and Annabelle began wheezing loudly. The sound racked her thin little body. I tried to put my arms around her as I struggled with the padlock, trying to reassure her that we were taking her away.' At last she was free and I gathered her stiff little body to me as the lawyer took off his coat and draped it round her.

When the coughing had subsided she looked at me as if she had no idea who I was. Then she looked at me again as I talked quietly to her, whispering her name and reassuring her. Then as her bruised and battered leg was freed,

Annabelle suddenly leapt to her feet and began violently rocking from side to side. The staff retreated to the outer door in panic. Ashamed at their behaviour I screamed at them,

' What? Are you scared of a poor sick child? You disgust me.' At the sound of my voice they peered round the door, anxiously waiting to see what would happen. I held her tightly and suddenly the rocking stopped as she froze in my arms. Her teeth were locked together but I continued to hold her. Slowly I felt her relax. I looked down at her small tired face, covered in sores, the bright eyes staring at my face.

'Aphra!' She whispered hoarsely.

I was overjoyed she had recognised me.

'She knows me!' I shouted.

'She don't know anyone. She is a lunatic,' the woman gasped as she stood peering round the doorframe.

'Yer better come out of there, 'fore she 'urts yer!'

Ignoring her comments I picked the child up and wrapped her in the rough grey blanket that lay on the damp mattress. Mr Stebbeds stepped forward to help and said loudly,

'I think that you had better fetch Mr Fanshawe at once. We need an explanation about how this state of affairs has occurred.'

The man nodded subserviently and rushed out of the anteroom to fetch his master. As he left the room I looked around the filthy chamber,

'Where are her clothes?'

'I sold 'em. I 'ad the right,' the woman replied insolently.

'You had no right. They are the child's clothes.'

"Ow do yer fink I can live wiv the money they pay me. Everyone knows when yer nursing a patient, you can 'ave their fings to sell.'

'I have never heard such nonsense,' Mr Stebbeds uttered, shaking his head as if he could not believe what he was saying or hearing. 'Your employer will hear of this.'

'Me employer! It's 'im wot says I can do it. Mr Fanshawe I says, 'ow can I feed me family on wot yer pay me, 'ere I am night and day, I gets bit and scratched, it's more than a body can take. Mrs Turnabout he says, if the patients 'ave any items of value, yer can 'ave them to sell. It is only right, payment in kind.'

All the time she was speaking I stood holding Annabelle, whose eyes were fixed on my face but her expression was blank, an overpowering smell of urine and ammonia wafting from her. The fumes were so strong that they made me want to gag. Frail as the child was, she was beginning to be heavy and I needed to be seated. The only other chair was filled by the nurse who had crept back in and was now sprawling on it. Mr Stebbeds glared at her,

'Get out of that chair!'

The woman grudgingly gave up her seat but defiantly stared at me with her bony arms folded across her flat chest. I managed to sit Annabelle on my lap as the door to the anteroom opened and in marched the Principal.

'Mr Fanshawe!' the woman screeched. 'You tells these peoples that I ain't no thief, yer said....'

'Shut up you stupid woman and speak when you are spoken to.' He turned to address the lawyer. 'What seems to be the matter here?'

Mr Stebbeds tutted and shook his head in disbelief.

'This organisation has been taking money from the Fitzroy family under false pretences. This child was supposedly having the best doctors and nursing that money could buy. Here we find her chained like an animal in a stinking room, no bigger than a cell. Explain yourself man!'

Mr Fanshawe's tone changed and he began to stammer.

'I do not know what you mean. I understood that she was being nursed.'

'Nursed, by a drunken hag,' I said, 'Look at the condition of this child. She is thin and covered in sores and has no clothes.' I was so angry that if I had not been holding the child I would have struck him.

'Well, I must admit, her condition is rather extreme. I understood that she was in a bad way when she came in. I can't be expected to know what is happening to all the patients, I leave the day to day running to my staff.' He looked desperately from face to face as if hoping for a means of escape.

'Leave it to your staff? This child is in the care of a drunk who has sold the child's clothes.' I raged.

'She will be instantly dismissed!' Mr Fanshawe replied angrily.

''Ere wot do yer mean? I ain't done nuffin.' the harridan interjected loudly.

Mr Stebbeds looked pointedly at the Principal.

'Whether you dismiss your staff or not is of no consequence to me. However, if this is how a child is offered the best medical treatment, I dread to think in what dreadful conditions the other patients suffer. We were lead to believe that you offered humane and respectful hospitalisation. I am appalled at what I have seen. Rest assured that I will inform the inspectorate of hospitals of what we have seen and I will ensure that you are the one that is dismissed. Meanwhile we are discharging this child from your care.'

'You can't do that there are papers to sign. If she is released we need a doctor's signature.'

'You can forward the papers and we will obtain the necessary signatures to be returned at a later date.'

'I am sure there is a misunderstanding, cannot we discuss this like gentlemen.......'

The old man brushed him aside and beckoned to me to bring out Annabelle.

'Come along my dear, let me carry the child and take her back to Whitefriars. He took Annabelle from me and as we walked out the nurse shrank back against the wall.

'Don't let that fing near me. She's got the divil in 'er. She is the daughter of Satan.'

Mr Stebbeds stared at the woman in disgust.

'Perhaps if you had treated her with kindness, you would not have suffered her violence.' As we walked out of that awful place Annabelle began to whimper and make strange noises and her whole body stiffened. I recognized that rigidity all too well from the past. She was so pitiful that it broke my heart.

Behind us the drunken women and the male helper came out and stood looking on foolishly as the door was locked once again. Mr Fanshawe ran along side us wringing his hands, pleading loudly.

'Do not do anything hasty. She has had the best of medical treatment. The child was restrained because she is violent. You do not know what you are committing yourself to.' I turned to him and he stopped in his tracks as I hissed,

'May you drown in the same mire of despond that you have condemned your patients to.'

Mr Stebbeds put his arm around my shoulders to calm me,

'They already have my dear.'

CHAPTER ELEVEN

'When sorrows come, they come not single spies, but in battalions'
                                                    Hamlet Act 4 Sc 5

We made our way out of the large building to the carriage. Meanwhile Mr Fanshawe, who had caught up with us, stood hovering by our side making his apologies. We carried the sick child in the blanket and managed to place her in the vehicle, ignoring his protests. The driver looked a little apprehensive at the party who were entering his cab, but a few pence placed in his hand was all it required for us to be driven away. As we set off the lawyer said quietly,

'Well we have stolen the prisoner away, but what is to happen now?'

'She will come back to Stoneleigh with me. I have made a plan to find Rosie and together we will look after the child as we did before. Only now it will be different. We can make a life there and we can live comfortably without any problems. I could not bear to say without 'Roland.' The name itself was like a curse on my lips.

'Rosie? The woman that Major Fitzroy has mentioned. His grizzled eyebrows rose heavenwards. 'Do you think that she is quite suitable?'

I sighed loudly. I was exhausted with the constant explanations and arguments and just wanted some peace.

'Please just do as I wish. I am grateful to you. You have been a kind and considerate helper in my hour of need. However, Rosie was my only friend when I first arrived at Stoneleigh. You know that I cannot take the child amongst society until she is well. My plan is to live quietly there and perhaps I can hire some local people to help me. Maybe even a woman who will nurse her with kindness, not like the sort of person in that dreadful place who had not a bit of human kindness.'

'Yes, perhaps you are right, but you cannot travel there now. Arrangements have to be made. Besides if, as they say, the child has exhibited violent behaviour, certain precautions are needed.' As he spoke we both looked at the frail child slumped in the blanket and that thought seemed so unlikely.

'Does she look violent?' I asked quietly.

'My child, I know how much she has suffered. There are things that child has endured that would turn the sanity of a grown woman. Let it just be said that she has been used abominably.'

I carried on speaking,

'You can't imagine what it was like when I found her in that filthy, neglected state. The child was starving, living in a fetid room, with only flies and maggots for company. Absolutely blue with cold. Staying there night and day alone whilst her father ignored and ill treated her. No one even aware of her existence.'

' I know all about it my dear. Please do not upset yourself,' he replied quietly. 'It is best that you try to forget it and look to the future. I think that you do not know or understand what has passed between that child and her father. It is best that you do not.'

I was somewhat taken aback by his words, he hinted at something I did not understand.

'What do you mean?' I asked.

'There is no more to be said. Let us just concentrate on the moment,' the old man said and looked at the child as if thinking deeply. Annabelle lay with her eyes closed but every now and then her body shuddered with a rasping cough. I pulled the blanket tightly around her as she was so cold. After a few moments the lawyer said,

'We will soon be at Whitefriars and we can best look after her there until arrangements can be made. What my wife will make of all this I don't know. He laughed merrily and his eyes twinkled and just for a moment I thought that everything would turn out well. He then added

'It will be nice for Betsy to have another woman to talk to. When I have warmed the chill that has invaded my old bones after the visit to that place, I may be able to decide what is best to do. I shall of course write to Major Fitzroy and explain the events but he has left me in full charge of his affairs, so the decision is mine.'

As he talked of Edmund I was sure I felt a sudden tremor like butterfly wings in my stomach and I held my hands to it in fear. Frightened that it would be obvious and I felt only hate as I realised that I could not escape the monster that was growing in side me.

Misunderstanding my reaction the old man smiled,

'Do not worry my dear. Everything will be sorted out and everything will be fine.' I nodded but did not answer and we sat in silence as we headed to his home.

The journey did not take too long, although we were delayed behind the carts and horses on the road as trade's people went about their business. The streets a throng of humanity. On arrival at a small whitewashed cottage, Mr Stebbeds helped me down and I tried to disguise the dreadful condition of the child. Rolled up in the blanket I held her against me, hiding the thin face and shaved head.

The cottage was set back from the main street and had a well-tended garden with a white wooden fence around it. The lawyer felt in his pockets and pulled out a key and opened the door to his home, calling out for his wife as he did so. Within a few seconds a little grey haired woman appeared. She was even smaller than her husband and her small birdlike face, surveyed the party interestedly.

The lawyer brushed a kiss against her cheek and entered the house murmuring.

'I've brought some visitors home Betsy!'

The woman bustled around us still unsure whether to be pleased or not.

'You could have sent a messenger Bertie. We are not prepared.'

The elderly man undid his collar and put his hat on a stand inside the main door.

'It will be fine. Ask Emily to prepare dinner for us.' He disappeared inside leaving me standing in the passageway, still holding my bundle.

'Come in. Come in,' she welcomed and before I could stop her she pulled back the blanket and recoiled with horror. Recovering she exclaimed,

'Mercy me, what on earth has happened to that poor child?' Then chiding her husband she called out.

'What are you thinking of Bertie? Bringing that child here. She looks as though she is suffering from some dreadful disease.' She turned on her heel and began huffing and puffing after him. I could hear whispering in the adjacent room and I was uncertain how to react. Mrs Stebbeds was obviously not too happy at our arrival. A few moments later her husband reappeared.

'It is quite all right. I have explained the situation to my wife. She knows what has happened and has agreed that Annabelle can stay whilst we seek medical advice.'

As he spoke the small woman came in and added,

'I am sorry I was so short with you my dear. Of course the child can stay. It is obvious she has been extremely neglected. Bertie just caught me by surprise. If he had sent a message I would have arrange things. A doctor would have been sent for.'

I nodded, 'I quite understand that our arrival has been an inconvenience. Major Fitzroy will ensure that you are more than compensated.'

At the sound of Edmund's name, the little woman visibly brightened.

'Are you the Major's young woman? Well why you didn't say so? Why we would not dream of asking for compensation. You are more than welcome here.' She turned and addressed her husband in a sharp tone.

'Fancy leaving the Major's young lady standing in the passage. Take the child through into the bedroom. She pointed down the hall way to a green painted door. As I passed she pulled the blanket back again and could not repress the look of distaste that appeared on her face. However, she gently replaced it and tucked it carefully around the sleeping child as she added,

'Well I hope she has not got something that we will all catch. That is all.' However, her expression was kind and I could not help but think that her bark was worse than her bite. As I went to follow her, still carrying Annabelle, she said in a brisk tone,

'Bertie! Where are your manners? Why are you letting that young woman carry that child?

'It is quite all right I assure you. She weighs hardly anything at all.' I responded,' However, as I arrived at the door I tripped on the carpet and nearly fell as she ran to steady me and said briskly,

'Bertie! Take this child.' The lawyer looked chastened as he took Annabelle from me and as his wife opened a nearby door, he placed Annabelle onto a small cot bed. I sank gratefully into a nearby chair as his wife's little button eyes looked at me with concern.

'You look extremely tired young lady. All this has been a strain for you. I only know a little about what has happened but this seems a strange situation.'

Mr Stebbeds took her aside and said,

'All will be explained in due course my dear. In the meantime, would you arrange dinner and we will talk of it later.'

The elderly woman pursed her lips and tossed her grey plait back over her shoulder. 'If I had known you were coming I would have had the girl put on some stew and had a meal ready. Now we will all have to wait and I am sure everyone is hungry.' Then with a busy movement she disappeared out of the room, leaving us with the child. The lawyer, now looking extremely sheepish and not at all business like in the presence of his wife, said forlornly,

'Tend to the child and I will call you when dinner is ready. The maid will bring some hot tea for you both. As Annabelle was still asleep I did not wake her but drank the warm liquid gratefully. The feeling of nausea that had welled up on the journey had passed and I found myself drifting off to sleep in the armchair. It was an hour or so later that I was called to dinner but as Annabelle was still sleeping it seemed best to leave her. We had no idea how she would react in her new surroundings. The maid came with a jug and water and having refreshed myself I joined my hosts at the table. The young girl was requested to check on the child at regular intervals whilst we ate.

Settled at the table I could only pick at my food. Although I was hungry the very smell of meat and vegetables, seemed to make my stomach swirl and nausea rise to my throat. It was only by strength of will that I managed to restrain myself from running from the room. I now knew the cause of my symptoms and I knew that I would have to hide away as soon as possible before the evidence would not be able to be disguised.

Mrs Stebbeds fussed around me, trying to encourage me to eat and I managed a little. However, I was grateful when the meal was at an end and the dinner things were cleared away. As we sat in the little room I took stock of my surroundings. Everywhere was red and gold and every nook and cranny was full of china and ornaments. Most of the shelves had small ornaments of children in various states of play. In the corner there was a large parrot in a cage, swinging violently on its perch. Every now and then it would whistle loudly and call out,

'Bertie what are you doing?'

It was obviously something that Mrs Stebbeds called out frequently and the parrot had mimicked her. The first time the parrot whistled during the meal I had started from my chair and inadvertently knocked over a glass of water. Offering my apologies, a cloth had been brought for me to use to dry off my dress and a cover had been placed over the bird to keep it quiet.

The elderly couple were clearly devoted to each other and Mrs Stebbeds constantly fussed around her husband, ensuring that he was comfortable. She ordered the maid to fetch his slippers, as she hovered around pouring him out some wine and he clearly enjoyed her attentions. After dinner I sat and talked quietly with Mrs Stebbeds, whilst her husband retired into his study to finish some paperwork. His wife seemed to enjoy having my company but she avoided asking any questions about the poor child who was still in a deep sleep.

After some time she suggested that I should retire as I looked so tired and I went to my bedroom where to my surprise Annabelle was still asleep. Her experiences had left her totally exhausted. I was frightened to disturb her. The last thing I wanted was to upset the household and yet I was conscious that Annabelle had not eaten for sometime. However, I deemed it politic to retire and Mrs Stebbeds left out some cake and milk incase the child awoke in the night.

'All children like cake,' she assured me. I realised that the business like woman that had greeted me on my arrival disguised a warm heart. As I bid my goodnights she commented that she and Mr Stebbeds had never been lucky enough to have children of their own. However, the lawyer informed me that his wife was fond of baking cakes and usually left them out for the local waifs and strays of the neighbourhood. They had come to expect it and would regularly knock on the door for their treats. Mrs Stebbeds was used to the starving orphans of the town.

I had left my carpet bag in the lawyer's office so his wife found me a nightgown and soon I was warm and cosy in bed. It was the first time I had been warm since my return to England. I had been cold in the dark at Stoneleigh and cold in the bright marble of Holland Park. However, unable to sleep I lay awake, thinking of everything that had happened. All the time watching the child, who was obviously dreaming as shadows flickered across her little face and now and again she uttered whimpering sounds, but still did not wake up. I constantly checked her breathing as she looked so pale and still but I would know she was alive by the occasional rasping cough.

Finally as night wore on I began to sleep only to wake with a start at the sound of Annabelle thrashing and hurling her body about. She began crying out loudly but the words were incomprehensible. This led to fits of coughing splitting the night. I was afraid that she would wake the household and I gently comforted her until she calmed down, although it seemed that she had been crying out in her sleep.

The night seemed an eternity, my mind full of images, people and horrors. Lying awake I couldn't stop thinking of Edmund but those thoughts always led me to start to dredge up images of a dreadful creature growing within me. Then I tried to pray but instead of a prayer I cursed it and hoped that my cursing would destroy it. Exhausted, it was with gratitude that I saw the dawn break and sun come up in the early morning. As the sun lit up the room, I noticed that Annabelle was awake. My arm was numb from having supported her, and holding her close I gently tried to prise it free. She looked at me watchfully, but did not speak,

'Would you like something to eat Annabelle? You must be hungry?' I asked. She didn't reply, but I eased myself out of the bed and uncovered the cake that had been kept in readiness by the bedside. Seeing the food, Annabelle's face changed and she leapt from the bed and ran to the bedside table and grabbed the food, devouring it greedily.

I was shocked at the ferocity of her actions. She was half crazed like a trapped wild animal. She had returned to being the ravenous child that I had known when I had first seen her at Stoneleigh. All the veneer of civilisation that I had given her had been lost in a few short months. I tried to restrain her incase she made herself sick but she pushed me aside as she crammed in the food in her mouth, screeching loudly. All the while she grunted and groaned in distress and fought with me.

Not knowing what to do, I sat and watched her spitting and salivating over the food. Although she was so thin, she was extremely strong and it was only when the food had gone that she became aware of her surroundings. The effort had exhausted her and she lay down in a curled up ball and to my surprise was once again asleep. I placed the bed coverlet over the small body and observed the purple and yellowing bruises around her ankles. The skin was split and encrusted where it had been damaged by the manacles. Her bony arms too were covered in bruises and scratches.

Just as I was beginning to relax as she was now quiet, there began the rasping coughing again and Annabelle sat up retching loudly. The child rolled around in a demented fashion, bent over double, clutching her stomach in pain. It had been foolish of me to allow her to eat all the food. Her system had been unable to cope with a sudden intake and I looked around for something for her to vomit in. I was desperate. I did not know what to do either to help or to stop her from making a mess in the bedroom. There was a porcelain bowl on a stand and I held it to her mouth as dark bile was brought up in, thick with clumps of undigested cake. As the moment passed it was with difficulty I prevented her from cramming it back in her mouth again. The whole episode was so disgusting that I was overwrought with the strain.

At last the crisis passed and Annabelle sat down on the edge of the bed, her head hanging down, shuddering with coughing. I poured a small glass of water and allowed her to sip it. I then poured some water on to my handkerchief and bathed her face. She sat quietly allowing me to wipe the encrusted dirt from her eyes and nose. We then sat together for some time, whilst I held her close to me as if fearful that she would disappear if I let her go. Annabelle, passively lay in my arms but did not speak and we rocked back and forth together.

After a time there was the sound outside my door of people moving around the house. I tried to separate myself from the child but she clung tightly to me. No amount of gentle coaxing or persuading would permit me to stand up without her. Finally, still carrying her, I opened the door and called out for Mrs Stebbeds. I was still in my nightgown and could not dress because I was unable to put Annabelle down. Soon there was the sound of footsteps and the small woman appeared. She was neatly dressed in a grey silk gown but still with her hair hanging down in the long grey plait. It was obvious that she had been up for some time.

'Come my dear, let me take the poor child and you go and dress.'

'I am afraid that she will not let me put her down,' I sighed and sat down again as the small, frail body began to weigh heavily in my arms.

'Nonsense!' Gently she put her arms out to take Annabelle from me and the child violently leapt from my arms spitting and hissing. Her arms and legs flailing wildly, lashing out at us with a surprising amount of force. I was unable to hold her and she fell to the floor still growling and coughing.

The shock of the sudden change in her behaviour quite took me by surprise and Mrs Stebbeds, fell backwards. Annabelle having caught her glancing blow that knocked her off balance. Hearing the noise, Mr Stebbeds came hurrying out, still trying to fasten his stiff shirt collar and managed to steady his wife who was winded. Rallying, and uncertain what to do, I called out sternly,

'Annabelle, stop it! As if slapped she suddenly stopped screaming and kicking and looked at me fiercely. Her eyes flickering over me as if trying desperately to understand what was happening and then she said in a hoarse high pitched voice,

'That ain't me name. Me name's Annie.' I felt a cold chill run through me at the eerie sound of her voice. I tried to explain to my friends how she had spoken to her doll like that when she lived at Stoneleigh. I didn't know where it was now. I had a sudden thought that if I mentioned the doll maybe Annabelle would remember who she was.

'You are not Annie,' I said sternly, 'You are Annabelle. Annie is your doll. Remember, Rosie gave it to you?' The elderly couple stood transfixed and we all watched the child in awe. Waiting to see what she would do. Annabelle then began to shake her head from side to side, rocking backwards and forwards. Nobody spoke as we suddenly heard her high pitched voice screech,

'My name's Annabelle!'

I tentatively sat down by her and kept up the conversation.

'Yes, remember, you had some pretty dresses and we used to walk to the village with Uncle Edmund.'

'Uncle Edmund!' She repeated, still nodding her head. I was uncertain whether she was just mimicking my words but at least she was constrained.

'I must get dressed now Annabelle. These kind people have allowed us to stay with them. You must apologise for behaving so badly.'

'Badly,' she repeated still rocking but now had moved herself to the floor and was sitting down with her arms around her legs. Then hugging her knees tightly began moving backwards and forward. Whilst she seemed calm I asked Mrs Stebbeds if she had been hurt but she shook her head.

'You had better leave,' I said to the shaken couple.' I am sorry to cause you this upset but I think it will be better if I deal with her.'

'Yes, you seem to have everything under control.' Mr Stebbeds said frowning, 'When she is settled, come and join us for breakfast. I think the child should just have sips of water and honey for the cough. I'll get the maid to tidy up the room later.' They left me to dress and I left Annabelle sitting and rocking. I tried to talk to her but now she was silent. I was uncertain whether to leave her, but I took the opportunity, having first locked the door incase there should be a repetition of her violence. I did not want her running out.

When I arrived at the breakfast table, Mr Stebbeds pulled out a chair for me with a look of concern.

'Do you think that this plan of yours is going to work my dear? If the child cannot be controlled, you will be unable to manage. The trauma of returning to Stoneleigh where she had such unhappy experiences may damage her nervous condition even more.'

'But what else can I do?' I asked miserably. I too was in a quandary. I had been so insistent on removing Annabelle but where could I take her?

Mrs Stebbeds buttered her toast in silence and then said in a matter of fact fashion.

'I think that you had better stay here for a few days. You seem as if you need looking after yourself, you are exhausted. A young woman of your age should be rosy cheeked and smiling not dragged down with care. Major Fitzroy would never forgive me if he came home to find you had wasted away. We will fetch a physician and a nurse for the child. That will allow my husband to make the arrangements for your return to Stoneleigh.'

The lawyer looked surprised and looked at his wife with relief. She however, continued with her toast ignoring him. There was a silence and then he commented.

'That is if you are still insistent on that idea?'

'I am,' I replied. 'I think that is best.' I could not tell him that I had no choice. I could not go to Edmund's estate at Threshingham Park. The demented child was not my only problem. To stay there would bring shame and degradation upon me. At Stoneleigh I would be hidden away. After a few moments I asked,

'Has there been any work undertaken at the house at all?'

'Well, it has been thoroughly cleaned and secured, but no re-decorating has begun.'

'If it is clean, then I can return there with Annabelle.'

'My dear, you ask too much of yourself. I've already told you it is impossible for a young woman like you to manage the household on your own,' Mrs Stebbeds interjoined, 'you need servants, a household cannot be run by a woman and a sick child.'

I did not want to hear their reasons. It was my only solution and yet I did not want to appear rude when they were being so considerate of my situation.

'All those things can be resolved as and when I am living there. If before we return Mr Stebbeds could arrange for the larder to be stocked. There was no food at all when we were living there. We relied on Rosie bringing in food from the village. I am hoping that she will help me, but I do not want to rely on her again.'

'That is why you should remove to Threshingham Park!'

'No, I cannot, I have my reasons, but that would not be suitable at all.'

'Well at least let me transfer some of the servants to Stoneleigh to help you to set up the household.'

'No, it is very kind of you, but until Edmund returns, I will live quietly at Stoneleigh. Perhaps I can find a girl from the village who will help me.'

'I see you will not be dissuaded.' the old gentleman smiled. 'What a stubborn young woman you are. I wonder if the Major know what he is taking on.'

'Bertie!' his wife chided. ' What a thing to say.'

Bertie laughed and took his wife's arm,

'Why he will have an imperious, young woman ordering him around and love every minute of it.' Betsy beamed at him and laughed loudly, showing little doll like teeth.

'How exciting! You must be counting the days until the wedding day?' Her husband frowned at his wife as if reprimanding her for broaching the subject. She looked puzzled, wondering what she had said that was out of turn.

I merely replied,

'There are no plans, it is not formalised. I am uncertain whether I shall marry Edmund. He is free until he makes his decision on his return.' Then I added disconsolately, 'I hope he returns soon. I know that he will take charge of everything and my future will be in his hands. I am beholden to him as a poor relative.'

Mr Stebbeds wiped his mouth with a white linen napkin.

'Poor relative! I do not think that he views it that way at all. Why he told me how much he was looking forward to his new life with a young bride. He loves you very much and who could not?'

To change the subject that was upsetting to me I stood up and said,

'I must check on Annabelle.'

'At least have some breakfast first,' Mrs Stebbeds responded, 'I am sorry if we have spoken out of turn.'

'Not at all.' I answered as I left them to return to my niece. Sadly thinking how different they would be if they knew my situation.

Unlocking the door, I was shocked to find the child threshing and rolling about the floor. Her eyes were staring from their sockets and there was deep red blood pumping from her mouth. I tried to mop up the blood and called loudly for my hosts to come and help me. Annabelle was soaking wet and bathed in perspiration. The Stebbeds called for their maid and we sponged her down until gradually the fit passed. However, each time she coughed, large globs of blood poured from her mouth.

Mr Stebbeds hastily sent a servant for the physician and we made Annabelle as comfortable as we could. However, she had become unaware of what was happening around her. Mrs Stebbeds helped me to put her to bed and we opened all the windows to bring down the heat as she was burning with fever.

'I wonder if she bit her tongue and that is the cause of the bleeding.' I asked with concern. The maid brought in a jug of fresh water and Mrs Stebbeds sat with me taking it in turns to sponge the child.

'Perhaps, my dear, but I feel may be it is something more serious, we will know more when the doctor comes. Her breathing is not regular and it sounds as though she has an infection. Her chest is bubbling'

I felt an overwhelming sense of foreboding. Surely, after all her suffering my dear niece was not going to undergo even more? I could not bear to think that in her young life all she had known was cruelty and unkindness. As if reading my thoughts the elderly lady put her arm around me and said quietly,

'You have done all you can for the child. You are hardly any more than a child yourself. I know something of the situation that the child was in at Stoneleigh. She has you to thank that for a short while, she knew love and care.'

'Yes, but knowing she was sick, Annabelle was placed in that awful place. Edmund assured me she was being well cared for. He surely must have thought that to be the case. How could he have let me think......'

'Ssh! I am sure, he did the best he could. My husband had to make a decision about whether to move her and he made enquiries first. That institution came highly recommended, but we are all in the hands of the doctors. You could not have cared for her yourself. You have no home of your own, and I understand that you too have been unwell. What is more the decisions had to be made urgently as the Major was abroad. It is a combination of circumstances that unfortunately all came together at the same time. You have nothing to punish yourself for.'

She tiptoed out of the room to await the doctor leaving me sitting with Annabelle, gently dabbing her dry lips whilst her breathing sounded shallow and wheezing. The bleeding had stopped, but her body racked with coughing fits for a while until shattered and exhausted she slept again.

Mr Stebbeds had left the house shortly after the servant had been sent for the physician and it was sometime before he returned. He arrived back home at the same time as the doctor who was ushered in to the room by Mrs Stebbeds. He was a thickset, stocky man, with a florid complexion and I left him to examine the child. I met Mr Stebbeds along the passageway. He was angrily waving the rag doll that Annabelle had tended so carefully when at Stoneleigh.

'I have been back to see the Principal. I have informed him that he will be receiving a letter advising him that I shall instigate court proceedings. I asked him to hand to me all the possessions that the child had when received into the asylum. All he had in the box were two items, the doll and this.'

He handed me a small gold locket, which I instantly recognised as one that had belonged to my sister. I prised the catch open to reveal a small portrait of Freya looking so young and happy. I felt a surge of pain as I looked at her lovely face smiling so sweetly.

I turned the locket over in my hand as Mr Stebbeds asked if I recognized it.

'It is my sister. The locket belonged to her. I never saw Annabelle with it. I wonder how it came to be with her. The doll she always carried with her and also a bit of dirty silk. It was her only comfort. That awful woman that guarded her room like a wolf at the gates of hell said that she had sold all her possessions. She can not have known about this locket as it extremely valuable.'

'This locket was entered into the register on Annabelle's arrival and locked away. The Principal advised that all possessions are locked away and although that so called nurse had sold items belonging to Annabelle, they were only clothes. He thought they were not of value as the child would outgrow them shortly. That does not excuse his behaviour in not checking that the child was being properly cared for. I shall be dealing with that issue through the proper authorities'

Still turning the locket over and over in my hand I mused almost to myself,

'She had no jewellery when we left Stoneleigh. If it had existed I am sure that Roland would have sold it long ago to pay all his gambling debts.'

The lawyer shrugged,

'Edmund must have given it to the child when he took her to the hospital. However, it seems unlikely. He would know that all personal property was at risk of being stolen.'

A thought struck me,

'I wonder if she had the items all the time and Roland never knew. I

BUT A WALKING SHADOW

know my sister had this gold locket. Perhaps she placed it on Annabelle as a baby and at some later date, Annabelle took it off and hid it.'

'Apparently it was found amongst the rags on the doll,' the old man added thoughtfully. I knew then why we had never seen it. That sad old rag doll that Annabelle had clutched so tightly and would not be parted from, had hidden the locket. No one had looked at the dirty object too carefully and the locket had been quite safe there.

As we were discussing it the doctor emerged from the bedroom and beckoned us in. I hung the locket around the doll's neck and placed the doll in Annabelle's arms. Her pale, thin face with the blue veins running so close to the surface was still like a stone statue. For a moment her eyes flickered open and she stared at me with those brightly fevered eyes.

'See dear, I have brought your doll for you.' I said and a faint smile played around her dry parched lips. She clutched it tightly in her cold hands. For a moment the fingers fluttered over the locket as if checking it was there.

The doctor was standing by her bedside looking very serious as he placed his stethoscope in his bag.

'Well doctor?' I asked quickly, 'How is she?'

'I am afraid that the situation is very serious. She has consumption. In a child so young there is not much hope.'

At his words, I felt my world crashing around me. Desperately I urged,

'But we can arrange for her to be sent to a sanitarium. They will make her well.'

'I think it is too late my dear. She is not strong enough to travel. I will leave a prescription for some medicine and when she is awake, feed her only liquids, soup or milk and I will call in tomorrow. At the moment she needs rest. I am appalled at her condition. This child is dreadfully malnourished. I suppose her head has been shaved owing to her fever? Some of the sores are badly infected and there is already the beginning of septicemia. I understand that she has been cared for privately!'

'Yes, in a dreadful place! We thought she was being privately nursed' I exclaimed vehemently. The physician did not reply but shook his head, and gesturing to Mr Stebbeds to accompany him, the two men walked out in quiet conversation.

Wearily I sat down on the edge of the bed. Would it never end? My dear niece had no hope but to fade away with the dreaded consumption and all I could do was watch and wait.

CHAPTER TWELVE

'O you Gods! Why do you make us love your goodly gifts,
and snatch them straight away?'   *Pericles Act 3 Sc 1*

The physician had left some medication and after a while Annabelle
became less restless. At last she ceased the desperate coughing and
her temperature cooled. For hours I sat by the bed just watching her sleep.
After some time Betsy insisted on relieving me to allow me to rest. I had to
admit that I felt exhausted and what is more I had the distinct impression
that the parasite I felt was growing inside me was beginning to stir. I shut out
the sensations and willed them away. My exhaustion was making me anxious
and I was experiencing strange feelings as if I was being watched by unseen
eyes. I kept turning, thinking people were behind me just as I had done in
the early days with the Westerhams but there was nobody there.

After a few days, Annabelle began to lie awake, her pale face peering
up from the pillows. However, her stillness was constantly broken by the
hoarse coughing. The child's body would rack and shake and large globules
of blood would spurt from her mouth as I dabbed it away and held her to
me. Gradually the coughing would recede until she fell back exhausted. As
I tried to lie her down the blood would erupt like a volcano, causing her to
choke and suffocate.

There was no sign of the wild animal that we had previously seen now as
she was too exhausted and frail. The small spark of life that was left in her
lingered on and all we could do was to sit and watch, offering her our small
token of love and care. The Stebbeds fussed around us as if we were their
own family, treating me like their daughter. Everyday Mr Stebbeds implored
me to change my mind and remove to Threshingham Park. Everyday I was

adamant that I would return to Stoneleigh. Tired and nauseous I tried to forget the disaster that would befall me in a few months. Sometimes I would stare in the mirror to ensure that no sign of the dreadful fate that waited could be detected by prying eyes. I knew it was nearly three months and soon the event would be obvious. When alone, I would look down at my belly and curse it. Sometimes if I slipped into sleep I would dream that I saw the monster that was growing inside me. It was the one that haunted my childhood dreams waiting to tear its way out.

The sound of Annabelle's hacking cough used to wake me from images of a deformed, hideous thing ripping from my stomach. I wanted to take a knife and rip it out myself and each day I prayed for it to die. If it was a sin to wish for such a thing, then I was a sinner. What did I care? I knew I would become one in the world's eyes when my secret was out.

I mused on how the elderly couple would change their opinion of me, when they realised that they had harboured an evil wanton beneath their roof. I knew I had to bear the predicament alone. It was my burden and I had to suffer it. I could not confide in them as they would be just as appalled as Lady Westerham and I could not risk it. I wanted them to love me and value me for a little while longer before the sword of Damocles fell. Sometimes, I was so tired I did not hear Annabelle's coughing and I would awake to find dear Betsy, as she now insisted I call her, bathing Annabelle's face. She would sit for hours watching and gently putting balm on the child's scabs and sores. Sometimes she would help the child to sip cool liquids to sooth the rasping cough and also mopping up the blood that gushed with each rasping breath.

The physician suggested that Annabelle should be given Ergatine to stem the bleeding. He advised that he would not usually prescribe it for a child, but there was no other treatment at this advanced stage. However, the medication gave her violent night terrors. Night after night she would sit bolt upright in bed screaming out at imaginary beings. Threshing in the bed like a thing possessed crying out 'Man! Man!' Gradually I would pacify her until she slept again. However, the medication seemed to alleviate the spurts of blood that had caused her such suffering.

The doctor called every day, but I could tell by his expression that the end was near. The small figure was wasting away before us, her eyes bigger than ever, bright with fever. The pale face flushed except for two large purplish circles on each cheek. There was something different about her that I could not explain. It was a sense of change. A sixth sense that she was dying, but I would not admit it to myself.

Suddenly one day, in the early dawn light Annabelle startled me by sitting up. She began nodding her head from side to side as though she was listening to someone. I thought that she was in the midst of the night terrors again but her eyes looked right past me. Her face lit up with a strange smile. I had that familiar sense of someone behind me and I turned to see who had entered the room, but we were alone.

I shivered and felt a cool breeze waft past my face and thinking that a window had been left open, I went to close it. As I did so I became aware of a figure in the shadows. However, I could not make out who it was. As I went to move closer, I found that I was transfixed. My feet felt as if they were bolted to the floor and I could not move. Not understanding what was happening I looked at the smiling child still staring, her eyes like saucers. Then through the gloom, with fear and trembling I saw Freya. I was sure it was her. I must have been so exhausted that I was imagining things yet she was there. My sister looked just as she appeared in that wooden casket in the family vault. I shuddered, surely my mind was playing tricks on me, I had hardly slept and perhaps my body was tired to the point of insanity. I thought to myself that perhaps I was asleep and this was all a dream as I stood unable to move. Telling myself I was having a nightmare and I would awake and find that Annabelle was fit and well and I was back living in Paris. I looked again at my sister, and a sense of calm descended over me and I wasn't afraid. My sister smiled at me and I was taken aback by how beautiful she looked. Her long red hair was flowing down over her shoulders and she lifted her hand and began to beckon to Annabelle who was sitting up and smiling back.

Shocked and shaken I tried to speak but Freya shook her head to silence me. I watched in awe as she began to shimmer in a golden glow. Then the shimmer began to fade and as quickly as the figure had arrived she was gone. Sensing that my legs were now free, I turned back to the bed expecting to see the child sitting there. However, to my surprise she was lying down with the blankets tucked tightly around her. There was no possibility that she could have been sitting up as the clothes were not disturbed. I was in a quandary and did not understand what had happened. Leaning closer to the sleeping child my heart leapt into my mouth as I realised the wheezing rise and fall of her thin little body had stopped. She lay at peace, like a little angel with a beatific smile on her face. All her suffering was at an end.

For a moment I could not take in what had happened and I hysterically, cried out in despair. Although I knew she was no longer suffering, the day I had been dreading had occurred. Sobbing loudly I gently kissed her little face and ran from the room screaming,

'She's gone! She's gone!'

Mrs Stebbeds collided with me in the doorway, her grey hair swinging as she caught me in her arms trying to console me. She ushered me back into the room with her husband close behind. In his haste he had only put on one shoe, and he limped in to join us as we stood sorrowfully at the child's bed side. I thought my heart would break at her passing. I raged at God for allowing that child to suffer so and then to take her at a time when she was loved and cared for.

Betsy tried to comfort me. Holding my hand and trying to reassure me that it was God's will. That Annabelle was happy now. Whispering that one day I would have a child of my own to love and care for. How could she know that those words were not a comfort to me? I did not want to hear them. The child I wanted was Annabelle, not this hideous thing inside me waiting to begin my ruin. I became demented and threw myself around in frenzy, ripping out clumps of my hair in my grief and the coils lay wormlike on the floor.

The couple were terrified at my reaction. They were so worried they sent a messenger to urgently fetch the physician. They did not know how to pacify me as I screamed and raged in my room, pacing backwards and forwards.

'She is quite all right,' he assured them. 'It is just a disorder of the nerves from the strain of nursing the child day and night. It will pass!'

How I hated humanity for the suffering it inflicted on a poor child and how I hated the Fitzroy family and everyone connected to it. I shut myself away in the room where Annabelle lay in death and refused to leave. How could I leave that little girl alone and I sat with the cold body, numb with grief, refusing all food.

Finally, extremely concerned that the grief was making me in danger of losing my mind, Betsy came and sat with me and also refused to leave. Over and over she gently persuaded me that the child needed to be laid to rest. That God required prayers to be said over her and it was not the child I knew and loved that I sat with. Annabelle was now in spirit and needed to be buried to be peace. I waited and waited in the hope that my sister would reappear but she did not and I was persuaded that my nervous condition had made me imagine it

We buried my darling Annabelle in St Stephen's churchyard on a bright sunny morning. The sun beaming down on this sad trio as we stood by the graveside and the parson read the words over the small casket. Mr Stebbeds had asked if I wanted her removed to the family vault at Stoneleigh, but I did not. How in death could she be at peace in the place that had caused such untold misery?

Feeling as if I was sleep walking I stood like a stone statue as the parson's words passed me by. I had the distinct impression that I was outside my body, looking down on myself standing in the graveyard. As a handful of earth was thrown into the open grave, I was oblivious to the stares of people around me as I mumbled to myself, trying to listen to the voices that were in my head. Before the coffin had been sealed we had placed the much-loved bloodstained rag doll in her arms and with it the gold locket. I had no need of either but it was all that Annabelle Fitzroy possessed.

I was brought back to reality as Betsy took my arm and shaken I looked into the grave. The coffin was lowered into a deep pool of slime and mud at the bottom. It made me sick to my stomach and I turned away in disgust. No amount of reassurance from my friends could convince me that Annabelle was at peace. Her whole life had been one of suffering and waste and now it ended in a six-foot hole, in a wooden box floating in murky depths.

Mrs Stebbeds murmured a few words of comfort as we walked along with the parson but I turned on them both. I pulled back and began to rage that there was no God. How could there be if a small child had to suffer so? The young, parson quickly turned away with embarrassment. I could hear Mr Stebbeds offering his apologies to him as Betsy tried to calm me as I struggled with them, refusing to get into the carriage. All the while a torrent of rain continued drenching us in the grey mist.

Almost as soon as we arrived home, I ran to my room weeping, throwing my belongings into the carpet bag. Then red eyed I placed it in the hallway. As I did so, Betsy appeared and led me unresistingly back to my room. Mr Stebbeds took my bag and later when I was more myself I found the maid had unpacked it. I wanted to leave but I did not know where to go. I became demented ripping the sheets off the bed where Annabelle had lain and when the name of Edmund was mentioned I became even more hysterical and I tried to strangle myself with a shawl. I was restrained and forcibly given some medication to make me sleep. Still shuddering and crying I howled crazily until the peace of sleep overtook me. When I next awoke and remembered she was gone, I felt only a dreadful emptiness. The Stebbeds constantly checked on me and I was conscious of people tip toeing around outside and gentle whispering but I did not move. I lay and stared at the ceiling unable to think or feel. Then one day I glanced down and saw that his ring was no longer on the chain around my neck. I leapt from my bed and began to search desperately through the cupboards and drawers trying to find it. Hearing the activity Betsy appeared asking what was wrong.

'My ring! My ring! I was crying. Taking my hand Betsy gently led me back to bed.

'We took it off when you were so unwell. It is quite safe. I will bring it to you.' She left and soon returned with the chain and placed it once again on my neck. However, I knew it was an omen. The ring that signified my commitment to Edmund had been removed. It could only be an omen that I was not meant to be his wife.

It was several days before I was myself again. I began to realise what a trial I had been for the couple who really were strangers to me. They had taken me in and shown me only kindness and I had repaid them with anger and rudeness. I was mortified at my behaviour but they brushed my apologies aside. They understood how I felt and they assured me that I would never be alone in the world whilst I had them.

Over and over the couple pleaded with me to stay with them permanently. I had been there a month and they loved me like a daughter. We had experienced so much that they felt as though we were meant to be together. I knew that I could not. As I was so thin my condition was still not noticeable but it would only be a short while before it would be. My immediate future was to live a life of isolation at Stoneleigh and to await news of Edmund.

I spent many hours writing long letters to him. Telling him of Annabelle's last moments and how much I loved him but I heard nothing in reply. The only news was that reported in the newspapers. I had no idea if my letters even reached him. I repeatedly told myself that I loved him but I had no sense of it. My emotions seemed to be deadened and I could feel nothing. I tried to conjure up images of him and found that I was beginning to forget what he looked like. My nights were filled with dreams of him and the dreams made me anxious. Sometimes he appeared looking thin and careworn. His cheery smile was missing and his face looked drawn, unlike the person I knew. Sometimes his face was completely blank.

The lawyer had found a small portrait amongst his papers and brought it home for me. I was overjoyed as now I had something to remind me of him. I liked to think that he had left it for me as I spent hours gazing at it. He looked so young and boyish, his thick blonde hair shining. It was worn much longer than I remembered, but he was smiling broadly showing white, even teeth beneath a full moustache. It had obviously been painted several years ago and was a small replica of the portrait at Stoneleigh.

When I told Betsy of my anxiety about the dreams she said that nothing had happened to Edmund. If it had the War Office would have notified us. She felt that my nerves were affected by recent events and this was colouring my dreams. However, the couple tried to hide the newspapers from me as I was upsetting myself poring over articles giving eye witness accounts of the horrors.

Mr Stebbeds' clerk returned from Stoneleigh to advise that the house had been cleaned from top to bottom, but most of the remaining furniture had been placed in store. There were only a few pieces left, mainly in the salon which had been locked. Before I could return, arrangements would have to be made to retrieve the necessary items. However, none of the planned re-decoration had begun and the firm undertaking the full renovation were unable to start until the winter. Edmund had led them to believe that there was no urgency as the property was not to be lived in. They had therefore committed to other work and had not begun the refurbishment of Stoneleigh. The company would now be reassessing the situation but the work definitely could not be started in the immediate future.

I was at a loss; I could not afford to wait. Soon the dreadful thing that was growing inside me would begin to make its presence felt, already I could feel it moving and I imagined it was warning me that it was desperate to emerge into the world. I was sure it was deliberately endeavouring to destroy me. When I heard about Stoneleigh not being ready I knew time was running out and I had to change my plans. I went to see Mr Stebbeds and told him that I was going to find Rosie and then if he could help me to find a small cottage near Stoneleigh, I would move out.

On hearing my plan Mr Stebbeds looked a little dismayed and had to admit that he had no knowledge of Rosie's whereabouts. The clerk had reported that the alehouse was closed and boarded up and none of the villagers had any news of her whereabouts. Her husband was apparently being held for the assizes after a drunken brawl. He had no news of his missing wife either. The news plummeted me into further depths of depression. I was desperate to leave as soon as possible.

One day, not long after a sudden thought struck me. I remembered that the first day that I had called at the office in Lincolns Inn, I had seen a robust woman in a doorway. As I caught sight of her she had reminded me so much of Rosie. Of course, why had I not realised before? It could have been Rosie! If her alehouse was closed, and she had no money and nowhere to go, then she would seek out her family. I knew that a sister lived in the East End of London.

I hatched a plan to retread my journey to Lincolns Inn and make enquiries. Mr Stebbeds would be able to use his contacts and although Rosie could not read, we could put up notices in case someone who knew her saw them. We would offer a reward and I was sure that someone would come forward. Speed was of the essence, as already I felt that my clothes were beginning to tighten. However, the comments from my hosts made me aware that they put it down to a healthier diet and their loving kindness. The nausea that had caused me to feel so ill when I had been staying with Leticia was passing and I was beginning to feel more like my old self.

I chattered feverishly to my hosts and I was so excited about my plan that Betsy was concerned that I was coming down with a fever. Mr Stebbeds looked shocked and advised me that it was impossible for a young gentlewoman like me to go a roving up and down the rank and dirty cobblestone streets of London. Apart from anything else I would not be safe. In addition he advised me that there were many women who looked as I described and it could not have been Rosie. He suggested that I advertised in the newspaper but I did not think anyone in Rosie's circle would read newspapers. It was essential to look for her myself.

Realising that I was serious, Mr Stebbeds arranged to accompany me on the condition that if we found the woman that I had seen was not Rosie, we would discontinue the search. He was sure we would not be successful and insisted that we only committed ourselves to the search for one week only. In the meantime he would arrange for his staff to seek out a property near Stoneleigh, where I could stay until Edmund's return. Not at all sure that he should be helping me he reprimanded me for my stubbornness and said that he would be writing to the Major, hoping that would dissuade me. However it did not. The Stebbeds could not understand why I was so intent on finding Rosie. The lawyer thought me a foolish and headstrong young woman and repeatedly told me so.

The next few days saw us, an odd couple, walking up and down the streets near Lincolns Inn asking if anyone knew of Rosie. The dank streets were foul smelling with open sewers running down the centre. The stench from sewage was overpowering and many times we had to quickly avoid buckets of effluent which were tipped uncaringly from a window, making us leap aside as its contents splashed at our feet. Unused to so much activity I found the noise of the crowded streets deafening. Young men pushed us aside with carts and barrows, cursing us for being in the way. Additionally, the heavy rain drenched and chilled us to the bone. After the first day my soft dove skin shoes were sodden and ripped on the jagged cobbles. When we returned home I could see Mr Stebbeds was tired and angry but I would not hear of ending the search.

The next day was the same as we attracted the attention of impudent young lads. Their shouts were added to by unhelpful comments from coarse, loud-mouthed women who cackled inanely at their own ribald remarks. My feet ached dreadfully and were covered in blisters and I was weary with disappointment, but I insisted that we continued for the week. At first we had been followed around by a group of little ragamuffins. They had found it great fun to tag along with us shouting out to by passers as we walked along,

'Anyone know Rosie Barnes?'

The elderly man and I had smiled at their cheeky behaviour and in a way thought that their actions might help our task. With their help the knowledge that we were looking for Rosie would be so well publicised that the grapevine might lead us to her. .

After a while the urchins had gradually lost interest and faded away. However, by the end of the second day we had found ourselves accompanied again, by a small thin boy who clutched a crossing sweeper's broom. Every now and then he would run in front of us whilst clearing a path with his tattered broom, making his way through the filth and effluent littering the dirty street. Yet, somehow his cheeky persona made us warm to him. I wanted to give him a few pennies but at the end of the day he disappeared into the shadows so I had no chance to do so.

The next day as we descended from the carriage at the top of Aldgate, there was the boy waiting. He had heard us discuss our plans the day before and turned up to meet us. His dirty face breaking into a broad grin he greeted us like old friends. He was wearing the same ragged clothes and a pair of boots without laces, on the wrong feet and full of holes. His grubby face had a knowing look but it was friendly. His cheekbones stood out prominently, and his thin body looked awkward and bony, and it was obvious he had not often had a decent meal. His short hair stood out in clumps as though someone had hacked at it. However, his face was very animated, full of energy and life. His large dark eyes shone like bright buttons and without asking he immediately resumed his duties sweeping us a way through the streets. The insolent expression on his face to some would have been deemed unpleasant but he endeared himself to me. He had such character as he tagged along with us. Mr Stebbeds shooed him away but I prevented him and enjoyed listen to his cheeky chatter.

As we walked along a roguish market trader with a thin face and protruding teeth, exchanged banter with us. Hearing of our search he led us to believe that he knew someone who had a sister called Rosie. He would not give us any details until we had handed over a few coins and then the weasel face had smiled broadly and had given us the address we wanted. We had excitedly trailed through the streets to the address, which had taken us down dark alleys and streets of running sewers. However, it was a wild goose chase. That Rosie was nothing like the woman we sought. I was beginning to realise it was useless as we walked street after street, jostled by the swell of humanity around us.

The third day my little friend arrived, his fragile body looking so cold and starved, that we bought him a pie, and he devoured greedily. Cheekily he would call out to anyone interested that he had been hired by the lady and her gentleman friend and his small frame seemed to grow in stature with the pride of it. He would attempt to thrash the insolent youths with his broom when they called out,

'Bit young for you Grandad!'

This would create much hilarity as did the sight of this thin waif squaring up to ungainly louts. As the costermongers called out their wares and nearly ran us down, the young boy, who informed us his name was Cobbles, whacked them heartily with his broom.

Mr Stebbeds insisted that he would no longer permit us to continue the search even though the week was not ended. We argued in the street as Cobbles stood watching, biting his lip in concentration as he leaned on his broom. It was nearing dusk as walked down a side alley and decided to make our way to the police station in Southwark. It was the first time I had looked at the old lawyer properly and I became aware of how tired and grey he was looking. He was breathing heavily and kept taking every opportunity to sit on an available bench or lean against the moss covered walls. I realised that I was being very selfish in making this old man walk the streets of London. The sergeant at the desk looked surprised when this bedraggled pair arrived. However, he found us a chair and he waved his fist at Cobbles to send him on his way, but I restrained him.

'Leave the boy alone, he is with us.' I said wearily, my body aching, grateful for a moment to sit. The sergeant was a big, bluff man wearing a uniform that seemed too tight around his thick neck. It made his face bulge over the top, reddened with broken veins and unsightly, wartish lumps.

'You don't know what these guttersnipes are like. They'd steal your eyes out of your head.'

Mr Stebbeds sighed and mopped his face.

'Quite so! Quite so, but we wondered if you could suggest where we might find a Rosie Barnes. We are searching for her and believe she might be in this area.'

The policeman laughed,

'Plenty of women around here, but none of them would be the kind that you would want to associate with.' The effort causing his eyes to bulge and he blew his large nose loudly. Seeing how tired we both were, the sergeant arranged for a drink to be fetched and whilst I sat with Cobbles standing guard at the doorway, Mr Stebbeds went into a side room with the policeman. As he did so I took the opportunity of having a conversation with my young friend.

'Tell me Cobbles, do you go to school?'

'L'awks no. I ain't got no book learning.'

'Where are your parents?'

'Ain't got none.'

'Surely you must have?' I asked looking at him with concern, 'Who looks after you?'

'I look after meself,'

I must have looked surprised and his grubby face crumpled into a smile,

'I does it real well. I got me place under the arches and I lives there. If anyone takes me place I sees 'em off, wiv me broom. Many a lout's got a clout I can tell yer.'

'You live in the street?' I was at a loss for words.

Just then the door to the side room opened and the elderly man came bustling out. I stood up eagerly but one look at his face told me that he had not been successful.

Although I was saddened I would not admit defeat. The lawyer once again insisted we discontinue our search but I begged again to continue for just one more day. The policeman joined in advising that it was all a lost cause but I would not hear of stopping. In the end the lawyer gave in but said,

'I must go to the office in the morning, but I'll return at lunchtime and we can go to the addresses the Police Sergeant has given me. If that leads nowhere than this futile exercise will end. I do not know why you have talked me into it as we can easily hire a woman to help you without it being this Rosie woman. We will now return home and rest.'

'I know I am being selfish, 'I sighed. 'I am sorry I can see that it is all too much for you?'

'Nonsense! My life is sitting behind a desk at Lincolns Inn. I needed the exercise,' he replied trying to persuade me that he was a fit young man and I could see he was not.

'I'll get a cab mister.' Cobbles shouted gleefully and before we could stop him he ran out into the street.

'Is he still here?' Mr Stebbeds said as we watched as Cobbles became tangled in his broom and his thin legs spun out of control and he crumpled onto the floor. Disentangling himself he immediately jumped up and headed off to the cab stand.

'He told me that he lives on the street and has no parents,' I sighed as we walked to the doorway.

'I know, it is very sad, there are a lot of children like that. Mrs Stebbeds gets very upset about it. That is why she bakes the cakes. She goes to the mission and serves soup when she can.'

I nodded,

'Can't we do something to help this boy?'

The old man frowned,

'My dear your intentions do you credit but what can we do for him.'

'I'll find him work. He can come with me to the cottage when I leave and do odd jobs.'

'My dear, you know nothing about him.'

'I know, but I like him, he makes me laugh. He has nothing and yet he is so cheerful. Look at him he must be cold, his clothes are soaked through.'

Mr Stebbeds shrugged and as we walked out I heard him mutter.

'We have not settled you in a property yet and already you are hiring staff?' At that moment Cobbles hurtled through the doorway, his knees bleeding from a fall.

'Cabs here Guv!' He called as he limped out. Concerned I said,

'You're hurt!'

'Ain't nuffin,' and his face broke out in a broad smile as he rubbed his bloody knees ruefully with his dirty hands. I felt in my bag and handed him my lawn handkerchief to stem the bleeding and his eyes widened,

'Blimey, I ain't putting that on me knee. There's some coves that earns a living pinching them from the gents and a selling 'em. I'd be right toff with a 'chief on me knee.'

As Mr Stebbeds helped me in to the cab, he turned to Cobbles.

'Can we take you anywhere young man?'

'Who me?' The boy's mouth opened in surprise. 'Yes guv,' he shouted and leapt nimbly into the carriage. As he did so his crossing broom became tangled in the doorway. Mr Stebbeds exasperatedly moved it and asked,

'Where do you want us to take you lad?'

Cobbles screwed up his cheeky little face and then looked sad,

'I ain't got no where to go.'

'But you must live somewhere,' I added

At that Cobbles brightened,

'Course I do. I told yer, I have me place under the arches. Well if I get backs early I do, but if I am late someone pinches me place and I have to find a doorway.' Seeing my stricken face, Mr Stebbeds laughed and patted the boy's curly head,

'I've an idea. Would you like some supper?'

I was even more surprised at Mr Stebbeds friendliness as I thought he did not approve of the boy. Cobbles bright button eyes widened and Mr Stebbeds continued,

'We will go to my house and see if my wife can find some soup.. Although I think she would insist on lots of hot water and give you a good scrub down before you could cross the threshold.'

Cobbles looked sad.

'Do I 'ave to 'ave a wash 'fore I can have me grub?'

'I'm afraid so!' The boy looked so downcast at the prospect of being faced with water before a meal that my heart went out to him. Mr Stebbeds put his arm round the child and said breezily,

'Surely a bath is not too terrible a punishment if it means a good dinner.'

Cobbles smiled brightly and settled back into the seat, clutching his broom tightly as we set off.

'Are we taking him back to your home. What will Betsy say?' I asked quietly.

'Well I find myself at a loss. He is probably a thief and a rogue but we will risk it. Perhaps Betsy can find something for him at the mission.'

'Oh you are such a lovely man' I beamed pleased that he wanted to help.

Cobbles meanwhile had leaned back against the leather upholstery, his eyes beginning to droop. If we were exhausted this child was even more so. In a few seconds he was asleep and his ragged head fell onto my shoulder where I let it rest, grubby as he was. His clothes smelt like the mould that permeated the alleys that we had traipsed through. I did not want to disturb him and Mr Stebbeds look disapprovingly at me.

'We should admit defeat. We have no real evidence that Rosie is in London. Why won't you do the sensible thing and remove to Threshingham Park?'

'Tomorrow afternoon, as you promised.' I urged. 'I will stop then. What is more I have been thinking. I do not need a cottage near Stoneleigh. Any where in the country will be acceptable.' I did not add that it would have to be somewhere that I was not known.

'If that is your decision then it makes sense then for you to take one of the cottages on the Threshingham estate.'

'No!' I retorted. Living near Threshingham was the last thing I wanted. Seeing that Mr Stebbeds had been taken aback by the vehemence of my reply, I apologised for my rudeness. As I had spoken loudly, Cobbles started up and stared round the cab as if unsure where he had found himself.

The lawyer shrugged.

'Very well my dear. However, I must say I do not understand it. You will be living at Threshingham Park when you are married. You could at least stay in the vicinity.'

'I have my reasons. I can't presume that I will be his wife until he returns.'

The lawyer laughed, 'Of course you will be his wife. I have never known a young man so in love as he is with you.' I knew he meant well but I did not reply and seeing my crestfallen face he squeezed my hand.

'We'll look again tomorrow.'

CHAPTER THIRTEEN

'Constant you are, but yet a woman: and for secrecy, no
lady closer'   *Henry IV Pt 1 Act 2 Sc 3*

e drew up outside the pretty white cottage at Whitefriars that
provided such a contrast to the dark and wet, stinking hovels that
we had passed on our way through the fetid streets of London. I was just
grateful to have left the noise and hustle and bustle of carts and carriages.
Several times we had almost been thrown from our seats as our driver tried
to avoid the seething mass of vehicles. I began to feel almost seasick at the
constant jolting and we narrowly escaped running down a passer-by who ran
out into the road in front of us. Cobbles' broom kept becoming tangled with
our arms and legs and repeatedly we had to free ourselves as it swung across
the vehicle, much to my amusement and Mr Stebbeds annoyance.

As we stopped outside the cottage, Cobbles peered excitedly out of the
window.

'Is this yer 'ouse?' he gasped as he climbed out of the cab, his broom now
tripping the old lawyer as he descended the steps. Mrs Stebbeds came out to
see what was happening and was aghast at the scarecrow before her.

'What on earth have you brought this filthy child with you for?' she
asked in amazement, trying to wrestle the broom from the young boy.
Cobbles refused to let go and as she held on he sank his teeth into her hand.
Betsy lost her temper and slapped him whereupon he emitted a loud cry and
rubbed his cheek his insolent expression now woebegone.

Mr Stebbeds pushed his way through and called out,

'Will everyone please calm down? Now lad my wife is not stealing your
broom. Give it to me and we will try to prevent any more accidents. I do not

want my knees to end up in the same state as yours.' I was taken aback at Betsy's anger and wondered if we had done the right thing bringing a feral child to her home. Cobbles sullenly handed over the broom as the lawyer grabbed his collar and began to steer him into the doorway. Betsy's small figure ran ahead and barred the doorway.

'You are not bringing that lice ridden child in my home.'

Mr Stebbeds sighed,

'It will only be for a few hours. He can have a wash and we will find him something to eat. I thought you might take him to the mission...' he was not allowed to finish.

'Definitely not. He is probably covered in fleas.'

I stood back from the argument, not sure what to do. After all it was not my home and I had been the cause of the disruption. As the debate continued Cobbles joined in, still firmly held by Mr Stebbeds.

'It's all right lady. I don't want ter come in yer 'ouse. I ain't having no wash. Sides I'll probably be murdered, I don't go off wiv no strangers.'

That brought a grin to Betsy's face and her attitude softened.

'Look at poor Aphra left out in the rain. You had better come in.' she pushed her husband aside and pulled me into the hallway and as she did so slammed the door. The other two were left outside as she opened a window and called out.

'That urchin can go round the back by the pump. He is not stepping inside this house until he has had a wash.' The lawyer shrugged and ushered Cobbles, still wriggling and squirming in his grasp, round to the back yard. As they reached the back entrance Betsy appeared with a bowl of warm water and threw it over the child, splashing her husband as she did so. He began shouting and so did Cobbles and then she opened the back door and grabbed the boy into the scullery.

'Wait there,' she said firmly. Chastened Cobbles stopped shouting and stood looking cold and miserable in his sodden rags. Mr Stebbeds closed the door and taking a towel began to rub himself down. The door opened again and the maid appeared bringing in a large metal tub, followed by Mrs Stebbeds. Her anger had faded as she was bustling around as jugs of water were brought in to fill up the tub.

'You, young man,' she breathed, 'are getting in that tub before we have dinner in this house.

Cobbles swung round and headed for the door but his path was blocked.

'Nobody ain't going to eat me fer 'is dinner.' With that we all burst out laughing including Betsy.

'This pot is for washing, not boiling children but we might change our minds if you don't behave yourself.' Without more ado she ripped off his clothes and lifted Cobbles into the tub. He had been taken by surprise and although small, Betsy was quite strong and Cobbles was in the water protesting loudly. The clothes were thrown into the fire as the squeals of protest echoed round the house as the lad fought to escape and Betsy ducked his head under the water. He came up screaming abuse and using language that I had never heard before in my life.

I took the opportunity to escape to my room to change out of my wet clothes, feeling guilty about bringing this trouble to Betsy's home. When I returned I found an unrecognisable small boy sitting dwarfed in the big armchair. The spiky, hair that had seemed a sludgy brown colour was lovely golden blonde curls and he now had an angelic air about him. His ragged clothes were still burning brightly in the fire grate, whilst he sat nervously clutching a towel around his thin little body, his sticklike legs protruding from below. They were black and blue with bruises.

'How did you get all those bruises?' I asked

'Them gents by the stews. When they comes out, if I ain't quick they kick me out of the way.'

'The stews?'

Mr Stebbeds interrupted,

'I think its best you don't enquire further, my dear, let us just leave it at that.'

Cobbles however, was now in full flow,

'I shout out to them about the ladies. If they go inside, then sometimes them girls give me a cake or some bread. Them gents ain't nice though, they got all them airs but they are cruel and they 'urt them girls.'

Mr Stebbeds who was warming himself by the fire fixed Cobbles with a warning look but it was ignored. He said sternly,

'Young man, I don't think we should talk about things like that. There are ladies present. Do not speak of such matters.'

Cobbles looked downcast.

'Sorry guvnor, I fought...'

'Never mind.' The lawyer changed the subject.

'Tell me Cobbles, what is your proper name?'

'That is me bleeding proper name!' The urchin called out looking uncomprehendingly at the old man just as Betsy entered the room and called out,

'Language!' Cobbles reacted and was about to argue but seeing her expression thought better of it as she said briskly,

'Put these clothes on!' She handed him a large shirt and pants that belonged to her husband. Cobbles' saucer eyes became even bigger at the thought of new clothes and he quickly pulled them on. He made quite a picture as they completely swamped him. As he dressed he carried on chattering,'

'Yer that's me name all right. Wherever I go everyone knows me. Here comes Cobbles they shout.'

'Didn't your family give you another name?' I asked as we made our way to the dining room. Betsy insisting that Cobbles remained where he was. Cobbles snuggled back into the warmth of the chair and looked serious.

'Me sister wot disappeared she gave me a paper. She says to me; never forget yer name is on it.'

'What was it?

'I dunno, I couldn't read it and it has got old and torn now.'

'Do you still have it?' I asked.

'It's in me boots,' he looked around and then his voice began to rise. 'Where's me boots. If you've stolen me bleeding boots.' This was followed by a cuff around the ear only this time from the lawyer.

'Remember to behave yourself young man, or there is no dinner for you.' Your boots are outside.'

Cobbles began to wail loudly,

'Them's mine. You ain't got no right to take them.' Betsy gestured to the maid and she went outside reappearing with the boots. She was holding them as far away from herself as she could, looking down her nose at the sodden items.

Leaping from his chair, Cobbles grabbed the old, worn out boots and put them on. This time on the correct feet. As he did so he felt inside and produced a folded, yellowing paper. Gently Mr Stebbeds unfolded it, trying to prevent it from falling into pieces and holding it to the light was just able to make out the faded writing.

'The best cobbler in London, bring your boots and shoes to be made as new.'

The paper did not contain a name at all; it was the remains of an advertisement with a tiny picture of a statue of King Alfred in the corner.

Mr Stebbeds and I exchanged glances. The name Cobbles had derived from a piece of paper advertising a shoe repairer. Meanwhile Cobbles waited eagerly,

'What do it say?'

A look passed between us and I felt terribly sad for this lost child. I became aware that Betsy's expression had changed and she gently put her arm around him. It was as if in that moment something about this waif had touched her heart. Cobbles winced, as she placed her arms around his shoulders as if expecting a blow.

'It says that your name is Cobbles, but I shall call you Cobham. Cobbles is short for Cobham and my father lived in the village of Cobham in Surrey.'

Cobbles smiled proudly and puffed out his chest,

'I have a name of a place? That makes me bleeding special don't it.'

'If you use that word again....' Mr Stebbeds did not finish as a look from his wife silenced him.

'Yes!' You are somebody special,' she said.

Cobbles sniffed and wiped his hand across his face as a bowl of soup and a crust of bread was brought in for him and he tucked into it ravenously.

'Where are your family,' I asked

'Dunno, my sister used to look after me, I don't know where she's gorn.'

Mr Stebbeds who had already gone to the dining room called out,

'I think that is enough of an inquisition. I am hungry and tired. Let us all sit down and have dinner and we'll decide what to do about our two problems after dinner.' As he spoke he pulled out his table napkin and tucked it into his neck.

'Two problems dear?' his wife asked as she joined him and the maid bought in the steaming tureen of soup.

'Yes, our charming Aphra will not do as she is told and the other is this impish rogue that looks as if he is going to move into our house.'

After the meal a bed was made up for Cobham in the scullery. The doors were locked just in case the angelic persona was only pretence and he ran off in the night with the silver. He settled down and was soon asleep. However, I was too tired to settle. My mind was full of sewers and smells, slum dwellings and toothless individuals, hovering drunkenly in doorways. My legs ached as I mentally walked those streets over and over again.

In the early hours of the morning a sudden noise woke me from my slumber and creeping from my bed I gently opened the scullery door to find Cobbles now asleep on the floor. He had left the soft cushions and instead preferred the hard stone. Beneath his head were the old boots and clutched to his chest was the broom, his most treasured possession. He looked so peaceful that I smiled to myself. Years of sleeping on the streets had obviously made a comfortable bed too difficult to sleep in.

As I turned to leave the room I became aware of Betsy Stebbeds sleeping in a nearby rocking chair. I was not sure if she was worried that Cobbles would steal her silver but something told me this elderly woman who had no children of her own had responded to something in this small boy. There was something endearing about him, we had all felt that. Despite his streetwise ways, he was just a small boy abandoned and alone. Not wishing to disturb them I quietly returned to my bed and when I next awoke it was daylight. Thankfully, the sun was shining brightly and when I made my way to breakfast, I found a small boy and old woman laughing merrily as Cobbles hungrily wolfed down large chunks of bread and mugs of chocolate.

As arranged, Mr Stebbeds went off to his office, returning at lunchtime with a cab to take us on our way. He had intended to take Cobbles back but Mrs Stebbeds would not hear of it. As we left I was surprised to see Cobbles standing to attention by the cab door. His mangled broom held as if he was a soldier on guard duty whilst his thin face shone with pleasure. As he opened the door to help me inside, his big eyes danced in his small face and he looked extremely proud.

He was still wearing the clothes that were too large for him and his old boots were firmly planted on the correct feet. The old man patted his head and whispered something. Cobbles looked surprised and then broke out into a huge grin. Excitedly he ran back into the cottage, calling Mrs Stebbeds loudly and she came running out thinking that something was wrong,

'Lord a mercy!' she said, 'What on earth is all this noise.'

Cobbles threw himself at her, his face pressed against her apron. Gently prising him off, she bent down and asked what the matter was?

'The Guv says, I can stay with you today. That you need a man to look after yer,' he breathed his eyes shining with happiness.

The elderly woman smiled benignly and winked at her husband.

'Yes, I do young man. You can be my protector.'

'Can I? Can I?' Cobbles shouted loudly and began to dance a peculiar scarecrow dance. His thin legs contorting in all directions and his old boots rattling on the cobblestones.

'I do not want to hear there has been any trouble whilst we are away. This lady and I will make our own way today. As he spoke a loud sobbing

185

broke out from the small boy who was now clutching Betsy Stebbeds' hand tightly as if frightened to let it go.

'What on earth is the matter child?' The lawyer asked as we climbed into the cab.

'You's bin so kind to me, and now you'll 'ate me.'

'Hate you! Of course we won't.' Mr Stebbeds stated looking at him waiting for an explanation.

'You've bin looking for Rosie all this time and I knewed where she was!'

'What!' Mr Stebbeds erupted, his face red with anger as the boy now hid behind Betsy, clutching her skirts.

'How do you know her? Why on earth did you not tell us? Instead of letting us wander the streets all this time Where is she you stupid little boy?' he hissed angrily. I was taken aback at his vehemence as it was so out of character. Betsy put her arm around the boy to comfort him and berated her husband loudly. Whilst Cobbles retreated behind her legs,

'Bertie Stebbeds how dare you raise your voice in that manner? Don't shout at the child! He must have had his reasons.'

Cobbles sniffed loudly and buried his small fists into his eyes as if trying to bore through to the other side. His face now grubby and tear stained.

'You'se was so nice ter me, and I wanted to stay with yer. If I took yer to Rosie yer would 'ave gone away and I wouldn't 'ave bin wiv yer no more.'

'Oh you silly child,' Mr Stebbeds exclaimed, trying to keep his temper. Then in a conciliatory manner added,

'Well now would you do me the kindness of telling me where she is? We do not what to exhaust ourselves on another fool's errand?'

'You'll send me away,' Cobbles began to wail, his thin body racked with sobs.

'No!' A firm response came from Betsy. 'We won't send you away.' You are here now. You are my Cobham.'

'But I don't...' her husband was waved into silence by her warning look and a flick of her arm.

'Come inside and we will resolve this matter. You had better return to the house my dear,' she gestured to me. I started to climb out of the cab as the driver becoming impatient banged on his box seat loudly,

'Do yer want this cab or not?' he barked.

Mr Stebbbeds glared, puffing out his chest,

'Yes we do, my man and I would ask you to wait a few moments until we ascertain the address of the place that we need to go to. This young lady may as well stay seated inside as we shall only be a few moments.' With that the elderly man turned on his heel and taking the boy sternly by the shoulders marched him back into the house.

I sat inside the cab waiting patiently and felt a surge of hope in my heart.

At last the door to the cottage opened and out strode Mr Stebbeds with the subdued boy firmly in his grip. Ushering Cobbles inside he instructed the driver to take us to Southwark and then taking his seat, he tapped on the cab roof and we set off.

'Is she in Southwark?' I asked meekly. I knew we had already searched that area.

'This young whippersnapper apparently knows the lady that we are seeking quite well. If you remember, he told us that he befriended ladies in a certain establishment. Well it appears that your friend is there. If it is the kind of place that I think it is, I am not at all sure that it is proper that you join us there. However, I need your presence to identify that the lady is the correct person. Indeed, I insist that you stay in the cab and I will fetch the woman out. You can then indicate if it is indeed she. On no account will you be permitted to enter the establishment. I will not brook any argument. If you do not do as I say, I will not take this trip. As it is I am appalled that I am discussing the existence of such places with a young gentlewoman. The area is full of thieves and vagabonds, but we will finally find out if it is the person we are seeking.'

I could see that he was resolved on this matter and so I addressed Cobbles.

'Are you sure that it is the right lady?' I asked.

Cobbles looked downcast and sheepish as he stared at the floor and replied,

'Rosie is 'er name and she is a big woman with blonde 'air. She told me once that she lived in a big 'ouse with her gentleman friend.'

'Why would she tell you?' I asked.

'Apparently, she used to stand under the railway arches when it was raining and chat to our little friend here.' Mr Stebbeds said, tapping his fingers angrily on the edge of the seat.

'Perhaps, it isn't her,' I stated. 'That description could fit anyone.' The excitement still bubbling in my stomach as I silently begged,

'Please let it be her. Please let it be her.'

187

Cobbles sat forlornly in the corner of the cab, his legs dangling over the seat.

'Why didn't you tell us before?' I asked also irritated and tired of wandering around and now it would seem led on another wild goose chase.

Cobbles sniffed loudly,

'Cos, at first I fought yer might be the police or somefin. Afterwards when yer was so kind, I didn't like ter tell yer I knew all the time.'

I shook my head and sighed loudly,

'Well we can't do anything about it now. If it is Rosie we will forget all about it.' At my remarks, Cobbles wan face broke into a smile and he settled back in the seat.

The elderly man huffed loudly and added,

'I am afraid that if this is Rosie, it would appear that she has fallen too low to be a helpmate for you.'

I settled back in my seat with indignation.

'I don't care. I will help her. I know that she came from a poor family and had to make her own way in life, but surely she should not be judged harshly for that.'

The lawyer frowned,

'I think you are being very naïve my dear. I don't know why I am allowing you to pursue this scheme. It can only lead to trouble even if we find her.'

By this time, Cobbles was looking excitedly out of the cab window as we rattled along the alleys and I recognised the tree lined streets of Holland Park. The sight of them made me think about Leticia and a well of sadness overwhelmed me. Lady Westerham was correct. My father would turn in his grave if he knew what my fate was. Then my nerve began to fail and I started to doubt my plan. It was true that Rosie was hardly someone that could be admitted to society herself and we would both fall together. Why was I being so foolish? I was clinging on to someone that was probably more of a hindrance than a help. All I knew was that she was the only person that I could rely on not to be disgusted by the news that I was with child. Who else could I turn to? I was damned with and without her. I needed her but what would I do if this woman was not my Rosie?

The panic in my thoughts must have reflected on my face as Mr Stebbeds tried to reassure me that all would be well. To change the subject I asked Cobbles who was excitedly waving from the window, if the woman he knew had told him the name of the person in the big house.

Cobbles shrugged.

'No miss, she just said she used to stay in a large house made of stones.'

My stomach somersaulted as I urged,

'Did she say it was made of stones or the name was something to do with stones?' I urged pulling his arm.

'I can't remember. She said many times that she looked after 'er gentleman friend until he became ill and died and she had to leave a stonely house.'

'Stoneleigh! It was Stoneleigh that she was referring to. It must be her! It must be!' I almost screamed with joy. Cobbles looked startled as I held him to me and kissed the top of his now clean head.

'I only said she lived in a stonely house,' he said rubbing the kiss from his head.

The lawyer interrupted,

'No young man, what she told you was that she lived in a house called Stoneleigh.' Cobbles looked confused and shrugged his shoulders, not understanding the difference.

As we left the stately houses of Holland Park behind, we soon began to travel the cobblestoned streets nearing to Blackfriars.

'Tell us when we find your railway arch.' Mr Stebbeds said firmly.

'Yes guv, it is near here.'

Suddenly, leaping out of his seat with such a force that he fell into my lap he yelled,

'There it is!' Cobbles excitedly pointed to a high brick built arch set to one side of the road. With a start the lawyer tapped on the roof of the cab with his cane and the cab driver stopped. The man and boy climbed down and just as I was about follow them, Mr Stebbeds prevented me.

'I think I remember insisting that you remain in the cab. We will see if we can find this woman!'

'How will you know if it is the right person?' I asked annoyed that I could not accompany them.

'I will make some enquiries. If I think this Rosie is the right person then I shall return to the cab and bring her with me.'

'What if she will not come?'

'I will face that obstacle when it arises.'

Giving the cab driver a coin he asked him to wait whilst I remained anxiously in my seat. I watched the two figures disappear into the blackness under the railway arch decorated with torn advertising posters and wondered how long I was supposed to wait. After what seemed an eternity the pair reappeared. Leaning out of the window I called to them excitedly, but by the downcast look of Cobbles I guessed that Rosie had not been found.

'Wasn't it her?' I quivered as they arrived at the cab door.

'We don't know. A person fitting the description of Rosie Barnes sometimes waits around the arches but it appears that she is not there today.' The lawyer said as he climbed aboard.

'Waits around the arches? Why would she wait? What is she waiting for?' I asked.

The lawyer brushed me aside.

'Let us just say that she is not there today.

'But surely someone must know where she lives?'

Sick with disappointment, I sat back in my seat and shut my eyes in despair. I opened them to see Cobbles staring at me in concern.

'I'm sorry miss. I should 'ave told yer before. I can still come back with yer can't I?'

I did not know how to respond. I wanted more than anything for this poor little boy to be able to stay at the Stebbeds cottage but the favour was not mine to grant.

'I do not know. You will have to ask Mr Stebbeds?'

The elderly man sighed and sat down heavily on the seat.

'If it was left to me, I would send you on your way. Leading us a merry chase and causing us to miss the very person we were seeking. However, it seems that my wife has over ruled me and is insisting that we do not come back without you.'

Cobbles put his curly head down and looked sad but did not speak.

The cab set off again and we sat in silence and as if in a trance I gazed out of the window desperately seeking that familiar body. Suddenly as we turned the corner of Blackfriars Road I saw a figure leaning against a broken fence and as if struck by lightning, I knew it was Rosie.

'Stop the cab! Stop the cab!' I shouted, banging loudly on the interior roof.

'What on earth is the matter?' asked Mr Stebbeds who had been gently nodding in the corner. Not stopping to reply I clambered out of the cab and begun running down the street. All I could think was that I could not let her escape from me. I called out her name as loudly as I could. I knocked into a boy carrying bundles of laundry which fell in the dirt and a great shout went up and people began to run behind me. One man pulling a thin, half starved dog on a string tried to bar my way, but I pushed him aside with such force that guffaws of laughter rang out from the idlers hovering around. Rosie had now left the fence she had been leaning against and was walking in the other direction. Hearing her name she turned and as she did so she suddenly caught sight of me. Instead of being glad to see me a stricken expression appeared on her face. Half running and half walking she began hurrying away. Desperately she looked around for somewhere to escape to, but the side street led to a dead end. As she was unable to run anywhere, I caught up with her. Realising that there was no way out, she sank to the ground in sorrow.

'Oh Rosie. I have been seeking you everywhere.' I cried trying to get my breath.

Rosie turned her head away from me, as she tried to catch her breath after the exertion of trying to avoid me.

'Go away. Leave me alone,' she gasped unable to look me in the eye.

'Why won't you speak to me? Why are you in London? I sent someone to find you at the alehouse, but it was boarded up. What has happened?'

'Me 'usband took everything and threw me out. I 'ad no where to go, what could I do? I 'ad to come 'ere.'

'Oh Rosie, come with me. I have a cab waiting. I want you to come with me. We can find somewhere to live together. Please help me?'

'Help you? I can't even 'elp meself. It's too late miss. I ain't fit company for a young gentlewoman like you. Best leave me. Forget you ever saw me.' She began to stagger to her feet as she spoke.

Helping her up I said,

'Rosie, please I beg of you. We can help each other. Come with me and we will discuss it properly.' As I tried to hold her up, I could not because she was too heavy. At that moment Mr Stebbeds arrived calling out furiously,

'What on earth are you thinking of charging down the street like a woman possessed?' He stopped as he suddenly became aware of the woman slumped by the end wall.

'Well! I assume this is the person we were looking for, and what a sorry sight she is?'

'Yes it is. Please help her to her feet.' We both took her arms and hauled her up. As we did so she noticed Cobbles, who had arrived behind. With a weary smile she said,

'So it's you young Cob, that I have to thank for bringing 'em after me.'

'I'm staying with 'em,' he stated proudly, drawing himself up to his full height.

Gathering her wits about her Rosie brushed down the muddied dress and sighed,

'So you are still collecting waifs and strays?'

'Come along!' Mr Stebbeds said with authority. 'We can't stay here all day, debating the situation in the street.' Gripping her arm so she could not escape he ushered her back along the way we had come. I was appalled how much older she looked. The hair that was a faded blonde was now greyer and there were deep lines around her eyes. Dishevelled, she weakly tried to resist but Mr Stebbeds did not release his grip. I took her other arm as we made our way back to the cab. She was wearing that same pink dress that I had seen many times at Stoneleigh. It was now ripped and torn and she had a Hessian sack tied around her shoulders. Her cheeks were rouged so violently that her grey face looked as if it was covered in a rash. I took her hand which was dry and cracked her fingernails were dirty and split.

The unruly group, that had set up a hue and cry parted to allow us to return the way we had come. Too tired to argue, she climbed aboard the cab whilst the driver was instructed to go to Lincoln's Inn. Cobbles had retreated as far as he could in the corner of the hansom and there was a brooding silence until we reached the lawyer's office. The lawyer took Cobbles away and I was left alone with the woman I thought of as my life line.

CHAPTER FOURTEEN

'And so, from hour to hour, we ripe and ripe, and then from
hour to hour, we rot and rot: and thereby hangs the tale .'

As You Like It Act 2 Sc 7

As we sat in an interior office Rosie leaned heavily on the table,
'You should 'ave left me miss, I ain't no good for yer.'

'Let me be the best judge of that Rosie. It isn't your fault that awful
husband of yours has taken your money. The last I heard he was waiting for
the assizes and was locked up in gaol.'

Rosie nodded forlornly,

'Best place for 'im.'

I leaned forward in desperation.

'Rosie, I need you to help me. You are the only one I can turn to.'

'I told you. I ain't no use to no one,' she yawned loudly as if my presence
was boring her. I ignored her rudeness and could not help but notice once
again how old and tired she looked.

'Where have you been? What have you been doing since your husband
threw you out of the alehouse?' I asked unsure whether I would like the
reply. At my question, Rosie began to cry, her rouged face streaking in dirty
rivulets, loud sobs racking her body. I was startled. I had never known her
to cry.

'The curate, you remember 'im, don't yer miss, he never liked me. Well
'e said that I 'ad to go to the work house. I told yer didn't I? When we was
at Stoneleigh. I ain't never going to no work house.' Trying to stifle the sobs
she gasped, 'They cut up yer bodies. Sometimes even when you ain't even

dead.' I put my arms around her shoulders and felt how bony the shoulders were that had once been so well padded.

I remembered how frightened Rosie had been of the workhouse and handing her my clean handkerchief to wipe her eyes I continued,

'So what did you do?'

'I came to London. I fought I could get some work, but all I could get was a job collecting that stinking Pure.' She shuddered at the memory. 'It was awful miss. I couldn't stand the smell, it made me sick. I just couldn't do it.'

I had never heard of Pure and was mystified,

'Collecting Pure, what do you mean?'

'Dog's dirt miss. They use it in the tannery to soften the leather, and it's disgusting. I spent hours walking the streets collecting it in a bucket. It took ages. You needed a lot to get just a few pennies. I had to fill a bucketful just to buy a bed for the night.'

Recoiling with disgust I felt my stomach churn at the thought of it. She smiled wanly,

'You see miss, you only 'ave to 'ear of it and you feel ill.'

'Oh Rosie how awful for you!' I sympathized, 'How did you manage?'

Rosie looked embarrassed and turned away as she mumbled,

'I just did odd things to get by.'

Realising that she was not going to enlighten me, I pushed back my chair and trying to make the best of it said,

'Never mind, what is past is past, but it is the future that I want to talk about.'

'I ain't got no future,' she sighed tugging at a greasy lock of hair.

'Yes you have and so have I,' I remonstrated, 'but we need to arrange things together.' Rosie stared at me blankly as if I was speaking in a foreign language. Biting the bullet I took my arms from her shoulders and looking around to make sure no one was in earshot I whispered,

'Rosie, I can't manage without you. You must help me.'

'The Major wouldn't like to think of us being together. He made it quite clear when he gave me the money,' she said sadly and edged her body away slightly.

'He gave you money?' I was shocked.

'Yes to see me right, but me 'usband took it.'

'Oh Rosie I didn't know. Anyway, that is past. I have some money and the Major is away with his regiment. He will not be returning for some time.'

'I fought you and 'im was going to be wedded.' She added as she peered into my face as if trying to understand.

'We can discuss that later,' I said impatiently. 'I need to make arrangements. Weddings can wait.'

Rosie nodded and said knowingly, 'You ain't going to marry 'im?'

I stood up and leaned against the wall for support, as she watched me in silence.

'Rosie, how can I? You know what happened at Stoneleigh, what can I bring him as a wife? I will ruin his life. Through no fault of my own I will be ostracized by my friends, besides I haven't told you everything.'

Rosie sat and waited for me to finish but she did not comment.

I knew that I had to persuade her to come with me and I could only do that if I confessed what I loathed to admit. Taking a deep breath I said,

'I am about to reveal something to you. I want a promise that you will never tell anyone what I am about to tell you.'

Rosie nodded without showing any interest as I continued,

'I am expecting a child.' A look of surprise flashed across her face and she started at my words but still didn't comment. She just leaned her head on her arms and slumped on the table. 'It is Roland's child. Nobody here knows and nobody must know. The Major is not aware of my situation and indeed I only found out myself a short while ago. I have been forced to make my own way now. The so called friends that know my secret have rejected me. The Major's lawyer, Mr Stebbeds, is unaware of my condition. He wants me to go to Threshingham Park and await Edmund's return. When Edmund returns and learns of this, can you imagine him still wanting me for his wife? Do you understand? I am lost! All I can do is to beg you to come and stay with me and help me when the time comes. I need a woman with me. Someone I can trust to keep my secret. What happens afterwards is in God's hands.'

Rosie sat up at the mention of Roland's name and her eyes flickered over my stomach as if trying to confirm that what I said was true. Then in a weary voice she sighed,

What a sad day it was for you when you turned up that night.'

I felt tears sting my eyes as I urged,

'Will you help me?'

Then she turned away and began murmuring to her self,

'It ain't fair. It ain't fair. Why couldn't...' Her words died away and she looked up with a strange expression on her face as if she had forgotten I was there. Shaking her head she mumbled again but I could not catch what she said. Standing she walked towards the door,

'There is nothing I can do to 'elp yer. What use is the likes of me?'

'Can't you see. You are the only one that understands what has happened. We'll find somewhere to stay, a place where we are not known.'

Rosie stopped in the doorway as if she had just remembered something.

'Will Annie be coming with us?'

I shook my head; I had forgotten that she did not know what had happened.

'Annie is dead.' I said quietly.

Rosie's expression changed to one of shock,

'Dead? Wot that poor child?' With that she began to cry noisily. The sound of which brought the lawyer in as I tried to quiet her.

The elderly man looked horrified at the sight before him and asked what on earth was the matter. I quickly replied, not giving Rosie a chance to respond.

'Rosie has just found out about Annabelle.'

He grimaced and it was obvious that he was not impressed with the woman before him. I continued,

'Rosie needs somewhere to stay for a few days until you have found a place in the country for us.'

He nodded, 'I have arranged for her to stay at Mrs Mardwell's lodging house, which is just in the next street.' Then with irritation he added,

'For goodness sake woman, stop that noise and let us go.' He took her arm as if to usher her out as she resisted.

'No! I 'ave a place. All me belongings is there.'

'What place? Mr Stebbeds spoke sternly to her and Rosie's eyes became downcast and she shuffled her feet silently like a naughty child.

'We will send someone to fetch them,' he snapped.

I was surprised at the old gentlemen's manner and it was a side of him that I had not seen before. He made it quite clear that he had no time for Rosie and he ushered her out making arrangements for her to go to her lodgings. I heard promises of money being made so that she did not disappear.

I only felt relief that I had told someone my secret, and I had a spring in my step when we returned to the lawyer's home. When we told how we had found Rosie, Betsy took me aside with concern. She insisted that Rosie was not a suitable companion. I brushed aside the concerns knowing that they were kindly meant. Again she begged me not to leave and to stay with them. That she thought Edmund would be angry that I was left to fend for myself. I argued that I ran my father's household in Paris, so I would be perfectly capable on my own.

As we talked I became aware of a sleeping Cobbles, in a corner chair still clutching the broom. I saw her face brighten as she noticed him.

'He is going to stay here. He hasn't any family of his own so Bertie and I are going to become his family.'

Astounded, I could only meekly say,

'Are you sure?'

Betsy continued to look fondly at the sleeping boy and said as though talking to herself,

'God has given this child to me. Cobbles will become my Cobham. You see it was obviously meant to be. I will talk Bertie round. However, the first thing I am going to do is to buy him a new pair of boots.' At that we both began to laugh at the little scarecrow's legs that were too short to reach the floor dangling from the chair, the boots once again on the wrong feet. The smiling woman gently shook him awake.

'Do you think tonight you could sleep in a bed?'

'Why, am I staying 'ere for another night?' he asked rubbing his eyes. 'What about me sweeping?'

'Betsy wants you to live here.' I said, 'You should be very grateful.' Cobbles looked puzzled.

'But wot about the Guv, 'e don't like me.' He began to snivel and rubbed his nose with the back of his hand.

'If you mean my husband,' Betsy smiled, 'of course he likes you, and if I say that you are to live with us, then that is the end of the matter. However, you will have to behave yourself. I don't want any of your shenanigans.'

'What's them? I ain't got none.' He replied, looking big eyed

'Never mind! But first you are going to learn to sleep in a bed.'

'What like a gent?' He asked and began to run around the room with glee. All the time he was bending low in a mock bow, kicking his thin legs out. Imitating what he believed was the way of an elegant gentleman.

Betsy and I laughed at his antics until the tears ran down our cheeks and I realised that it was the first time I had laughed so much since I left France.

A few days later, Mr Stebbeds advised that a suitable place had been found for me to set up home. He made the necessary arrangements and still hoping that I would change my mind he saw Rosie and myself off in a hired carriage. I thought that we made an odd couple, I was small and although I had put on a little weight I was still thin. Rosie thinner than I had known her was still robust and brightly dressed now in a purple cotton dress and cape. I could not but notice that her nails were now clean but the rouge was just as bright.

It was early evening when we arrived at the cottage at a place called Motts Clump. When we saw it my eyes lit up as it was such a pretty place. It was a stone built whitewashed cottage, with ivy clad walls and a thatched roof. The garden was full of hollyhocks and delphiniums with roses gathering around the trellised doorway. It was obvious that the little cottage had been carefully tended, and the rooms though small were well furnished, with an ingle nook fireplace. I fell in love with it at once. There were two bedrooms and a small anteroom with a water closet, leading into a kitchen. Mr Stebbeds had arranged for the kitchen to be well stocked and I thought that I would be happy in this welcoming place.

That night I went to bed feeling quite optimistic about the future but woke with a start in the early hours in a cold sweat. I felt nervous and agitated and I knew that I had been dreaming. Although the dream had unsettled me, I could not quite remember what it had been about. I just knew that it had left me with an overwhelming feeling of anxiety. Afterwards I felt that an upsetting dream on the first night was a bad omen.

I had been so preoccupied searching for Rosie that I had viewed everything through rose coloured spectacles. Now I realised that everything would be my responsible and it weighed heavy on my shoulders. From the first day I realised that it had been a mistake to rely on Rosie for support. She was hardly ever there and when she was she would sit around all day lost in daydreams. Meanwhile my nights passed with more and more terrifying dreams only now I remembered them when I awoke. There was the smell of burning powder and all around me the screams of men and horses. It was a nightmare of tragedy and chaos and I would wake up in a panic only to find that I was safe and well in my bed. However, it made me unsettled and anxious all day. I tried to talk to Rosie about my dreams but she laughed them off.

The newspapers were full of the situation in the Crimea and I thought that the terrible news that I was reading was the cause of my vivid dreams.

Thoughts of Edmund and the danger he was in filled my head. Despite this I devoured the articles over and over again until sometimes I almost knew them off by heart. Every night I awoke in fear and trembling, knowing that I had been in the midst of disease, death and turmoil.

Sometimes I was sure that I had dreamed of Edmund but I could not remember how or why?

The days passed with my hated body becoming bigger. Every morning I would wake feeling tired and exhausted and creep out of my bed and stare at my body in the mirror. I would stand for hours in front of it and cringing at the reflection, would harangue this thing that was growing inside me. Additionally, I kept myself out of sight as it was all too obvious that my secret could no longer be hidden.

No matter how I cursed this being inside me, my stomach grew and grew and I knew that this horrible thing would not disappear. I had to face the fact that soon the child would come and nothing would prevent it. When I berated my fate in Rosie's hearing she became upset. Once she became angry shouting that it was not the baby's fault that it was given life and it was a wicked thing for me to curse the poor child. She said that it was a Fitzroy and had a right to live. From that day our relationship seemed to deteriorate.

I would often stay in my room and hope for everything to come to an end and sometimes we did not see each other at all during the day. Rosie often went down to visit people in the village. She would return singing to her self obviously in a very happy frame of mind. I did not know who she went to visit and although the local people were friendly I did not socialise. I had spread the word that I was a widow and that seemed to have been accepted. Rosie had totally adapted to her new life and was enjoying accepting invitations from the community whilst I was deemed as 'that strange widow woman.'

I was spending too much time on my own thinking and felt that I was going mad. Sometimes I was sure that I could feel this monster trying to climb out of my body. The baby moved more noticeably now and with each kick I thought that this thing would soon tear through the skin and rip my body to shreds. I raged at myself and at the child and spent a lot of time on my knees pleading for Edmund to come back and help me. I would pace the room for most of the night and be tearful and exhausted during the day. I began to loathe my life and this unborn child so much, that my thoughts turned maudlin and I convinced myself that when the child was born I would die and I welcomed it. I counted the days to the impending birth as the remaining days of my life.

Occasionally Leticia came into my thoughts and I wondered what was happening in her life that was so different to mine. No doubt Lady Westerham, the great gossip, had spread the news of my condition far and wide and many of my father's friends would be dining out on the tale of my disgrace. These thoughts reinforced my view that there was no way that Edmund could marry me with Roland's bastard attached to my side. Even if he felt that he had a sense of duty to marry me, I owed it to him to refuse.

The Crimean situation continued to deteriorate and all of the articles in the newspapers were full of the chaos that reigned. Disease was rife and the military had not organized themselves in a way that kept the regiments in supplies and equipment. Mr Stebbeds wrote that he regularly checked the military lists and Edmund was safe. However, he had heard that the Major's regiment was encamped at Sebastopol in Turkey. Apparently it was taking some months for mail to be forwarded and he advised that I should not worry if I did not hear from him.

Each night I would gaze at the miniature portrait I had of Edmund for hours on end. He looked so young and boyish and I would kiss his face in its silver frame. The ring was now on my finger to add to the subterfuge of being a widow and I had turned it over so much my finger was quite sore

Rosie went out more and more and most of the household chores fell to me. As I was becoming increasingly unwell it was becoming too much. Day after day, I sat looking out of the window, watching the seasons change. The trees changed from green to red and gold and then began to shed their leaves. Meanwhile when Rosie was not out visiting she would sit in an armchair nodding.

Sometimes when she thought I wasn't looking, she would steal money and buy sweetmeats. I would find her hiding away, greedily eating them in secret. As a result she had put on weight and was now quite fat. However, I could see the remains of the handsome woman that she must have been once. Our roles seemed to have reversed and I sometimes wondered who the mistress was. If I chided her over her laziness she was insolent and then would sulk for days. Then she would take great delight in constantly talking about what would happen when the child came. It was getting nearer to my time and she was aware that I did not want to be reminded of it but she seemed to go out of her way to provoke me. Then when she had raised my anger she would march off with the slam of the door and I would not see her for days. I had no idea where she went.

Some days she would stay home and sit in reverie, daydreaming about the child being a boy and what an important man he would be when he took his place in society. She seemed to have no idea of the reality of our life. Meanwhile when she wasn't around I began to hatch a plan to remove this evil from within me. Rosie didn't know that there would be no baby. I had been secretly boiling pennies and drinking the liquor in the hope that I would poison the monster. Night after night I crazily concocted this magic potion and drank it. It was disgusting and it caused me severe cramps and vomiting, but the monster still fed off me. As a result whenever she was in the cottage I would rant and rage at her and once in a temper I even slapped her face. I was beginning to hate her and when she disappeared I was glad as I could escape to my room and secretly drink my poison. It made me so ill that I could not stand and had to retire to bed in agony. I wanted Rosie to leave but when I thought these thoughts I realised that if she went I would be completely alone and then when she threatened to go I demeaned myself by begging her to stay.

One day when she was sitting inside looking forlornly out of the window, bemoaning the weather, I asked her to make enquiries to see if there was a young serving girl that we could hire locally to help with the housework. Rosie had not undertaken any household duties for weeks. Meanwhile, I was too tired to do anything as my body became thinner and thinner the child seemed to grow bigger and bigger. It was a parasite draining the life out of me.

She was only too glad to get another person to help out and after making enquiries found a young girl called Violet. The girl was quite plain being tall and lanky but was very pleasant and a lively chatterbox. I stayed in my room and Rosie now acquiring airs and graces began to act the mistress of the house. She ordered the girl around and I left her to it. However, the cottage was noticeably cleaner.

One day thinking I was alone I found Violet, cooking and seeing my wan face she fussed around me and began to look after me like an invalid. There was something nice about her and I began to enjoy just sitting and talking to her. One day she told me that her mother had been unsure of letting her come to work for me, as they were not sure that Rosie was a respectable person. I nodded but said that Rosie meant no harm and that she was always receiving invitations from people in the village.

'That might be,' Violet replied as she busied herself, 'but who from?'

'I believe there is a Mrs Hardcastle.'

'Mrs Hardcastle!' Violet exclaimed loudly. 'She is the proprietress of the local inn at Dersingham. It's a terrible place, full of drunken oafs and gamblers!'

I was taken aback. It had not occurred to me that Rosie might have been associating with undesirable people.

'Surely Dersingham is too far to walk.' I said thinking to myself that when she disappeared for days that was obviously where she had been staying.

Violet laughed and wiped her hands on her apron,

'She don't walk anywhere, I've seen her. She is always hitching a ride in the carts with the men. My mum says she is too friendly with the farmhands by half.'

My heart sank; Rosie had not taken long to resume her old ways.

'I shall have to speak to her,' I told Violet. 'I am afraid as I have been unwell, I have been remiss in checking what was happening in the home. I hope that your mother has not judged me to be an undesirable person.'

'No, of course not,' Violet replied pulling up a chair by my side. 'Anyone could tell you are a lady. My mum said that you seemed so lost and sad that she felt sorry for you. It was because of that she agreed to let me come. You being a widow woman and all. You go and help that woman Violet she said. Give her some of your home cooking like I learned you. I suppose you are so sad because your husband is in heaven and will never see the child. My dad died before I was born so my mum says she knows how you must be feeling. Was your husband the man in the little picture?' She pointed to the miniature that I had placed on my lap and I said that it was even though it was a lie.

One day as I was poring over the newspapers, Violet came to my side and peered at the newsprint.

'It must be good to be able to understand them letters,' she sighed. I asked her if she would like me to teach her to read. She was pleased to accept my offer and for a while in our daily lessons I thought of something else besides myself. I had offered to help Rosie in the past, but she made it quite clear that she had no intention of trying as she reckoned that,

'No good never came from any reading.'

Meanwhile, I was beginning to dread the nights. Each morning I awoke having been dragged through a mire of soldiers, horses, and guns. I was exhausted. Rosie was unsympathetic stating loudly it was because of them papers. It proved what she already knew, that reading was not good for me.

One day, there was a knock at the door, and Violet went to see who was there and returned holding a letter. She handed it to me and I weakly turned it over in my hand. I could see that the writing belonged to Betsy Stebbeds but I was too disinterested in anything to even open it. Violet looked at me anxiously and enquired if I was well as she thought that I looked ill and should look after myself or it would affect the baby. She told me that her mother would help me when the time came as she had brought many babies into the world. They were all alive and well and growing up to be strong and healthy.

Her constant chatter just faded into the background as I drifted into a haze, locked in my own thoughts. Tears began to roll down my face and I let them trickle down my face, too weak to brush them away. I suddenly became aware of Violet's voice again as she handed me a linen handkerchief, her face crumpled and anxious,

'Don't be sad miss! Just open your letter it might be good news.'

Forcing myself to break the seal, my eyes scanned the familiar writing. However, my heart sank when I read its contents.

'We have been made a party to some alarming news. It appears that there are rumours about that you were turned out of Lady Westerham's house because you were expecting a child. Of course, we have tried to quash such falsehoods, as we do not believe them to be true. However, with you living in the country, it has been difficult to convince people of the truth of the matter. It is said that you are staying away until your lying in. What is even more scurrilous, they are saying that Major Fitzroy is the father of your unborn child. I am sorry to apprise you of this, as I know it must be upsetting for you. However, you must return to London to give the lie to these stories once and for all. Mr Stebbeds wanted to write to Edmund and inform him but it is very difficult to contact him at the moment. We have had some news via officers who have returned from the Crimea, but have had no news from him directly. As you know he was at Sebastopol. However, the situation is just as dire as reported. I know he would be appalled to think that you have been left to be the subject of rumour and falsehood. Please my dear, do come and stay with us and let people see that what Lady Westerham has been telling people is a lie.'

The letter then continued telling me news of Cobham and how well he was doing. That in a few short months had turned into quite the little gentleman, and was learning to read and write. I crumpled the letter and let it fall in my lap. I could read no more. It felt as if a heavy black cloud had descended upon me and there was no escape. This thing that was tormenting me and growing inside me, was drinking my blood like a vampire. I tore the letter into tiny pieces and threw it up in the air in disgust. Sighing, I idly picked up the newspaper and flicked through its pages to read again the descriptions of the tragedies in the Crimea. The headline seemed to leap at me from the page even though I had read it before

'*From the Heights of Sebastopol, Oct 25.*' Sebastopol was the place that Betsy had mentioned in her letter. It was where Edmund's regiment was stationed. Quickly I read the newsprint unable to really take in the details of the fighting. There had been a battle at a place called Balaclava. The Scots under Sir Colin Campbell had fought off four squadrons of Russian cavalry with the help of the Turks. Following this Lord Raglan had realised that the Turks were in need of help and ordered eight squadrons from the Heavy Brigade, under Brigadier-General the Hon James Scarlett to support them. They were outnumbered but managed to carve a way through the Russians. The enemy had halted when the British sounded the charge. It was all so confusing and I could read no more.

Deeply depressed I tried to stand, but a wave of giddiness overtook me and I stumbled knocking over my drink. Violet rushed to my aid and helped me to my bed saying that I had to lie down. I remembered that Edmund had mentioned a James Scarlett and friends in the Heavy Brigade. It was obvious that he must be in the thick of the fighting. The paper had said that 3000 men had been routed with a loss of 80 casualties. There were highland regiments and the Lancers all in the battle I was in despair, even if Edmund could have survived a battle, according to reports men were dying of sickness and disease. Constantly the news stated that Cholera raged in Sebastopol and that the soldiers were cut off from their supplies and dying of cold and starvation. The whole campaign had been a disaster. I glanced at the paper again and looked at a photograph of Lord Lucan and Lord Raglan that appeared there. As I did so I noticed with a gasp what I most dreaded. I could not imagine how I had missed it before as the words almost leapt from the page,

'*Amongst the missing is believed to be Major Edmund Fitzroy. He was seen rallying the men at the start of the battle at Balaclava but there have been reports that his horse was shot from under him. However, in the tumult that ensued, a lot of the wounded had been unseated and at the time of writing many of them were still straggling back to base camp.*'

My whole being froze. I stood as if paralysed, clutching the newspaper, feeling nothing. The horror that I had faced night after night had been a premonition of what was going to happen to Edmund. I stood unmoved for several minutes as the door opened and Rosie came gaily in. Seeing my ashen face she stopped in her tracks and asked what was wrong,

'He is dead Rosie.' I said calmly.

'Who?' she asked and flinging herself on the bed sighed loudly showing her lack of interest and then seeing the crumpled letter suddenly became very animated. 'Not the Major?' she gasped.

My veins turned to ice as I shivered and said blankly,

'This newspaper says that Edmund is missing, in the Crimea. He might be dead.'

She stood silently watching me and then said angrily,

'I told you no good came from reading.'

'You stupid woman,' I said coldly. 'Do you think that such a thing does not happen if you do not read about it?'

The large woman shrugged and she went back to the door and began to whistle nonchalantly,

'The Major will be all right. He can look after himself.' She called out over her shoulder as she did so I grabbed a large vase from the shelf and threw it with all the force I could muster and it broke into tiny pieces. Violet came running in and stood foolishly in the doorway as Rosie pushed her aside and I heard the front door slam.

CHAPTER FIFTEEN

'Shake off this downy sleep, death's counterfeit, and look
on death itself! Up, up, and see the great doom's image!'
Macbeth Act 2 Sc 3

I yelled at Violet to get out and then I began to claw at myself in frenzy until I drew blood. Crazed, not knowing what I was doing, I tore at my clothes, and raked my stomach with my nails. All I knew was that my life was over and I had to put an end to this terror once and for all. Tipping out my bedside drawers in a demented fury, I searched for an implement to end my torture. Hysterical and deranged, I found a long button hook and pulling aside my petticoats I rammed the instrument between my thighs. Forcing it deeper and deeper inside.

I didn't care about the excruciating pain that ripped through me as I did it again and again. Stabs of agony racked through me, but I laughed insanely. I was destroying this thing that I had endured like a parasite feeding off me. I was taking my life back. I experienced an overwhelming sense of relief, that I had at last gained control of my body and my life. With an enormous feeling of joy, I was rewarded with a hot sticky dark liquid pouring down my legs, soaking into my linen. Swaying with light headedness and pain, I fell down. A torrent of water flooded from between my legs and mixed with the sticky mess that was oozing on the floor in a glistening pool. Screaming and laughing as a violent pain ripped through me, I collapsed amid the thick black slime. I crawled around the room doubled up rubbing my face and hair in the gore as I rolled around in a demented state suffering terrible pain but exhilarated. Again and again I stabbed myself viciously trying to rip my innermost being to pieces.

In the distance I heard the door open and Rosie shouting,

'It can't be the baby it's too soon, it can't come yet.' Her wailing echoed around me as she screamed,

'Don't let him die! Don't let him die!'

Still laughing like an insane creature, I could taste blood where I had bitten my tongue and the salty liquid seeped from my mouth. Horrified Rosie stood transfixed as Violet came running and leapt to action trying to stop me throwing myself out of the window. The implement I had used to torture myself slipped under the carpet and they had no idea what had happened. Rosie rallied a little and between them they managed to get me on to the bed and restrained me as I began to sob. The initial feeling of power was beginning to fade and I was only aware of the agony.

Screaming in agony I begged, 'I must lie down. I must lie down'

Violet ran to get her mother. Rosie found some rags and began soaking up the blood that gushed from me. Packing the material in between my legs.

'You'll be all right,' she fussed. Violet's mum, knows about babies.'

'Make it stop!' I screamed as I threshed around the bed, unable to keep still.

'I don't know what to do Miss. Babies come when they're ready. I don't know anything about it. I ain't ever had any.'

'You said you did, you said your mother had twelve children.' I sobbed

'Yes but I never seed them born.'

'Rosie! Rosie! I gasped, 'You said you'd help me.'

'I will when the baby comes, I'll feed 'im and wash 'im..........she stopped in her tracks as I began to flail at her with my fists. Screaming and shouting at her to get out and let me die. Rosie tried to fend me off as I suddenly became aware that some others had entered the room.

Someone held my hands and then as I struggled everything became still and I was floating above the bed, looking at myself and the people around it. Then as I hovered I found myself floating along a long dark tunnel and all the agony ceased. I was so happy and felt as if I had been wrapped in a cocoon of warm love. Although I was completely alone, I was not afraid, but felt myself drawn swiftly along towards a light that shone in the distance. My body felt as though it was immaterial with my feet barely skimming the ground beneath me. I had a tremendous feeling that once I reached the light that my life would be over and I was transfused with joy.

At last I reached the light and eagerly floated out of the darkness waiting for the calm and peaceful end, pleasantly drifting into oblivion. However, with horror as I came out of the darkness, I was greeted with a scene of such unimaginable chaos that my feeling of happiness turned into one of terror. Desperately, I tried to retreat and return to my cocoon of safety, but an invisible force prevented me. Try as I would, I could not return to the safety of my womb like tunnel, but could only gaze in terror at the scene of carnage as dead and dying men suffered their death agonies. Cannons and gun carriages were upended with their owners trapped beneath them; their mouth's contorted as they screamed silently in terrible agony. All around me severed limbs and sabre slashed bodies, sprawled in grotesque postures, piled on top of each other, their stomach's ripped open, bloodied entrails trailing in the dirt and mud. Yet there was no sound.

Crowds of panicking horses threshed about wildly, some on the ground with terrible injuries. The animals fought to stand their eyes rolling in their death throes, white froth bubbling around their mouths. I stood as an observer in a scene of hell, trapped amongst it, but not a part of it.

Although I was aware of the suffering around me, I could not touch the dying men, as their mouths silently cried out for help. When I bent down to see if I could help some poor soldier it soon became obvious to me that they were completely oblivious to my presence. As far as they were concerned I did not exist.

I made my way through this scene of carnage, heart pounding with terror as I was drawn on. Floating above the men, yet touching nothing. Wanting only for this horror to end. Then suddenly through the silence, I became aware of children's voices and through the pall of smoke that hung all around I saw two children playing. Overwhelmed at such an unnatural sight, amongst the carnage I could not believe what I was seeing. A boy and a girl were playing hide and seek amongst the debris, oblivious to the terrible scene around them.

Following them I tried again to reach down and help some of the men who were screaming in silence for their mothers, their faces contorted in agony but it was to no avail. I was frightened and shocked by what I was seeing and I did not understand what was happening to me. Suddenly I became of aware of some sound. This time it was a familiar voice. I was sure that I could hear Violet crying. Someone shouted,

'She's going. Oh Lord please don't let her. We have got to get her back.' I was puzzled, and could make no sense of it, but suddenly I felt myself being pulled backwards in a great rush, struggling to keep my balance. As I heard my name called over and over. I tried to cry out but everything went black and then the bright light returned. This time I found myself hovering above a large rock where I could see the same two children again. I watched for a moment, and then the girl looked up and for the first time noticed me. I was surprised as I had believed that they, like the men around me were unaware of my presence. However, she waved a greeting to me and beckoned me towards her. Intrigued I did as I was bid and followed the children as they frolicked amongst the rocks. All the men around me had no knowledge of my presence but this child did. Then I realised that her little piping voice was calling out to me by name. Her voice being the only thing I could hear among this disastrous scene of horror.

As the child waited for me to catch up with her, the smoke cleared and with a great joy I recognised my beloved Annabelle. However, she looked so happy and healthy in a way that I had never seen in her in life. The small boy, still a baby, with little plump legs and a mop of red curls, was unfamiliar to me. He stood by Annabelle studiously watching me, chewing his thumb absentmindedly. I was sure that I had died, otherwise how could Annabelle, appear so fit and well. However, I did not understand how she appeared to be so happy as we wandered through this vision of hell.

Stunned by the horror around me, I drifted in a strange despair, happy to see Annabelle but deeply affected by the slaughter around me on the battlefield. All around me lay dead and dying men, in their death throes, bloodied uniforms of indecipherable colours, soaked in mud and blood. The few survivors were straggling out of the chaos supporting each other as they clutched their slashed and ripped bodies.

Then I heard loud voices echoing around me. A strange voice I heard say that we would have to wait, that time would tell. I could hear sobbing and then the distinct voice of Rosie wailing,

'What shall I do?' I smiled to myself but then to my dismay I found myself being pulled back again. Struggling I fought against it. I wanted to stay with the children, even though surrounded by horror. I felt myself dragged back the way I came and then suddenly I was dazzled by sunshine. It was difficult to see but as I managed to focus I was greeted by a sea of faces around me. They were all blurred and featureless and I looked blankly seeing but not seeing as I heard someone say,

'I think she is conscious.'

I tried to speak but no words would come out. My mind formed words but my mouth would not say them. I shut my eyes with the effort and to my absolute pleasure began to float away again. All around were bloodied Dragoons and their horses now a tangled melee of flesh. Infantry men were wearily sitting on any available surface, rocks, gun carriages or the carcasses of their dead mounts. The uniforms of the enemy now merging into that of our blues and greys. Men in large fur busbies crawling through the mire, their heavy coats dragging them down to their deaths in the mire. All around me I was aware of the silent cries and groans of the suffering and dying. I was deeply disturbed by it but I was powerless and could do nothing. I didn't understand it what was happening. How could I one minute be in the midst of the dead and dying and then hear recognisable voices from the cottage.

Carefully, I tried to tread a path through this terrible scene, hardly able to see through the arid smoke, uncertain where I was going and unable to place my feet on solid ground. Bundles of papers blew around all containing writing in a foreign script. On an on I drifted making my way past the magnificent horses as they trampled on the bodies of their riders. Guns tipped into the mud trapping the men who manned them; crushing them into bloody pulp until soon it would be as if they had never existed. Their bodies would just be reabsorbed into the slime and mud around them.

Through the smoke filled haze, I could see the children again and Annabelle was waving me on and the little boy with the serious expression, tottered behind. However, each time I thought that I had reached them they seemed to move further away. I also noticed that like me, their feet did not touch the devastation that lay beneath them.

Soon I observed what seemed to be hordes of dark crows coming out of the shadows. Picking at the bodies. As they came closer I realised they were women. Some were checking the pockets of the dead to find anything of value. Some others were wandering around the battlefield in a complete daze, weeping profusely as they searched forlornly through the devastation. These women were looking amongst the dead and wounded for their husbands or lovers. I watched silently at the terrible tragedy around me.

Through this carnage, the children giggled together. The two red heads would come together whispering some secret to each other. Each time I was distracted by the scene around me, Annabelle would seem to hang back and beckon to me to follow them. As I did so, I became aware of a strange dark looking woman walking amongst the soldiers, pushing a cart loaded with all kinds of jars and pots, balms and ointments. She too was calling out in silence, but her large face was open and friendly. She would stop and help the injured men as they tried to struggle to their feet. The woman was of a large build, with tight braided crinkly hair of a kind I had never seen before and her skin was darkened and black. She was wearing a heavy, long nurse's cape, with a frilled cap, hidden beneath the hood of the cape. As each man called out in his silent anguish she would stop and tend to their injuries as best she could, there being far too many for her lone administrations. Some men followed behind and placed the wounded on stretchers and carried them to a place of safety.

Watching her in awe, I suddenly realised that my little guides had stopped and were pointing down at the ground, near an overturned gun carriage, that was wedged behind some large boulders. Excitedly they shouted to me to hurry up, but I could not walk any faster, my body could only drift at the same speed. I felt paralysed; I knew I could not be dead as I would not have heard the familiar voices. I was sure that I was dreaming. As I reached the children they both vanished.

I was in despair. I called out but no sound came and panic flooded through me. I tried to run but my bare feet were so heavy that I could not move. Fixed to the spot, I looked around desperately and then in a moment knew why I had been led to this place. There trapped beneath the body of a mangled and bloodied grey horse was Edmund. His blonde head, dark with blood as he sprawled against the wheel of the gun carriage, a sabre slash across his shoulder. The lower half of his body was wedged between the horse and the wheels of the broken gun carriage.

Foolishly I called out to him, even though I knew that he could not hear me. Desperately I tried to reach him, but I was unable to move. He was sprawled in a strange posture; the whole area seemed like a scene from an ancient painting. Suddenly the force of gravity that had restrained me seemed to snap and I was by his side. I did not know how, it was as if I had wanted it so much that it happened.

He looked so ungainly and bloody that I was sure he was dead. I tried to hold him, but his body was trapped and I could only hold his hand. One arm was flung awkwardly above his head, as if he had tried to pull himself free. He'd desperately tried to haul himself up, clinging onto the wheel spokes, but the effort had been too much for him. As I tried to hold him, my hands past through his body as if he was a phantom. However, to my joy I could see the rise and fall of his chest and knew he was alive but unconscious. The blood from his head and shoulder congealed in a sticky mess.

Although I knew he could not hear me, I called his name but he did not react to it. I desperately tried to lift him, willing him to be alive but my touch had no effect on him at all. Then he audibly sighed. I bent to kiss his dry lips even though I could not feel them beneath my own and as I did so, his eyes opened, and he whispered my name. I was sure I heard it. The sound being so gentle that the words brushed my cheek like a cool kiss, so softly that I thought that I had imagined it. He stared at me and through me. I knew he could not see me, yet I could hear him mumble incoherently. There was no sound from all the carnage but I could hear his soft voice. However, nothing I could do could make him aware of me.

There was a gaping wound across his forehead and I tried to touch it but as before my hands felt nothing beneath my fingers. He looked pale, with a purplish tinge around his nose and lips, his face thin and worn, exactly as he had appeared in my dreams. I looked around desperately, wanting to find him aid but had no means of doing so. All I could do was watch him as he stirred and groaned, unable to help in any way. Suddenly he half raised himself, trying to pull against the wheel and desperately called out loudly. With relief I realised that the noise had attracted the attention of the strange dark lady with the cart and making her way through the bodies she came to his side. She began shouting out instructions in dumb show and some of her helpers appeared carrying a stretcher. I watched as she bathed and bandaged Edmund's head and shoulder as he lapsed back into unconsciousness. As I watched she stitched the jagged sabre wound in his shoulder, but he was beyond pain.

It seemed like an eternity as I watched the carnage before me. Edmund unaware of his helpers moaned in his delirium. The black woman muttering words of comfort to him and yet they had no knowledge of my presence. She called for the men to move the horse and gun carriage and free Edmund. As they did so they laid him carefully on a stretcher and began to remove him. I managed just for a second to take his hand and I was sure that he had squeezed it in response. I tried to follow him, but my legs seemed to be stuck in the quagmire around me and I was fixed again.

Suddenly I found myself back amongst the corridors of dead and dying men. I was inside a low roofed building where the smell of gangrene and sickness and death was overpowering. Now in shock at what I had seen I realised that I could now hear the men's screams as their shattered limbs were sawn through by surgeons. It was a living hell. I walked through the filth from the latrines, and the smell of ordure engulfed me. I ran through corridors of wounded all lying on straw bedding row upon row and realised that I was in hell. I was a sinner and this was my punishment.

I tried to escape but I could not. All I could do was to drift past each bed, seeing each young man's face that looked no older than me, calling out for water. Young women bustled around the beds, trying to treat the terrible injuries. I saw shattered faces, and destroyed limbs each horror worse than the last. I tried to leave my torture but an invisible wall prevented me from returning to the safety of my tunnel. In desperation I fought to leave and then suddenly I was outside again. There with a surge of hope I saw Edmund was still being carried away on the stretcher. It must have only been a few moments that had passed. I could only blow him a kiss, and for a moment he stirred as if aware of my touch and then was gone. Soon the distance between us grew further and further as the dark lady continued on her way, helping other soldiers that called out to her.

As I stood there I felt cold and strange and began to shiver. Until then I had been covered in a strange heat and looking down I realised for the first time, that I was wearing my white cotton night-gown. Shocked at being out in my shift, I knew that I must be experiencing a dream as I would not be out in the world at large wearing only night clothes. Then a thought struck me. Perhaps it was the gown that I had been buried in and I was dead after all.

Shuddering with the cold, I rubbed my bare arms for warmth and as I did so a strong gale force wind seemed to blow up and buffeted me back through the battle scene. Like a tornado picking me up in the air, spinning and spinning out of control until suddenly I was back in that warm cocoon of the tunnel again. With relief I allowed the darkness to envelope me. Giving in to it, drifting like a baby returning to the womb. It was so safe and secure and I was so happy and carefree. Then as before, my peace was interrupted by the sound of my name being called out. I tried to ignore the voice as it disturbed me and made me angry. I wanted to continue my secure existence, but the voice kept calling and disturbing me and struggling to float my body became rooted to the spot. A icy coldness descended over me and I started to shake. The voices were louder now and seemed to all merge into an incomprehensive gabble. I shivered uncontrollably, my teeth chattering loudly and as I opened my eyes I was dazzled by hot sunlight and my dark tunnel disappeared. Warmth and heat flooded through me, melting the icy cold that had permeated deep into my bones.

Slowly I looked around in confusion uncertain where I was, but gradually the blurred, featureless faces staring over me began to become familiar. Violet's tired, anxious face was peering at me excitedly and she shrieked so loudly I felt my head almost explode with the sudden noise.

'She's awake. She's back with us. Oh mum come quick!'

I was devastated. Overwhelmed with a feeling of sadness and longing, I tried to sit up but was too weak and sank back wearily into my pillow. Violet held a drink to my parched lips and I sipped it gratefully.

'What has happened? Why am I here?' I croaked my voice sounding strange an unfamiliar to me.

'You've been so bad miss, but you are all right now. My mum has been looking after you.'

I tried to look around my room but the brightness hurt my eyes.

'Have I been ill?' I gasped

'Yes, but we'll soon make you better again.' Violet fussed around me, encouraging me to drink more but I could not. Looking around I realised that I was back in my bedroom at Motts Clump. I sighed and lay back, overwhelmed with the misery of being back with the living.

The days passed as an eternity but every day I became a little stronger, whilst Violet and her mother fussed around me. They helped me to sit up and fed me like a child as I listlessly lay there, not caring what happened to me. One day, feeling a little better, it occurred to me that I had not seen anything of Rosie. When Violet came in with my breakfast, I asked her to help me to get out of bed and sit in the chair. As she did so I enquired about the missing Rosie. Violet looked uncomfortable and turning her head away, muttered something. . As I did not catch what she said, I struggled to stand and Violet anxiously rushed to help me,

'You've got to take things easy. You've lost a lot of blood. The doctor says that you must rest.'

'I have been resting; I cannot stay in bed forever?'

'Don't upset yourself. You came before your time and we nearly lost you, but my mum saved you. My mum's delivered lots of babies.....' She stopped suddenly as she looked at the expression on my face. What was she talking about? What baby? I was confused, was she telling me that I had a baby? Surely that could not be, the thought was abhorrent to me. Surely I could not have forgotten. Then as if an avalanche of ice descended upon me I remembered. I had been expecting a child, a satanic monster and horror flooded through me. Turning my face miserably to the wall I asked bleakly,

'Where is it?'

'It's gone.'

Relief flooded through me. Everything would be all right and for the rest of the day I sat numbly by the window, looking out at my pretty garden, which Violet's brother had tended for me. When Violet brought me some dinner I asked again,

'Where is Rosie?'

'Gone away.'

'Gone where? She had nowhere to go.'

'I don't know. She just packed her clothes and left. Whilst you were ill. She took all the money from the food tin and we haven't seen her since. My mum says that it is good riddance to bad rubbish, if she could run away and leave you when you were so ill. After you had been so good to her and all, my mum said that she always thought she was a bad lot'

'It doesn't matter,'

Neither the child nor Rosie were mentioned again. Gradually I resumed my strength but in my dreams I spent my nights wandering through the corridors of sick and wounded. Hearing the cries, smelling the rotting flesh and searching for someone who was never there. Each bed I stood before I expected to contain the shattered body of Edmund but it did not. Every morning I awoke remembering the stench and filth. Then so gradually that at first I did not realise it, my dreams began to change. Although I knew that I had been in that same dreadful place, I had a strange feeling that I had been standing somewhere that was peaceful and calm. I remembered that I was at the foot of a bed watching a soldier but I could not see his face. It left me unsettled but somehow with an unexplained feeling of hope.

When I was up and about again, and thinking more clearly, I had thoughts again about setting up a little school for the local village children. I enlisted Violet to help me prepare a school room in readiness. Violet's brother Tom helped with the carpentry and ran errands. He often brought us some meat from the butcher wrapped in newspaper and would ask me to read him the news that seemed always to be about disasters in the Crimea. Everyday I turned my ring for good luck but the feelings that I had for Edmund seemed to be locked away somewhere in my heart and I could not reach them.

There was no more news of him except a letter that I received from Mr Stebbeds confirming that Edmund was missing. He tried to reassure me by stating that as communication was in such a disastrous state, that it was probable that Edmund had not been able to communicate with his regiment. He was probably amongst the wounded at Scutari. I could only hope that what I had witnessed in my imagination, that had seemed so terrible, meant that Edmund was safe and being tended somewhere.

One day I was unwrapping some provisions wrapped in newspaper. My attention was drawn to the headlines. It said that there had been another battle in the Crimea which had resulted in a great number of casualties. Then I spied something in the small print that made my heart leap. There in a reporter's eyewitness account stated that amid the unimaginable scene of carnage, he had been surprised to see a large Jamaican woman called Mary Seacole. She had been pushing a cart filled with medicines and potions giving aid to the wounded. The men called her 'Black Angel.' He mentioned that she had set up the British Hotel to provide soldiers with accommodation, food and nursing care using her own money. The article described this woman exactly as I had seen her. The woman that I had seen in my dream was a reality. If what I had seen had really happened, then perhaps it was proof that my beloved Edmund really was alive.

I knew then that I had to find out for sure and the only way to do so was to go to London. There I could make enquiries at the War Office with the help of the lawyer.

Excitedly, I called out to Violet to pack me an overnight bag and without any more aforethought was soon catching the coach to London. Violet and her mother tried desperately to dissuade me from such a journey, saying that I was not well enough. They worried that I was travelling alone and wanted me to take Tom but I would not listen. Besides I wanted no one to let my friends know what had happened since I left them. I hoped that my arrival would be welcome as they had not been advised of my visit.

We stopped at a coaching inn and whilst we changed horses, I sat quietly in the waiting room. A young woman tried to engage me in conversation, showing concern for my health as I did not look well. However, I was in no mood for talking and politely rebuffed her. It was nearly dark when I arrived in London so with trepidation, I hired a hansom to take me to Whitefriars.

CHAPTER SIXTEEN

'If we shadows have offended, think but this, and all is mended. That you have but slumbered here whilst these visions did appear.'

A Midsummer Night's Dream Act 5 Sc.2.

As I anxiously waited, it was sometime before I heard the sound of footsteps. At last the door was opened by the maid who recognising, me smiled and ran off to fetch her mistress. Suddenly I was overwhelmed by Cobham throwing himself upon my neck and hooraying loudly in my ear. Freeing myself with some difficulty, I saw how much he had grown since I had last seen him. He now looked quite the young gentleman.

'Look at me.' He shouted, spinning around for me to see him the better. 'Ain't I the toff.'

I heard a familiar voice in the next room call out,

'Cobham, what have I told you? We do not say ain't.'

Cobham laughed loudly and added

'Her ladyship is always telling me off.'

'I'll give you her ladyship...the voice tailed off as Betsy came to the doorway and crying out in surprise, urged me inside.

'What on earth are you doing standing there? Oh how nice it is to see you. Cobham, behave yourself and let Aphra get inside. Why didn't you write and let us know that you were coming?'

Unable to restrain the grief I was feeling about Edmund, I waved the newspaper I was clutching and a torrent of words gushed out, not making any sense. She tried to pacify me by saying that her husband had already been making enquiries. However, so far, there was nothing concrete. I told her of my dream and she reassured me as best she could. Then Betsy insisted that I stayed in my old room and would not hear of me booking into lodgings. When I was sitting in the parlour with some tea and cake, Betsy looked at me with concern and commented that I was still too thin. However, she did not refer to her letter.

The lawyer returned from visiting a client and he too greeted me like a lost friend informing me that it was difficult to find out any news. Many of the soldiers in Edmund's regiment were only now returning to London. He had consulted the War Office and enquiries were being made amongst the troops returning.

That night I lay awake in that little room which I had left only a few months ago unable to sleep. I could only think of Edmund and his sufferings and in the candlelight I stared at the miniature portrait willing him to be alive. At last exhausted I fell into a restless sleep but there were no dreams.

The next day when we were alone, Betsy took me to one side and quietly said, 'Do you know my dear; I am so pleased to have you here. When you did not reply to my letter I thought that perhaps you were angry with me for writing to you in such a fashion. I did it to help; I could not bear it that people should think ill of you. It was only by chance that Mr Stebbeds found out what had been bandied around the town by Lady Westerham. Of course we have made it known that it is an untruth and in fact Bertie has written to the woman to state that he will sue for slander should the falsehood be repeated. I wanted you to dispel the rumour by being seen. Anyone can see by looking at you that the scandal she has broadcast could not be true. If it were, you would be near your time and there is nothing of you.'

I turned away, not wanting to look the kind woman in the eye and simply allowed her to believe the lie.

'I know that you only have my best interest at heart,' I said sadly and then shrugging off the conversation, changed the subject. 'Well anyway I am here now and all is well!'

Mr Stebbeds returned to the War Office and came back to inform us that everywhere was in such chaos, that no one knew anything. It was not even known whether in fact some of the troops listed as missing had returned to England. The lists were being posted but as quickly as they were issued, the details changed. Many of the wounded had not been accounted for. He tried to reassure me that there was every hope that Edmund was in one of the casualty stations. Seeing how anxious I was he consoled me by saying that in the heat of battle many men became separated from their regiments. If the chaos that had been reported in the Crimea was true then, it was difficult for information to be reported back. In the meantime the more I heard about the situation the more I pinned all my hopes on my dream. If it had been a premonition then Edmund was alive. If the dark lady was a reality then perhaps the rest of the dream was too and if we traced her then we could find out more.

When I suggested it to the lawyer he shook his head.

'My dear child, it is impossible given the conditions, anyway it would take a long time for any letter to reach the authorities. By that time we would possibly have heard about Edmund officially. Everyday I have someone checking the lists of the wounded that are returning to the Central Station. There is nothing more we can do. I have spread my net far and wide to find out where he might be. He is as important to me as he is to you, after all,' he laughed trying to reassure me, 'he is my most important client.'

Against my will I was persuaded to stay with my friends until we knew more. Betsy enquired after Rosie but I let them believe she was still at Motts Clump. As I had nothing to do to pass the time I offered to give some lessons to Cobham. I enjoyed sitting with Cobham, who was an unruly pupil but was very quick to learn. However he could not concentrate for long. By lunchtime he would either be dancing on the table pretending to be a coster monger, shouting out his wares or singing unsuitable music hall songs that were cut off when Betsy came into the room and cuffed him around the ear. He would dodge and dance about to avoid the blow, but was always led away by the small woman who gripped him by the earlobe. As he was a good head taller than her, the pair made a comical sight. Sometimes Betsy chased him with his beloved broom that was still kept near at hand.

After several days, Betsy and I were sitting in the drawing room when the conversation turned to the Westerhams. She could not understand why Lady Westerham had been so unkind. I merely said that she was unhappy that I had become engaged to the Major and there had been a quarrel. Betsy looked at me searchingly as if she did not quite believe me but did not pursue it. Then she suggested that when I went to Threshingham Park I would have many friends. I sighed,

'Perhaps one day everything will be different. However, all I know is that my sister Freya and I rue the day that we ever went to Stoneleigh and our paths crossed that of the Fitzroys.

'But my dear, your intended husband is a Fitzroy,' she smiled in the kindly way she always had.

'Yes, by name but not by nature.'

Betsy looked puzzled and said with concern,

'As the Major's future wife, you must be seen out in society. You cannot stay hidden away here whilst in town. It is also important to be seen to quash any of the lies that have been spread about your condition.'

'Well, would you suggest that I attend all the ball's that I have been invited to?'

'Yes, you must. I did not realise that you had received invitations,' she said brightening.

I realised that the elderly woman had not understood that I was being sarcastic. I had not received any invitations. I changed my tone and added,

'I cannot be seen in society, because society does not wish to see me.'

'That is nonsense.' She sighed waving to the servant to clear away the remains of the dinner. 'Tomorrow, we shall venture out to the stores and order some material for some dresses. If you are to attend a ball you will need to have a new dress.'

I sighed knowing that to argue was useless.

The next day, at Betsy's insistence, we went shopping and I found that I quite enjoyed the pleasure. It had been ages since I had chosen material for clothes and feeling the lovely textures of the silks and satins was an indulgence that I was beginning to revel in. As we walked around the store, I became aware that occasional sideways glances were coming my way, but I ignored them. Then as I was unravelling some bolts of cloth I glanced into the mirror and to my astonishment, I saw Leticia. She was looking through some pattern books. Seated a short way from her, looking decidedly bored, was the gangly young man that she had met at the ball.

I quickly tried to avoid her but at that moment she looked up and caught my eye. Immediately she glanced down at my body and her eyes searchingly returned to my face. I so wanted to speak to my dearest friend but with cold disdain she turned away from me and I was ignored. The way she cut me hurt as much as anything could. I was devastated! My once close friend, whom I had loved almost as much as my sister, had spurned me. As I stood in despair I saw her quickly take the young man's arm and usher him away. He stood up protesting with irritation but catching sight of me, the colour rose in his cheeks and they both rushed away.

I wanted to cry but I had no tears left. I was determined not to give them any satisfaction so I turned away and pretended to look at the materials.

Locked in my thoughts I did not hear what Betsy said until she caught me by the arm and said,

'You look distracted my dear. Are you all right?'

'Yes, I am quite all right,' I murmured putting back the cloth, 'but I want to leave now.'

'But we have not finished our purchases.'

'No, but it was foolish of me to come. I am tired of being the subject of interest.'

'But that is what we want. It will give the lie to the rumours.'

'I do not care about the rumours. I have just been completely ignored by my dearest friend, and I want to go home.'

'Of course my dear. Whatever you want.' Betsy looked anxiously around, to see to whom I was referring, but Leticia and Garrick had long gone. Paying for our purchases we made our way outside and returned home.

On arrival, there was a message from the lawyer. He wanted us to know that he had ascertained that the dark lady named Mary Seacole had a hotel where she treated injured soldiers during the battles. It was possible that if Edmund was not in the hospital at Scutari he could be at the hotel and there were no listings of the soldiers there. My despair lifted as I now had a degree of hope, as more and more my strange experience when I was ill was beginning to gain credence. However, I just wanted to go back to Motts Clump. I had no wish to have another day like this one where I was the subject of the conversation of those around me. There was nothing to be gained by staying in London and I definitely would not be attending any balls. I wanted the security of my little cottage and knew that I wanted to follow my dream of setting up a school for the village children. I explained this to my hosts and they did not argue. However, the lawyer asked that I should accompany him to his office to sign some papers before I left. This I did and we were greeted by his thin clerk fussing around nervously. The man settled himself on a high stool and leaned over a pile of ledgers, occasionally seeking out one stored away, blowing out clouds of dust. As he did so he sneezed continually and apologised profusely, blowing his nose loudly on a grubby handkerchief.

Whilst we were there Mr Stebbeds explained that although we were hoping for good news about the whereabouts of Edmund, certain arrangements had to be made. Edmund was the sole heir of the Fitzroy family. Threshingham Park was being maintained in his absence by a legion of staff but Stoneleigh had been more or less abandoned. The lawyer had been left with a responsibility towards me. Although he did not agree about my plans for the school he said that he would help me in any way he could. However, Edmund had ensured that I would not be without means.

I told him that I wanted to be independent and not reliant on Edmund. At my words the lawyer's expression changed to one of astonishment.

'My dear child,' the old man said, stroking his sideburns thoughtfully, 'I don't think that you understand the position. Your fiancé has a considerable fortune and an elevated standing in society. As his wife you will take your place as you should.'

'I thank you but should Edmund decide that he no longer wishes to marry me on his return, I must have a plan so that I can live a comfortable life.'

'What on earth would make you think that Edmund would not wish to honour his promise? You are a beautiful young woman, every man would envy him?' As he spoke he stood and paced the small office thoughtfully, staring out of the window. An atmosphere descended and there was silence between us. The old man looked as though he wanted to say something but then changed his mind. Finally he returned to his seat and uttered the words that I did not want to hear.

'We have to face the fact Aphra, I want to be optimistic but there is a possibility that Edmund will not return. Arrangements would have to be made on that basis'.

'I feel very strongly,' I replied my voice quivering with emotion, 'that Edmund is alive!'

'I know! I know! I hope it is so. However, he left instructions, that God forbid, should he not return and they concern you.'

'I know I have an allowance. That was arranged sometime ago, when I left Stoneleigh. It was given to me to ensure that Annabelle would always have someone to look after her, when she was well. I supposed that allowance to be at an end with her death.'

'No my dear, the allowance is yours in perpetuity. Whatever the circumstances. However, he has added a codicil to his will to include you as a beneficiary should he die.'

'Well that is irrelevant as he is not dead.' I said refusing to accept the possibility and pulled on my gloves, preparing to leave.

The elderly gentleman returned to his desk and patted my shoulder,

'That is true, but I have instructions that involve him being missing or injured and I must follow them through now.'

'What instructions?'

'You are to live at Threshingham Park. When he returns you will be his wife. Should he not return you will be permitted to live there for your lifetime. There will also be an income of £10,000 per annum.'

'No!' I said firmly, 'I do not wish to live at Threshingham Park without Edmund. I wish to return to Mott's Clump and await his return. I do not want the income. He is a free man, I am promised to him only conditionally, and it is not right and proper for me to assume that I will one day be Lady Fitzroy.'

'Why do you fight against it, Aphra, most young women in London would be overjoyed to have such an offer from someone of Major Fitzroy's standing.'

I felt my bravado weakening as I replied,

'You misunderstand me. I love Edmund with all my heart. However, he asked me to marry him out of kindness and pity for my situation, of that I am sure. When he has time to reflect and sees that I am independent and running a little school, he will no longer feel pity for me. He says that he loves me but I am sure that he said that because he is such a kind and decent man with a loyalty to his family. However, I am not unaware that there are many young women of title and money that would be only to happy to be his wife. He should marry according to his status and not a poor relative that is unworthy of him.'

'Now you listen to me young woman,' the old man said standing up and pushing back his chair. He addressed me in a stern tone as if speaking to his daughter.

'That man loves you more than life itself. When he came into the office to prepare the codicil all he could talk about was you. Your strength of character, how you rose above adversity, how beautiful and independent you were. I have never seen a man so in love before. He was exhilarated at the prospect of your life together. I am appalled, what reason would he have to feel pity?'

I could find no answer except to say softly,

'He may have a change of heart.'

The lawyer looked exasperated and pursed his lips, shuffling papers as he did so and then speaking to me once more like a father added,

'I suggest that you return to Mott's Clump and think things over. I hope to hear something soon. However, everyone of authority that I have spoken to does not appear to know what another department is doing. I do not wish to alarm you any more than is necessary, but we have to face facts. The men are facing dreadful conditions, there are no supplies and dysentery is rife. It is not at all the sort of thing that I should be discussing with a young woman. However, if they are the conditions that Edmund has had to face, should he return, he undoubtedly will be in need of medical attention.' He pushed the papers on his desk angrily aside as he continued,

'What on earth could this government have been thinking of, sending troops out with no proper supplies and organisation? Forgive me, my dear, but I feel so angry at our young men being sent out to fight under such conditions. I am sorry but it makes me so annoyed that I am forgetting myself and upsetting you.'

I waited for him to finish his tirade and then quietly responded,

'I am not a child. I understand the situation. I have seen for myself the carnage there. I have walked along corridors of filth and ordure, and listened to the screams of men and suffered the dreadful smell of gangrenous flesh. I have seen it all in my dreams.'

'Goodness gracious, Aphra that such sights should have filled your imagination!' He offered me his arm and began to escort me to the door, telling his clerk to fetch me a hansom to take me to the coach. He seemed to suddenly look much frailer and old as he stiffly stood there and I noticed that he had difficulty walking. For the first time I became aware how much all the work that he had undertaken had been a strain on him. He seemed diminished and dejected. As we came out into the street I became aware of a youth leaning against the exterior wall of the office in an insolent manner. The lawyer watched him carefully as the youth shouted out.

'Hey mate! Do you know some old cove who works here called Stebbings?'

He grinned in a leering fashion and tipped his cap, which was worn at a rakish angle. He was wearing a dirty hound's tooth check jacket with a red neckerchief tucked inside the neck, and looked rough and ill mannered. The lawyer ushered me back into the doorway and said briskly,

'Who wants to know?'

'Me that's who!' Came the insolent reply. 'Go and tell 'im I have a message for 'im!'

The lawyer pulled himself up to his full height and asked,

'What is your business here? Loitering outside my office. Be off with you!'

The youth tipped his hat again and said loudly,

'I fink you might want to hear what I've got to say. If you be old Stebbards or whatever 'is name is, I have a message. You're to come to the Cock Tavern in Southwark.'

'Why on earth should I want to do that?' The lawyer replied with irritation as I listened in the doorway.

'Cos there's a toff there who's taken sick and we was told to tell yer.'

'Go away or I shall summon a constable. I am not going off to Southwark with the likes of you.'

The youth's manner changed and his eyes flashed angrily,

'Please yerself, but we was told that you would need to know about this toff.'

'What's 'is name? Who is he?'

'Well as you've been so rude, it'll cost yer.' The youth leaned back against the wall and began to whistle.

'If you think I am going to give you money, or go off on some wild goose chase you are mistaken.'

'Suit yourself, but some woman called Rosie said you'd want to know!' Shrugging he turned to walk away and the whistling became louder. Hearing the name I ran out.

'Don't let him go. Perhaps he knows something about Rosie?' I gasped.

'The man's a rogue. It is probably a trick!' Mr Stebbeds said with exasperation and tapped his foot on the cobbles.

'But he knows something about Rosie. Please? I implored.

The elderly man looked at me in dismay. 'Well if it is so important to you.' He then called out to the youth to wait and the lout stopped in his tracks and then swaggered back.

'Changed yer tune have yer!'

'What has this person Rosie, got to do with you?'

The youth held his hand out in silence, intimating that he wanted paying and Mr Stebbeds felt in his pocket for a coin. On receiving it the youth smiled in a wolfish fashion.

'Don't ask me! Some woman by the name of Rosie, fetched this cove in saying he's been ill. Lost 'is memory or somefing. She paid for a night's stay and said to fetch yer. If yer don't come, he'll be out on the street tomorrow. Sick or not. We run a business. We can't be tending sick toffs. It puts off the customers.'

'I certainly have no intention of running off to Southwark on a fool's errand.' The lawyer snapped.

'Up to you, Guv. She paid me two pence to come and that's what I've done.'

'Describe this Rosie,' Mr. Stebbeds challenged as I listened eagerly.

'A big tart with pale 'air. That's all I know.'

Desperately I gripped the elderly man's arm,

'It must have been Rosie. We must go and find out what is happening? 'I begged.

Mr Stebbeds prised my fingers from his arm,

'Nonsense. I thought you said she was back at Motts Clump. Why would she be here?'

I looked downcast and replied,

'No she disappeared. I didn't like to tell you after all you did for her.'

'Then why should we care about her now?' The lawyer turned away and was about to return inside.

'But who is this person that she has taken to the inn?' I asked in desperation.

'There probably isn't anyone.' The lawyer replied. 'How can we trust anything that this person is up to? It might be a trick to entice me to the inn to rob me.'

'Why that's a damn lie.' the youth shouted angrily. 'We run a respectable business. As it is we only took the gent in cos he was a toff, for all we know she is landing us with one of 'er customers.'

'I suggest you watch how you speak in front of a lady Sir.' Mr Stebbeds retorted. Just at that moment the clerk returned with the hansom and I pleaded with the lawyer to go to the inn and find out what it was all about. Much against his will, Mr Stebbeds climbed in and refusing to be left behind I sat beside him. As we were about to leave he instructed his clerk to contact the constabulary if we did not return in two hours. The youth made a great show of being offended and the clerk still looking mystified nodded his affirmation as we set off. However, the lawyer insisted that the smirking youth make his own way. As we drove along the lawyer muttered with annoyance about going on a foolish errand. He could not understand why I would be interested in Rosie but for me she was my only contact with the past and Edmund. I felt a rush of excitement and didn't know why. Certainly I had no reason to thank Rosie for anything.

CHAPTER SEVENTEEN

'My bounty is as boundless as the sea, my love as deep; the
more I give to thee, the more I have, for both are infinite'
Romeo and Juliet Act 2 Sc 2

We travelled through the dismal streets and passed the run down
hovels, trotting along behind the jostling traffic of horse drawn carts.
Neither of us spoke as we gazed out at the black smoking chimneys through
the window and the raggle taggle children playing in the dirt. It did not take
long to arrive at Southwark and the driver stopped outside one of the dingy
doorways. The buildings were three stories high, with large wooden cellar
doors on the broken, cobblestoned pavement. Alongside the gutter was an
open sewer that ran along the length of the road. Mr Stebbeds insisted that I
stayed in the cab whilst he went to investigate. Even outside there was a smell
of beer fumes which mingled with the foul stench from the effluent fumes.
The horse began to bang its hooves noisily against the stones and the driver
began to mutter restlessly at having to wait in such a dark and dingy area.

The street was very noisy and thronged with people. There was a coal
merchant tipping large sacks of coal through a nearby cellar door and a
knife grinder not far away was busily sharpening knives so loudly that it set
my teeth on edge. As I waited I saw the youth arrive and he sprinted ahead
into a side alley, where there was a side entrance to the building that had
a weather worn sign portraying a cockerel hanging above the door. This
groaned and creaked as it swung in the breeze. I watched as Mr Stebbeds
stood on the steps leading into the inn. As he hovered, the door suddenly
swung open to reveal the youth who must have run round from his side
entrance and with a cunning expression he beckoned the old man in. The

lawyer disappeared inside just as the driver began to complain loudly about the wait. I was impatient to know whether Rosie was inside the inn and finally having listened to the driver's irritated complaining; I gave him his fare and sent him away.

The roadway was disgusting and I made my way through the stinking liquid and filth on the pavement. My shoes totally inadequate for the wet muck that soaked through. There was an abattoir at the end of the road and the roads were covered in rotting offal, and congealed blood. The smell of rotting meat took my breath away and holding a handkerchief to my mouth I tried to peer through the dirty windows. The inn's windows were caked with dirt and grime and there was no way that I could see inside. Scrubbing at them with my free hand I was still unable to see. In desperation I tried to push open the heavy door that had closed on the lawyer. It was padded with large oak panels and stiff metal bolts and it was difficult to open. At first it resisted but then I managed to force it by holding my shoulder against it. The effort hurt my arm, and I exclaimed aloud as the door swung open, and I almost fell inside. The room was filled with smoke and crowded with people. Large tankards of ale were being downed noisily but I eagerly looked around hoping to see Rosie.

The room was mostly full of men but there were some women sitting amongst them, laughing loudly. Looking up to see who had entered so ignominiously, they called out a few ribald comments whilst I quivered with embarrassment by the bar. An oafish man came over and pushed his face close to mine, his breath stinking of ale was hot on my face as I tried to edge away. Looking nervously around I saw Mr Stebbeds deep in conversation and just at that moment he looked up and seeing me, he stopped in mid sentence and angrily rushed to my side and gripped my arm firmly.

'What do you think you are doing? I asked you to stay in the cab. This is no place for a young woman.'

'The driver did not want to wait. I had to pay him, besides I wanted to know if Rosie is here.'

'As far as I can ascertain she is not!'

Disappointment flashed across my face and as I turned to leave a tall man, running to fat joined us from behind the bar counter. He wiped his hands on his dirty butcher's apron and lifting the bar flap squeezed his large bulk through. As he did so the surly youth reappeared on the stairway and seeing me made a facetious bow.

'Come in yer ladyship,' he said grandly. 'You and the old gent should come this way if you want to see the toff.'

'What about the woman you mentioned? Rosie?' I asked

'I thought yer wanted to see the toff she brung?'

'Toff! What toff? Who are you talking about?' I asked.

Mr Stebbeds indicated to me to go back to the doorway saying,

'We are certainly not, ascending the stairs to God knows where until we have an explanation as to why you have brought us here!'

'Will Rosie be returning?' I asked eagerly, desperate for news.

'Dunno about Rosie. Haven't a clue!' The youth laughed from the top of the stairs.

The large man in the apron, signalled to the youth to be quiet and added,

'If you're talking about the 'erm.....,' he paused for a moment as if trying to find the right words, and then coughing in an affected manner, continued,

'Lady!' If that's what she calls herself. Anyway, her what brung him. Well I dunno, she paid his rent for two nights. She never said if she'd come back. I ain't never seen her before. We just thought one of her customers took ill and she didn't know what to do with him'

'Customers?'

'Oh sorry yer ladyship. I must watch my mouth, I was a forgetting that I was speaking to another lady' and he sneered knowingly at me. We stood in awkward silence as the barkeeper pulled out a large green leek from his apron pocket and began chewing the end, spitting pieces out as he did so.

The lawyer pushed me towards the door,

'Come along my dear. I knew we were wasting our time coming on a fool's errand. These people do not know where Rosie is.' As he did so, the fat man chimed in,

'What's all this about Rosie? I thought you came to see the toff! He's sick; we don't want nobody a dying here. We've got our reputation to think of. We ain't spending our money fetching no doctor for him neither. She said you would see to it. So let's see your tin. You either help him or he'll be out in the street. This woman comes in 'ere and brings this toff with 'er. We didn't know 'e was sick else we wouldn't 'ave let her bring 'er rubbish for us to look after. She only paid for two nights. If we'd known he was a going to take sick, we'd have told her to find somewhere else to leave him. She had the tin. He had the room.'

'Oh for goodness sake,' the lawyer responded. 'Let us resolve this situation once and for all and find out who this so called 'toff,' is. If he is ill then common decency would insist that he receives medical treatment whoever he is.'

'Well we ain't paying. You tell 'em pa!' The youth shouted.

The fat man banged on the counter of the bar and shouted,

'Shut yer mouth and use it to cool yer soup with. Now this lady and gent don't want to get the wrong impression do they? We don't know who he is. This tart comes in here and rents a room for this bloke. I thought he was drunk as he was staggering a bit. Anyway, she gave my lad some tin to fetch a Stebbings. Is that you?' He picked up a large jug and washed down the leek with a mouthful of ale. Then wiping his thick lips with the back of his hand, he added. 'Well is it?'

'My name is Stebbeds,' the lawyer replied and we noticed that a hush had descended as the raucous clientele had stopped their noise to listen to our conversation. Just for a moment there was silence and then a drunken woman fell into a nearby man's lap and began laughing loudly. I was becoming increasingly uneasy standing amongst these people.

Looking with disgust at the woman the lawyer finally spoke,

'To sort this matter out once and for all, I suggest that you go back to the man and ask him his name! Then I suggest that he comes downstairs to see me.'

'I told you he's sick.' The large man replied and took another swig of ale.

'Why do you think this person is anything to do with me?' Mr Stebbeds asked now becoming even more irritated.

'She said to fetch yer. That is all I know!' Grinning he wiped his fleshy mouth with the back of a blackened hand with raw knuckles.

The youth began to join in now and called out,

'Tell 'em to cough up the tin pa. Don't stand there all day talking about it!'

'Come on my dear let us leave. I am not venturing up the stairs to be robbed by some vagrant skulking in the shadows!' The lawyer urged as I stood routed to the spot not sure why I did not want to leave.

'There ain't nobody going to rob yer mister.' The youth called out. 'All we want is for someone to take charge of this toff before he dies on us!'

'If you require money to call a physician, then I will as a gesture of humanity give you the necessary tin as you call it!' With that Mr Stebbeds felt inside his coat pocket and taking out some coins flung them on the counter.

'Will this be enough?'

'I expect it will.' The large man sneered, 'But what are we supposed to do with him?'

'That is your business!' Mr Stebbeds opened the door and pulled me out onto the street where I noticed a young girl cleaning in the courtyard.

'Perhaps we could ask this girl about Rosie?' I said, not wanting to give up so easily and I ran over to the girl who looked anxiously at me as I began to address her. She looked around as if uncertain whether she should speak or not,

'Do you remember a large blonde woman called Rosie coming to the inn?'

'The one that brung the sick 'un?

'Yes, do you know where she lives?

'No, I ain't never seen her before!'

'She came with a man?'

The girl nodded.

'Did she say anything about who he was?

'No! She said he needed a room and then told Trader to fetch old Stebbings.'

'How did this Trader know where to find Mr Stebbeds?' I asked

'The lady said it was at Lincoln's Inn and had a sign outside with 'is name on. She couldn't write it down as she didn't know learning?' I thought how often I had tried to teach Rosie to read and she had said it was of no use to her.

'But surely the man she was with must have given his name?'

'No, he looked a bit strange like. As though he didn't know where he was. All she said was old Stebbings will know what to do as he conducts 'is business!'

'Is he a client of my legal firm? Mr Stebbeds looked astounded.

'She said that the man was her friend and that she'd met him at the Station?'

'What station?'

'The one where all them lads is. Coming back from the wars, soldiers and the like.'

'You mean he is a soldier?'

'Yes, 'e was wearing a uniform?'

Mr Stebbeds looked disconcerted, 'The only way to settle this is for me to go to his room. Can you show me where it is young woman?'

The girl smiled, her peaky white face looking happy at being given the task.

'I'll take you round the back way and then yer won't 'ave to go back through the bar.'

A hot flush washed over me and my heart began to race with excitement. Rosie had brought in a soldier, someone that was known to Mr Stebbeds' law firm,

'It's Edmund, I know it is.' I gasped and started to run ahead of the girl to the iron railings that supported the back stairs. The girl looked surprised at my excitement but caught up with me and led the way to the door at the top and taking a key from her sleeve undid the lock. I tried to go in but was restrained by Mr Stebbeds who had breathlessly followed behind.

'Wait a minute my dear, let me go first and see who it is? I don't want you to be disappointed. Who knows what people, Rosie associates with? I doubt very much that it could be Edmund. He wouldn't be wandering around London. If he has returned, arrangements would have been made........' I didn't wait for him to finish as I rushed ahead, calling Edmund's name loudly.

'Please let it be him! Please let it be him!' I said to myself over and over as the girl murmured,

'Well he looks proper poorly, for one of the Queen's men.'

As we arrived at a landing with three doors, one of the rooms opened and the insolent lout, that had led us to the inn, barred our way.

'Out of my way,' Mr Stebbeds said angrily and pushing past the lout.

'Who told yer to bring 'em up 'ere Molly?'

'They wanted to see the soldier!'

'Cost yer!' The lout sneered.

The lawyer looked at him with disgust and threw another handful of coins down on the floor and as the youth bent to pick them up, Molly led us into a side room. It was very dark inside and as our eyes adjusted to the light we became aware of a figure lying on a bed. As I approached him, heart pounding I heard Molly say,

'I think 'e 'as a fever. I've been giving 'im some water but 'e don't know what 'e is doing.'

Looking down at the prone body I cried out with joy. It was Edmund. Not the Edmund I remembered but a shadow of him lying on a stained mattress. Restlessly tossing and turning, mumbling in delirium. Across his forehead was the livid red scar, just as I had seen it in my dream. His chest was bare and around his shoulder was a dirty bandage, which was congested with dried matter and festering into the wound.

'Good God!' Mr Stebbeds exclaimed as he reached my side, and turning back to the landing urgently shouted at Trader who was now lolling against the wall, tossing the coins in his hand.

'Send for a physician immediately.'

Back came the typical response as he grinned wolfishly,

''ow much yer going to pay?'

'Enough of that. You have had money and I suggest you fetch someone immediately or it will be the worse for you.' The old man puffed out his chest and clenched his fist as if ready to strike the lad who towered over him. The youth leered and also clenched his fists,

'That was for the quack. I want money fer going.' There seemed to be a stand off as both men glowered, the older man dwarfed by the rude youth. As they glared at each other the lawyer said firmly,

'In that case I will send for a constable and have this place closed down.' The youth started to retort angrily just as his father's large bulk appeared, huffing and puffing up the staircase. As he reached the top he grasped the banister and breathing heavily gasped,

'Do as he says son.'

'But Pa....,' the lad didn't finish as a warning look was flashed from father to son and the lout shrugged and set off down the stairs whistling defiantly. I wrung out a damp cloth that was placed by a bowl on a nearby chair and began to gently place it on Edmund's forehead. He was soaked through with perspiration as he threshed about on the urine soaked mattress, burning with fever. I looked around for his military jacket and found it torn and crumpled under the bed. I called out for someone to bring me a jug of fresh water but no one came. I ran back down the stairs and shouted at the bar tender who had returned to his place at the counter. I shouted so loudly that a hush fell over the customers and even the thin woman with brown hair that had been laughing non stop since we first came, stopped for a moment and was quiet. Molly appeared with a dirty jug and I returned to Edmund's side whilst Mr Stebbeds hovered around me.

The room was damp and musty, so I flung open the window to let some air in the fetid room and as I did so, smoke from a nearby factory drifted in. Tearing a piece of clean linen from my petticoat, I dampened it and placed the cloth between his lips which were dry and cracked with fever. All the time I whispered to him telling him that a doctor would be coming. That we would soon take him home and that I loved him. As I bathed his face, he suddenly opened his eyes, but they were crazed and unseeing and he sat up shouting loudly. Men's names were barked out. Orders shouted! Over and over he relived the experiences that he had in the Crimea. As he threshed around I tried to pacify him until at last he sank back with exhaustion onto the striped flocked mattress and unconsciousness.

I comforted him and as I did so, he became less restless but I felt inadequate to help him. Mr Stebbeds stood by my side in dismay,

'This is not a sight for your eyes, my dear. There is nothing you can do. We must wait for the doctor and then we will arrange for a nurse to tend him.'

'A nurse! I shouted. ' I know how nurses, look after their patients. Like the one poor Annabelle suffered. Shall we give money to some drunken hag to sit by his side and do nothing? No I shall nurse him myself.'

'We must remove him from this place. Once the doctor has attended, I will start to make the necessary arrangements. He must go to Threshingham Park where he will be well looked after. However, I believe at the moment that he is too sick to make the journey.'

Leaving me, tending to Edmund, the elderly man went back downstairs to arrange for clean bedding and wait for the doctor. As he did so I found a wooden stool and sat by Edmund, constantly reassuring him. I sat alone in the filthy room, watching him constantly. How changed he was. He had been so muscular and strong but now he had lost weight. His face was drawn and haggard. His thick blonde hair was unkempt and long and darkened with dried blood.

I gently traced my finger over the livid scar on his burning forehead. I then tried to remove the bloodied bandage around his shoulder, but it was stuck with pus and infected matter. I asked Molly to bring me some warm water and salt and using that I tried to clean the wound and remove the bandage by gentle soaking. However, the wound had healed around the bandage and could not be freed. All this time Edmund was oblivious to my ministrations, mumbling unintelligibly to himself.

As I sat with him I tried to make sense of what had happened. How had Rosie found Edmund? Why was he sick and ill in an inn in Southwark? Where was she now? After what seemed an age the physician arrived and the lawyer escorted him up the staircase. The man took one look at Edmund shook his head despairingly,

'I'm afraid it's serious. We must try and bring down the fever; until the crisis has passed we will not know what the outcome might be. The wound is infected and I can cut away the diseased tissue but I understand he has been abroad. Who knows what has caused the fever. I know there is cholera and dysentery rife out there. All we can do is wait and time will tell.' He opened his large leather bag and took out a stethoscope and listened to Edmund's rasping breathing.

'Well his heart is sound, so that is a good sign.'

'Do you think we could move him?' Mr Stebbeds asked taking out his watch as if pressed for time.

'Good heavens! No! He must rest. It would be dangerous to move him in this condition. I could not be responsible for the outcome. I will leave some physic to bring down the temperature and if the young lady will leave the room, I will deal with the shoulder wound.'

'I am not leaving!'

'Really, my dear, the doctor knows best,' Mr Stebbeds said taking my arm.

'I am staying.'

'Very well!' As he spoke the man took out some scissors and began to cut away at the suppurating bandage. He then felt for a scalpel in his bag and began to slice away at the open gash that was sceptic and stinking. As he did so Edmund moaned with pain and although half conscious tried to raise himself from the bed. The physician gestured to the lawyer to hold him down and I had to force my hand into my mouth and suppress my cries of dismay. As the man cut more deeply Edmund struggled and cried out and then thankfully at last fainted. Finally, the physician poured some powder over the wound which he subsequently lit, the flames sizzling viciously as Edmund gasped in his unconscious state. He then began to bind up the blackened wound and washing his hands in the bowl, said with a serious expression,

'That wound looks very bad.' With that he poured out some liquid into a smaller corrugated glass bottle and squirted some into Edmund's mouth with an eye dropper.

'Give him drops of this in water and if he lasts the night I shall call again tomorrow. It is essential that he is not dehydrated so keep giving him boiled water in little sips.'

'Lasts the night?' I gasped, 'He will live! I know he will!'

Mr Stebbeds, patted my shoulder,

'Of course he will my dear. He is a strong young man, but he has been through so much. Hopefully, the fever will break. Once he passes the crisis, we will know more. The medicine will help. It is essential that he is not moved.'

'How can he stay here, look at this filthy hovel? The wound is already infected. How can he recover in this disgusting room?'

The doctor put the cork back in the medicine bottle,

'We'll get some clean linen, a clean mattress will be obtained and I'll send a nurse.'

'No, I do not want any nurse. I will stay and look after him, day and night.'

'My dear, you can't stay alone in this tavern, a young woman alone. That is impossible; this is not at all a respectable place.'

'I shall stay. How can I leave him to suffer? He has been through enough.'

The physician shrugged and seeing my mind was made up snapped his bag shut and went on his way. Meanwhile I was still arguing with Mr Stebbeds who insisted that I should leave. Realising that I would not, he stomped out of the room to chase up the bed linen. After a short while, Molly appeared on the landing staggering under the weight of a stained mattress that was at least dry. Mr Stebbeds followed with a bag of clean linen and between the three of us we managed to change Edmund's sick bed. With a bucket and cloth Molly set about cleaning the room, scrubbing the surfaces furiously. Her thin little body was working so hard, that I took the scrubbing brush and helped her to finish the task.

At last the room had a semblance of cleanliness and against his will Mr Stebbeds left me to resume my role as nurse. He advised me that he would return to his office and arrange for his clerk to come and stay at the inn to ensure my safety. Edmund was still tossing and turning violently and mumbling incoherently and I tried to make him comfortable, giving him sips of water. It was not a chore for me to have to tend him so patiently; I had spent many hours at my father's bedside. It was something I was well suited for and being so overwhelmed with relief that Edmund had been found, I could have sat there forever.

Some time later there was a knock at the door and Molly reappeared with a dish of food covered in a muslin cloth.

'What is that?' I asked getting up and stretching my legs, which had stiffened from sitting.

'It's your dinner. The old gent paid for it.'

'Thank you, but I am much too worried to eat anything.'

The girl brushed her mousy brown hair out of her eyes and sniffed loudly, and then walking closer to Edmund she looked at him with interest.

'Is he your fancy?'

I did not understand what she meant and replied,

'He is my fiancé,'

'Yes that's right! Your fancy. He's beautiful ain't he?'

'Yes he is!'

The girl looked at me sadly and said quietly,

'What would I give to have such a toff? I bet he looks pretty in his regimentals.'

'He looks very smart.' I replied as I continued to bathe his face.

'Is he going to die?'

I felt my blood run cold at the words,

'No he will not,' I replied firmly, 'I will not let him.'

The girl nodded again and sighing loudly went towards the door but just as she reached it, I called her back.

'Molly, will you help me? I want to know if the lady that brought him here returns to the tavern. I will give you a sovereign if you tell me if you see her.'

The girl's pale face broke out in a broad smile and something about her face looked very familiar to me, but I could not think why. She laughed loudly,

'Lord, I ain't never had a sovereign,' she then looked crestfallen.

'But what if she don't come? I won't get no tin.'

'If by the time we have left this place, she has not reappeared, then I will give you the money in advance so that you can let me know in the future. Do you know Rosie?'

'No, but I seed her come in with the gent. I was serving at the bar and I couldn't take my eyes of 'im cos he was so pretty. We don't normally get no toffs in 'ere.'

'Did he walk in as though he was fit and well?

'Well 'e was walking, but 'e was leaning on her shoulder. She kept saying, "Edmund! Edmund! that's yer name," but 'e didn't take any notice. He just looked as though he didn't know where he was. I thought perhaps he had been on the ale and was drunk.'

I was dismayed. Why would he not know his name. Could Edmund have lost his memory? Was that how he had been found by Rosie?

'Thank you, for your help Molly.'

'That's all right. Shall I fetch yer some more water?'

I asked her to do so and her face broke into a smile again and then her expression changed, a frown wrinkling her forehead.

'This place is full of thieves and vagabonds, they'd cut your throat for tuppence. Make sure you bolt the door if you are staying on your own. If they think you have money, they'll try to steal it. Trader is the worse, they took the toff's jacket and rummaged all through his pockets but he didn't 'ave anything.'

'Thank you Molly, I'll take care. Was that why his jacket was under the bed?'

She nodded, then added,

'Ain't you got pretty 'air miss?'

I smiled to myself as I remembered the trials of managing it, '

'It is a lot of trouble.'

'I think it is wonderful!' She then went on her way singing to herself. Her thin body looking as if it would break in half at the slightest breeze.

I sat quietly for some hours just staring at Edmund's face. Drinking in every aspect of it. Although he was brown from the sun, there were deep lines around his sunken eyes. I wanted to etch every thing about him firmly into my memory so that I would never forget. Sometimes his pale blue eyes would open and look around unseeingly. Then every now and again he would sit up in panic, waving his arms around and shouting. It was with some effort that I managed to calm him. However, it was not long before the clean sheet was also soaked with perspiration.

After some time the light began to fade and there was an overpowering smell of damp wood and stale beer drifting through the floorboards. In the distance I could hear singing and the heavy sound of footsteps. As it began to grow dark, my courage began to fail and I began to be nervous about staying in the tavern, even though I had bolted the door. Suddenly I was startled by an unexpected knock and I called out to see who was there. Relieved I heard the familiar voice of Mr Stebbeds who had returned.

'I am worried about you staying here, my dear.'

'But I must, if Edmund cannot be moved, what else can I do?'

'We could hire someone....'

I interrupted him, 'No they cannot be trusted!'

'Perhaps you are right, but Fothering is coming along. I have sent him off to have some supper and then he will stay here with you.'

'If you feel that would be for the best, then I would appreciate the company, but I am quite all right I assure you. There is a large bolt on the door to that I am quite safe and I have found a friend in the little maid Molly.'

As I spoke we heard the sound of footsteps and she appeared in the doorway with candles,

'Oh, I didn't know you had a visitor, I thought you might like some candles as it will be dark soon.'

'Thank you very much Molly,' I replied, 'Yes I would like some light.'

'I brought this along as well, to help you pass the time, perhaps you can read it to the gentleman' she held out a battered and well-thumbed book to me.

'What is it?' I asked

'I don't know! I can't read. I just like looking at the pictures. I thought you being a lady will know what it says.'

Mr Stebbeds took the book from her small, rough hands that looked chapped and sore, and read the title,

'Why it is Pilgrim's Progress,' he laughed.

'Thank you Molly. I would like very much to read it.'

'Perhaps, if you don't mind, when I've finished me chores, perhaps I could listen to it.'

'Of course Molly, you come back when you are ready, and we will read it together.'

'You won't mind will you guv?'

Mr Stebbeds half smiled at the thin, wasted girl.

'No of course not, I am glad that this young woman has such good company.'

Looking very pleased, Molly disappeared out of the door and the elderly man closed it behind her,

'It looks as if I am worrying for nothing!'

'It was very kind of her to fetch the book. I will need something to help me stay awake as I sit through the night and its words will be a comfort to me.' He nodded and then said,

'Well I must leave but Fothering will be along soon, and I will suggest that he stays outside the door just to ensure your safety.'

I smiled, the thought of the thin stooping figure who was prone to loud sneezing fits, being my guardian, I found somewhat amusing. However, I was reassured to think that there would be someone else for me to rely on.

When I was alone again I thought that Edmund seemed a little less restless but he was still racked with fever and mumbling incoherently. Mollie came along later with some milk and bread and whilst I ate it, she took over my role of sponging down Edmund. Whilst, she worked I made conversation with her trying to find out more about her. She told me that she lived and worked in the tavern. That it was better than her life before, when she had been cold and starving and sleeping on the streets. She didn't remember her mother as she had died when she was young. The owner of the tavern had said she could stay at the inn for free if she worked. Everyday she told me, she would arise at 4 o' clock in the morning and start to clean the counters and tankards and swill out the butler sinks. Then she would prepare the breakfasts for the guests. She would sweep out the yards and the tavern and change the taps on the beer barrels. Sometimes if there were no guests she could have a few hours to herself but she wasn't allowed to go out of the tavern as the owner, Bill Streamer thought she might disappear. He constantly reminded her that she owed him for her living.

'But surely, he owes you wages for all the work!'

'No, he says I am repaying me debt.'

I asked her how old she was but she did not know? I thought she looked about fifteen years. Apparently there had been brothers and sisters but they had all either died or disappeared and she had no idea where they were now. I felt so sorry for her, a young girl worn out with years of slaving and working and not even being paid a wage. She seemed a very kind girl and soon we were sitting reading the John Bunyan whilst we tended the patient.

Suddenly, we were interrupted by the sound of feet on the landing and a raucous shouting of her name. Molly visibly paled and began to shake,

'I must go Miss. He'll kill me and call me a lazy good for nothing. I don't want no beating.' As she was explaining a loud banging started on the door and Trader's voice echoed through it.

'I thought you'd be a skulking in here. Get downstairs. There's chores to do and people to serve.'

I refused to open the door but called through it,

'How dare you shout like that through the door?'

Molly quaked and desperately asked me to open the door which I did. She then ran down the stairs, trying to avoid a glancing blow. Angrily I stood my ground,

'You ought to be ashamed of yourself. That young girl has been working non stop all day. It is now nearly 10 o'clock, surely she should be retiring for the night and resting, I understand she has been up since 4 o'clock in the morning.'

'Go to bed at 10 o'clock. I don't think so, she'll be lucky if she gets to bed before midnight. We can't have her a skulking about. She lives here for nothing as it is.'

'That may be, but you ensure that you get enough work out of her in recompense.'

'Of course we do. Me dad did 'er a favour. We could have left her out in the street to starve. This ain't no alms house.'

'Well in that case, 'I hissed. 'I wish to hire your girl for the duration of my stay. How much will it cost? I think that these coins should cover it.' As I spoke I took some money from my purse and threw it at him. He stooped to pick it up, saying with a sneer,

'If your ladyship wishes,' and his eyes glinted nastily.

'Her ladyship does wish.' I ordered. What is more should I hear after I leave the premises that this young girl has been chastised or beaten, I shall return with an officer of the law. Also I insist that you bring an additional chair.' He shrugged and biting the coins to test their validity, put them in his pocket and jingled them loudly. Molly reappeared on the stairs, her brown eyes staring with alarm at the way that I had spoken to Trader. As the youth passed her he pushed past her and catching her off balance she nearly fell down the stairs. I managed to catch her and prevented her from toppling down.

'Oh miss, what did you mean you want to hire me?'

'I want you to stay and keep me company. You can help me tend my patient.'

'I can't Trader will beat me.'

'No he will not. I have paid him to let you help me. I will not permit him to harm you as a result of it.'

We returned to the room, and just as we were about to bolt the door Trader reappeared carrying a stool,

'We ain't got no other chairs. This stool will 'ave to do for her ladyship.'

He placed the stool on the floor and mockingly said,

'Anything else your ladyship requires? Perhaps some silk and satin cushions or gold plated tea cups!'

I ignored him and gestured to Molly to sit down. Trader went to speak but he obviously thought better of it and left us, jauntily ripping off a piece of the tattered brown wallpaper that was hanging in shreds by the door post. Holding it in the air, he tore it up in a meaningful fashion and then threw the pieces aside and went off still whistling. Molly looked fearful and anxious and I realised what a dreadful life this poor girl lived at the mercy of the uncouth men who ran this tavern.

'Does he threaten you?' I asked when we were alone.

'No, but sometimes he plays tricks on me and 'urts me.'

'In what way?'

He trips me when I am carrying the beers and pushes me over in the yard. Sometimes he kicks me when I am not looking and laughs. Look!' She lifted her tattered dress to show her thin bruised legs.

'What of his father? Doesn't prevent him from doing it?'

'No, he beats me for spilling the beer.'

Just then there was another knock on the door and I heard Fothering calling out that he had arrived, and that Mr Stebbeds said he was to sit outside. Slightly opening the door and peering through I saw him smiling at me.

'Old Steb.... ! Oh beg your pardon, Mr Stebbeds said I was to get you anything you want,' he sniffed. I asked Molly if she would like something to eat and asked Fothering to obtain some supper.

'I ain't never 'ad no supper before, I usually just get bits that's been left from the kitchen.' I didn't answer but resumed bathing Edmund's livid forehead. All the time wondering how this situation I had found myself in would resolve itself.

CHAPTER EIGHTEEN

'Out of this nettle, danger, we pluck this flower, safety'
Henry IV Pt 1 Act 2 Sc 3

I must have fallen asleep for a moment. However, something startled me into wakefulness and with a feeling of panic I looked down desperately at my patient. It was with relief that I saw the rise and fall of his chest, and noted that his breathing was a little easier. I steadied my nerves and saw that the young girl was also asleep, probably too exhausted to stay awake. The scarecrow like figure was slumped on the stool, leaning against the wall, her head drooping on her chest. As Edmund was much quieter, I felt his forehead. Although his hair was wet with perspiration he had cooled and was now clammy and cold. The rasping noise that had been coming from his throat had ceased and he seemed to be sleeping normally.

The sound of my chair moving woke Molly and with a start she looked around the room, as if uncertain where she was. Seeing me standing over Edmund's prone figure she feared the worst.

'He 'asn't gone 'as he?'

'No, Molly, I think the fever has passed. Feel his head, it is quite cool now and he seems to be sleeping.' Molly leaned over and placed her rough hand on his head,

'Lord miss, the fever must have broke, 'e's sleeping like a baby.'

Happily I picked up my cloak and draped it over his body,

'I think we need to keep him warm now as his temperature has receded.' Molly nodded and sat back down on the stool, hugging her bony knees. I listened closely to Edmund's heartbeat, my head pressed against his chest.

I could feel the slow thud of his heart, now beating evenly, not racing as it had been before.

Trying to restrain myself from crying with joy I smiled,

'Oh Molly I think he is going to recover.' I was so happy that I hugged her, at last being able to allow myself to believe that what I most dreaded would not happen. My nerves had been so fragile at the thought that after all the strain of waiting and worrying about him in the Crimea; he would die after all, when at last back to the safety of England.

Molly a little taken aback by my joy said quietly,

'Well 'andsome, will be a donning his regimentals and being a toff again all right.'

'Yes he will Molly, and very handsome he will look.'

The girl's wan face broke into a grin and again something about her reminded me of someone but I could not place who.

'You will make him a lovely bride. What a pair you'll make, you with your lovely red 'air, and him with his pretty face.'

'We'll see!' I nodded and wiped Edmund's face with a clean towel.

'I suppose I had better go, it will be getting light soon and I 'as me work to do!'

'No Molly, I have paid for you to stay with me. If Edmund is sleeping now, then we can do the same. Can you fetch some cushions?'

'Yes, I know where there are some.' She swiftly unbolted the door and as we looked out we found Fothering sound asleep. He was wedged on a beer barrel, his feet pushed against the wall, snoring loudly.

'I had forgotten that Fothering was out there.' I whispered. 'Can you squeeze past without waking him?'

Molly giggled, putting her hand over her mouth to stop the sound,

'I can't see him being much use as a protector,' she smiled and crept out of the room returning a few moments later dwarfed by some large pillows, a bolster, a grey blanket and a large velvet curtain. This time the noise disturbed the sleeping man who leapt up looking sheepish and immediately uttering apologies helped Molly carry in the items. We then bolted the door and he returned to his post. Molly settled down on the floor, placing a bolster under her head. I suggested that she put a cushion under her body to support her but she declined.

'I'm used to it Miss. It beats the pavement on a cold night.' and settling the rough grey blanket around her thin body she was soon fast asleep. I pulled the curtain around me and tried to make myself comfortable, and soon I too was fast asleep.

Suddenly I was awakened by a cool breeze blowing through the cracked open window. Shivering, I anxiously looked down at Edmund and with a start I found our eyes met. His eyes were wide open and staring at me intensely,

'You're here again,' he croaked his voice hoarse and parched and I quickly held some water to his lips.

'What do you mean?' I asked brightly.

He stirred a little and reached out to touch my hands that were holding the glass and he sipped the liquid for a moment. Then as he did so, a flicker of surprise lit up his face and then he shut his eyes tightly for a moment, opening them again a few seconds later.

'Still here!' he said almost in a whisper.

It was most strange and not understanding, I asked him again what he meant.

'You're real this time. Every night you stand by my bed, but when I reach out to touch you, you disappear.'

'Oh, Edmund, you have been so ill, we thought you would die,' I cried urging him to drink again. 'You can touch me now. I won't disappear ever again.'

He didn't reply but his eyes flickered over my face as if trying to imprint it in his mind. Then sighing he tried to raise himself to a sitting position but was too weak and fell back, groaning as he jarred his shoulder.

'Be careful, your shoulder is injured.'

'I know. It's damned painful, sorry!'

I smiled, for a moment there had been a flash of the old Edmund as he croaked,

'What am I doing here with my guardian angel sitting by my bed?' His voice was dry and cracked and I quickly poured him some more water which he drank thirstily.

'Rosie found you at the railway station. I don't know anymore than that!'

'What that little scrap?' He waved a limp arm at Molly who was still asleep.

'No that's Molly. She works here.' Anxiety swept over me. Why had he thought that Molly was Rosie?

'Don't you remember Rosie? Your brother's friend.' Still he looked blank and I did not want to continue, the memory of the brother too upsetting for me. For a moment he looked as if he was mentally struggling to put his thoughts in order. Closing his eyes, he put his hand to his forehead and feeling the livid, scar looked puzzled.

'Have I hurt my head?'

'Yes, you were injured in the Crimea, when you were there with your regiment. You have just returned to England. 'That injury is healed now, but your shoulder had become infected and you have been ill with fever.'

Edmund tried to ease his body into a more comfortable position but could not find a place that did not cause him pain. I tried to help him by placing a cushion behind his head. As I did so, he gazed at me blankly, but did not speak. I felt uncomfortable, there was something strange about him but I told myself it was because he had been so ill. To control my sense of foreboding I bustled about, trying to organise the bedding. Endlessly plumping up the cushions in a business like manner.

'Would you like something to eat? Mr Stebbeds' clerk is outside. He can get something light for you.'

He shook his head,

'Just some more water if you don't mind.'

'Of course,' I reached over for the jug and poured him some more. 'I don't think you should drink too much, the doctor said to just have little sips.'

He drank a little and handed me back the cup,

'It has been very kind of you to stay and help me.'

'I could not leave you.' I smiled 'We are waiting for the physician to call this morning and then we will take you back to Threshingham Park. Mr Stebbeds will make all the arrangements and I am sure you will be permitted to travel now the fever has broken.'

Edmund stared at me as if he did not understand what I was saying. Then I felt a cold shiver run down my spine as he said,

'When are you going to tell me your name?'

'Don't you remember me?' I asked with shock and apprehension waiting for his reply. Edmund smiled a strange secret smile, as if he had been thinking about something and my heart leapt only to be dashed in the same moment,

'You're my guardian angel!'

'My name Edmund! My name?' I urged.

'Do you work here?' He smiled wearily and closed his eyes again leaning back against the pillow. I was devastated after all this time of waiting and hoping Edmund had no idea who I was. To him I was a phantom that had appeared to him in dreams. A ghostly spectre that had somehow become reality.

'Oh Edmund, I am Aphra.' I could not bring myself to admit to him that we were betrothed. Edmund pursed his cracked lips but did not speak. As I sat beside him in despair, Molly stirred and sitting up, rubbed her eyes. Seeing Edmund awake she stood up quickly,

'Thank 'eavens. We've been so worried about yer?'

'Thank you for your concern,' he said weakly without opening his eyes but his fingers idly traced the scar on this forehead.

Wanting to help, Molly rushed off to fetch some broth for him. Meanwhile I sat by the bed and watched him. Suddenly I felt him reach out and take my hand as if reassuring himself that I was still there. Holding it he drifted back to sleep with a faint smile on his face.

Forlornly I sat by his side. I had waited so long for him to return, so that my life would change for the better. Hoping that I would be able to put the nightmare behind me, and that Edmund would still want me for his wife. Even if he no longer wished to marry me I thought he would always care for me and ensure that I did not go without. Now my dreams were shattered. He did not remember me.

Molly returned with the broth and fresh water. Not wishing to wake him, I quietly used some of the water to wash my own face to try and remove some of the dirt that settled from the air. My body felt stiff and cold and although I had slept I was extremely tired. I beckoned to Fothering to come into the room and he greedily ate the broth whilst we waited for the physician to return. When the man finally arrived he was accompanied by the lawyer. He looked at me nervously as if trying to judge from my appearance whether the news was good or bad.

'The fever has broken and he has been awake!' I said quickly.

'Thank goodness for that,' he said. 'I am afraid I feared the worse.

He opened his bag and took out some tinctures and undid the bandage on the shoulder wound and pronounced that it was clean, but it would need bathing regularly. Edmund, now awake, winced as the bandage was removed but did not utter a sound.

The doctor looked at the scar on his forehead and tutting loudly said,

'You are lucky to be alive young man. I really thought when I left yesterday that I would be making your funeral arrangements this morning.'

'Well I'm glad you were mistaken!' Edmund smiled painfully, shifting uncomfortably.

'So am I Major,' Mr Stebbeds chimed in. 'We have been so worried about you. Still we will soon have you home where you belong.' He then asked if we could take the patient to Hampshire by carriage. The physician advised that although Edmund was weak from loss of blood, he would probably be better off made comfortable and transported in the carriage than being at risk of more infection from this dirty room. He then wrote some instructions on a paper and handed them to Mr Stebbeds saying,

'I assume he will see a medical professional at Threshingham Park?

Mr Stebbeds accompanied him downstairs but as he left I whispered,

'He doesn't know who I am!'

'I beg your pardon?'

'He doesn't remember my name. He asked me if I worked here. Oh what am I to do?' I gripped the banister on the landing in my agitation but could not speak loudly for fear Edmund would hear.

'Don't upset yourself, he has been very ill. His memory will come back I am sure, he is still very weak. When he is back at Threshingham Park having good food and being well looked after, slowly his memory will return of that I am sure.'

The doctor nodded in agreement,

'I have examined his head and I am sure there is no injury to the brain. However, such an injury would cause a tremendous shock to his system. His memory is bound to be affected.'

Leaving me in the depths of despair the doctor went on his way and the lawyer and I stood at the bottom of the stairs.

'If he does not remember who I am, then I am as nothing to him?'

'Please do not be despondent, everything will be well. You will see!' The lawyer patted my hand and left to make the arrangements. I watched him go. What would happen to me if Edmund's memory did not return?

When everything had been arranged, Edmund was gently carried down the stairs to be settled in to the carriage. He was unable to stand as he was so weak, and some of the men frequenting the tavern were enrolled to help him inside. Wrapped in a fur coverlet he was soon asleep again and we were on our way to Threshingham Park.

All thoughts of my returning to Motts Clump at the moment I pushed aside. If Edmund needed to be cared for, then I would make it my responsibility, whether he remembered me or not. As far as anyone was concerned I was staying with him as a member of the family. I instructed Mr Stebbeds that on no account were any of the household staff to be made aware of my betrothal to him. Before I left I gave the gold coin that I had promised, to Molly and asked her to send a messenger to Mr Stebbeds if there was any news of Rosie at all. As the loutish son of the bar owner knew where the office was, I advised her to tell him to make the contact if necessary and to inform him that that he would be well paid. I also advised her not to tell anyone of the money I had given her and to use it wisely. As she cheerily waved us off into the distance, I felt sad that the nice young girl had to stay in such a place. I made a vow that if I could do anything to help her in the future then I would endeavour to do so.

Edmund slept for the whole journey, and in only a few hours we arrived at the Threshingham Park estate. As the carriage swept over the rolling countryside, I could not believe the beauty of the Fitzroy house as it appeared in the green vale beneath us. As we drew nearer, I was overwhelmed by the majesty of it. The Palladian building stood back at the end of a swirling driveway butted on either side by landscaped grounds with box trees and a fountain. The main house was built from brick with stone quoins. Thank heavens it was so different from the gloomy design of Stoneleigh. As the carriage came to a halt in front of a semi circular colonnade, above which was a balcony, the door opened and the household lined up before us. One by one they came out to stand on the marbled steps, waiting to greet their master.

The head footman stepped forward to open the carriage door and some of the other servants moved to help Edmund descend weakly from the carriage. He struggled to do so unaided but was unable to. I could see the look of shock and concern on the faces of the servants at the sight of their master. He had left them a strong young man, and returned as weak and helpless as a baby. The lawyer went with him leaving me to be helped from the vehicle as the housekeeper stepped forward to welcome me. As we entered I stood apprehensively in the entrance hall, which was embellished with large-scale decorative schemes and paintings.

As the men of the household, helped Edmund to his room, the housekeeper, a severe looking woman, insisted on showing me where I would be staying and introducing me to my personal maid. As I had nothing with me except for the clothes I was standing up in, I told her that it would not be necessary to have the maid. The woman sniffed in a critical fashion and I immediately felt inadequate, just as I had done when being addressed by Lady Westerham. I explained that we had left London in a hurry and I would have to wait for my luggage to be forwarded on. She made me feel as if I was lying but with a shrug she disappeared out of the door leaving me to my own devices.

Not sure what to do, I left the room and wandered along the corridors where room after room led off though white panelled and gilt edged doorways. Alone and feeling extremely isolated, I wandered through a suite of grand rooms. The high ceilings were ornately decorated with scenes of nymphs and shepherds. Everywhere was light and bright but elaborately decorated with gilded wood and plaster.

As I returned to the entrance hall I saw that Mr Stebbeds was in conversation with one of the senior male servants. He was arranging to return to London and I joined them to ask that arrangements be made for my clothes to be sent on from Motts Clump. The lawyer left and I walked around this cold house where everywhere seemed silent and strange. I was uncertain what my role would now be in this well ordered household. I found a parlour maid busily laying tables in the dining room and enquired where Edmund had been taken. She advised that he had retired to his bedroom and the housekeeper had given orders that he was not to be disturbed. I was unsure what to do? I had seen myself as his nurse but now I had been relegated to the position of house guest.

I resumed my wanderings around the house and found myself in ballroom which was decorated with gold leaf, the walls lined with silk damask. All the décor was so extravagant. It had been such a long time since I had been anywhere so ornate and grand that I stood in awe gazing at the crystal chandelier that was suspended from the coved compartmented ceiling. Meanwhile the sunlight flickered brightly, casting rainbow shadows and prisms on the walls. Just for a moment I could imagine the room filled with friends and relatives dancing the night away at a grand ball.

As I stood lost in thought, a short, well-built man was busily polishing the furniture and seeing me, asked if he could assist me. I explained that I would be staying and was just trying to make myself familiar with the residence. He offered to show me around the building and we walked through a gallery of paintings. Most of them were of military men. There was even one of Roland and Edmund's father who looked nothing like either of his sons except he had Edmund's blue eyes. Amongst them I was taken by an ornate painting of a beautiful woman with very small features and thick blonde hair. Looking closely at the nameplate at the bottom of the painting I read that it was of Lady Caro Fitzroy, Edmund's mother. Now as I looked again I could see that there was a marked resemblance to Edmund. The man was helpful and friendly and I began to relax as we continued on our tour until the severe looking housekeeper found us and insisted that I should return to the drawing room. Feeling chastised, I sat down on a horsehair sofa, feeling lonely and vulnerable whilst she sent in the maid with some tea. I enquired after Edmund and was advised that he was asleep and that I would be sent for when he was able to receive a visit. The family physician had been notified.

I felt useless and unwanted. All I wanted to do was to nurse Edmund to regain his strength but I seemed to be banished to be an onlooker. Every time I walked out of a room a servant would appear at my elbow to see if I required anything. Several of them enquired what had happened to their master, as he seemed so unwell. I could only tell them that he had been ill. The household did not seem to be aware that he had been reported missing in the Crimea.

At last I decided to escape to my bedroom which, like the rest of the house, was ornately decorated in blue and gold with matching embroidered cushions and coverlets. There was a dark blue velvet chaise longue with ornate cabriole legs and a magnificent Robert Adam fireplace that overpowered the room. By my bed a set of silver combs and brushes had been laid out and a bone china pitcher and bowl. I was desperate for the luxury of a bath to wash away the dirt of the tavern. As a maid hovered around as soon as I entered the room I asked whether it could be arranged. Soon I was relaxing in the warm water enjoying its soothing and healing properties and wondering what life was going to be like in this mansion.

When I next emerged from my room I discovered that the physician had called and prescribed rest and recuperation for Edmund. However, I had still not seen him. I took dinner alone in my room and decided that I could not stay away any longer. I made up my mind that I would visit Edmund, even if only for a few moments. I asked to be shown to his room and refused to accept the response that the doctor had prescribed no visitors and rest. I insisted and as I suddenly spied a footman who was about to take in some food on a tray. I took the tray and uncertain of my welcome, I knocked timidly on the bedroom door and heard Edmund's familiar voice bid me enter. I walked in and was surprised to see him sitting up in bed; his pillows propped behind him. His eyes looked hollow and there were dark shadows beneath them, and it hurt me to see how haunted he looked. The livid scar across his forehead seemed to stand out angrily, but he brightened on seeing me enter and his voice still dry and cracked said sweetly,

'Why it's my guardian angel. I thought I had dreamed you again.'

He laughed as he used to do and white teeth flashed in the weather beaten face, the skin drawn tightly against his cheekbones.

'I've brought you something to eat.'

'I hope it's not invalid's food.'

'I expect you would think so, but you need to eat very lightly until you are quite well again. I understand that you have seen the doctor.'

'Well a rather pompous chap came and said I needed to rest, which I thought rather strange as I have been asleep for hours. Perhaps you could enlighten me as to where I am staying.' A look of shock must have passed over my face. It had not occurred to me that Edmund would not be able to recognise his family home. Noticing my expression he frowned as if realising that he had said something wrong.

'It is your family home Edmund!' He looked puzzled and I could see he was trying to make sense of it and then he sighed loudly,

'It is no good, I can't remember! I do not recognise anything here. I remember being in a hospital where day and night the noise was driving me insane. I remember the calm voice of a strange woman called Mary clanking around with jars and pastes. Sometimes I think I remember being on a ship and then I was with a lot of people and there was a fat woman but everything else is a blur. If I try sometimes there is a flash of a face or a place. Then I try to think who or where it is and it disappears. It has all jumbled into a great puzzle except for you.' He smiled at me but it wasn't my Edmund's smile but that of a patient grateful to a nurse who has been kind to him. He nodded at me and his hollow eyes crinkled, 'My guardian angel, you were always there standing in the shadows. I thought you weren't real because when I reached out you always disappeared. I thought you were a figment of my imagination.' He laughed a soft laugh and added, 'But you were real all the time.'

'Yes Edmund! I am real. Perhaps given time and rest you will be able to remember things.' I said, trying to reassure him but he seemed locked in his own train of thought as he continued,

'I know you are familiar to me, but I don't remember who you are.'

'I am your sister-in-law. My sister Freya was married to your brother.'

'We're related?' he responded, looking askance at me, the livid scar furrowing in astonishment.

'Only by marriage. They are both dead now.'

'I see!' He sipped at a bowl of soup quietly and I watched every expression on his face as he struggled to make sense of it all. This man who had been so confident and assured was now a blank page. All his past a mystery to him, having to rely on people for any information that he could glean. I watched quietly as he pushed the bowl away unable to finish it.

'I'll leave you to rest.'

He sat up trying to raise himself out of the bed,

'No! Don't go, sit with me a while longer, I have rested enough for eternity.'

'Shall I read to you?'

'Yes, but first talk to me. Tell me about everything, I want to know more about you. Perhaps if you tell me things about myself and my family, gradually my memory will return. I certainly do not recognise this house and to realise that it is my family home and to have no recollection of it, is appalling to me.

'Are you sure that it will not tire you?'

'No, I want you to stay.' He picked up my hand and turned it over and looked at the palm but then held on to it like a child does for comfort. I left it there and sat by him and told him about Freya and my father and Roland and Stoneleigh, but revealed nothing of the recent events. Then I mentioned Annabelle and he seemed to suddenly brighten.

'Did she have red hair like yours?'

'Yes,' I replied. 'Why do you remember her?'

'Sometimes I remember seeing a girl in my dreams. She was always with a boy who was younger. They both had red hair. When I saw them they were always standing on a rock looking down at me and beckoning to someone to join them. I couldn't see who it was but they were often there.'

I shuddered as if someone had walked over my grave as I replied softly,

'I saw them too, in my dreams,'

He nodded as if it was the most natural thing in the world for us both to have experienced the same dream.

'Did you see who she was calling?' I asked

'No, or if I did I don't remember. I only know that I was suddenly lifted up and I felt someone hold my hand and I knew at that moment that I would survive.'

'Yes I saw it in my dream! I knew that you were alive. No matter how many times people said that you must have been killed, I knew that you had not.'

'There you are. I knew you were my guardian angel.' As he spoke his voice faded away and I realised that he had drifted off to sleep. I sat with him for a while until the maid came to advise that the she had made the bed ready for my rest and I was returned to my bedroom.

Unable to sleep I tossed and turned and wondered what I should do. Should I stay at Threshingham Park? Would it make more sense to return to Motts Clump? It seemed that Edmund did not need a nurse and I felt strange in this household. Thankfully, it looked as if his body was on the way to recovery, as for his memory only time would tell. When morning light came I decided that I would tell Edmund that I would return to Motts Clump as soon as possible. If he had no memory that we were to be married, then our betrothal was at end. I loved him so much. More than ever now that I saw how frail and weak he was but I was a realist. How could I hold Edmund to a promise that he did not remember? Yet, a little part of me felt a ray of hope. Perhaps if Edmund had no memory of what had passed, he would grow to love me? He would have no knowledge of the dreadful event at Stoneleigh and my secret would be safe. There would be no sense of pity as perhaps he would learn to love me for myself.

With that hope I lay in bed restlessly fingering the exquisite ring he had given me. He told me it had been his mother's ring and I knew that it must be returned but I wondered how I could return it without acknowledging that our relationship had been anything other than friendship. I decided to seek a suitable place where valuables might be safe and hide the ring away. However, I would reveal nothing of this to him.

The next time I was permitted to visit the patient I spoke about returning to my cottage but he became anxious and began to show signs of the fever again. The doctor was called and I was told in no uncertain terms that the Major wished me to remain and he was not to be upset by any change in my arrangements. As it was obvious that the thought had made him ill I remained. As it was with the rest and medication he did seem a little better each day and soon insisted on coming downstairs to sit in the drawing room and demanded that I join him. However, once there he would sit passively looking out of the window, unaware of everything around him. The doctor visited often and soon the news of his return began to circulate amongst his friends on the neighbourhood and friends began calling with invitations. However, Edmund could not be persuaded to see them, as he could not remember them.

Many hours would pass with me sitting by his side and reading to him.

When he felt stronger he would sit at his desk in the study and peruse all the papers as if trying to force his memory to return. Mr Stebbeds would send business papers for signing and as Edmund had no choice but to trust him, he merely signed as requested. Day after day he would sit and disconsolately shuffle papers, but always insisted that I sat in the study with him. If I did not he became nervous and anxious. I loved to sit with him but it made me sad to see him so ill at ease. He had put on weight and the scar on his head was not quite so livid, so he was beginning to look like his old self but he was not the same person. I remembered how kind and sensitive he had always been. How that bright smile used to light up his face. Now he hardly smiled at all.

My luggage had arrived from Motts Clump and Mr Stebbeds had sent someone to check on the situation there. They reported back that everything was fine and that Violet and her mother were looking after the cottage until I returned. As Edmund would not let me leave it seemed my school was once again postponed. He suggested that as the cottage was rented, I cancel my tenancy. I insisted that I did not want to do that because Motts Clump gave me a sense of security and a feeling of independence. I did not know what the future held as each day I became more worried about him.

In the evening Edmund and I would play cards to pass the time. I tried to teach him some games but he could not remember how to play and it was difficult for him to concentrate. Sometimes when he was feeling very low, we would walk along the gallery and he would look at the generations of Fitzroys on the walls but they meant nothing to him. Even the painting of his mother brought no response. Sometimes he would ask me to play the piano for him. I was unsure at first but I did so and he would sit and stare into space as if the music took him into some dark recesses of his mind but he never spoke of it. Then I began to become aware that after I had played for some time, he would suddenly become excited about some image that had flashed into his memory. It would always be scenes and pictures but none of it made any sense to him. Only occasionally did I recognise the description as something familiar

As he became stronger he started to become impatient to go outside so on fine days we would walk together around the estate in silence. Edmund deeply lost in thought. As I had never visited Threshingham Park before, each corner we turned was a revelation to us both. The gardens were landscaped, with a walled Tudor garden full of roses in bloom. There was also a large pond full of water lillies. Sometimes when the weather was chill, the fish would hide at the bottom, so we spent many hours peering into the murky water, to try and spy a fish. Sometimes, Edmund would pale visibly and clutch his head as if in pain and we would have to sit and wait for the moment to pass. On these occasions, I knew that he was seeing images of the past in his head.

After a while I realised that the scenes that occurred the most frequently, always involved Stoneleigh and Roland or Annabelle. I would find him staring at the picture of his mother as if trying to will himself to remember her but he could not. Some nights I would hear voices on the landing and I knew that it was Edmund walking around, pacing the floor unable to sleep because of the dreams and recurrent flashes of unremembered scenes. The servants would always lead him back to bed in his confused state. I no longer had the ring as I had found a tortoiseshell box in a dresser with thick red velvet padding inside. It had obviously been used as a jewellery box because there were some paste pieces inside and I lovingly laid my ring in it and hid the box in a place of safety.

CHAPTER NINETEEN

'Excellent wretch!! Perdition catch my soul but I do love!
And when I love thee not, chaos is come again.'

Othello Act 3

One morning I was awoken by my maid, whom informed me that Edmund was waiting for me in the drawing room. I was surprised that he had arisen so early, as lately he seemed to take longer and longer before appearing. In fact quite often I breakfasted alone and he would not appear until nearly lunchtime. I quickly washed and dressed and hurried to the drawing room, to be greeted by his tall figure pacing angrily around the room, clutching a piece of paper. Hearing me enter he swung round and glared at me with such a violent expression, that I was quite taken aback.

'Why Edmund what on earth is the matter?'

He waved the paper at me, and thrust it into my face making me draw back with surprise.

'What does this mean?' He shouted as he angrily strode around the room again, rubbing his forehead furiously, as if trying to rub the purple scar away.

'I am sure I do not know. Is it a letter?' I felt sick, my mind was in turmoil. Had somebody known of my secret and now it was all to be revealed. I sank into a chair, and gripped the rail, my hands clammy with perspiration as I tried to control the quiver in my voice.

'It is an invitation to a wedding!' He snapped, thumping his fist on the table as he threw the paper aside. This was not at all what I had imagined and overwhelmed with relief, I stared at him in astonishment.

'But why would that make you angry?'

'Look at it!' He demanded and not comprehending, I bent down and picked up the crumpled item. Flattening it out, I read the words and my relief turned to dismay as the names of the friends that I had left behind me appeared on the card.

> 'Lady Westerham invites Major Edmund Fitzroy to the wedding of her daughter Leticia to Mr Garrick Henby-Smythe to take place on 2nd August at 2.30 p.m. St Martins in the Fields London.'

Shrugging I handed back the paper. So, Leticia and the young man that she met at the ball were to marry but that was no reason for Edmund to become so disturbed.

'Why does this anger you?' I asked. 'Lady Westerham knows you very well. Of course she would invite you to her daughter's wedding. Are you upset because you can not remember who she is?'

'You know I do not remember who she is.'

Thinking that was the reason for his frustration I began to explain the connection.

'Lady Westerham lives in Holland Park,' I began. You have attended many balls and parties at her social events. It would be surprising if you were not invited.'

Edmund's expression darkened and he sneered,

'Have you been invited?' His face was contorted in fury, and his behaviour seemed bizarre and out of character. I could not understand what was wrong.

'No! I would not expect to be. Leticia and I quarrelled, we are no longer friends.'

'You are a liar!' he raged.

Stunned at his nastiness, I was at a loss for words and went to speak as he signalled to me to be quiet and said vehemently,

'Turn it over!' As I went to do so he took hold of my hand, bending back my fingers as he forced the invitation into it. Shaken, by his tone I freed myself and turned over the gold embossed card and began to shake as I read,

> 'Dear Edmund, we have sent you an invitation as you have been a valued friend to this family. It would be unthinkable for us to exclude you from any of our social occasions. However, we are not

able to include your fiancée Miss Aphra Devereaux. The reasons are well known to her!'

'What do you think of that?' He stormed still pacing the room.

Still uncertain what to do or say I was silent and unable to form the reply until sighing I said,

'I told you we quarrelled. Doesn't the invitation confirm it?'

'Are you deliberately trying to anger me?' As he spoke he ripped the paper from my hand and ripped it into pieces. I could stand it no longer and stood up and began to leave the room but he gripped me by the shoulders and shook me. His eyes maddened with anger and I shouted back,

'Stop it! Stop It! Why are you behaving in this fashion? What have I done?'

'Pick up the pieces. Go on! Read it! Read it out loud.' He raged at me as he stood over me in a threatening fashion. Bravely I pushed him aside.

'No I will not! How dare you address me in this fashion? You are obviously not well. Shall I ring for someone? Perhaps you should take your medicine.'

'I'll read it then shall I?' He scooped up the pieces and laid them on the desk like a puzzle and began barking out the words on the invitation and I still did not understand. The rage was all out of proportion.

'Look again. Look again.' he commanded. 'It says *fiancée* Do you understand now?'

Then realisation dawned. It was the fact that I had been described as his fiancée that had made him so angry. I was at a loss as to why Lady Westerham had referred to me in those terms. The last occasion that I had spoken to her she knew that I had refused Edmund's offer of marriage. He wiped the pieces from the desk with his arm and glared at me in silence.

'What do you want me to say Edmund?' I asked quietly.

He began to pace again like a caged wild animal as he continued,

'I want an answer. I want to know what this means.'

Taking a deep breath I walked over to the window and watched as droplets of rain pattered down on the window panes. Unable to look at him as I said,

'Does it make you so angry to realise that I am your fiancée?' As I said the words there was the crash of glass breaking and I swung round to find he had thrown a water jug across the room.

'Of course I am angry.' He raged, 'All this time you have been staying here as my sister in law and never once told me the truth!'

I bent down to pick up the glass pieces saying,

'Stop it Edmund you are frightening me. ' I whimpered

'I am frightening you, am I?' he sneered. 'That is the fate of liars.'

The words stung me and I quivered tearfully,

'How could I tell you that we were betrothed? Even though you once declared your love for me, you had no recollection of it. You did not remember me at all. How could I add to your frustrations by reminding you of something that you did not feel? We did become engaged to be married before you left with your regiment. However, at the time I insisted that it remained a secret until your return. I did not want you to be held to your promise in case you changed your mind. No one else knew of it, apart from your lawyer. I am unable to understand why Lady Westerham should have written of me in those terms, she knew the situation. As far as she was aware I had refused your offer of marriage.

Edmund snatched the last remaining pieces of broken glass from my hand and gashed his hand as he did so, but seemed unaware of it. He threw the pieces away and trampled on them, grinding them into the carpet. As he did so the blood dripped onto the antimacassar on the back of the chair. Hearing the noise the door opened and a footman appeared only to disappear quickly as Edmund screamed at him to get out.

'So you refused me did you? Why? Why did you think I would change my mind? He glared at me furiously and pushed his face up close to mine, and placing his bloodied hands on either side of my head seemed as though he would crush me into eternity. I wanted to scream but could not do so as I struggled to free myself from his grip. I only managed to snivel,

'I thought that you asked me to marry you out of a sense of duty. That you did not love me.'

My words seemed to stop in his tracks and then his expression softened. For the first time he became aware of the dripping blood, which now stained his shirt and smeared on my face. In only a few seconds he was quiet and the storm having passed he took the cloth from the back of the chair and wrapped it round his hand. Shaken I began to rub the blood from my face with my hand and we both turned away from each other. Then in a quiet voice he said,

'What duty may I ask?'

Surprised at the sudden change of tone, I looked at him and realised that the face that had been so dark with rage, now looked ashen and grey. I felt such sadness but I was in a quandary. What could I say? I felt my face start to burn and knew that I could not reveal to him all that had passed between us. The rain outside seemed to permeate the room and it seemed to me that the dampness hung like a dark, wet curtain. I could see him despondently waiting for an answer and could not leave him nor tell him everything.

'Because I was a woman alone. You felt a sense of duty to a family member.'

'Poppycock!' he exploded. Fearing another outburst I felt waves of anger well up. I was tired of suppressing every thought and emotion for fear of saying or doing the wrong thing. Wearily I said,

'There is no need to be upset at the prospect of being united with me. As I have I told you, when you had no memory of me your promise was at an end. What was the point of telling you of it? It meant nothing to you.'

He leaned back against the chair, his shoulders sagging as if he had the weight of the world on them. The bloodied hand began tracing the scar on his forehead again and closed his eyes.

'Do not talk such nonsense. It is you that has stayed here because of a sense of duty.' I did not know how to reply but just at that moment the sun began to peep out from behind the clouds and it seemed to lift the gloomy atmosphere in the room. I heard him say,

'Was there a ring?'

'You gave me the family ring and I have returned it to its rightful place, here at Threshingham.'

He slumped further into the chair and seemed to have diminished in size as he asked,

'Please sit here next to me,' he gestured to the sofa. I hovered uncertainly wondering whether it would be better to leave. Seeing my indecision he said,

'I am sorry, I would not hurt you for the world but don't you realise that is why I am so angry. I do love you! I have loved you since the time you were my guardian angel during those dark days in the Crimea.' He did not look at me but seemed lost in his own thoughts as he continued almost talking to himself.

'Every night I would lay listening to the sounds of the dead and dying and you would come to me. I would wake and see you standing at the foot of my straw palliasse, your feet bare. Your long red hair would be flowing around you in a haze and you were wearing a white linen gown.'

I was astounded by his revelation. Just as I had seen his misery in my dreams he had been aware of me in his. Confused, I did not reply. I was so shaken at his earlier outburst that I could not respond to his declaration of love for me. However, as the sun continued to light up the room I had a strong feeling of hope. That perhaps everything would be all right after all. I took the bloodied hand and tried to hold a compress to it as he carried on speaking.

'I thought you were a phantom. Something I had conjured up from a past that I could not remember. However, when I was ill at the tavern and awoke to see you sitting there, you can't believe the joy I felt when I realised that my vision was a reality. I have always loved you but had no idea that we were once engaged to be married. Then I receive this invitation and find out that you had not told me that we were engaged. That you stayed here only to nurse a shadow of a man out of a sense of duty.'

I could stand it no longer; the words began to tumble out.

'Edmund, I stayed because I love you. However, until you remember all that has happened, my feelings had to stay locked away. You can not imagine what it has been like to love someone so much and yet be unable to express it because they can not remember the past.'

He smiled that old familiar smile and it broke my heart.

'Oh Edmund! I want nothing more than to be your wife, but until you remember everything, I cannot. You love a phantom that comforted you when you were ill. Not me, the real person. I could not bear for you to love the woman you thought I was only to realise that it was a mistake. The woman you left in England is not the woman you see before you now.'

'I am sure that is true. After all I am not the same man.' He laughed and there was no sign of the anger that we had just experienced. There was lightheartedness about him as if he was the same Edmund that I had always known. However, I did not respond and he stood up and kicked a footstool petulantly. In a moment I remembered the way he had kicked the balustrade when Leticia had interrupted us at the ball and it made me smile. Edmund looked out of the window for a while as I waited and then turning he said,

'So what do we do? Consider our betrothal at an end until my memory returns?'

I had no answer only to mutter something about fetching a dressing for his hand. As I reached the door I knew I could not leave without saying something. Turning I said,

'You have a status in society that I do not. It would degrade you to marry me.'

'Oh please!' He said sarcastically. 'What difference would it make? I have enough fortune it appears for both of us. However, it seems that you do not wish to marry me.' I began to become nervous again as his tone was once more becoming nasty.

'You misunderstand me Edmund. You love the person that you have known in the last few weeks. However, that is because I have cared for you. It is not the feeling you had for me before. Of course I want nothing more than to be your wife. It is what I dreamed of when you were away. But it seems unless your memory returns it will never be a reality. I do not want you to marry me out of gratitude or because I am some dream woman from your illness.'

He sank back down again onto the sofa with his head in his hands. I just stood and watched as he began to bang his forehead viciously.

'How can I make myself remember? Every time I shut my eyes, I see people and places, dead and dying. I can't sleep, and I think I am driving myself into madness. If it was not for you, I think that I would have ended it all. My one hope is that you will be my wife and help me to make sense of it all.'

'And what if we marry and then you remember who you are and realise that you do not love me?' He looked up with despair written on his face and my heart went out to him. However, there was nothing I could say or do to help him as he continued,

'Of course I will love you? When I saw you by my bed I knew we had loved before, it was an instant recognition. If you had told me that you were some stranger passing by, or a hired nurse I would not have believed you. I knew that you were a part of me, past or future. However, you were so formal and correct that I could not understand why I had these feelings. Don't you see it has confused the situation even more? Try as I would to remember our relationship, your formality made me think that I was mistaken. Then I discover that we are betrothed and you had said not a word on the subject. That is why I am angry.'

'I have explained why. Because of the agreement when you left for the Crimea. You did not remember therefore, it was best to let it lie. I loved you and wanted to help you. The rest was of no importance.'

'Of course it is important. I know there is more. I keep trying to remember. I keep seeing a room and a piano, and you are playing. Someone comes in and the playing stops, but I can't see who the person is. I know it is vital to remember and it has some importance but I can't do so.'

I felt the hairs on my neck begin to prickle at his words as I tried to subdue the shudder that flooded through me. Despite myself I answered.

'I used to play the piano at Stoneleigh.'

He nodded and then standing up shrugged and said with despair,

'So where does that leave us?'

'I think we should wait. However, I can promise that I will never love anyone as I love you and I will never marry anyone should I not marry you.' I smiled a smile that I did not feel as he searched my face for a commitment.

'Are we betrothed?' He asked desperately.

'In my heart.'

'What of this invitation, I have no wish to be seen in society with people that I have no memory of.'

Walking back to him I took his gashed hand and kissed it.

'Then refuse on the grounds of ill health. No one will be slighted. News of your return has spread far and wide and people know that you are still recovering from your injuries and illness.'

He nodded,

'Perhaps you are right.'

'I love you Edmund. Always remember that.' I turned to go, my mind exhausted with the situation. I just wanted to leave the room and try to make sense of what had happened.

'I cannot remember anything, that is the trouble,' he said and strode out of the room nearly colliding with the footman who had returned.

I was unsure what to do. He had been so nasty and threatening and then so calm and sad. I no longer knew what to say or do. It was as though I had to always creep about for fear of his moods but this had been the worse and it had frightened me. I could never be sure how he was going to react. I knew for my own sanity I would have to take matters into my own hands and make arrangements to leave. Opening the Davenport desk I took out some paper and pen and ink and hastily wrote a note to Mr Stebbeds informing him that I wished to return to Motts Clump.

It was with relief that I did not see Edmund at all for the rest of the day. However, after a few hours, I became aware that there was activity in the household. On making enquiries I discovered that Edmund was unwell and the doctor had been sent for. When he attended, I hid in the drawing room until I heard the sound of his departure. As I heard his voice in the hallway I came out much to the disapproval of the housekeeper who was accompanying him to the door. The doctor was a small man, with a pinched weasel like face and a nervous air. When I called to him he stopped and looked anxiously around as if caught doing something that he should not. Seeing me, he briskly walked over to me and asked after my health.

When I explained about my concerns he reassured me, saying that Edmund was just tired and depressed over his memory loss. That could only be expected as he had been through so much. As his patient was having difficulty sleeping he had prescribed a sleeping draught and insisted that Major Fitzroy would soon feel more like his old self. He added that he had also left some powders for the headaches. Patting my arm in a fatherly fashion he insisted that Edmund only needed rest and hoped that I wasn't worrying unnecessarily, as I looked a little pale.

'How long will it be before his memory returns?' I asked.

'That I can't answer, he replied in a patronising manner. 'It may come back slowly, but some people who have an injury to the head, never regain their memory.'

'Is there nothing that anyone can do?'

'No, but time is a great healer!'

He then bid me goodbye and continued on his way leaving me more unsettled than ever. Disdainfully told by the housekeeper that the master was resting, I did not see anything of Edmund that day and deeply depressed I retired to bed early.

I began to sleep for a while but was awakened in the dark by voices outside my door. For a moment I was filled with dread and thought that I was back in Stoneleigh. Slowly I remembered where I was and as the voices became louder, I recognised that it was the footman speaking. Pulling a shawl around my shoulders, I padded barefooted to the door.

Surreptitiously opening it, I peered out and could see that the door to Edmund's room was open. Everywhere inside was a mess and the housekeeper, clad in her nightclothes was busily trying to disentangle the bedclothes. Meanwhile the footman had lit a candle and was mopping the floor. Seeing me standing in the doorway, the footman tapped the housekeeper on the shoulder, to signify that they were observed and she quickly turned round.

'It is alright madam. Go back to bed. The master had a nightmare and knocked over his water jug and his medication. He has gone downstairs now as he cannot sleep. We are just changing his bed linen and cleaning up the mess.'

A strange aroma hung in the air that seemed familiar to me.

'What is that smell?' I asked.

The woman yawned noisily.

'It is the medicine that the doctor left. The master was supposed to take it with water to help him sleep. I suppose he knocked over the jug when he was trying to pour it out.'

In an instance, I recognised the smell. It was the pungent odour of chloral. That awful liquid that Roland had drowned himself in. The smell that had permeated the whole house at Stoneleigh, seeping into every room. It had caused the downfall of one Fitzroy. Was it about to do the same for another? I immediately felt nauseous at the recollection and all its associations. I swayed for a moment and the footman quickly steadied me,

'The master is all right, now Madam, do not concern yourself. He says that he will stay downstairs and read for a while. Go back to your room and rest.' They gathered the bucket and mop together and went off down the stairs leaving me standing forlornly in my doorway shivering in the cold and feeling an overwhelming sadness.

I wondered what had provoked Edmund's nightmare, and thought that possibly it had been the smell of the medication? Had this brought pictures of Stoneleigh into his head? I shuddered dramatically at the memory. Could he have relived that dreadful night at Stoneleigh in his dreams? I silently prayed that it was not the case.

Too awake and unsettled to sleep I decided to go downstairs and check that Edmund was not unwell. All was quiet as I made my way down the staircase. Although the door to Edmund's room was now closed, the smell of chloral still hung in the air. Braving the chill as my feet turned to ice on the highly polished floor, I wandered along the marbled corridors. Everywhere was still and dark, as I felt my way along the gold leafed recesses, the shape of the embossed decoration pressing into my numb fingers.

I was uncertain where Edmund would be. The footman had said that the master wanted to sit up and read so I headed for the library, but he wasn't there. Then a premonition swept over me and I knew that I would find him in the music room. Gently I tried the brass doorknob and opening the door looked into the room. The moon was shining brightly through the leadlight windows, casting an eerie glow around. At first all I could see was the piano and the moon reflecting off its shining lacquered surface. I was just about to shut the door, thinking that Edmund was not there, when I saw him. He was sprawled out asleep on a grey heavy velvet sofa. A book he had been reading had dropped down and was lying open on the floor. His arm was draped over the side as if he had fallen asleep whilst reaching for the book and his body was hanging half on and half off the sofa. The sleeping draught must have taken sudden effect. He looked uncomfortable as his head was dangling awkwardly downwards. As the candle on the side table had melted down and had burnt out, the moon was the only source of light, casting shadows around the dark room.

He had obviously dressed quickly in the night as he was bare chested, and only clad in breeches, his braces dangling down by his head. The picture that he made in the moonlight quite took my breath away. He looked like a fallen angel, the moonlight reflecting on his thatch of blonde hair. Wanting to reassure myself that he was breathing, I silently padded across the deep pile of the woven carpet. As I reached his side, I tripped on a wooden claw foot of a chair and stubbed my toe. I inadvertently cried out and the noise caused Edmund to stir. Opening his eyes he stared straight into mine as I leaned over him just as he had at the inn. Embarrassed, I turned to leave but he caught me by the wrist and quickly screwed his eyes shut and then opened them again as if testing to see if I was really there.

'I am sorry that I have woken you,' I murmured, 'I was worried I......' Before I could speak any further, Edmund reached up and pulled me towards him and instantly I was in his arms.

'Oh my darling!' He breathed, 'How long I have waited to hold you like this. I just want to touch you and kiss you and know that you will not fade like an apparition.' Swept away, by a tide of emotion, my heart beat furiously as he kissed my face and hair and held me to him. He slipped my nightgown down from my shoulders, and buried his face in my naked breasts, as his breathing quickened. The closeness of him was overpowering, the masculinity of him frightened me and despite myself I started to tremble and I struggled furiously. Pictures of Roland began to flash into my mind and I couldn't breathe, and I began to suffocate with panic.

'It's all right. It's all right!' he whispered reassuringly and then his lips sought out mine and they were so soft and tender as he whispered how much he loved me and I was lost. All I knew was the touch, sense and smell of him and I exulted in it. I just wanted to dissolve into his body that was so desperate for comfort and love. All I was aware of was pure sensation and nothing else but an overwhelming love for him that took over my whole sense of self and I no longer existed but through him. The joining of our bodies being the most natural thing in the world as if we had united and transcended every reality and ceased to exist except in the moment. He whispered his love to me as his body blended with mine and tears of joy

267

rolled down my face whilst he kissed them away in the moonlight. At last exhausted we drifted into sleep, locked in each other's arms with no thought of tomorrow.

As day began to break I was brought back to reality with shock as I realised what I had done. Shivering with the cold I gazed down at Edmund's sleeping figure looking so contented and was overcome with shame and embarrassment. In desperation I pulled my nightclothes about me dreading that the sounds of the household beginning to stir would be confirmed by servants arriving to find us together. Anguished with guilt I just wanted to get away and struggled to free myself from under his sleeping body, wrapping a gold and blue embroidered cover around me. My movements woke him and smiling he lovingly pulled me to him and kissed the top of my head.

'It was real,' he sighed and held me too him and began again to kiss me as I tried to avoid his kisses.

'We must go.' I urged. 'The servants are beginning their duties. I do not wish to be found here we must return to our rooms. Please let me go,' I begged.

'To hell with them! Just stay here with me.' He whispered holding me closer.

'Edmund, please. It will be a scandal. We must not allow the household to discover us here.' I could not bear the thought of being the subject of servant's gossip again. He studied me for a moment and there was a twinkle in his blue eyes as if he relished the thought of causing a scandal but as I implored him he laughed,

'No you are right, as usual. I can always rely on you to be the sensible one.' Then to my surprise he added,

'Do you remember when I first saw you standing on the stairs when I arrived at Stoneleigh?'

'Yes,' I laughed, 'You thought I was...' I tailed off. I could not believe it. Edmund had remembered something from the past.

'Edmund, you remember me then?'

'What?' He looked taken aback as if wondering why I would ask. 'Oh, I don't know, I must do. I don't know why I said it'

'You remember me at Stoneleigh?' I laughed and he put his arm round me and kissed my cheek lightly.

'As I awoke, just for a moment in my mind I saw you. Standing on the stairs in a brown dress looking startled. All I could think was how lovely you were, but how sad you looked.'

Stunned I looked at him in amazement and exclaimed excitedly, 'Your memory is returning that is wonderful.'

'Perhaps!' He looked thoughtful and I was surprised at his reaction. To have his memory return was what he had been desperate to happen. He stood up and pulled his braces back over his shoulders,

'I think we need to discuss this.'

'Of course, but we must get dressed and we can talk later,' I urged.

Edmund nodded but the lightheartedness that had been there a moment ago had disappeared and the serious expression was back. He walked with me to the music room door and carefully opened it checking if any of the servants were outside. As I went to leave he pulled me back and kissed me roughly. It was, almost as if he was frightened that if I left the room, the feelings we had for each other would not be remembered.

'I must go my darling,' I said as I freed myself and ran out of the room. All the while anxiously looking around in case the housekeeper appeared. Luckily the house was still and I arrived back at my room, relieved not to meet anyone on the way. However, I was in turmoil, how could I have been so foolish to have let my emotions run away with me. I did not know what to think or feel. I was exultant over the hours we had spent together and yet I felt as though I had committed a foolish act and I would suffer the repercussions. Surely fate did not have more scandal in store for me.

I just managed to return to my room, when the maid came to help me bathe and dress. Although she knew nothing of what had passed I felt awkward and embarrassed and it was some time later that I felt brave enough to come down for breakfast. I was also nervous about facing Edmund. When I arrived in the breakfast room, I found him pacing the room in an agitated fashion and for a moment my heart was in my mouth. However, as he saw me he stopped and taking my hand said,

'I think I have remembered something.'

'Yes, I know. It was the vision of me standing on the stairs at Stoneleigh.'

'No something else!' It was last night when I came downstairs.'

'You had a nightmare, the housekeeper told me. I replied, 'You spilled the water jug and the medicine.'

'I didn't have a nightmare. I was trying to sleep and I tried to pour out some medicine from the bottle and I dropped it. The smell of that stuff was so overpowering that I couldn't think straight. Then I saw it as clear as anything in my mind.'

I felt a wave of apprehension pass over me as I listened intently. Was my moment of happiness now going to be destroyed forever with Edmund's memory returning.

'It was that scene again.' He began, 'The one I see when you play the piano, and the man who is always there in the shadows. I saw him this time.'

'Who was it?' I said trying to sound calm.

He stood up and began that familiar pacing again,

'The man in the painting. The one in the picture gallery. The dark man that people keep telling me is my half brother Roland.'

I began to toy absent mindedly with my cutlery, uncertain how to react.

'I expect it was the smell of the medicine, they say that perfumes can bring back memories. I smelt it too when you spilled it, it made me remember Stoneleigh. Roland used to take it all the time. The whole house reeked of it. His addiction to it had made him paranoid and agitated.' I looked up but I could see that Edmund was distracted and wasn't listening to me as he continued,

'You were playing the piano. I could hear you. I didn't recognise the piece but it was very light and you sounded very happy. I heard you humming a tune.'

Pretending a calmness that I did not feel I said brightly,

'Yes, I was. You were in your room all yesterday. I passed the time by playing in the music room. I hope I didn't disturb you.'

'No I mean in the vision in my head. You were there playing the piano and Roland was there.'

I swallowed nervously, as I tried to suppress the feeling of panic that was arising in me. Would there now be a revelation? I did not answer but looked at him, biting my lip nervously.

'He hurt you didn't he?' He said quietly, the pacing ceasing. He then looked at me intently.

I stifled a sob by putting my fist into my mouth and in an instant he was by my side, his arm around my shoulders,

'Tell me.'

'I can't. It was too horrible. Roland was mad.'

'What happened?' he insisted, 'Don't you see I have to separate the reality from the scenes I see in my head.'

I knew that the moment that I had been dreading had come. Now I would have to tell him and I was devastated. What would I do if he was disgusted and wanted nothing more to do with me? Tears streaming down my face, struggling to find the words I sobbed.

'He attacked me. I was playing the piano and he came in and dragged me up the stairs. I tried to fight him but he was too strong for me. He forced himself on me in front of Annabelle. You were there. You rescued me, there was a fight and you knocked him down. Rosie, the lady who found you at Central Station, helped me afterwards. That is why I will always be grateful to her. Later you took me to stay with my friends in London.'

'Lady Westerham?'

'Yes!' I said meekly with my head bowed, unable to look him in the eye.

'Does she know?'

'A little, but she was angry and did not believe me.'

'So I didn't imagine it. I saw him, in a small room, there were papers blowing about all over the place and that dreadful smell. He was slumped over the desk, blood pouring from his head.'

'Yes, he shot himself.' I gripped his arm almost hysterically. 'He was a sick man. He didn't know what he was doing.'

'He shot himself? I didn't kill him?' There was such relief in his voice as he sat down as if he could bear it no longer.

'Thank goodness. I thought that I had killed him.'

'No! You didn't kill him.' Distraught as I was there was a feeling of relief that at last I had been able to tell him at least part of what happened.

'And the child?'

Horrified, my heart sank, how could he know about the child?

'The child?' I asked nervously.

'Yes, Annabelle, what happened to her?'

'She died, I told you. You made arrangements for her to stay in a hospital in London as she had a disorder of the mind. When I was better, I went to find her but the hospital that was supposed to be looking after her was a disgrace. I took her to stay with your lawyer and she died there.'

'Why were you not with your friends?'

'Lady Westerham seemed to think that what happened was my fault. That I would cause a scandal. She made me leave.'

'A fine friend. It seems the Fitzroy family have caused you only grief!' He leaned down placing his head in his hands and we both sat in silence.

Then he seemed to come to a decision and looking up he said in a matter of fact tone.

'You should have told me!'

'How could I? I loved you Edmund. I do love you, but I wanted you to be free to choose on your return. When you did return, you had no memory of me. What happened at Stoneleigh would always hang over us. If you found out about Roland after we were married you might have hated me.'

'Hate you. How could I hate you for something that was beyond your control? I love you. I have always loved you. I knew when I saw you at the tavern, sitting there so demurely, with the long red hair tied up in that ugly snood. I realised then that the ghostly apparition who came and offered me comfort in my terrible days, was a reality. I love you so much that I do not think it is possible to love anyone more. No woman has ever been to any man what you are to me. I feel as if I have been taken from the darkest dungeon into the light and you are my sun. Since the day that we returned to Threshingham Park, I have sat with you, dined with you and my heart has been eaten away with love for you and all the time you gave no indication of anything except friendship. Then last night...'

I felt my face burn at the mention of what had passed as he said quietly,

'Put the ring back on and marry me. Whatever has happened cannot be undone, but I want you and need you to be my wife.'

'Oh Edmund, it can not be. There will be scandal. Lady Westerham will have made sure that the world will know that I am a fallen woman...'

'Sssh!' He whispered and taking me in his arms he kissed away my tears.

'We will face the world together, if my memory comes back or not, there is nothing that can hurt us. We are united by adversity. It is a bond that is so strong it cannot be broken.'

'Come, let us go find the ring and return it to its rightful place!'

CHAPTER TWENTY

'The end crowns all, and that old common arbitrator, time,
will one day end it.'   *Troilus and Cressida Act 4 Sc 5*

I took the amethyst and pearl ring from its hiding place and with great
ceremony, Edmund placed it tenderly on my finger. Then kneeling at
my feet he kissed the hem of my dress and said,

'Miss Aphra Devereaux, would you do me the honour of becoming my
wife?'

I was ecstatic. My sorrow was over. I was to be Edmund's wife and all
my doubts and fears were as nothing. Edmund was aware of it all and he still
wanted me. Nothing could ever hurt me again, and I replied quietly

'Yes, I will!'

Edmund excitedly, threw his arms around me and picked me up,
sweeping me from my feet,

'We will announce it in the Times, and we shall throw a party. I have
hidden away too long. I have my strength back now and who knows, perhaps
seeing my old friends will enable my memory to return.'

I was unsure how to react. The exuberant behaviour was out of character
and immediately I was concerned. His maudlin depressed state had suddenly
disappeared and in its place was this manic whirl of activity. This sudden
interest in local society filled me with apprehension. Since his return he
had insisted on complete isolation and he could not even bear the company
of servants. The thought of him hosting a dinner party was unthinkable.
Gently I reminded him that it was too soon.

'Perhaps, it will be better to take it one step at a time?' To my surprise
he laughed and in such a normal tone like the Edmund of old,

'Perhaps you are right, as usual,' and gently kissed my forehead. Then turning on his heel he ran out into the hallway and banged on the dinner gong loudly, to call the entire household together to announce our engagement. The servants came hesitantly out of their various rooms and seemed unsure of what was happening. They had been so used to tiptoeing around in fear of disturbing their master and now there was this sudden call to arms by the very man who insisted on silence. Edmund announced the news and the senior footman grandly responded on behalf of the rest of the servants who stood in a line looking bewildered. I meekly stood to one side as the housekeeper looked at me with astonishment. After a few moments Edmund dismissed them and they all drifted off amid a hubbub of chatter about the strange turn of events.

Then without more ado Edmund rushed off and locked himself away in his study shouting out that he was composing an item for an announcement in the Times. I was left wondering what to do. It was all most strange. It was as if I had been forgotten. There was a niggling doubt in my mind that this happiness could not last. As usual I retired to my room when there was a knock at the door and the housekeeper appeared to inform me that her master wanted me to send out invitations for a small supper party. It was all most odd as I did not understand why he had not asked me himself but sent a servant. I was uncertain whether a party would be a good idea. Since his illness his friends in the area had hardly seen him as he rejected all their overtures and they had become strangers to him. Since his loss of memory he did not even remember who they were. However, doing as I was instructed I dutifully sent out the invitations.

A few days later I mentioned my dream of starting a school but Edmund dismissed my suggestion. He stated almost condescendingly, that a school was not at all the kind of thing that his wife could undertake. I was dismayed at his sneering tone when he dismissed my idea. It was a plan that I had thought about so long, but his ridiculing of it unnerved me. I lost confidence in the idea and thought that perhaps he was right. It had been a plan for a woman alone to make her living. If we were to marry, I would have a status that had not been in my thinking when the plan had formed itself. However, it was becoming more and more difficult to speak to him as he seemed always to be in a flurry of activity now planning the wedding and the supper party had been cancelled.

Any suggestions I contributed were brushed aside. Each day, he would begin making lists and calling out orders to his staff but I did not seem to be included in the arrangements. It was a strange situation in which I was to be a bride but appeared to be totally excluded from the arrangements. When I tried to protest he looked at me with astonishment, but still ignored any input I made.

Things came to a head when he announced that he had to visit his lawyer in London and insisted that I accompany him. It seemed odd that he always referred to Mr Stebbeds as the lawyer and not by his name even though they had been friends for so many years. Now Edmund seemed unwilling to view him as a friend. The Stebbeds had invited me to stay with them for as long as I liked but I had not mentioned it to Edmund. Then out of the blue he announced that we were going to visit them together. I was not sure that I wanted to do that and I tried to persuade Edmund to leave me behind but he would not hear of it. He insisted that I joined him as it would enable me to purchase items for my trousseau. There was a nagging doubt about how long this new outgoing, dominating behaviour would last. More and more I was concerned about the way he was organising things. I was uncertain how he would behave when he arrived at the lawyer's office. However, although worried at Edmund's intensity I was looking forward to seeing my friends again.

A few days later we set off for London, our first stop was to call at the office in Lincoln's Inn. As we arrived I was surprised to be greeted at the door by Cobham. He told me excitedly that he was now working in his father's firm. I was overjoyed to see how he had grown. Whilst Edmund attended to his business affairs, Mr Stebbeds suggested that Cobham and I took the carriage back to Whitefriars to see his wife. As we left the office I became aware of the sinister figure of Trader, lurking by the doorway.

'Is the old man 'ere?' he asked lounging against the wall. As usual the customary smirk was on his face.

Cobham protectively ushered me back inside, calling out that there was someone making a nuisance of themselves and Edmund angrily ran out shouting

'Be off with you!'

I caught his arm to restrain him,

'It is the man from the tavern.' I said.

Sneering Trader commented,

'Molly said yer wanted to know if the doxy came by again. I came to tell the old 'un that she's back. She comes every day. If yer going to be difficult about it, I'll be on my way. I only did it as a favour to Molly.'

Excitedly I gasped,

'Rosie is there! Edmund, I must go and speak to her. If she is at the inn there is so much I want to say. She saved your life. Who knows what might have happened, if she hadn't helped you. We owe her so much.'

To my dismay I saw a blank look of disinterest flicker over his face. The same expression he would wear when I tried to intercede in the wedding arrangements. He didn't speak for a moment and then shrugged.

'If it is so important to you then we will go!'

Turning to the youth, he ordered,

'If this is a trick, it will be the worse for you.'

'It's no trick guv. Come or not, it's up to you.' Trader responded with a sneer. 'I've done my bit. The old tart comes in everyday about this time. She always asks after yer. If we go now she'll still be there, too drunk to move.'

Edmund frowned, telling me to go to Whitefriars in the carriage but I refused and insisted on going to see Rosie. To my surprise he didn't argue but helped me into the vehicle and were soon clattering along the cobblestoned streets. When we arrived at the tavern in Southwark, Edmund leapt from the vehicle and told me to wait inside until his return but I could not. I climbed down and followed behind and immediately inside I saw her. She was slumped over the bar clutching the remains of a glass of green liquid. The liquid had spilled and she was lying face down in it, mumbling to herself incoherently. As I stood in the doorway I became aware of Molly standing across the room. Her small face brightened and she ran through the smoke filled haze to greet me calling out excitedly. Hearing my name Edmund, who had not noticed that I had followed, turned and his face darkened at seeing I had disobeyed him. I did not care as I ran to the large woman calling to her but she was too drunk to react.

Edmund meanwhile strode up to her and prodded her harshly. Startled, she looked up, and tottered unsteadily on the bar stool, her eyes bloodshot and glazed. Then fixing a bright smile on her sad, care worn face she ran her hand up Edmund's sleeve.

'Ain't you an 'ansome one? Got any tin for me tonight, I'll make it worth your while.' He brushed her off with a look of disgust as if swatting an insect. As he did so a look of shock came over her face and she gasped out loud. Through the blur of alcohol there came a realisation of who was standing there. Her smile faded and her lip quivered as she slurred

'Blimey! It's the Major ain't it?'

She looked so pitiful as she pushed her glass away and tried to stand.

As she did so she almost fell as the effects of the drink made her unsteady on her feet. Edmund caught her to prevent her falling, and with disgust said coldly,

'Is this slattern the woman you have been seeking?'

I put my arm around her shoulders, which were now shaking.

'Edmund, how can you be so cruel?' I gasped. 'Surely you can afford her a little kindness? Have you forgotten how she helped you?'

'How can I? You keep reminding me.' He retorted angrily and then twisting my arm roughly, he began to steer me out of the room through the small throng that had gathered to watch the proceedings. Meanwhile, Rosie began talking to herself in a loud incoherent voice and slipped down from the stool, clinging on to the bar counter. The people in the room began laughing and joking at the sight. Their interest infuriated Edmund even more as I struggled against him, unwilling to leave.

Ribald comments were called out and there was much jeering, so much so that the noise brought Rosie back to reality. As I remonstrated with Edmund, she looked up and for the first time saw me. Distressed, she gave a loud cry and began to flail around, trying to push people aside and make her way through the bar, trying to leave. As she did so she inadvertently knocked Molly over and the thin girl sprawled awkwardly in the sawdust and dirt. Looking around wildly, Rosie became crazed like a trapped animal trying to find a way out. Her tangled, greasy hair had become unpinned and was now hanging in clumps around her shoulders. I managed to free myself and run in front of her to block her path.

'Rosie, I am so glad we have found you! Please let us help you.' I shouted trying to prevent her from leaving. Seeing there was no escape, she stopped as if struck and suddenly began to wail loudly,

'Oh my gawd! I fought you was dead. I fought you was dead. Don't 'ate me. Please don't 'ate me.'

Edmund picked up the bar stool which had tipped over in the melee and helped Molly to her feet as I steered Rosie to a nearby seat. She tottered drunkenly, unable to steady herself. Molly awestruck was gazing at Edmund in admiration but came to help me. Seeing the young girl more closely I was shocked to see that she had a large purple bruise on her face that was yellowing. Additionally one of her eyes was half closed and swollen. Seeing me looking at her face, she quickly placed her hand over the bruise, trying to conceal it.

Meanwhile Edmund snarled in my ear,

'We are making a side show here. I suggest that we adjourn to somewhere more fitting, if there are matters to discuss with this creature.'

'I won't go without her.' I said firmly, unhappy that he was so cold and unyielding. Rosie fell down and as she struggled up again a fat drunken man called out,

'Cheer up Luv. Give 'er a tot of muvver's ruin, that will get 'er going.' He then thumped Rosie so hard on her back that she fell down again. I could hear Edmund ordering me to leave but I ignored him. As I tried to talk to Rosie a thin woman wearing a black hat with a large feather, shouted to a man covered in coal dust,

'Comes to something when yer can't 'ave a quiet drink without some toff coming in and causing a scene!'

Another woman leaned over and shouted much to the amusement of the others,

"E might be a toff but my ain't 'e an 'ansome one. Is 'e yours dear?'

I tried to ignore the comments but Edmund was outraged and he again tried to drag me away.

'What on earth are you thinking of?' he hissed at me. 'We are leaving. Leave this woman in the cess pit where she belongs. I command you to come with me this insistent and leave this place.'

'No, I will not!' I cried standing my ground. 'I must help her. How dare you command me? I am not one of your servants.' My voice rising in hysteria.

'That's right luv you tell 'im!' a rat faced youth called out, to more hilarity from the crowd.

Edmund pushed aside some of the gawping men and said in a cold tone that chilled me to the bone but I refused to acquiesce.

'Madam, you forget yourself. I insist that you leave immediately or suffer the consequences.' and he strode out of the pub closely trailed by Molly who was still gazing at him in awe. I was in a quandary, I could not stay but I would not leave now that I had found her.

Rosie began to sob,

'You'll 'ate me. You don't know what I've done.'

'It doesn't matter. Where do you live? We will take you home.' I breathed propping her up and trying to walk out with her leaning heavily on me.

'I ain't staying nowhere. I ain't got no 'ome. I ain't got no money!'

'But what happened to the money you had?'

A look of pain crossed her face. She knew I was referring to the money she stole from Motts Clump. Suddenly, she freed herself from my support and seemed to become conscious of how bedraggled she looked. Standing apart she tried to assume some dignity by pinning her hair. Securing it she rebuttoned the front of her dress to hide the grubby white linen under clothing. Molly, who had watched Edmund leave, came back to say that he was waiting impatiently by the carriage, angrily walking up and down. I knew those signs only too well.

I whispered to Rosie quietly and tried to usher her out.

'Come with me. You can't stay here.'

'I don't deserve it Miss! Not after what I've done. Even the Major can't stand the sight of me. Look how 'e despises me. Yet I never done him no 'arm. We was friends.'

A ripple of laughter went round the room

'Is that what they call it?' A voice shouted from a dark corner, just as Edmund reappeared in the doorway, the comment infuriating him even more. He strode over and gripping Rosie by the arm forced her out of the tavern. As he did so he glared at me saying,

'I may have lost my memory but I have not lost my self respect.'

He threw a few coins into the sticky mess on the bar counter and shouted to the bartender who was looking on with interest.

'I am sure that will more than recompense you.'

Rosie had stopped resisting and now walked forlornly outside, as I said quietly.

'Edmund, please show Rosie a little kindness. You owe her your life. Perhaps we can ask the driver if he knows a place that we can take her.'

He looked at me with such animosity that I braced myself as I thought he was going to strike me. However, the moment passed and his eyes narrowed as he said

'As you wish! For God's sake let us get out of this hell hole.'

He manhandled Rosie into the vehicle as she began resisting again. I looked back and noticed Trader smirking in the doorway and holding onto Molly.

'What happened to your face Molly?' I asked. She looked at Trader as if frightened and answered with a sullen,

'I fell down!'

As both Edmund and Rosie were in the carriage and I was still on the wet pavement I walked over to the grinning youth and said,

'You ought to be ashamed of yourself, treating this poor defenceless girl in such a fashion.'

'She told yer. It was an accident.'

'You know it was no accident.' Then turning to the girl I said, 'Molly get in the carriage. You are coming with me.' Molly's saucer eyes widened and again she reminded me of someone that I could not place. Then timidly looked at Trader who was still holding her by the arm. She went to walk away but he raised his other arm to her.

'Don't you dare touch her or I shall call a constable!' I shouted.

'I don't think so,' he smirked, pulling himself up to his full height as if trying to dominate me.

'She owes us board and lodging. Me dad did 'er a favour taking her in when she had no where to go.'

'You did yourself a favour misusing a starving girl and treating her worse than a dog.' Angrily I opened my beaded purse and found two gold sovereigns and threw them at him. He flinched as they hit him in the face and bounced into the dirt. He cursed me and then bounded across the pavement to retrieve them. Trying to wipe of the filth before biting into each coin to test the gold.

'I am sure that more than covers any food and lodgings this girl owes.' I snapped.

'Who do you thing you are Miss Hoity Toity?' he shouted and advanced towards me threateningly, Molly screamed and tried to flee. As he came towards me I steeled myself for a blow but I was pushed aside and to my surprise Edmund leapt from the carriage and knocked him down. Trader crumpled into a heap in the gutter amongst the ordure. The throng of people now poured out of the tavern and began jeering at him as he sprawled on the floor. At the sound he sat up and began looking around, blinking foolishly, as I helped Molly to climb into the carriage and she shrank into a corner. As soon as we were seated Edmund said grimly,

'I see we have acquired a waif and stray.'

'I couldn't leave her there Edmund. Don't you remember she was helping you when you were so ill in that place?'

'Nonsense! What would I be doing being ill in that place. All I see is that we have made a ridiculous show of ourselves for such as that bag of rags.' He gestured to Rosie who had fallen into a drunken sleep in the opposite corner and was snoring loudly. Her mouth hanging open to reveal discoloured teeth. My heart sank. What was I thinking of? Rosie was a lost cause and would never change and yet I could not abandon her.

'Please do not judge her too harshly?'

'How can I agree to my future wife being in the company of a woman of that kind?'

'Edmund, you don't remember but she has been a good friend to your family. Whatever has happened, it is not her fault.'

I could see by his expression that I was wasting my time, but he did not reply as we continued on our journey to Whitefriars. However, after a few moments I noticed that he was looking at Rosie intently, as if trying to dredge up memories. Meanwhile, she slumped in a deep sleep, unaware of anything around her. Molly sat quietly by her side, occasionally dabbing at the string of spittle that seeped from Rosie's open mouth as she dribbled in her sleep. With a look of disgust, Edmund moodily began to stare out of the window and I smiled reassuringly at Molly, who sat forlornly, looking anxiously around.

After a while I became aware that we were heading in the wrong direction for Whitefriars. I asked Edmund where we were going and he replied that whilst I had been making an exhibition of myself he had found out from the driver that there was place called Sisters of Charity. This was a home for gentlewomen and we were taking Rosie there. He added that he had no idea if they would accept her as she certainly did not look like a gentlewoman. I gazed across at her. She looked older than I remembered and her once blonde hair was even greyer. The torn grubby dress she was wearing was still the pink one she had been so proud of at Stoneleigh but now the pink had faded into a dirty beige.

As I sat lost in thought, the atmosphere suddenly changed and Edmund's expression softened. He took my gloved hand and held it tenderly and whispered,

'I am sorry if I have seemed unhelpful.'

'I am sorry that we caused such a sensation. However, you have no memory of how ill you were when Rosie found you.'

'I am sure you are right,' he nodded, but I could see that he was not comfortable with the thought. Suddenly, the carriage jolted to a halt and Edmund opened the door and almost vaulted out of it, and indicated to me to climb down. The sound of the driver's voice awoke Rosie who looked around uncomprehendingly. She rubbed her eyes with a grubby hand and then seeing me began to sob loudly, the same words as before.

'I am sorry Miss! I am sorry! I thought you was dead.'

'Come along, Rosie. We have found you somewhere to stay.' I said trying to help her out, but she was still unsteady and was heavy. Edmund tutted impatiently and took her arm and manhandled both of us down.

'Ain't no one who can help me. I done a wicked thing.' She snivelled and wiped her nose with the back of her hand. Then she looked imploringly at Molly who was sitting demurely in a corner of the cab as if trying to be invisible.

As Edmund escorted the woman up the steps he looked back and with a sudden shock I noticed that there was something about his expression that reminded me of Roland. My whole being shuddered. I had never thought that the brothers were anything alike. Roland was dark and swarthy and Edmund although burned by the sun had much lighter colouring and finer features. Rosie too must have caught the look and a terrified expression appeared on her face as she cried.

'Don't hurt me! Don't hurt me!'

Ignoring her pleas Edmund frog marched her along the pavement as I tried to keep up all the time trying to reassure her that she would not be injured. Edmund did not release his grip but twisted her arm, forcing her to stumble up the stone steps angrily saying,

'I have had enough of this nonsense. Let us get this over and done with!' His tone had the desired effect and stopped Rosie in her tracks. From then on she stopped struggling and meekly allowed herself to be escorted. Arriving at the door Edmund loudly banged on the brass lion's head door knocker. Nobody came and he was just about to bang again when the door opened to reveal a slim, young woman wearing a large white apron, her hair tied back in a scarf.

'We wish to speak to the person in charge.' Edmund stated.

The woman bobbed a curtsey and asked us to come inside and went off to fetch someone in authority. We walked into the long entrance hall which disappeared into dark corridors. The walls were heavy oak panelling decorated with embossed Tudor roses. There were several doors leading off from the entrance but the décor was very plain. There was also a strong smell of carbolic in the air.

After some time, the young person returned, followed by a tall angular woman severely dressed in black. Around her waist she wore a thick leather belt with many keys suspended from it.

'Can I help you?' She asked looking down her long nose, her expression one of disapproval.

As she addressed us, she gestured to some plain wooden chairs lined up against the wall and indicated that we should be seated. The pair of us meekly sat down whilst Edmund ignored the gesture and remained standing,

'I understand that you help women who have no visible means of support.'

'That is a correct! Gentlewomen!' The woman emphasised the last word, her steely eyes glittering as she fixed her gaze in our direction, seemingly weighing up our suitability to fit the description. Then she continued,

'However, we are a religious organisation and we expect the women who come to us to be God fearing and church going. We also expect them to work for their keep. The young ones go into service. That young woman will not be a problem, although she will have to do something about that unruly hair. However, the older one may find our rules too prohibitive.'

I was astounded. The woman had assumed I wished for a place. Edmund responded angrily,

'Who do you think you are talking to? That young woman is my fiancée and does not require any assistance from you.' Realising her mistake, the woman's face flushed and her long pointed nose took on a purple hue. The thread veins bulging and becoming more marked.

'Oh I do apologise, but as she was........' she stopped realising that she was digging herself in more deeply and merely pursed her lips into a thin line.

'Can you help this woman or not?' Edmund asked anxious to leave.

'I think we need to go to the office to discuss it.'

'Well, please lead the way.' The woman nodded her assent and looking vexed, turned and led the way into a side office, closely followed by Edmund. Rosie and I were left sitting against the wall like naughty children. She looked so unhappy and miserable as I tried to reassure her.

'You must stay here if possible. You can't go on drifting from one crisis to another. I can't spend all my time looking for you.' I laughed trying to make light of the situation. 'If you have no money left, these people will help you. Where have you been all this time?'

Rosie ignored my question and began to ramble again.

'I thought you was dead miss. You were so ill I didn't know what to do and then there was the baby. I am so sorry!!!!!'

I felt a chill descend over me at her words and my veins turned to ice. Anxiously I looked around in case Edmund had been in hearing distance. I could not believe that I had heard that dreadful word. I clenched my teeth and gripped her hand so tightly that I hurt her. Taken aback she cowered away from as I hissed into her face,

'Never, ever mention the baby again!'

Rosie went white and started to reply but I fixed her with such a contemptuous look that she visibly shrunk. She closed her eyes and turned away, leaning her head on the panelling. As the moment passed I was angry at myself for reacting so badly, but I had almost convinced myself that there never had been a child. I did not want it ever mentioned again. However, I had been trying to help Rosie, and instead, at the mention of something I would rather forget, I had been just as cruel as Edmund.

Neither of us addressed each other as we sat waiting. Rosie's eyes were downcast as if she could not look at me. After some time, the side office door opened and Edmund reappeared with the officious woman. I stood up expectantly,

'Is everything arranged?'

'Yes, Rosie can stay here, as long as she obeys the rules.' The woman's attitude had softened a little, but she sniffed disapprovingly, as she helped the larger woman to her feet.

'I am sure you will be happy here. There are three meals a day. However I must remind you that this is a teetotal establishment and no drinking is permitted!' As she spoke she sniffed disparagingly. The aroma of alcohol fumes that permeated the air around Rosie was so strong that I was surprised that the woman had agreed to her staying.

'Of course,' she continued. 'We will have to arrange for an examination by the doctor first.'

Rosie's face turned ashen and she began to struggle in panic.

'They will cut me up. I've 'eard about it. Just like I told you afore. Just like the workhouse. I ain't seeing no doctor.' She began to wail loudly again.

The woman brooked no nonsense and said firmly,

'You will do as you're told. No one is cutting anyone up here, so just behave yourself immediately. This is not a work house.' Rosie seemed to wilt before her. She sank back onto the wooden seat, whilst the woman sniffed loudly, and taking out a large white handkerchief blew her nose loudly. Looking at Rosie she added,

'I suppose you can walk unaided?'

Rosie nodded miserably and followed the woman into the depths of the building. Seeing her disappear into the dark recesses I felt ashamed at my

outburst. All the life and spirit that had marked her personality had gone
from her.

'I'll come and see you as soon as I can,' I called out but she did not
look back. Edmund was already on his way out of the doorway as I asked
unhappily,

'She will be alright here won't she?'

'Anywhere would be better than the streets. Mrs Ecclestone did not want
to take her. Women like that are past redemption. Why you insist on helping
that drunk I do not know. However, I promised to pay a contribution to her
keep so they will permit her to stay for the moment anyway.'

'I wish she could have come back with me.'

Edmund turned and stared at me in astonishment.

'Are you mad? A woman like that. We have done all we can. I do not
want to hear her name mentioned ever again.'

'But Edmund?'

'Never!' He stared at me with such fury that I said no more and meekly
followed him out and he handed me into the carriage. Seeing Molly's little
figure crouched in the corner he was taken aback. It was as if he had forgotten
she was there but said grandly,

'I want to see Stebbeds. He will not be at his office now as it is too late,
so I suggest we call in to see him at Whitefriars.' I was confused as we had
started our journey intending to go to the lawyer's home. However, I didn't
respond. I felt tired and anxious and as we left I looked back and I was
sure that I saw Rosie's white face staring miserably out of an upper window.
However, it could have been my imagination.

There was a sense of doom hanging over me and the building reminded
me of that hospital where poor Annabelle had stayed. It left me with such
a bad feeling and I was depressed all the way back to Whitefriars. However,
I comforted myself with the thought that at least Rosie was safe and had a
roof over her head. However, I would not even be able to write to her, as she
had never learned to read.

When we arrived at the Stebbeds' cottage, the front door opened and
as usual Cobham hurtled down the path,

'Let me help yer down miss. I'm quite a gent now. I knows how to treat
a lady.' Edmund looked surprised at his exuberance but disappeared inside
leaving Cobham to help me down. The young boy had changed so much.
His face had lost the streetwise knowing look it had always worn, but he still
had the bright button eyes and the smooth round face. Suddenly, he looked

passed me and his mouth fell open. I turned to see what he was staring at and found Molly looking just as horror struck.

'Why Cobham, what's the matter?'

I heard him make an intake of breath as he almost whispered,

'Molly!'

'Oh my! Is it you?' The young girl suddenly became animated as she climbed out of the cab in excitement. Then added, 'Why are you done up like a gent?'

'Do you two know each other?' I asked with surprise.

'It's me sister.' Cobham shouted. 'The one I told you about.' In a moment the pair began to hug and kiss each other excitedly as Molly gasped,

'Why yer twice as big as me now.'

'This lady found me a new ma and pa didn't you? Me name's Cobham now ain't it.' He looked to me to agree as he began to prance around imitating his idea of a gentleman, just as he had that time he was first allowed to stay with the Stebbeds.

'Cobham?' Molly repeated, looking puzzled but did not speak as she flung her thin arms around his sturdy body. Strong and healthy now, he towered over his thin undernourished elder sister as he led her away to meet his new father. As he did so Betsy appeared and began chiding Cobham for the noise he was making.

'Look ma,' he shouted, 'Miss Aphra's found me sister. The one I've told you about. I thought she was a dead un that's for sure!' Betsy stopped in her tracks, not sure what was happening. Seeing the stick thin, young girl, her manner immediately softened.

'Good heavens! Young woman you look as if you could do with a good meal. Whatever next Aphra? You are always finding lost souls. What happened to your face dear? ' she said with concern looking at the yellowing bruises.

Molly began to babble an explanation but it was all too much for Betsy to take in and she silenced her with a wave of her hand.

'This is all too complicated for me! Let's ring for the maid and serve some tea.' Soon we were all settled in the warmth of the drawing room eating Mrs Stebbeds scones. Seeing brother and sister together I remembered how Molly had reminded me of someone when I had first met her, now I realised why. Her bright button eyes mirrored Cobham's. The likeness was so obvious I could not believe how I had not realised the connection. When we had finished the plate of scones the pair disappeared into the kitchen seeking more, leaving me alone at last with my dear friend.

'Molly is coming back with me to Threshingham Park.'

'That is kind of you, but are you sure?' Betsy asked. 'She looks a poor young thing but you can't be too careful.'

'Like you and Cobham?' I smiled. Betsy beamed, her rosy face crinkling with pleasure, 'What of the other lady? Rosie? What has happened to her?'

'Edmund found a place of charity that has taken her in. I believe that they were not too happy to do so, but he has settled the problem with the promise of money. I hope she will be happy there. I did not know what else to do and Edmund seemed to be very angry that I was concerning myself with her.' Betsy tutted with disapproval.

'You must be careful my dear. Edmund has a position in society and you will have too. As his wife your behaviour must be above reproach. It will not be thought right to associate with women of her class.'

I shook my head,

'I owed her so much. It was through her that we found Edmund again. I had to help her. I know she is not all she should be but does that mean we can't offer her assistance. Why was Edmund so difficult about it? I do not understand his moods these days. He was even nasty to me.'

Betsy patted my hand fondly,

'You have to remember that Edmund has been very ill. His memory is affected it must be very unsettling and frustrating not to remember who you are.'

'I know and I try to understand. He has remembered some things, but it seems to come in flashes of past events in his dreams and the thoughts give him dreadful headaches. In the past he was so depressed and then recently he has been so elated, rushing around, organising things. Then today, he seemed different again. I had not seen him like it before. For a moment.......' I stopped.

'What my dear?'

'For a moment, he seemed like Roland. Even Rosie noticed it and it frightened her.'

Betsy frowned,

'Sometimes when people have suffered a head injury it can change them. Nobody knows what the result will be. However, I am sure with love and kindness Edmund will recover. Remember, he is not Roland they were only half brothers after all. I have heard that Roland Fitzroy was a man of some repute, before he became a dissolute. He was master of his own fate, everyone has choices and Roland made his and suffered the consequences. Edmund has always been a dear sweet person, and always helpful and kind. Perhaps he was just protecting you.'

I smiled,

'It is true that the owner of the charitable institution did for one moment think that he was trying to find a place for me. That seemed to infuriate him.'

'I am not surprised. Heavens! What a thought. What did she say?'

'She said that I would have to do something about my unruly hair.'

'What insolence, she was probably jealous. Your shining, red hair is beautiful my dear. Any woman would envy having such a cloud. People pay a fortune these days to have false hair to pad out their own and yours is rich and curling naturally.'

'That's as maybe, but I spend an eternity trying to tie it down neatly and it always escapes.'

'That is part of your charm my dear!'

'Edmund seemed so angry at the suggestion that the place was for me.'

'Men are strange creatures. We women have to learn to judge their moods. When Bertie and I first met I was not at all enamoured of him and he chased and wooed me until I gave in and we were married. As soon as we were married, I hardly saw him. Of course he was only a clerk in his father's office then and he worked all the hours that he could to improve himself. I understood that, but it was hard coming to terms with the besotted romantic lover, turning into a disinterested husband.'

'Yes, but Edmund has changed even before we are married. He was so unkind and even when he is arranging the wedding it is as though it is nothing to do with me.'

As I finished speaking Edmund entered and I hoped that he had not heard what I had said. However, he seemed very relaxed and smiled warmly,

'It is too late for us to return to Threshingham Park today. Mr Stebbeds has asked that you stay here with them and I will go to my flat at the Albany. It will be interesting to see it. Especially as I haven't the slightest recollection of ever being there.'

CHAPTER TWENTY ONE

'Unkindness may do much; and his unkindness may
defeat my life, but never taint my love' *Othello Act 4 Sc 2*

The next day Edmund came to collect me. However, he was in a
morose mood and it was obvious that staying at the Albany had been
a disappointment for him. I assumed that his stay there had not sparked any
memories and thought it best not to discuss the matter. I wanted to stay with
the Stebbeds for a few days more but Edmund would not hear of it. He was
agitated and wanting to leave urgently and my friends could not help but
notice how different his mood appeared from the day before.

Once back at Threshingham Park, Edmund regained his buoyant frame
of mind but the manic behaviour revealed itself again. Sometimes he was
fired up insisting that he was going to become more involved in the running
of the estate. He would then set off galloping around the countryside, but
when we discussed his visits with the land agent and the estate manager, they
had not seen him. He would be away for hours and we would have no idea
where he had been. As fast as the excited interest in everything occurred it
would die away and he would shut himself away and not speak for days.

Some days I would spend hours on my own reading or playing the
piano. If he heard me playing his mood would become depressed, nervy and
irritable. On other occasions he would demand that I played musical pieces
for him and when against my will I did so, he would sit and listen, morosely
lost in thought. If I tried to play a lively piece he would become angry and
claim it gave him a headache. Once he even stamped around the room like a
maddened beast, bellowing. As he reached my side, he slammed down the lid

of the piano with such force onto my fingers that I screamed out in pain. He trapped them underneath causing me such extreme agony that I cried out,

'Edmund, stop it. What is wrong?' There was a strange, malevolent expression on his face that I had not seen before. He then leaned towards me and pressed down harder on the lid to compress my hands even more. I wriggled and squirmed trying to release them, begging him to release me. Finally he threw the lid up and with a scornful laugh stood back. Now free, I started to run away from him, but as I passed he began to bellow again like a trapped animal. Turning I saw that he had clasped his hand to his head and was careering around the room banging his head against the wall, clutching his forehead. I did not know what to do as the servants arrived drawn by the noise. They stood, mouths agape, looking on as Edmund pushed his way through them still crying in pain and disappeared up the stairs. The group of us stood there uncertain what to do until the footman asked formally,

'Are you all right madam?'

'Yes. 'I replied, shaken and upset. 'I have injured my fingers but they are only bruised. Please see to the Major as he needs assistance.'

He nodded and ushered interested servants away leaving me alone. Looking down at my hands, I could see the skin was split and my fingers were swollen and bruised. My knuckles were grazed but worse had been the embarrassing scene in front of the servants. No doubt the people in the local area would soon hear of it

'I do not know what to do.' I cried to myself rocking backwards and forwards, holding my painful fingers. Molly, who had been making herself useful as my maid, ran down to me on hearing the tumult. We both retreated to my sitting room and tired and dispirited, I showed her my hands. She fetched some witch hazel and bathed them saying as she did so,

'I don't understand it Miss. I really don't. He is so nice and kind. It's like he's two people, 'e must have something wrong with 'is 'ead. Broken like! I seen it before. I remember in the tavern there used to be fights. Men used to fight each other for money. I used to hide outside because it was so awful. They'd be all battered and bruised and when it was over there would be blood all over the floor and I would have to clean it up. Sometimes I found broken teeth amongst the sawdust, it used to make me sick to me stomach. There was this one chap 'e was a strange looking cove. His nose was flat and his ears were all thick and twisted. He was always shouting that he would 'take on all comers. He never talked no sense, and the guvnor said it was cos he'd taken too many blows to the 'ead. Lost 'is senses. Sometimes he would sit in a corner talking to himself and if anyone took him unawares, he used to nearly kill them. He 'ad to be restrained, there was some talk of locking 'im in the asylum.'

'Do you think that his head injury has caused something like that to happen to the Major?'

'I don't know miss, but 'e 'as had 'is 'ead damaged. Who knows what's going on in 'is mind? The other day he called me Tilda, but there ain't no Tilda in this house. I asked Dorothy, the parlour maid who Tilda was and she said she worked here in Lady Fitzroy's time, when the Major was a boy. She says that she looked a bit like me. He got confused like!'

'I do not know how long I can go on like this.' I sighed as she carefully brushed and detangled my hair. 'I love him so much Molly but this cruel side occurs without any warning. I feel so tired and anxious when I am with him. How can we marry? There could even be a scene at the church. How awful it would be if we stood at the altar and when the vicar says, "Do you take this woman?" Edmund denies even knowing me.' Despite myself a wan smile flickered over my face at the thought.

'Oh no, Miss, you must marry him. He loves you. Anyone who sees you together can see that. I ain't never seen a gent so taken with a lady as the Major is with you. His eyes follow you everywhere, 'e never stops looking at you. I hope one day I find someone who loves me like he loves you.'

'I know he loves me, but since his return he is not my Major. The one I depended on and who was so kind and gentle. I can't bear this.' I sighed.

Every day I dreaded what mood I would find him. I began to realise that when he demanded I play the piano that he would see flashes of past incidents in his mind. It was the only way that he could try to rekindle his memories. Afterwards he would lay on the purple velvet chaise longue looking exhausted and pale. I would sit by him placing cold compresses on his forehead, bathing the scar that still stood out angrily as a constant reminder of his injury. His shoulder also bothered him but he would cry out exclaiming that agonising headaches were driving him into insanity. After raging in a frightening manner, he would fall into a comatose sleep, so deep that nothing seemed to wake him. I would leave him to rest and then he would suddenly re-appear at mealtimes as if nothing had happened.

Everything about his behaviour worried me but I tried to be a calming influence. I spent hours reassuring him that his memory would return. I would pass days recalling events from the past so that I could help him. The hours I spent with him were exhausting as I felt as if I was walking on egg shells. Any moment I would make a wrong move and his mood would become aggressive and confrontational. When he fell asleep it was a relief to retreat to my room. I felt totally isolated and alone but every time I walked out of a room a servant appeared at my elbow wanting to know if they could help me. It was easier to stay closeted in the library or my room.

One day Molly, who had settled in to not only being my maid, but also my companion, sat talking to me whilst she tried to untangle my hair. After a while she said quietly,

'Can I ask something Miss?'

'Of course you can Molly.'

'Why did them kind people call my brother Cobham?'

'Well, when Mr Stebbeds and I first found him he told us his name was Cobbles.'

Molly pursed her lips and tutted to herself,

'I suppose that is what they called him, after I lost him.'

'What was Cobham's name?'

'Alfred, 'she said brightly

I winced as she tugged at my knotted hair and added,

'But there was a piece of paper in his boot that he said had his name on it.'

'Yes, I gave it to him. There was a man who mended shoes where we lived and he had bits of paper that he said were advertisements. They had a picture of King Alfred on them. Of course I couldn't read them but I said to Alfie, always remember your name is Alfred King.'

I started to laugh, I remembered that there had been a little picture of King Alfred on the torn paper but we had only looked at the printed writing.

'I think that he's rather stuck with Cobham now!'

She nodded,

'It doesn't matter now does it? He ain't me little brother is he? He's a proper gent. I'm glad. When I left he was so small and I was so worried about him but old Barney wouldn't let me go fetch him.'

'Old Barney?'

'The landlord at the tavern. I ain't never told anyone about this before.'

'You told me that he gave you board and lodgings and said you had to work to cover the cost of your keep.'

She looked pained and after a pause added,

'That's true but before that I used to go out begging. Trying to get food for me and me brother. I used to go down to the mud banks on the Thames and see if anything had been washed up that I could sell. I was only about ten years old and me brother must have been about five. I was standing in me usual spot when this man comes along and says that he'll take me to this place and buy me some food. I was starving 'ungry, we 'adn't eaten for days. Well we went along by the Tower and we fetched up in Wapping. I was a wondering how I was going to get back to me brother, but the man said he would take me. We had been walking for quite a bit and I was beginning to get worried because he never stopped at any pie shops or nothing so I refused to go any further. He grabbed my arm and twisted it. 'E really 'urt me miss, I thought he broke me arm it was that painful. He pushed me against a wall and tried to 'ave 'is way with me. I was only ten years old. I never thought that he was after anything like that. I thought he was just being kind,' she sniffed and I realised that she was becoming distressed by the memory.

'You poor girl. Please don't upset yourself. You don't have to tell me anymore.' I said putting a reassuring arm around her but she continued,

'But I want to miss. This man was hurting me and I didn't know what to do. I was kicking and punching him. Finally, I bit 'is ear and for a minute 'e let me go and I ran but he grabbed me again and somehow, I found a large brick in me 'and and I 'it 'im with it. Oh miss, the blood from 'is head, it was 'orrible and he lay there on the floor. He looked dead. I didn't know what to do. I was frozen to the spot. Just then Trader came along and seeing this man on the floor 'e starts whistling,

'Well, well, what 'ave we 'ere?' He says. 'Why if it ain't old Hebsworth and you 'ave gone and killed 'im. I think we'll 'ave to call a Rozzer and take yer before the Beak.'

I starts begging and pleading that it was an accident and he says,

'Never mind little girl, he 'ad it coming. There's many a geezer round 'ere will fank you.' With that he takes me hand and leads me to the tavern and says I can stay there. It turns out that man that I killed, was always coming round threatening Barney. Saying 'e had to pay 'im money like or 'e would ruin 'is business.'

Unable to believe what I was hearing I was lost for words until at last I managed to say,

'Oh Molly, how awful for you! Is that how you came to stay at the tavern?'

'Yes, that's 'ow I lost me brother. When we got to the tavern, Trader said that I was a murderer and I would be hanged. I couldn't leave not for nuffin, else I would be arrested. That I had to work me keep cos they was saving me from the 'angman.'

'But you were a child! It was self defence.'

'But who would believe me. I was terrified of the drop. I was so grateful that I had somewhere to stay, but I cried everyday for me brother. I stayed there two years hiding away. If people came in what looked official like, I stayed out of sight until they'd gone. Then one day who comes in but that man I thought I killed. 'E wasn't dead! There 'e was large as life, but it was too late then. Barney said I owed all me board and keep and I 'ad no idea where me brother was so I just stayed with nowhere else to go. 'She looked up brightly the big eyes sparkling and added,

'Then you came and rescued me'

'I was grateful to you. You helped us when Edmund was so ill.'

The young girl sniffed and wiped her eyes that had filled with tears and then as she resumed brushing my tangled locks asked,

'Is the Major going to get better?'

'I hope so Molly,' I sighed.

'It's so sad to see 'im when 'e locks 'imself away. Raging in pain with the 'eadaches.'

'What do the servants say?'

'They say, 'es changed. That 'e is losing 'is mind. That's not true is it miss?' She asked sadly.

I did not know the answer.

As the days passed, the familiar pattern of Edmund's behaviour continued. Some days I would wait in the breakfast room and he would rush in, beaming with smiles so pleased to see me. He would kiss me warmly and brightly and outline the plan for the day, which usually involved a lot of activity that never developed into anything definite. On other days, we would walk to the village or sometimes sit quietly writing our correspondence or reading. If Edmund had been busy in the study dealing with his business matters, he would constantly come to check on me, wanting to know what I was doing. He could not bear to be parted from me for too long. If I went out for a walk on my own to escape, or even ventured into another room, he would become agitated. From room to room he would follow me like a lost child, unable to function without me. His constant presence became overwhelming. I was a prisoner in a bright, gold ornamented prison. I was unsure if I was happier when he was locked away or with me when the moods were upon him.

On the bad days I would sit and breakfast alone, my heart sinking knowing that what lay ahead was a day of nastiness. When he materialised he would be argumentative and start ridiculing Molly and her attachment to me, calling her a gutter snipe. Then he would return to the study and stay closeted for hours on end. When he finally emerged he would ignore me and become even more morose and argue with the servants. Within a short time his face would turn an ashen grey and clutching his head in agony, he would rage around the room calling out and shouting insanely. There was nothing that anyone could do, to help or placate him. The doctor would be sent for but by the time he arrived the moment had passed and he would prepare a dose of chloral and Edmund would sleep.

I was in despair. I saw in Edmund the behaviour that Roland had exhibited at Stoneleigh and wondered if it was caused by his injury or if there was a strain in the family that went much deeper. When he was my dear Edmund, I loved him dearly but the other person that I did not recognise frightened me.

One bright sunny morning, I awoke feeling in a positive frame of mind and came down to breakfast looking forward to spending the day with Edmund. I sat waiting for him to join me and when he did not arrive my heart sank. I asked the footman to check whether his master would be joining me and he came back to report that his master was not in his room and was closeted in his study. I took that as a good sign as he had obviously arisen early. However, when he did not join me after some time, I made my way to the study and knocked on the door. He did not answer and I softly opened the door so as not to disturb him. He did not look up and continued writing furiously as if unaware of my entrance.

'Edmund!' I whispered gently, 'I am sorry to interrupt you. Will you be joining me for breakfast? If you are busy could I arrange for some food to be sent to you in here?'

Edmund looked up at me blankly and then in a sneering tone said,

'I'm glad to see that you haven't got that awful green dress on today.'

I was surprised by his manner.

'I have no green dress Edmund.'

'The one you keep for special occasions!' Then dismissing me, he returned to the furious writing and scribbling. Wondering what he was writing in such a determined manner I peered over his shoulder and was shocked to see that he was not writing sense at all. The script was rambling, meaningless phrases. There were swirls of disjointed hieroglyphics filling up sheet after sheet of paper. All were signed with a flourish. Some of which he had screwed into a ball and thrown across the room.

'Edmund, why do you not leave your work and come and come and eat with me?' I was trying to distract him from the fury with which he was attacking the sheets of paper.

'I haven't time for that. I have this work to do!'

'But you need to rest.'

'Rest? How can I rest, don't you see that I have to get my business affairs in order. What is wrong with you? Why aren't you lying on the chaise in the green dress weeping like you usually do?'

'Edmund, I think that you are confused. I do not own a green dress. Perhaps you are confusing me with someone else.

He laughed scornfully,

'Do you think my memory is defective? You wore that green dress every time I saw you. Why you even had your portrait painted in it.'

At first I was confused, there were no portraits of me anywhere. Then shaken I realised what he meant. He had confused me with my sister.

'Edmund, do you know who I am?'

'What a ridiculous question, just go away and let me continue my work. Can't you see that I am busy? Go and pester Roland, you drive him to distraction with your moaning and weeping. Please do not bother me.'

I was in turmoil. I did not know what to say, he was obviously having some memory lapse and did not recognise me at all. What is more he was disparaging of Freya. Yet he had always shown such sympathy and concern for her. Uncertain what to do or say, I said,

'I think you are not well Edmund. Why do you not come for a walk with me and we can pay a call on the doctor and ask his advice.

Angrily he rose to his feet and standing over me in a threatening fashion raised his fist and struck me in the face, bellowing

'I told you to go away. Can't you see your snivelling drives me insane?'

The force of the blow nearly knocked me off my feet and putting my hand to my face I felt blood trickling from my nose. Tears stung my eyes as I steadied myself, steeling myself not to faint. Clutching my cheek, I stumbled back to my room trying not to draw attention to myself. As I did so Molly appeared in the stairwell and seeing my distress came running toward me and tried to help.

'It's nothing! Nothing! I am afraid that Edmund is not well, I think I should ask the doctor to call.'

'Did he strike you miss? I can't believe it. That lovely gentleman, he must be ill ma'am, he would never do such a thing.' She helped me to my room and fetched some water and cotton to bathe my face. My nosebleed stopped and apart from a red mark on my cheekbone there was nothing to indicate that Edmund had struck me.

'What could have provoked him miss?'

'I do not know. He was busy at his desk writing furiously, but when I looked he was writing nonsense. Then when he spoke to me it was in such a dreadful fashion, he seemed to think that I was my sister. Even if he thought I was she, I am sure that he would never speak so unkindly to her as he did to me. I am afraid that something is seriously wrong Molly and I do not know what to do. I thought that when he recovered from the head injury his memory would gradually return. However, his nature has changed to someone cruel. He is not the same person and yet I cannot be angry with him because he is ill. Please do not mention what has happened to the other servants.' I sighed and lay down on the bed.

'No miss, of course I won't but you can't manage this alone. You must ask someone to help you. I know what it is like to be at the mercy of someone cruel and hurtful and having no one to turn to.'

I smiled at her forlornly and squeezed her hand,

'Of course you do!'

I looked at her bright, eager face, now looking more round than the poor, thin waif that had first come to work to Threshingham Park.

'Do not worry Molly.' I said squeezing her hand to reassure her. 'Fetch my cloak and I will walk to the village. I am going to see the doctor and demand that something is done. The chloral is not helping at all.'

Molly nodded and quickly left the room returning with my brown, velvet cloak and after helping me to fasten it, I left her and made my way out of the house. As I passed the study door, I could see it was now slightly ajar and Edmund was slumped over the desk. His head buried amongst the papers that were littered all around him. I shuddered with despair. How reminiscent that scene was of the times I saw Roland at Stoneleigh.

As I came out the servants appeared at my elbow insisting on setting up the carriage but I wanted to walk and clear my thoughts. I walked through the country lanes and past the manicured hedges of the Threshingham lawns. My mind was in a whirl. Could it be that the head injury had not merely caused loss of memory? The doctor had seemed to believe that Edmund was healthy apart from that. When he had first recovered Edmund had been so kind and gentle, as he always had been. I thought to myself that was it possible that his medication had changed his personality? I was sure that Roland's decline had begun after he became addicted to that vile liquid. Could the same thing be happening to Edmund?

I was overwhelmed with the responsibility of it all. I was embarrassed that Edmund had struck me, I hoped that nobody but Molly knew. I did not want to be the subject of gossip. I felt so guilty that I had provoked him and told myself that it had been my fault that I had driven him to it. He had asked me not to interrupt him and I had persisted. Yet the meaningless writing that he was so engrossed in was an indication that he was not in his right mind.

Lost in my thoughts, I was oblivious to my surroundings, when I suddenly saw the spire of the church where we hoped soon to take our vows. Instead of being elated I wondered whether I should try to postpone the marriage. How could we live as a married couple, if I had to spend my time as a prisoner, fearful each day of the moods of my husband? I was in desperate need of help and yet there was no one I could turn to.

I passed the church and made my way down the side alley to the bevelled window of the apothecary next to the doctor's house. I hoped that he was at home and had not been called out to one of his patients. As I arrived I noticed that the door was slightly ajar and I knocked on it and pushed it open further. Abigail, the doctor's plump servant came rushing out and stopped suddenly in a fluster.

'Oh Miss Devereaux, was the doctor expecting you?'

'No, Abigail, but I was hoping that he was at home. I want to discuss something with him.'

Surprised at seeing me, she asked me to wait a moment and went to see if the doctor was available and returned a few moments later saying that the doctor was free. She asked me to wait in a side room, as he was just finishing his breakfast. Before she left she made sure that I was comfortable, asking if I would like a drink? I realised that I had not eaten or drunk anything since arising from bed and the walk had made me hungry. I gratefully accepted and the servant brought me some tea and some biscuits. I had just started to eat them when the doctor appeared, dabbing at his mouth with a napkin.

'Well this is an unexpected pleasure Miss Devereaux. To what do I owe this visit? I hope it is a social call. There is nothing is wrong I hope.' Unable to restrain myself I blurted out,

'Yes there is. I need to speak to you about Major Fitzroy. I am very worried about him.'

The doctor nodded although hardly listening as he folded his napkin.

'I told you before that it takes time to recover from his injuries. What on earth can you expect? It all takes time. More haste less speed young woman.' His attitude angered me but I persisted.

'He is still suffering from terrible headaches. Sometimes he is in such agony he does not know what he is doing.'

'Of course. His injury was very serious you can not expect his recovery not to cause problems. That is why I have prescribed the medication to alleviate the suffering whilst he recovers.'

Becoming more agitated I snapped,

'But he is not getting better. In fact he is worse. Before if his head ached he would rest or take willow bark and it would pass. Now the headaches seem to be more frequent and make him rage with pain and nothing anyone can do eases it.'

The doctor yawned loudly as if he was bored by my conversation and something inside me snapped. I was so angered by his cavalier attitude that I lost my temper. I shouted at him that he had no business being in the medical profession if the serious condition of his patient merely bored him. The doctor's manner changed and he said brusquely,

'I hope you are not questioning my professional ability. I would take that very seriously indeed. I suggest young woman that you are forgetting yourself. I have left strong medication for him and that should be enough. As I have told you, rest is the best cure.' Angry at myself for losing my temper, I burst into tears and sobbed,

'How can it be helping? Sometimes he doesn't even know who I am.'

The physician's manner changed and softening his tone he put his arm around my shoulders and gently said,

'Please do not upset yourself my dear. Everyone is irritable sometimes. We men can't be bothered with interruptions concerning women's trifles. If he has a headache, then he probably does not want company.'

This was the final straw and I began to go into a rage.

'Why will you not listen to me? This morning I found him poring over piles of papers in his study, they were sheet of sheet of scrawls and squiggles.

Apparently he had been there since the early hours. He doesn't sleep but walks around all night.'

'A man has business......'

'I have not finished.' I interrupted, shrugging off his arm. Of course I realise that men have busy lives? I know the difference between a man going about his tasks, and someone driven along by something outside his control? Do you think I am stupid?

'The man blinked nervously at my outburst and opened his mouth to speak but I carried on regardless. 'He seemed to believe when he was talking to me that I was my dead sister. When I tried to reason with him he...' I caught my breath, realising I had gone to far but it was too late to stop. 'He struck me across the face.' As the words left me I quickly hid my bruised hands not wanting to admit that Edmund had also done that.

The doctor looked uncomfortable, his bushy black eyebrows lifted in alarm and he sat down, biting his bottom lip. I was shaking with rage as after a few seconds he said, 'This indeed is quite out of character. It seems strange behaviour as whenever I see him he looks quite well, except for the scar on his forehead of course. Even his shoulder has completely healed. I thought he was well on the road to recovery. What is more his memory is beginning to improve. I was given to understand that he was occasionally remembering things from the past.'

Taking the bull by the horns, I said desperately,

'I believe that the medication you are prescribing is the cause of his problem. Roland Fitzroy was addicted to chloral and suffered extreme mood changes and paranoia. Edmund is behaving in the same way.'

The man stood up quickly, obviously annoyed by the accusation.

'Nonsense,' he responded. 'Allow me, my dear, to know what the correct medication is. The Major is only taking an occasional dose. He is not taking anywhere the amount that could cause addiction. That is a ridiculous suggestion.'

'Please,' I begged, 'you must do something to help him. I do not know which way to turn. He spends most of his time in the house and does not wish to see anyone. I am thankful that people who knew him before do not see how he has changed. I just feel so powerless to help him.'

The doctor patted my hand,

'Rely on my knowledge my dear. I have examined him and he is a fit and healthy young man! I am sure that there is nothing more to it than the frustration caused by his memory lost. He must have been extremely provoked. You have suffered no lasting injury?' he asked. In despair I realised that I was wasting my time. The physician was not taking my concerns seriously. I walked to the door saying,

'My nose was bleeding but it is all right now. My cheek feels a little tender, but it will pass.'

He turned my face to the window to look more closely and then said seriously,

'Everything looks all right but I must say that to strike a woman is unforgivable and I am sure that Edmund will be waiting to apologise to you when you return. In what frame of mind was he when you left?'

'He was slumped over his desk, as if exhausted.'

'Go home dear and do not worry your pretty head. He was probably frustrated trying to deal with his business and you caught him off guard. It is difficult when your memory is not all it should be. I will call in a few days and you will see that all this will have been forgotten.'

Taking out a pad of paper he made some notes and opening his bag took out small brown, corrugated bottle of liquid and handed it to me.

'If he truly can't stand the pain, make sure he takes some of this medicine.'

'Is it better than chloral?' I asked.

'It is Calomel and will help. Do you want me to send for the carriage to take you home?'

'No I want to walk and think. I am afraid this morning has been a strain on my nerves and I am trying to walk myself into a clearer frame of mind.'

'Yes! Yes! I see!' he replied absentmindedly and he began writing on the notepad again. As I said with annoyance,

'If and when you call, I would be grateful if you would not refer to our discussion. I do not want to suffer the consequences should he become even angrier.'

'I am sure you are exaggerating the problem my dear. I will overlook your rudeness as you seem tired. Perhaps I should prescribe you a tonic for your nerves.'

'I have told you the reason for my nerves.' I snapped, 'And the cure is not your medication.'

The man's eyebrows rose again and he snapped the bag shut as I picked up the bottle and stalked out.

I was beside myself with anger and despair. The thought of returning to my prison in my present state of mind was impossible. Passing the small church again I decided to call in and try to gain some peace of mind. I made my way through the overgrown tombstones in the graveyard, absentmindedly reading the names of the local people who were buried there. Pulling back the rusty iron bolt of the church door, I entered the peace and tranquillity of the church. Although I often attended morning service, as I looked around I had not noticed until now that amongst the stained glass memorial windows and plaques, the name of Edmund's mother appeared quite often. She seemed to have been one of the main benefactors of the church. It was only then that it struck me that Edmund never mentioned his mother at all.

When I arrived back at Threshingham, Molly fussed around me, taking my cloak and bonnet and said that Edmund was waiting for me in the breakfast room. As it was now lunch time, I headed there, tentatively opening the door, unsure what to expect. To my relief I saw him sitting quietly eating his food. Hearing my footsteps he swung round and standing up he pulled out a chair for me.

'I waited for you, but Denham said that you had gone for a walk. Why didn't you wait until after breakfast and I would have come with you?'

'Breakfast was hours ago.' I said wanly. To my surprise he put his arm round me lovingly and kissed the top of my head,

'What a lot has happened in so short a time,' he laughed, his blue eyes twinkling as they used to. That familiar smile brightened his face but around the corners of his mouth, there was a nervous tic. Seeing him so friendly and calm I was unsure how to react. I longed so much for the old Edmund but I was so worn down, that I distrusted every mood. Fearing that I would say something that would spark his anger, I found myself too apprehensive to speak. He meanwhile began to talk about arrangements.

'Our wedding day is due in a fortnight. After the ceremony we will entertain our friends at Threshingham Park. Then I think we shall stay in London with Lord Haverstock. I met him in town recently and he has invited us to the London ball and asked us to spend some time with him after the wedding by staying at his town house.'

This was most strange as Edmund had not met anyone recently, unless he was referring to the time that he stayed at the Albany. This man was a friend of Lady Westerham. It would not be possible for me to go there.

'Is he a friend?' I asked, not sure if he would strike me again.

'Haven't a clue,' he laughed. 'But he seemed to know me well enough. I dined with him in town and he told me many things about the past. It will give me time to find out more things if we stay there.'

I was perplexed and did not understand why he had suddenly come into Edmund's mind now.

'Edmund, I don't think it is a good idea to stay in town. You will be unhappy when you can't remember things. If you stay with Lord Haverstock there will be parties and balls. People will want to talk to you and you won't remember them. It will be too difficult. The doctor advised you to rest and live quietly until you are better.'

'What rot. I am better.' He breezed confidently.

I knew I had to be honest with him and quietly I added,

'Remember that I told you I am unwelcome in Lady Westerham's company. Lord Haverstock is a good friend to her family. I am sure I will not be welcome.'

'Not welcome. What nonsense. Why he told me himself he was looking forward to meeting my wife.'

I sighed knowing it was useless to discuss it now. I was sure he had forgotten our conversation about my quarrel with Lady Westerham. He had also forgotten the day's earlier events.

Taking his rough brown hand which was resting on my shoulder I said gently,

'Edmund, do you remember what happened this morning?'

'What?'

'You struck me!'

A look of astonishment flashed across his face and he pulled his hand free. I watched in dismay as he began the familiar pacing back and forth. I recognised the pacing as the precursor to his change of mood and sat waiting for the eruption but it did not come.

'Did I hurt you?'

'A little, but it was mainly my dignity. My cheek feels bruised but it will pass.'

Edmund turned and gathered me to him as I sat unresistingly in his arms.

'My darling! I am so sorry. I would not hurt you for the world. In my regiment if one of my men struck a woman I would have him flogged. Now I am as low as a man can be and yet I have no recollection of it. How can that be?' He held me tightly to him and as he did so I suddenly realised that he had mentioned being in his regiment.

'Edmund, do you remember being with your regiment?'

Edmund looked puzzled for a moment and then added

'Why do you ask?'

'You must have remembered something. Otherwise, why would you talk of something that you would have done in your regiment?'

'I spoke without thinking.' He looked lost for a moment then added, 'Perhaps it means my memory is returning?'

'If that is true then perhaps you are getting better. It would be a good idea to postpone the wedding until your memory returns.' I said in excitement, relieved that I could broach the subject at last.

Edmund turned on me in astonishment and the expected mood change occurred. His expression became dark as he snarled,

'I see! You wish to delay the wedding. Don't think I have not seen you skulking in the corridors with that little gutter snipe. Conniving and colluding, all the time, talking about me behind my back. Pretending you were going to be my bride.'

There was no hope despite trying to be so careful, I had managed to provoke him.

'No my dear,' I sighed, my moment of optimism diminished. ' I just want you to be well. This morning you struck me and you do not remember. You are beginning to frighten me.'

'Frightened of me?' He sneered and then laughed in an affected manner, as I sat in silence.

Sadly I said,

'Perhaps it will be better if I go and stay in London for a few days. Molly can come with me and spend some time with Cobham. If the wedding is to go ahead I would like Betsy to help me. I have no family and a woman needs to make a lot of arrangements before the wedding. I have still to order some material for my dress. If we are to stay with Lord Haverstock I will also need to purchase some fine clothes especially if we are going to a ball. I only have one ball gown and I have worn that many times.'

"Why on earth would you want to stay with that old woman?" He asked, beginning to rub frantically at the livid scar. 'Why don't you stay with someone of your own class?' The agitation growing more marked.

'I don't know what you mean Edmund. I thought that the lawyer and his wife were your friends?'

'Business only my dear! If you are to be my wife you had better start acting your class, not fraternising with people of the gutter.'

Offended I retorted,

'Mr and Mrs Stebbeds are not from the gutter. Edmund that man has handled all your business affairs. When we thought you were dead we searched for you and his only concern was for your happiness. How can you speak in such derogatory terms about them? '

He shrugged and the pacing continued,

'We are visiting Lord Haverstock and that is the end of the matter.'

'I told you Edmund, when you were invited to Leticia's wedding, that I am not welcome in Lady Westerham's house and that man is a close friend of hers.'

'Not welcome! I have never heard such nonsense!' His pacing increased and he began slapping his forehead as I noticed the signs of his fury beginning and standing up to make my escape said calmly,

'I told you we quarrelled. You have forgotten.'

'Well we shall have to see about this. My wife has the right to visit any person she wants.'

'It doesn't matter Edmund, I will make arrangements to stay with Betsy.'

He stopped in his tracts and his eyes narrowed and he looked at me with such hate that I quaked under his gaze.

'I do not want to hear anymore about postponing the wedding. People will talk about you. I can not have that. I am a Fitzroy. What is a young woman doing living under my roof, using all the facilities without my permission. Propriety is everything.'

I felt my face flush with embarrassment at the word propriety. In a flash the memory of that night that we spent together made me giddy. Yet he seemed to have no memory of it. I sat with my head bowed, not even able to raise it, as he said casually,

'You are looking tired. Perhaps a holiday will improve your looks which are fading fast. I can not have my bride looking old before her time. I will write immediately to my agent and state that you will be calling and he must put himself at your service. We will visit London together.' As he spoke he fingered the package containing the medicine which I had taken into the room.

'What is this?'

'The medicine from the doctor, he asked me to collect it.' I lied.

'Collect it?' His eyes blazed at the thought. 'It is not your place to carry out duties like a servant. How dare he suggest it and you should not have agreed. Skulking around like a timid little mouse. I can not stand timid women.' His words cut me like a knife. I was no longer Miss Sparky. In my concern not to say or do the wrong thing in his presence, timid is just what I had become.

How alone I had felt at Stoneleigh. It had been so threatening and dark and Threshingham Park was so different. Yet I also felt so alone here even though there were always servants bustling around and intruding on my every move and it was unbearable. Their presence was suffocating and more and more I tried to escape by wandering for hours amongst the country lanes. Often I went to the churchyard and just sat. One day I saw the tall figure of the apothecary coming through the hedgerows. He was a pleasant young man who always enquired after the Major and I always enjoyed his conversation. As we passed time just talking I told him that Edmund was still suffering from the headaches but the doctor had now prescribed Calomel to take when the pain was too great. The apothecary looked surprised and leaning towards me in a confidential manner whispered,

'I would advise you not to allow Major Fitzroy to use the Calomel on too many occasions. It is mercury based and can cause complications, sometimes it can lead to mercury poisoning and brain disease.'

My blood ran cold.

'Surely the doctor would not prescribe a medication that would make Edmund ill.?'

'Quite so. Quite so.' He uttered, puffing out his cheeks. 'However, there are conflicting views on its uses.' He bid good day leaving me unhappier than ever.

CHAPTER TWENTY TWO

'Would you have me false to my nature? Rather say I play
the man I am'   *Coriolanus Act 3 Sc 2*

That night I was awakened by a noise outside my bedroom door. For a moment I was completely disorientated and thought for a moment I was back at Stoneleigh. However, becoming aware of my surroundings, and with heart pounding, I took down my robe and went to open the door. As I did so I heard the footsteps again and I was certain that they stopped outside my room. I listened again, but even though I knew that I was not at Stoneleigh and there were servants in the household, I was too frightened to open the door. Then I heard the sound of voices but I could not understand what was being said. One voice, louder than the others, was recognisable as belonging to Edmund but the sentences were muddled and confused and he seemed to be giving orders. I waited with baited breath for my bedroom door knob to rattle, just as it had at Stoneleigh, but it did not. Then the footsteps started again and I recognised the familiar Edmund pacing on the landing.

As I listened I heard more voices and eased open the door open and peered around it. The sight that greeted me was amazing. Several of the servants were gather around Edmund who was standing there in full dress uniform. He appeared to be confused and the servants were trying to make sense of it all. There was a lot of head shaking from Edmund and waving of arms, but none of his words made any sense. Feeling braver now I knew that I was not alone, I asked,

'What is happening here?' In an authorative tone that I did not feel. The servants immediately stood back and began to ask for instructions as they did not know what their master wanted.

My nerves on edge I snapped at them.

'If you are not here to help will you please return to your rooms?' There was a flurry of activity as they disappeared, looking chastened. Only the Major's man servant remained, looking foolish and uncertain what to do as I ordered,

'Please take the Major to his room and ensure that he goes to bed.'

The man looked disconcerted,

'I have been trying madam, but he will not take any notice of me. He keeps saying that he is waiting for someone. That his leave is over and he has to return to his regiment.'

'It doesn't matter what he says. You can see is unwell and confused.' I said firmly. 'Can't someone please help him? How long can we stand here in the cold watching a sick man in his agonies?' As my voice rose Edmund stared at me as if having no idea who I was or what he was doing there. He looked down at his uniform and then the blank expression disappeared and he became irritated.

'Why am I standing here in the middle of the night?' he snapped, looking around and then he blasted, 'What are you two staring at?' His servant looked at me as if waiting for me to reply and I merely responded,

'I think you have had another nightmare Edmund. Your manservant found you walking in your sleep, didn't you?' I gestured to the man to confirm what I was saying and stammering he agreed.

'Well I must get out of this uniform. Things to do tomorrow, I need my sleep.' Then confirming that he was in his right mind again he smiled and kissing my cheek breezed, 'You had better go back to bed Aphra, you are frozen. What on earth are you doing standing there in the cold?' With that he wandered off to his room with his servant following anxiously behind. I retreated to my room and fell into bed with relief and despite myself was so exhausted that I slept until morning.

The next day to my surprise I was greeted by a happy, smiling Edmund.

'Are here you are,' he beamed, 'I thought you would never come, I've had a good idea, why don't I come to London with you? I can stay at the Albany and then I can sort out some of the business that I have been remiss in dealing with since I have been here.'

Already he had forgotten that our discussion about the visit following his anger about Lord Haverstock's invitation. He laughed and handed me a plate to serve up the food, and suddenly noticed my hands, which were still quite bruised and scabbed over.

'What happened to your hands?' he gasped with concern.

'It is nothing.' I casually responded as I placed my plate on the table.

Edmund frowned,

'Nothing! You have hurt your hands. What have you been doing? I was uncertain whether this light mood would change if I made him remember the piano incident but he kept badgering away, wanting to know how it happened. Finally I admitted defeat and told him.

'You did it Edmund. You flew into a rage the other day because I played the piano and.....'

Taken aback he gasped,

'What are you talking about?'

'You slammed the lid down on my hands because you were so angry.

For a moment Edmund was disconcerted, as if he was trying to make sense of my words until sinking into a chair he said in despair.

'Oh my God! What is happening to me?'

'It's not your fault Edmund. You can't help it, but we must seek help in London, from someone who understands about such things. The apothecary told me that the medicine that the doctor has now prescribed is not good for you.' Perhaps it will be a good thing that we are going to London. We will seek an expert who understands your injury. I think you must see someone my love.'

'Yes, maybe you are right. Sometimes I think that I do remember things and just as I try to recall them they slip away. If I try to make them stay the headaches start.'

'You had a nightmare yesterday,' I stated almost as an afterthought.

'Did I? I don't remember doing so!

'Yes, the servants found you wandering around on the landing in full dress uniform. Perhaps it is the Calomel, having a bad effect. Perhaps you should refrain from using it.' I said lightly.

'Yes, that is probably it.' He looked relieved as though it was a hope he could cling to. That there was nothing wrong it was purely the side effect of the medication. He pulled his chair up to the table and began to eat his breakfast. He then continued in such a normal way that I felt relieved, hoping that today would be a good day.

'When I first returned to Threshingham Park after I was ill, I thought that my memory would improve. I was sure that it would soon return. I wandered around the house from room to room trying to recollect someone or something but could not. Then I consoled myself with the fact that as I was away with the regiment so often, I probably spent only a little time here. That it would not be so familiar. The only person I remembered was you. Standing at the foot of my pallease in the dressing station, night after night. Yet you could not have been there. It could not be a memory. It must have been a fantasy. Something that my inner thoughts conjured up. When you became reality, I could not believe it. Yet it still seemed that it was unreal. After a while the images kept looming up in my head. People I did not know or remember and no amount of explanation as to who they were, meant anything to me. It was if you were telling me a story and I was imagining things. I understand that they are pictures of things that took place, but I can't remember them. At night I see you in a long dark corridor sitting on a wooden settle surrounded by paintings and clocks. There is a strange sense of foreboding as if something terrible is about to happen.'

I put my arms around him as if to reassure him, 'That dark place is Stoneleigh. That is where you found me again. Nothing terrible will happen. Every thing that could happen has already taken place.'

Sighing loudly he said almost to himself,

'Sometimes I do see a child. She is a poor neglected thing, I feel like an observer watching her cold and alone. I want so much to help her and yet I am powerless.'

'You did try to help her.'

He patted my hand,

'I know. You have told me and yet I feel so guilty as if I could have prevented everything and I didn't. That house haunts my dreams. Night after night I walk the house and yet there is no one in it.' He shook his head despairingly adding,

'Perhaps you are right. We should not marry in haste. I am hardly suitable husband material in this state.'

'You will be well again,'

'God willing, I can't bear to think that unknowingly I have hurt you. Let me see your hands?'

I held them out and pulling me up from the chair he kissed them tenderly,

'Don't ever leave me will you?' He sat me down next to him on the chaise and placed his head against my breast whilst stroking his hair, I held him to me,

'I promise that as long as you want me, I will never leave you.'

He smiled and murmured,

'I will always want you.' and in a few seconds he was asleep, still resting on my breast like a child.

I sat there in silence holding him to me for what seemed an eternity until he suddenly awoke with a start. He then walked out of the room as if I was invisible and my sense of isolation was complete. There was no sign of him for the rest of the day. I was uncertain if the arrangements for both of us to visit the Stebbeds were arranged or not.

That night I heard him as usual pacing around the landing outside my door. The sounds that had become commonplace. However, I was startled to hear him banging on my door and calling out but the words made no sense. At least they were not the depths of foulness that I had experienced with Roland but I could not understand anything he said. Some of it seemed to be giving orders to his men and others were in a foreign language. Many times he referred to "horses" or "cannons," and there was a lot of shouting and screaming out of commands. It was obvious that in his dreams he was back in the heat of battle. The dreams had become a nightmare of reliving his awful experiences.

I felt so sad and upset but his behaviour bought back all the terror of Stoneleigh and I was terrified. Too afraid to open the door, I sat up in my bed quaking with fear. At last, I thankfully heard the servants lead him away. Sick at heart I knew that although I loved him so much, our life had become one of despair. There was something seriously wrong with him.

At last the day came to travel to London and I arose in a nervous and anxious condition. I was uncertain whether Edmund's behaviour would be controlled or there would be more scenes. At least I was thankful that I was going to escape the nightmare at Threshingham Park for a while. I insisted that Molly should visit her brother and was relieved that Edmund seemed in a reasonable frame of mind. We set off with him talking excitedly about the plans he had for Threshingham Park but more than once he commented on how tired I looked. I was so exhausted that I soon ceased to listen and drifted off into a heavy sleep. It was some time later that I was woken with a start by someone shaking me firmly.

At first I was disoriented but realised that we had arrived at Whitefriars when I saw the cheery face of Cobham staring at me. Edmund and Molly had already made their way to the door as the young lad helped me down from the carriage. Betsy rushed forward and hugged and kissed me. As she did so Edmund looked back and I saw his face darken and my anxiety returned. I recognised the look and knew he was seriously displeased. It was the look he adopted when I interrupted his frantic scribblings in the study. Betsy was too busy chatting to me to notice his displeasure but he began the foot tapping that indicated all was not well.

As we went inside, Edmund asked in a business like manner where Mr Stebbeds was? Betsy told him that was working in his office at Lincoln's Inn. Edmund frowned. And then to my surprise announced grandly that he would call in there. He then issued instructions to the driver and climbed back into the carriage, calling out as he did so that he would also be seeing his commanding officer, and would return in three days. He ignored me completely and our little group stood awkwardly in the doorway uncertain what was happening. I was devastated. He acted as if I was not there whilst Betsy looked on in astonishment.

'What could he be thinking of?' She asked, 'I thought he was joining us for dinner this evening'

I did not know what to think. There had been no mention of him visiting his commanding officer. Betsy looked at me as if expecting me to explain and I tried as best I could. Miserable and embarrassed I said that Edmund had some official business and was somewhat preoccupied. The old lady shrugged,

'Well never mind, men are strange creatures! Who knows what is in their minds?' Whilst Molly unpacked my clothes, we sat in the sitting room drinking tea and I poured out my troubles, but only telling my friend a little of Edmund's behaviour as it was too extreme to admit to.

Betsy listened intently and asked,

'Have you spoken to anyone about it?'

'Edmund's physician calls to see him and I have talked to him about my concern but he seems to think I am a silly woman fussing about nothing. He insists that the headaches are merely the after affects of his injury and will cease with rest. He has also prescribed medicine that I have concerns about. In any case the medication does not help him.' Finally unable to keep my anxieties to myself any more I added tearfully, 'He walks about all night, and flies into rages. Oh Betsy he frightens me. Look!'

I held up my hands.

'Edmund slammed the piano lid down on my hands, because I was playing the piano without his permission.'

The elderly woman looked aghast and stood up angrily.

'That is appalling and unforgivable. I can not believe it of him.'

'Betsy, he doesn't know what he is doing. Afterwards he does not remember and behaves as if nothing has happened. We must find a physician who understands about such head injuries. Do you think Mr Stebbeds would be able to find one?'

She patted my hand fondly,

'I am sure that he could make enquiries after all if the behaviour is as you say, the poor man must have treatment. It is tragic that you have no family of your own, and have to bear this burden alone.'

I sighed despondently,

'Even after all this I do love him, but I do not know where to turn. How glad I was that he was alive after that dreadful time when we had no news from the Crimea. His injuries are healed but I think that his mind is not. I am sure that night after night he relives those experiences from the battleground. I am not equipped to help him. Nothing I do seems to make any difference and most of the time I make him lose his temper.'

Betsy smiled,

'You must not worry my dear. Bertie will know what to do!'

'I hope so!

We sat passing the time and after a while I asked if she had any news of Leticia. Betsy said that she had heard that she had been travelling abroad.

'I do hope she is happy,' I added almost as an after thought as I asked the question that had been on my mind since my arrival. 'Is my betrothal to Edmund common knowledge?'

Betsy looked uncomfortable,

'People will always talk. Edmund has hidden away all these months. You know the artificiality of society. If someone is not seen in it, all kinds of stories are made up. Remember I wrote to you when you were at Motts Clump telling you to show yourself in society as there were rumours about you. However, you chose not to. People see that as an admission that you are aware that you will not be received. I am afraid my dear the cutting you received from your friend the last time you were in town, may continue.'

'I thought that would be the case. Edmund says that he has no use for the gossip and busybodies of society. However, it is important for him to retain his good name. I would hate people to judge me and ostracise him because of it.'

'Well, if you are going to live at Threshingham Park, it will not matter. However, I believe that Lady Westerham has done your reputation a great deal of harm. She spread abroad that you were with child. That you had tricked Edmund into marrying you. It was such nonsense. Anyone could see how he loved you. How on earth anyone can believe that a man like Major Fitzroy could be tricked by the wiles of a young lady I do not know. If it was that easy he would have been tricked many times. The number of times the most important ladies set their daughters on a path to ensnare him. Some of them were quite rich too. There is a lot of jealousy. So many young ladies had their hearts set on winning the handsome Major. For a young woman to come from outside their social circle and capture him makes you no friend.'

'They can't understand why such a mouse could be his wife?'

'Mouse? Is that how you see yourself? You are allowing your concerns for Edmund to affect your self esteem. You are a beauty. You have a lovely face, you come from a good family and with that cloud of red hair I defy any man not to desire you for a wife. Never do yourself the injustice of underestimating you attractions. That is what has caused the jealously. When you are married it will all be forgotten, he is too rich and important to be slighted.'

As we spoke the door opened to reveal Mr Stebbeds' wizened face, his eyes twinkling merrily as he greeted me.

'How nice it is to see you my dear. I hope I am in time for dinner?'

'Is Edmund with you?' I asked hopefully.

The lawyer shook his head,

'I haven't seen the Major today. Was I supposed to?'

Betsy explained that he said he was going to the office at Lincoln's Inn.

Almost immediately I began to worry. However, I clung to the hope that he had gone straight to see his commanding officer instead.

The lawyer nodded to reassure me,

'Yes, I am sure you are right. I am sure he has a lot of pressing matters to attend to. Not least regarding his commission. How is his memory, my dear? Is it any better?'

Unable to check my concern any more I burst into tears.

'He does remember some things but he is not Edmund anymore. You must find a doctor to help him. He can not go on like this.'

Deeply concerned the couple tried to reassure me and Mr Stebbeds agreed to make some enquiries about a suitable physician. However, he felt sure that with rest and time Edmund would be fine. However, I was not so sure. I told them what had happened recently.

'Something is terribly wrong. He locks himself in his study writing for hours on end. When you peruse what he has written, it is all nonsense.'

The lawyer whistled loudly, 'Well! That explains it,' and standing up stiffly he disappeared out of the doorway to return clutching a sheaf of papers, and handed them to me.

'What are these?' I asked, uncertain what the papers were.

'Look at them!'

Turning the papers over, my hand went to my mouth in amazement. Page after page was filled with heavy black scribbling and words that made no sense. All of the sheets were signed with a flourish in the name of Edmund Fitzroy.

'But where did you get these?' I asked.

Shuffling them together he said,

'They are delivered by the post every few days.'

'Then he must think that he is sending letters of instructions to his lawyer and yet it is disjointed ramblings. This is what he is doing locked in the study all day.'

Mr Stebbeds shrugged and nodded in agreement.

'Is he aware of what he does?'

'I do not think so. He seems to be intensely writing for hours on end. Sometimes he seems perfectly normal and then something provokes him into a violent rage. He does not remember the outburst afterwards.'

'You must help the girl Bertie!' Betsy added waving away the maid who came to clear the dinner things.

Settling himself down into a comfortable armchair, the lawyer idly looked over the papers again adding,

'I will see if there is someone who can advise on such matters. Some of my clients are men in the medical profession I will ask them to recommend a physician. We will try to make an appointment for the Major to see someone urgently before you leave for Threshingham Park.'

I explained that Edmund had said that he would be back in three days but I had no idea where he was going. The lawyer advised that he was probably staying at the Albany as before and feeling less anxious and strained now that I had some support, I retired early.

The next day there was still no news of Edmund and he did not appear at the office in Lincoln's Inn. However, the lawyer felt that we should wait for the three days before being concerned. During the day I started to think about Rosie and decided that I would take the opportunity to visit her. Betsy tried to persuade me against it. However, I was resolute, I sent Cobham for a hansom cab and we set off. As the place where Rosie lived meant a journey passed the Albany, I secretly asked Cobham to go and make enquiries without telling my friends. He left on route and I continued on alone.

It did not take long to arrive at the premises of the Sisters of Charity and soon I was pulling on the large bell cord that hung down from the heavy doorframe. The door was opened by a pretty, young woman wearing a black calico dress, hidden by a large white apron. It was not the same young woman that had greeted me on our arrival previously. I explained my wish to see Rosie and the girl directed me into that same unfriendly hallway. I stood and waited for the harridan from last time to descend upon me. There was something overpowering about the dark corridors and high ceilings, and the strong smell of chlorine and carbolic.

A different young girl arrived at the end of the corridor with a bucket and began scrubbing the tiles that already looked well scrubbed and the overwhelming chlorine fumes made me blink and gasp as my eyes smarted. The girl seemed oblivious to it.

As I stood waiting there was the sound of footsteps and a bespectacled man came hurrying towards me. He seemed in a hurry as he stretched out a pale, podgy hand.

'Miss Devereaux I believe. I am the proprietor of this establishment. We have not been introduced, my name is George Remington.' His voice had a sing song tone that reminded me of someone leading a church service, as he took my hand and shook it with his own clammy one.

'I thought that the lady I was introduced to on the previous occasion was the Proprietor.' I said standing to greet him.

'Are you are thinking of Mrs Ecclestone! She only deals with day to day affairs,' he added rubbing his hands together as if trying to warm them. Then he continued in the same sonorous tone. 'I understand that you have expressed a desire to speak with one of our residents.' He smiled but the smile did not reach his eyes as he added, 'I am afraid that is not permitted. We do the Lord's work here and visits are only earned by repenting their sins.

Ladies are only allowed visitors when they have been in the residence for at least a year and have been suitable shriven. In that time it is hoped that they will have learned to do the Lord's work and be ready to return to the world in a suitable profession in service or some such. I believe the lady in question has only been one of our guests for about eight months.'

I frowned but persisted.

'I understand, but I shall be leaving London soon and it will be some time before I can return.'

'No my dear lady! The rules cannot be broken there are no exceptions.' He smiled that cold smile again adding, 'This is a religious establishment. Sinners have to be punished and that involves no social calls for my ladies. This is a place of work not idle chit chat. That is my final word on the subject so I bid you good day.' With that he turned on his heel with a flourish and began to walk back along the corridor.

I was shocked at his rudeness and unable to restrain myself I shouted angrily,

'It may be your final word but it is not mine. I insist that you permit me to see her.' The man stopped in his tracks and turned back towards me the false smile now wiped from his face.

'I am afraid that I shall have to ask you to leave the premises.' He said firmly his eyes narrowed as he stared at me not being used to being challenged.

I refused to be intimidated and with a bravado that I did not feel I said sharply,

'I think that you will make an exception in my case or do I need to remind you that my fiancé Major Fitzroy makes large donations to your establishment.'

The man stepped back angrily and tripped over the bucket that had been left by the young girl who had stopped her scrubbing and was staring with interest from further down the corridor. As he glared at her she quickly gathered her brushes and cloths and in a flurry of activity tried to escape. In exasperation he kicked the bucket out of the way and as the girl panicked to retrieve it, he turned back to me and taking a deep breath, he took off his glasses and began cleaning them. There was a silence for a moment and then he commented in an obsequious tone,

'Well, I suppose an exception can be made on this occasion only. If you will come with me. I will send one of the girls to fetch the lady in question.' He then marched ahead with large strides as I danced along behind him trying to keep up. The reference to Edmund had done the trick. As we arrived at a side room, he walked in and I meekly followed. He then furiously rang a brass bell that sat on a desk that was bare except for a neat pile of bills and receipts on a spike. After a few minutes the same young woman that had opened the front door appeared.

'Agnes, would you be as kind as to fetch Mrs Barnes please. Tell her she has a visitor.' I never thought of Rosie as Mrs Barnes, the term seemed so strange. The girl bobbed a curtsey and went to fetch her whilst Mr Remington hovered around for a moment pulling off and replacing the papers on the spike. He completely ignored my presence and unnerved I stood foolishly by his desk. Tired of standing in silence and not even being offered a chair I sat down and broke the silence,

'How is Rosie? Is she well?'

'Yes. Mrs Barnes has settled in much better than one would have thought. As you are aware she is much older than the ladies that we take under our wing. However, she has settled in very well. Yes very well! She has put her trust in the Lord and he will save her from hell. She will be led to the paths of righteousness.'

I sniffed loudly at his dramatic response. There was no brotherly love in his voice and I wondered how Rosie would have found life in such a cold joyless establishment. Just at that moment there was a knock at the door and he called out for the person to enter. The edged open slowly and revealed a much changed figure of Rosie. For a moment I did not recognise her as she looked so different.

Mr Remington stood back disdainfully.

'I see you are surprised Miss Devereaux. I think we have made a silk purse out of a sow's ear. Don't you agree?' I was uncertain how to reply. Rosie stood in silence, her posture meek and dignified. Her faded blonde hair was tied back neatly into the nape of her neck with a black snood holding all the stray hairs in place. Her hair was parted in the centre so that it framed her face, which was pink and shining as if well scrubbed. I had been so used to the powdered and rouged face. Now without the artifice Rosie seemed much younger. She was wearing a plain brown, bombazine dress, covered in the requisite white apron and she stood demurely with her hands clasped in front of her. None of the defiance of the old days was there.

The proprietor seemed to scrutinize us both as if comparing the well scrubbed look of Rosie with my untidy hair and fashionable outfit. Then peered down his nose and said,

'Well, I shall leave you. I hope you understand that this visit is an exception and we can not have social interludes of any length. The allowance will entail an extreme work penance. Mrs Barnes will have to have two extra hours bible reading this evening and there will be extra duties in lieu of time wasted. 'I stood to protest that Rosie should not be punished for my offence but he stared me down and then repeated his mantra,

'This is a place of work not chit chat,' and walked stiffly out of the room. As he passed, to my surprise Rosie bobbed a curtsey and was so humble that I was shocked.

I went to greet her but she was stiff and unresponsive, unsure what to do or say I pulled out a chair for her to sit down. There seemed nothing of her old spark left. I asked her if she was happy in this establishment. I knew it was a foolish question having seen the behaviour of Mr Remington but could think of nothing else to say. She did not answer but sat there meekly. Her head was bowed down and she avoided my gaze, merely placing her hands that were sore and red in her lap. After a few moments I said quietly,

'Please speak to me Rosie.'

She sighed and like an automaton said,

'I have put my trust in the Lord and the Lord has saved me!' The words sounded so strange coming from her lips. It had been virtually impossible to make her attend church when we lived at Motts Clump. Now she was talking of the Lord in such a pious way, it was most unlike her. Remembering that Mr Remington had mentioned bible reading I asked,

'Can you read now Rosie?'

She didn't respond for a moment and then said,

'The wages of sin is death, Romans Chapter 6 verse 23.' Then she stood up and walked to the door as I watched in dismay. Then as an afterthought she said in a voice that sounded nothing like her East End origins,

'I am pleased to see that you are well but you should not have come.'

Catching her by the arm I prevented her leaving.

'Rosie, what is wrong with you? Are you not pleased to see me?' I asked. Not looking me in the eye, she turned away and said quietly,

'I have learned the error of my ways. I am a servant of the Lord. I am his instrument. My deeds reflect the sinner that I am. Now I have repented and the Lord will be merciful.'

I could not believe what I was hearing. The words were chanted as if reciting them from a book. Rosie's dead eyes reflected the tone of voice reciting the maxims of the establishment. I remembered the sad face at the window when she was first left here and I felt so guilty. I thought we had done a terrible thing to her.

'I wanted to see you Rosie. I wanted to tell you that I am soon to be married to the Major.'

I saw her eyes flicker in recognition but she did not answer.

'Aren't you pleased for us?'

'I am sure you will be very happy,' she said meekly and then her expression softened and she added,

'Is he better?'

'A little.' What else could I say? I then smiled and continued,' He doesn't recall hardly anything from the past.'

Her expression resumed its blankness and she began to chant again,

'The past is dead. We should only look to the future and live in the path of the Lord.'

I sighed and looked out of the window at a bare stone courtyard.

'Yes the past is dead! But Rosie, why are you speaking to me as if I am a stranger?'

Her voice continued to drone on like an automaton,

'Mr Remington says that we must only speak when spoken to. Noise and gossip are sins of the flesh and only leads to evil. I have put my evil ways behind me and have become a servant of the Lord.'

'And are you happy here?' I asked taking her hand. However, I recoiled at the touch of it being so roughened. She almost recoiled from my touch and a strong smell of carbolic wafted from her. I realised that her hand must have been constantly in lye and carbolic to have made them so chapped and bleeding. I held onto her hands and turned them over and she pulled them away and tucked them inside the bib of her apron out of sight. It was strange that she smelled so strongly of chemicals when once she had always been surrounded by an aroma of cheap perfume.

Pulling it away she stated,

'Yes, I am 'appy!' This is my punishment. I am a guilty sinner. There is no hope for me in this life only in the next?'

'Rosie, that is ridiculous. We are all sinners.'

Then she lifted her head and for the first time she looked me in the eye and said quietly,

'If you knew what I had done you would not wish to speak to me. I have committed a dreadful sin and I have to pray for forgiveness.'

I smiled trying to comfort her,

'Rosie I am sure that anything that you have done could not be so terrible. Think of the good and kind things you have done. You helped poor dear Annabelle and if it had not been for you, Edmund would probably be dead. Don't these good deeds become your redemption?'

She didn't answer but tried to push passed me and leave the room but I was in her way. Then I noticed that her expression was one of terrible agony her eyes full of tears.

'How can you be so kind to me? I have done a terrible thing to you and yet you are always so kind. I don't deserve it. I must be punished.'

'Rosie, what are you talking about? You have not done anything to me. Forget about the money you took, it doesn't matter.'

As I spoke Rosie began to wring her hands frantically and bowed her head dramatically,

'I didn't mean it. I did not know what I was doing. I loved him so much. You hated him. He was mine! He was always mine. It was my right. I wanted it. I did, more than anything. More than life itself. I thought you was dying. They said you would die. It wouldn't make no difference to you if you was dead. So I took it. I am sorry! I am sorry!'

'What do you mean Rosie? I've told you, the money does not matter. 'What have you done?'

'I stole your baby!'

CHAPTER TWENTY THREE

'There is nothing either good or bad, but thinking
makes it so'   *Hamlet Act 2, Sc 2*

y world came crashing down as Rosie suddenly became animated
and shouted,

'You didn't want him! I know you didn't! I know what you did, but they
didn't. They thought that you had the baby before your time. I know what
you did! I have seem 'em many times. Getting rid of the unwanted ones! I
found that metal thing that you used, but they never knew. Then you was
so ill and Violet's mother was fussing around and I heard them whispering.
They said that you would die and the poor baby with you. He was just a little
boy, so small, it was more than I could bare. I took him and wrapped him
in wool and I left with him. I told 'em that 'ed died. 'E wasn't christened, so
I told 'em I buried 'im in the churchyard where they puts the unsaved ones.
Like my baby was done, till you made 'em move 'im. They believed me, they
never checked, they was too busy looking after you.'

Stunned I staggered back against the wall for support unable to speak,
my mouth dry and parched with shock. I started to gag with nausea as a pain
of anguish ripped through my stomach. A flow of bile burned through my
chest at her words. The baby that I had almost convinced myself had never
been, was alive. I gripped the edge of the table to steady myself and held it
with such force that my knuckles were white and the veins stood out angrily
on the back of my hands. Struggling to speak I choked,

'Where did you take him? This child?' My words sounded strange. I
could not bring myself to say "my son." I did not recognise my own voice as I
tried to restrain myself from picking up a nearby paper knife and slashing her

with it. The tone of suppressed fury in my voice startled Rosie into silence, and she sank into the chair and whimpered,

'I had a man friend in the village. He 'elped me. He fetched 'is cart and we went to me sister. She just had a baby. That little scrap needed a wet nurse and I made her take him. I 'ad to pay 'er. We kept him warm by wrapping 'im in a sheepskin and placed 'im in a drawer.'

Gripping her arm, my finger nails burrowing into her flesh. I hissed,

'Again, I ask you where you took him.'

Looking up at me her face full of fear she sobbed,

'Near Blackfriars.'

I was beside myself with rage the tears stinging my eyes as I fumed,

'Why? Why?' I gasped not expecting a reply as I twisted my fingers more violently into her arm and she gritted her teeth with the pain but would not cry out.

As I glared at her in my fury she wilted.

'You don't understand Miss. How much I loved Roland.'

Scornfully I sneered.

'Roland! What has it got to do with him you stupid fat slut?' The sound of my words shocked me and I shuddered and put my hand to my mouth as I tried not to vomit, the gorge rising in my throat. Disgusted with us both, I released my grip and too devastated to speak, I bent over the desk gagging and retching as Rosie looked on.

Rubbing the bruises where my fingers had done their work she said quietly,

'I deserve yer hatred. Yer only did me good but I 'ad to take 'im. The child is with me sister. That's why I needed the money that I took from Motts Clump. Me sister already has five children and one more mouth was too much. I sent money to 'er as much as I could.'

Sighing she leaned back against the back of the chair looking tired and strained, the blood drained from her face as she sighed,

'You didn't want 'im! You didn't want 'im.' She reached out to me imploring me to understand and I ignored her unable to think or speak. Sick at heart I was uncertain what to say or do. I felt as if everything that I had wished and hoped for was about to be destroyed. Roland's child was alive to haunt me like some spectre at a feast. Stung by my rejection she hovered uncertainly,

'I am a sinner I knows it. This is my punishment living 'ere. Having to do as I'm told. Listening to old Remington reading out the bible and having to learn his lessons day after day. Scrubbing out the privys on me 'ands and knees. Me hands is so sore but that is my penance. I am to suffer for me wrong doings. If it weren't a sin, I would kill meself.' As she continued with her reciting of her sufferings we were suddenly interrupted by voices outside and there came a loud rap on the door and it opened slightly.

'Get out.' I shouted rudely, to the small girl who was nervously standing there. Timidly she said,

'Mr Remington has asked me to tell you that you have had enough time and must leave.'

She looked startled and shifted anxiously in the doorway as she stared at the forlorn figure of Rosie who had slumped in the chair.

'Go away! I snapped. 'You can tell Mr Remington I will leave when I decide. Not him!' With that retort I slammed the door shut and turned on Rosie.

'I want the address of your sister. I want to see this child.'

She snivelled and rubbed her eyes which were red and swollen.

'I don't know the address.' Then she brightened adding, 'But I can recognise it when I see it. It is near the bridge at Blackfriars down one of them side streets.'

I gripped her arm again and pinched her hard and she flinched but still would not cry out although I wanted her to. I wanted her hurt her and revenge myself on everything that had happened.

'Then you are going to come with me and show me where it is.'

She backed away again, pressing against the wall.

'I can't leave. He won't let me. I am a sinner a loose woman and its hell and damnation that waits for me in the world. He will make me scrub and clean till the skin on me 'ands....'

'Be quiet and let me think,' I snarled, wanting to slap her face every time I looked at her. 'You are coming and that is an end to it. You are here because I wanted to help you, Lord knows why? Edmund was right you are not worth a candle. Edmund has funded your stay and you can leave when I decide. If he stops paying for your place they will turn you on the streets soon enough. This is not a prison.' Although much smaller than the large woman I managed to haul her to her feet as she tried to resist me.

'Get up' I hissed, 'before I slap you.' She looked at me as if unsure what I would do and said quietly, still snivelling and sniffing,

'I fink I can find it. I ain't seen her recently. I ain't sent any money as that old snake don't give me any. I know I done wrong, but this ain't living. It is death.' She began to howl loudly and this time I could not restrain myself and I slapped her face leaving a large red mark on her cheek. Tears filled her eyes and her expression was one of shock but still she did not cry out. Instead she looked sullenly at me as I glared at her and snapped,

'Pull yourself together. We are leaving.' Opening the door I pushed her protesting out of the room. I was beside myself with rage, almost driven to madness by the revelation she had made. Now all my thoughts were concentrated on that child. My despair had changed into fury and anger but with those emotions came a feeling of power and control. We both marched along, with me leading the way and Rosie hanging back looking anxiously around expecting Mr Remington to appear at any minute. I heard her still muttering and did not catch the words but as we reached the outer door she said,

'Please forgive me. I wouldn't never 'ave dun it , but yer didn't want 'im. Yer know yer didn't!'

I responded with sarcasm.

'I forgive you Rosie. You are right. It was all my fault. I was near death and you took my baby. Of course it was my fault.'

She looked downcast but then became agitated as she saw me start to tackle the bolts on the door.

'But I can't go out. You mussn't. I ain't allowed out. I can't be trusted not to return to my sinful ways.' She tried to return to the room but I blocked her way. As we stood defying each other a loud bell began to ring violently and there was a stampede of footsteps from somewhere on the next floor above our heads. A side door at the end of the corridor opened and Mrs Ecclestone appeared her face a picture of displeasure.

'Where do you think you are going? Her high pitched voice quivered.

'We are going out to visit someone.' I retorted still wrestling with the bolts.

'I am afraid that is unacceptable. Mrs Barnes is not allowed to venture outside. The rules of the establishment have already been broken by allowing her a visitor.'

I ignored her and in my distress began to kick at the hinges trying to release the catches, but they were too stiff. The woman smiled and mocked.

'It is useless to try to open the door. It is locked and I have the key.' I was desperately trying to keep my temper under control as I urged,

'Please open this door or it will be the worse for you.'

325

'I don't think you understand the rules of the house.' She responded and indicating by a shake of the head to Rosie, continued, 'Mrs Barnes I suggest you return to your quarters.'

'Mrs Barnes, stay where you are.' I shrieked at her as she cowered in a corner unsure what to do. Meanwhile other women and young girls appeared in doorways, amazed at the scene before them. Angrily, I felt in my bag and taking a handful of coins threw them. They scattered along the corridor and there was a scramble among the women as they dived to pick them up.

Affronted, the thin woman's face darkened with displeasure as she barked, without even looking back at the scramble behind her.

'Leave them!' Immediately, the women disappeared into the shadows, the coins remaining where they fell.

All three of us stood, refusing to move with Mrs Ecclestone silently challenging me with narrowed eyes, whilst Rosie nervously watched. At last there was sound of more footsteps as Mr Remington ran down the stairs two steps at a time. Seeing that she now had support, the Mrs Eccelstone's red nose twitched and she said coldly,

'Under no condition can this woman...' but was not able to finish as her employer shouted from the staircase.

'What on earth is happening here? I make an exceptional case for you and this is how you repay me. This behaviour is quite unacceptable.' He reached the door and leaned on it to catch his breath, ensuring that I could not reach the lock

'This lady is trying to take Mrs Barnes off the premises,' she stated her pinched face a mask of displeasure

'That is enough,' he ordered, waving her away. 'I will deal with this. Return to your duties.' Angered by his tone but unable to respond, she pulled herself up to her full height and then silently nodded ascent and walked stiffly away, her back rigid with anger.

'Leave the key.' I screamed out, now in a complete temper but she did not look back.

Mr Remington looked at me disdainfully and murmured,

'I suggest you control yourself young woman. I understand that you wish Mrs Barnes to leave the premises.'

Refusing to be intimidated I shouted,

'Yes she is coming with me. I demand you unlock the door.'

He looked discomfited and was obviously unsure how to deal with the situation. His response was clipped and strained.

'I think young woman you are taking too much on yourself.'

Still overwrought and determined that I would see my child I snapped,

'How dare you? My fiancé pays for this woman's keep and she is going out on a visit.' Unable to risk losing his benefactor he began to try and placate me.

'You must understand my position. If we start contravening the rules for one. This is a house of sinners; they are here to work for God. He sees their sins and they will achieve eternal life with out Lord when they have worked.....;

'Please do not quote the bible at me,' I replied beginning to calm down. 'I am not one of these poor women used like household skivvies.' He started back in amazement unused to being interrupted as I continued,

'How much will it cost for Rosie to leave with me now?'

'It is not a question of money. We are here for the Lord's work.' He rang his hands together and I remembered how damp and clammy they were when we had shaken hands earlier.

I rummaged in my bag again looking for more coins stating,

'I do not want to remind you again that my fiancé is....'

'Yes! I know who he is.' Remington responded, biting his lip nervously. Almost as if trying to prevent himself from saying too much. Again there was a silence and he seemed to be struggling with his conscience. At last after a few moments he smiled an artificial smile which reminded me of a crocodile baring its teeth as he continued,

'Well I suppose if you are acting as guarantor. However, you are only a young woman yourself. It is most irregular, most irregular.' He took his glasses off again and cleaned them with a large white handkerchief and in doing so held out his hand for some money. I found some coins and pressed them into his hypocritical hand just as Mrs Ecclestone reappeared and indicated to Rosie that she should go upstairs. Rosie turned to meekly obey, but again I positioned myself in her way. The woman looked to her superior for support.

'Mr Remington, may I remind you that we have rules for a reason. We can't have our ladies coming and going at all hours.' The proprietor had not been aware that she had reappeared and was startled at being caught taking the money which he quickly secreted in his pocket. Angry at her presumption and being made to appear foolish in front of us, his manner changed.

'Leave this to me and go about your duties.' He hissed, ' I am the proprietor here and as such I have made the decision.' The woman began to argue but was silenced by his furious expression and sniffing with disapproval, strode off down the corridor again, jangling her keys loudly. As she did so, he called out,

'Mrs Ecclestone, the keys.'

She sullenly returned and dutifully handed them over as he slipped the bolt and turned the key in the lock. As we went out into the fresh air to escape the smell of urine and chlorine I said coldly,

'I do not want to hear that Mrs Barnes has suffered any repercussions because of her outing. She will return in a few hours. You may keep the coins on the floor.'

Mr Remington had been unaware of them. Now his eyes fell on them and his expression was one of cold fury but he merely replied,

'That is unnecessary. It is now two o'clock. I wish Mrs Barnes to return before five pm. Should she not return as directed her place here may be at risk. We have made an exception this once only.'

'I quite understand. Now will someone please fetch Mrs Barnes an outer garment and send someone for a hansom as we have a short journey to make.'

His mouth pinched and tight he rang the bell and a hansom was sent for.

We waited outside on the steps for its arrival and the fresh air made me begin to think more clearly. As we climbed aboard the cab, I had no idea where we were going. After probing Rosie to try and remember something of where her sister lived, she could only repeat what she had already said that it was somewhere near Blackfriars Bridge. Instructing the driver to take us there we soon arrived and began to make our way through the dark, cobble stoned alleys running with open sewers.

As I looked around I was overtaken by a sense of horror at the dense crowd of humanity that thronged in every corner. The smell of ordure was stomach churning. Stinking rubbish was piled high in the streets and now and again a large black rodent would scuttle past making me scream with fright. Rosie seemed unperturbed by her surroundings. All the while I was urging Rosie to try and remember a landmark or something that would make us know we were somewhere near her sister's house. We occasionally stopped some passers by and asked if they knew a woman called Daisy Green, but nobody could help. It dawned on me that the name might not be correct as it was Rosie's maiden name. I felt that Daisy would not be known by her maiden name if she was married with five children. When I mentioned it to Rosie she looked at me incredulously,

'Lor, Daisy and Arthur never married. They ain't into no churching.'

Suitably corrected now in the cold light of day, I wondered what on earth had made me decide on this course of action. She was right I had not wanted this child. Surely I should have left the situation as it was. I was bathed in a conflict of emotions that I could not explain. No one would be aware of his existence if I just left him where he was, but I could not. Having walked around for at least ten minutes, my feet were sore and beginning to bleed where the sharp stones ripped through the material. Additionally, my shoes were torn and sodden with the slimy effluent that ran through the streets. In addition to the stink of sewers another strange smell was beginning to waft our way.

'Are you sure that she lives around here?' I asked beginning to feel tired, cold and wet and the adrenalin rush that had made me so intent on finding the child had long worn off.

'Yes, I know she does.' Rosie replied cheerily. The nun like persona that had greeted me on my arrival at the Sisters of Charity had long worn off and out in the streets that were so familiar to her she had resumed that cheery attitude that had marked her before. We had walked over the bridge and down the side alleys all running off the main Blackfriars Road. However, to my dismay the drizzle now began to rain heavily, making the streets even more disgusting and we had to seek shelter. After waiting a while the weather did not look as if it would cease, so we had to continue on our way, cold and drenched right through. We stopped under a shop awning as I tried to prise some useful information from Rosie that would at least make us realise we were on the right track.

'The street had a funny name, like work house or somefing.' She said in a childlike fashion

'A street with a name like work house?' I asked with exasperation. 'That could be anywhere.'

'Yes! I'll recognise it when I see it. I think we are nearly there now. It can't be far.' As she spoke we turned a corner of a narrow alley and came across some ramshackle cottages that looked in urgent need of repair. The windows were broken and there were holes in the roof, which had been patched with odd bits of refuse. These were blowing about and only hanging by a thread.

'I think this is it,' she shouted excitedly, 'I remember there was a funny shaped building at the end by the cottages.'

Looking ahead I saw a tall thin narrow building, which went into an L shape cutting across two streets. In large letters across the front it read,

'Glass House and Co.'

'Is that the name you were thinking of? The reason that you thought of the work house?'

'Yes that's it! Glass House, I knew it was like it. Daisy lives behind that funny building. I think they make shoes there. It stinks somefing terrible don't it?' She smiled as I wearily sat down on the edge of a stone horse trough, tired and dispirited. My whole body was aching and my unsuitable clothes were soaked and weighed me down. Moreover the terrible smell of effluent that hung over the filth strewn streets, had changed into a stronger, foul smell that took my breath away and stung my eyes. I could hardly see and started a coughing fit and Rosie patted my back helpfully. Surely I thought to myself, nobody could survive in this filthy atmosphere. I began to despair. Rosie had not had any communication with her sister recently. There was no proof that the child was still alive? I tried to dismiss the thought but the surroundings were so awful and the miasma so terrible that if I could not breathe how could a child?

'Nearly there miss. Just put a hankie over yer face, it will help.' I looked around at the street strewn with rotten vegetables and other refuse. There was an overflowing dust-heap and all around were pools of unwholesome water; the whole place was filthy in the extreme. I was shocked that people could live in an area like this with the putrid fumes day after day.

As we turned the corner we came upon a large water tub that some children were filling containers from and its water was fetid. I held my hand up to protect my face certain that cholera was just waiting to pounce on anyone who came by.

Just behind it was a ramshackle cottage that was hardly more than a lean to shack. The building had subsidence down one side, so that it seemed to be tottering on a slope with one side higher than another. Smoke poured out of a hole in the roof, as I looked on in amazement at what was no more than a shed, Rosie suddenly called out,

'This is it. This is it' and then ran down the path calling loudly,

'Daisy. Daisy! It's me Rosie.'

The door opened to reveal a slim, blonde woman, who was a miniature replica of Rosie but with a more aggressive stance. On her hip rested a snivelling baby and the woman looked exhausted. She could not have been much older than me but she seemed much older. Recognising her sister she reacted angrily,

'Where the 'ell 'ave you been? We fought you'd been kidnapped by someone. We fought yer must be dead. Yer never sent no more money. 'Ow we s'posed to manage on what Arfur brings 'ome?' Suddenly becoming aware of my presence as I hovered behind, she stopped shouting and looking me up and down disparagingly, said,

'Who's yer friend?'

'My name is Aphra Devereaux. Could we perhaps talk inside?' I asked, aware that a small crowd of people had gathered around us. The woman surveyed me for a moment and then said mockingly,

'Oh la di da! Well yer ladyship would you do me the 'onour of visiting me humble habode,' and making a mock curtsey gestured to me to enter.

At first I could not see inside as it was so dark, there being no natural light. In addition the room was filled with smoke that emanated from a pile of wood in an ashy grate. It blurred my eyes and made me cough even more. As my eyes became accustomed to the darkness, I saw that the fire that had been smoking so fiercely was the only means of providing light. Additionally, there was a large pot bubbling away merrily on it.

Slowly I became aware of unkempt and dirty children coming out of the shadows and circling around me. Their faces pinched and thin as they stared at me in awe. Their hair hung down greasy and lank and their clothes were ragged and patched. A couple of the younger ones clung to their mother's skirts, whilst others sat on the bare dirt floor, hugging their knees. They all had a haunted look with large eyes, in small pinched faces. As I peered through the gloom I saw a small figure lurking in the darkness, hanging back. Even through the smoke there was an instant recognition that brought me up with a start. Dirty as he was, the bright, red hair glowed in the firelight and his piercing blue Fitzroy eyes stared up at me. His clothes were torn and covered in filth and he had his fist forced into his mouth chewing on it furiously. In addition he repeatedly coughed the noise rasping and hacking. As I looked something happened and a great feeling of love washed over me and a bond was forged. This was the little boy that had haunted my dreams of the battlefield. The child that had been with Annabelle and led me through the carnage of the battlefield. A wealth of emotions flooded through me and I wanted to clutch him to me but I did not. It was apparent that he had been crying as his dirty face was covered in dirty streaks, where the tears had run down and mixed with the green slime that was oozing from his nose.

'Why has he been crying?' I asked.

'Crying? We're all crying 'ere. More mouths to feed and no money coming in. He ain't even mine and I have to feed him. Well he'll have to wait, if there is anything left over then he can have it. If not he'll have to go without like the rest of us.'

I realized that the fist in the mouth that he was chewing so furiously was to stem his hunger. The child was starving. I quickly opened my purse and gave my few remaining coins to Rosie suggesting that someone could go and fetch some pies and milk for the children.

Daisy immediately snatched the coins saying,

'John will go,' and began to call him loudly. 'John, get yer self ready. There's a lady here wants yer to go and get some vittals. Move yerself.'

A boy of about twelve years appeared, as ragged and dirty as the other children.

'This is Arfur's brovver. Another mouth to feed. I don't know what he finks this is? Some sort of charity home. 'Ere what did you say yer name was?'

'Aphra Devereaux!'

She repeated my name then suddenly looked back at her sister.

'Ere ain't that the name of that woman yer lived with......?' She tailed off and looked intently at me and then at the poor scrap with the red hair and tearstained face, but did not comment.

All this time Rosie had stood silently in the shadows and merely said quietly,

'I live at the Sisters of Charity now.'

'What that place where yer gets religion.' Daisy laughed scornfully. 'I never fought you was churchy?'

Rosie didn't reply. We just stood in the darkness, my chest tight from the smoke and listened to the sound of constant coughing. Whilst all my thoughts were revolving around that little boy standing there. He was Roland's son. A man that I despised, but he was a Fitzroy. Edmund's blood ran through his veins. I stared at the child and knew that whatever happened I wanted my son. I could call him that now. He was a Fitzroy and he was mine.

'I want to take the boy!'

'Want the boy!' Daisy said, 'Yer can have him, but it'll cost yer, I've been feeding 'im all this time. I needs to have repayment.'

Rosie gasped, 'Daisy 'ow could yer.'

"Ow could I? 'Ow could you lumber me with some other woman's child, then clear off. Not sending me any money or nuffing. He should have been in the workhouse.'

'I did send some money, I don't earn any now.'

'What 'cos yer got religion?' Anyway, what yer done to yer 'air. Yer look like a nun. I never fought I'd see the day!"

Tired of the constant haranguing I interrupted,

'Never mind all this. This child has been starved and neglected, if any money is owed for food, it was not because it was given to him. I can see he is starving.'

'Yer don't pay. Yer don't get 'im. I'll sell 'im for a chimbley sweep.' She laughed.

Desperate to leave this stinking hovel I asked,

'How much do you want?'

'That's better. I fink a sovereign should cover it.'

'That's a fortune yer can't ask her for it?' Rosie interjected

'Can't I! Well I have. If 'er ladyship wants that snivelling, ginger brat she can pay.'

I waved Rosie to silence.

'It is quite all right. I will give you two sovereigns. Just make him ready.' I said remembering that I had two coins stitched into my petticoat that I always carried with me and I hastily ripped at it to take out the money. It was the last money I had on me but I was willing to pay. I saw her eyes light up greedily as she sneered.

'Make 'im ready. 'E he is ready! What more do yer want?'

At that moment, the older boy returned with some meat pies and a bottle of lemonade and all the children descended upon him greedily. Each of them grabbing the food and forcing it into their mouths like starving animals. All the time fighting and squabbling and in their haste, falling over each other. However, my little red haired boy stood back and waited patiently. He was obviously used to always being last. I pushed some of the children out of the way and handed him some pie and he began to chew on it furiously.

Taking the boy's free hand, as he crammed the pastry into his mouth, I pulled him to my side. As I did so I pressed the coins into Daisy's hand and she snatched them and crammed them into a pocket at the top of her torn grey dress. Rosie, who by now was looking ashamed at her sister's behaviour, argued with her, as I walked out of that dark rat hole with the child. I had

333

no idea what I was going to do with him or where I was going to take him. The two women were still name calling as Rosie ran after me,

'What are you going to do miss? Yer can't take him back to Threshingham Park. What about the Major?'

'I don't know. All I know is that I could not leave him that hell hole.'

Rosie looked stung.

'I'm sorry about me sister but yer ain't never been starving. At least she has a roof over 'er 'ead. If it weren't fer us he would be dead by now.'

I knew she was right but I did not reply. Looking down at the grubby boy, who wiped his nose with his hand and munched on another bite of pie and smiled. In that moment I recognised a Fitzroy expression that was pure Edmund. The child's colouring was Devereaux, but he had the blue eyes of Edmund and his Fitzroy grandfather. There was nothing of Roland in him.

'Let me help to look after him miss. I love him so.'

'How can you look after him? You can't even look after yourself. You are living in a charitable institution. I do not think they will take too kindly to you arriving with a child.'

Stung she said archly,

'Quite a few of the young ones there have had children. The older ones are in school. There is a separate house for the young ones. He can go there.'

'No, he will not.'

We three walked along, aimlessly amongst the rat infested streets as I tried to think what I could do. The child's thin legs slowly trotting along as he held my hand tightly. He was obviously used to keeping silent, as nothing that I said to him merited a reply. He just looked solemnly at me with his big, blue eyes, wiping his nose with the back of his hand.

We arrived at Ludgate Hill where the streets were teeming with people, horse and carts. An apple cart had tipped over and all the apples had fallen in the gutter. Crowds of small children had appeared and begun stuffing apples in their pockets and carrying them off. Rosie bent down and filled her shawl tying it into a makeshift bag and handed it to some of the children. I remonstrated with her as the cart driver began shouting at the thieves and tried to retrieve his apples. Just then a policeman arrived blowing his whistle loudly and the children scattered,

'It may be thieving to the likes of you, but you ain't never been starving!'

She said sullenly patting the child's head and he flinched as if expecting a blow.

As we walked aimlessly in the rain I desperately tried to think what to do. I could not take him to the lawyer's house even though they would be kind I was sure of that. However, they were unaware of his existence. Threshingham Park was also out of the question. I did not know what could I do? I had acted rashly, without thinking. Then a thought occurred to me.

'I will send him to Motts Clump. Violet and her mother are there. Perhaps Molly could take him, if I made the arrangements. They know of my child, when they know it was stolen away they will help me. Everyone thinks of me as a widow. I will resume my life there and do as I had intended, open my school.'

'But the Major?'

Sadness welled inside me and I gulped,

'I think that it was foolish of me to have believed that we could ever have been married.'

Rosie looked thoughtful,

'Just let me pretend for a while that he is mine. Let me be like his mother, till you make the arrangements, I'll tell them at the Charity that I had to collect my child and they will take him. I know they will. Especially if you say you'll pay for his keep. It will only be a short while, please let me.'

I thought quietly for a moment and then admitted defeat.

'I suppose I have no choice. Not until I can make the arrangements. It was true that whatever she had done it was thanks to her that the child was even alive.

She smiled broadly and then as the child stumbled on the uneven cobbles I noticed a cab stand. As we walked over to it we were heckled by lads who seemed to find it a great joke to see two ladies dressed so smartly clutching the hand of a little ragamuffin.

"My ain't we refained. Quaite a laidy,' one youth loafing by the roadside called out. I tried to ignore their laughter as Rosie turned and shaking her fist at them sent them on their way with her robust language. As the youths disappeared she suddenly realised what she had done and apologised profusely but I just shook my head in astonishment. Was it only a few hours ago she was quoting religion and now was berating the local boys with the language of the gutter?

'Do you want to come back to Motts Clump Rosie? You seemed so sad in that place.'

'No, it won't work miss. I'll fall back into me old ways. That old geezer knows me best. He knows that me sins will be forgiven, if I stay there. It's for the best, but I'll keep an eye on the boy till you're ready.'

Soon we were in the cab with the dirty child fast asleep on my lap, as I desperately hoped there were coins for the fare at the bottom of my bag. I wondered what sort of greeting we would get at the Sisters of Charity when we arrived with the child after my ignominious exit. Bracing myself for an unwelcome reception, we pulled the bell rope loudly and the door was opened again by the same pretty young woman as before,

'Can you fetch Mr Remington, please?' I was calm but inside I was feeling anxious. If he would not let me leave the boy there, I would be in extreme difficulty. My authoritarian tone now not representing what I was feeling inside. I was unsure of my ground with the proprietor now, after my behaviour, he had no reason to help me.

The girl did not comment but looked at the scruffy child, shrugged and went off to fetch the proprietor. Within seconds he came rushing out in an agitated fashion, his eyes flickering with dismay.

'What's this? What's this? Why is that child here?'

Before I could reply Rosie leapt in.

'It's me son, Mr Remington. I told yer when I came 'ere I had a child. Well 'e's got nowhere to stay for now, and this lady is going to find somewhere for him. I wondered if 'e could stay with the other children fer the time being.'

The man looked astounded,

'What on earth are you thinking of. We can not have every little guttersnipe brought here. It is not an orphanage. If he needs a home send him to the Foundling Hospital.'

'Doesn't the Lord say suffer the little children to come unto me?' I asked saying the only thing I could think of. I obviously hit a nerve as his mouth began to twitch at the corners and he added.

'That's as may be but we have rules. Mrs Barnes, you know the organizations view about children. We would have to investigate the situation. We would need to know that you and his father were married and.....'

I took control of the situation as the man was obviously in a quandary,

'Mr Remington, I will stand surety for this boy. If you would permit him to stay here for two months until such time as a small boarding school that I know of will be available to take him. I will pay his board until that time.'

'You continue to overreach yourself young woman.' He snapped peering at me through his round glasses. I buckled under his gaze but stood my ground.

'I will pay anything that is required.'

He smiled that obsequious smile again and looking down his nose at the dirty boy said quietly,

'Well I suppose if you are willing to pay it would be acceptable. However, it is most irregular. Why can't he go to Coram's place? They look after the children and get them apprenticed when they are old enough. We don't have any room, besides he has a cough. They have physicians there. Yes that's the place he should go.'

'No! I said firmly. 'He will not. Mrs Barnes is in charge of him and I will pay for a doctors services. It will only be until arrangements are made for him.'

Mr Remington blew his nose loudly as he admitted defeat, blinking nervously. '

Two months you say?' He looked away as if thinking what to do.

'Yes, if you would like to prepare a contract I will sign it.'

'Wait a minute.' He uttered and disappeared for a few moments, coming back clutching a sheaf of papers. He was closely followed by Mrs Ecclestone, who on seeing the child gasped,

'Just look at him Mr Remington! He is filthy. He is probably ridden with lice.'

'Yes, quite so! Well I suggest you take him away for a bath and have the physician see to that cough. You had better go with her Mrs Barnes and help her see to the child. This time he put a great emphasis on the Mrs.'

'She is married is she not?' he enquired almost in a whisper, his face reddening.

'Yes she is married, but her husband left her without any money.'

Mr Remington sighed with relief,

'Well that is something I suppose.'

The boy, who stood watching, silently began to hack again with the rasping cough much to Mrs Ecclestone's horror.

'Look at him? He has a nasty cough. We do not want everyone catching it.' The angry woman continued with exasperation.

'Please do not worry. I am sure that the cough has been caused by the place that he lived. The premises were full of smoke. It is not catching all he needs is a steam kettle. I will return in approximately two months to remove the child. Until that time I would be grateful if you would send me a report on a weekly basis. I do not wish to hear that Mrs Barnes has been harshly treated because of any of my actions. Send the bill for my attention please.' I wrote out my address, and leaving the disgruntled management with Rosie and my son I made my way back to Whitefriars, with a strange feeling of happiness and thoughts of the future.

On my arrival Betsy urged me to get out of my wet things. Sitting me down with some tea she told me that Cobham had returned from the Albany and had been told that Edmund had been there, but had left a day ago. Bertie returned to his office in case he arrived there, but there was no sign of him. Nobody had seen him at the War Office or the Barracks either. The lawyer had learned from Edmund's commanding officer that he was not even expecting him. They knew that he was still recovering from his injuries and not heard from him.

'Where can he be?' I sighed too tired and dispirited to cry.

'We do not know my dear. However, he did say that he would return to take you home so we must wait until tomorrow and see if he arrives. You know what men are? They get easily distracted. It probably all has an innocent explanation.'

'I hope so, but I know he had business matters that he wanted to discuss with Mr Stebbeds. There are matters to be resolved about Stoneleigh. I know it was playing on his mind that it was closed and being allowed to run down. Although neither of us had any thought of living there after we are married.'

That evening I took the opportunity to ask Mr Stebbeds if he had any luck in finding a doctor that could examine Edmund. He advised that one of his clients had a practice in Harley Street. He had sent a message to him to see if he could recommend anyone and he had forwarded the name of a surgeon. He was apparently very experienced with head injuries of all kinds and had written papers on the subject for scientific journals. Mr Stebbeds had sent a message to ask if an appointment could be arranged but we would need to persuade Edmund to attend. I was sure that it would not be a problem as Edmund was desperate for someone to help him with his headaches.

The next morning I was awake bright and early hoping that nothing was wrong and that Edmund would return. Molly had been busily packing the bags for our return home and Mr Stebbeds went off to the office as usual. Cobham stayed at Whitefriars to see Molly, before she left. As we arranged our things, Molly said,

'Can I ask you something miss? Do you think you will marry the Major?

I sighed uncertain how to respond.

'What makes you ask?'

She shrugged and said

'Well 'e ain't the same is he. He's just as 'andsome. Lord a right picture with them bright blue eyes.' Then realising that she had overstepped herself quickly added, 'If you don't mine me saying,' and blushed a beetroot red.

'It is all right Molly. He is handsome,' and feeling in my bag I took out the small portrait that had always been my comfort. Molly gazed over my shoulder and sighed loudly and then said astutely,

'The light 'as gone out of 'im.'

I nodded there was no more to be said. Then almost as an after thought she continued,

'If you don't marry the Major, you won't send me back to Trader will you?'

'Goodness no Molly. What makes you think that?' She visibly brightened and smiled broadly.

'Thank you miss, I couldn't bear to go back there. Just like me brother we will be living new lives.'

I smiled forlornly,

'Yes, I think that is true. We are all starting a new life Molly.' However, I did not reveal that mine now included a child.

CHAPTER TWENTY FOUR

'When love begins to sicken and decay, it useth an enforced ceremony. There are no tricks in plain and simple faith.'

Julius Caesar Act 4 Sc 2

All day we waited in readiness expecting Edmund to arrive, so we could make our way back to Threshingham Park, but he never came. At last the lawyer returned from making his enquiries, concerned that he could find no trace of him at any of the usual places. He had definitely not visited the War Office. Seeing my stricken face, my friends tried to reassure me, but I was filled with gloom and foreboding. The elderly man sent his clerk out to make more enquiries but the youth returned saying that he too had failed to find out anything. It was a mystery and sick at heart I was undecided whether to return to Threshingham Park without him or to remain at Whitefriars and wait.

The next day as we were discussing what to do, an official looking letter was hand delivered to Mr Stebbeds. Puzzled he opened it and immediately his expression changed to one of surprise. Telling the messenger that there was no reply, he read out a communication that advised that Edmund had subsequently arrived at the War Office and there seemed to be some kind of mix up and he had caused a scene and left. Excitedly I urged the lawyer to take me there and we immediately hailed a cab. After being sent from one office to another in the grand building, we located the official who had sent the letter. There we ascertained that Edmund had left some hours before after insisting that he was reporting for duty, having just returned from leave. When he was refused permission to speak to his senior officer because he had no appointment, he had lost his temper and there had been an ugly commotion. It was only when a brother officer called Paget arrived by chance that he had managed to calm Edmund down and they had left together. Mr Stebbeds obtained an address for the person named Paget and we immediately headed in that direction.

I knew something was dreadfully wrong. Edmund was not expected to report for duty, he was on permanent sick leave. Why would he have turned up when he had not officially been recalled? Additionally, it was out of character for him not to contact us in any way. I felt a gnawing lump of anxiety eating away at me. It was as if he had forgotten we existed. I thought back to the time he left just three days ago and that had been the impression he had made then.

Soon we arrived outside a grand, red brick building. There was a brass plate on the door listing several names of which one listed was Lieutenant Joel Paget. Mr Stebbeds rang a brass bell pull sharply and after some time, there was the sound of footsteps. The heavy oak door was opened by a large man with a handlebar moustache, dressed in a red and gold braided military uniform. The jacket was pulled tightly, straining over a large stomach.

Mr Stebbeds explained that we wished to see Lieutenant Paget and the burly man insisted that we needed an appointment, barring our way as we tried to enter. When the lawyer showed his card and mentioned the name of the man that we had seen at the War Office we were told to wait. The door was then shut firmly in our face. We were left hovering foolishly on the well scrubbed steps. The lawyer's face was now dark with irritation and I was cold and strained with nervous anxiety. After a few seconds he banged loudly on the door and it was opened again, to reveal the same man. He peered down his large nose at us and in a disdainful voice said,

'Lieutenant Paget says he'll see you. Follow me.'

We followed the man who marched briskly along the corridor as if he was on the parade ground. As we did so we passed imposing red doors decorated with more large brass nameplates. At last our guide came to a halt and rapped respectfully on the nearby door. In answer we heard a refined, male voice call out for us to enter. As we did so I desperately hoped that Edmund would be there, but it was a foolish hope. We entered a large office that contained several hard leather chairs lined up against the wall, a row of dark wood filing cabinets and a heavy oak desk covered in papers. The walls were covered in large maps and there was the sound of brass band music playing loudly through the open window. As we entered a tall, young officer quickly stood up from the desk and walking to the open window closed it and drew the heavy brocade curtains blocking out the daylight.

'Forgive the noise,' he said as he smiled broadly and offered his hand. 'They are organising the parade in the courtyard below. What can I do for you?' He gestured to me to be seated and began sorting through the pile of maps and papers to clear a space on his desk. The Lieutenant had a pleasant round face with large brown eyes, spaced wide apart and looked quite young, although I assumed he was Edmund's age. My heart lurched at the sight of his uniform as it was the same one Edmund had worn. The officer's face was weather beaten and I assumed he must have been a fellow officer in the Crimea.

I gratefully sat on a hard backed chair whilst Mr Stebbeds remained standing. He formally told the young man about our visit to the War Office and what we had heard. The officer confirmed that he had seen Edmund, and that they had served together. I became conscious that he was staring at me and it made me feel uncomfortable. Every time I caught his eye he turned away quickly and addressed the lawyer. He commented brightly,

'I was overjoyed when we heard that he was still alive after that dreadful business when he was posted missing. What a mess that whole expedition was. Still it is over now. Hostilities have finally ceased.'

'So I understand,' Mr Stebbeds continued, eager to come to the point, 'I believe that you left with Major Fitzroy after that altercation?'

The young man frowned.

'Yes I did. There must have been some mix up. I called in on army business and was surprised to see him there. As far as I was aware he was still on sick leave. He flew into the most dreadful rage. Strange that! In all the time I have known him; I have never known him to lose his temper. He is one of the most amiable of chaps..' He broke off, and then almost as an afterthought added, 'The odd thing was that he didn't seem to recognise me.' The young man glanced my way again and smiling went over to the window and opened the curtains slightly and looked down at the parade ground below where the sound was coming from. Then turning, rubbed his hands together cheerfully and said,

'Well anyway, it was good to see him. I hadn't seen him since... Well anyway that is all I can tell you.' He looked at me as if waiting for me to speak but I did not. I meekly sat with my head bowed not knowing what to think. The lawyer pulled out a chair and sitting down said with exasperation,

'Three days ago we were under the impression that he was going to call into my office at Lincoln's Inn. He was also expected at Whitefriars to collect this young lady who has been waiting for him. We are extremely worried because no one appears to have seen him apart from the people at the War Office. Did he say where he was going?'

The young man looked puzzled,

'Well we left together but we parted on the steps. Edmund said that he had an urgent appointment and rushed away. He did mention a lady but I thought...' He stopped for a moment as if trying to recollect something and then with a wave of his hand added, 'It doesn't matter.'

Mr Stebbeds gestured towards me still sitting forlornly by the wall and apologising for not doing so earlier, introduced me.

'This lady is Miss Devereaux. The Major's fiancée.'

The young man smiled again,

'Forgive me. I had no idea! Well if this beautiful young lady is his fiancée, Edmund is a very lucky man. May I offer you my congratulations?' He gently offered his hand and as I shook it I could restrain myself no longer.

'Lieutenant Paget, I am very worried. Edmund has been unwell since his return from the war. He suffered a head injury you know and it has not yet healed. Surely he said where he was going?'

The young man shook his head,

'No I am sure he didn't. He did not quite seem himself. I thought he had become irritated at the mix up. However, it was strange he didn't recognise me. We spent a lot of time together in Varna.'

'What did he say as he left?' Mr Stebbeds urged.

Frowning, as he tried to remember, Lieutenant Paget continued,

'He said that he had pressing family problems that he had to tend to. He mentioned some names but I can't remember what they were. Edmund was extremely agitated and not making a lot of sense. I just assumed he was in a hurry.'

The young man sat down and began idly shuffling the papers on his desk as he tried to think what Edmund's parting words were as we sat and waited hopefully. Then as he racked his brain he suddenly noticed a large vase of flowers filled with large pink and red roses and his face brightened.

'That is it. I remember now. Forgive me Miss Devereaux; are you also known as Rosie?'

The lawyer tutted with annoyance,

'No of course her name is not Rosie. What on earth are you thinking of. What made you think she was anyone by that name?'

'It is quite all right,' I interrupted also surprised. 'We do know someone of that name. Why do you ask?'

The man shrugged,

'He said that he had a letter from his brother and he had to leave immediately as the child was with Rosie.' He looked rather embarrassed and then apologising added,

'Forgive me. He said that she could not be trusted. He never mentioned a fiancée.'

My heart sank and I must have looked so pale that the young man's expression changed to concern.

'Can I get you something Miss Devereaux? Have I said something upsetting? It was not my intention I....' He looked chastened and sat down with embarrassment. Mr Stebbeds sat down next to me and put his arm round my shoulders.

'Do not upset yourself my dear. We will sort all this out.'

The young man poured some water from the jug on his desk and offered it to me, but I declined it. Meanwhile Mr Stebbeds shook his head and sighed loudly.

'You have been most helpful, but I am afraid that the Major is very unwell. His brother has been dead for some time. This Rosie that you mention was his housekeeper and the situation he was referring to happened several years ago. The child was his niece and she is no longer alive. '

The young man looked confused.

'I don't understand. Why would he say he had to leave now?'

'I am afraid he is not thinking clearly. The head injury has obviously still not healed.'

The officer still shuffled his papers and replaced them in exactly the same place they had already been.

'He said several things now I come to think of it that did not make sense. All that business about reporting for duty.' He frowned trying to recollect what had been said. 'I know he mentioned Rosie, and then something about a house and appointments had to be made.'

'Did he mention Threshingham Park?' I asked.

He shook his head,

'No that wasn't it.'

Then with dread I asked,

'It wasn't Stoneleigh was it?'

The officer thumped the desk excitedly, looking pleased and rubbing his hands together again in triumph at recalling the name.

'That was it. Stoneleigh. Is that any use?'

The lawyer grimaced.

'That place has been closed since his brother's death. There is nobody there. He was supposed to return to Threshingham Park with his fiancée.'

'Oh I see.' He looked disappointed, 'Well he left several hours ago. I expect that he is already there by now. Is it far?'

Mr Stebbeds buttoned the top of his jacket and offered his hand to the officer saying,

'I think we had better leave. If Major Fitzroy has gone to Stoneleigh we will need to make arrangements to find him.'

The young man nodded and escorted us to the door whilst he and the lawyer began a discussion as I tried to make sense of it all. My thoughts were in a muddle and I did not take in anything that was being said, until I heard the lawyer tell the young man that he would take me back to Whitefriars and go on alone. Immediately I argued that I wanted to go to Stoneleigh. It was obvious that the officer was embarrassed by our heated discussion, but I would hear none of the lawyer's arguments. Seeing that I was intent on going, Lieutenant Paget offered the use of his carriage to take us to the lawyer's office to fetch the keys and we would then take the coach. Having rolled up some of his maps he went off to make the arrangements. Whilst he was away, Mr Stebbeds again tried to make me agree to stay at Whitefriars but he was wasting his time.

After a short time the officer returned and escorted us out to the courtyard passed the parading soldiers marching in the sunlight. My mind was filled with the memory of my dreams of the Crimean battlefield. These soldiers seemed so young. Immediately my mind was full of the death and decay in my dreams and it contrasted so dramatically with these soldiers in their red and blue.

On making enquiries we found out that there was only one coach a day and it was leaving almost immediately. We bought out tickets and set off for Stoneleigh knowing that it would be dark by the time we arrived. The journey seemed an eternity. Part of me was dreading seeing that house again as all it contained were horrible memories. The other part was desperate for the coach to arrive so that I could put my mind at rest and that I would find Edmund there fit and well. That it would all be a misunderstanding.

It was dark when the coach arrived at the village stopping place. We alighted and the pair of us made our way down the country path in the cold and damp moonlight. The lawyer walked slowly, bent and stiff, but although shivering with cold, I was almost running to get there as quickly as possible. It started to rain and we battled against the wind and had to duck and dive to avoid the overhanging branches. They looked like long, gnarled fingers grabbing at us in the darkness. I had a terrible premonition that these fingers were like the grip of death trying to haul us down into hell. I pulled my cloak around me tightly as I remembered how I had walked these paths alone, the first time. So much had happened since then.

At last ahead of us, the castellated building of Stoneleigh loomed large, lit up in the moonlight. It stood out like a forbidding mausoleum. The turrets disappearing into the darkness of the night sky, we finally entered the portico, at last sheltering from the icy blasts of rain that beat against my cold face.

There was no light to be seen in the house and the area looked deserted. I involuntarily shuddered as if someone had walked over my grave. As I did so the old man began to cough and I was concerned that he would come down with a fever from being so cold and wet.

As we stood on the marbled steps, a shutter banged loudly, making me jump and cry out as the lawyer felt for his keys. The lock was stiff and it needed some force to free it. As the door swung open I looked into the shadows and thought that it was like entering the doorway to hell. I looked up almost expecting to see a sign saying,

"Abandon hope all ye who enter here."

There was no hint of light or sound, only an overwhelming smell of mustiness and damp.

'I do not think he is here.' I said shivering, 'If he was here he would have needed some light. Besides the door is so stiff, no one has opened it for a long time.'

'Perhaps so. Perhaps so! However, he could have entered by the rear stable entrance. I shall not be very happy if we have travelled all this way and he is sitting back at Whitefriars enjoying a nice supper with Betsy and Cobham.' The lawyer said with exasperation.

'Perhaps he is out in the grounds, or perhaps had an accident in the carriage.' My voice began to rise with emotion as I hurried down the corridor looking in the doorways and staring out of the windows into the darkness.

'And perhaps not, my dear.' He began to stroke his whiskers thoughtfully.

'I think all we can do is stay for the night and catch the coach back tomorrow.'

I refused to listen.

'No, I cannot stay here. It has too many memories and none of them good. Besides, there is no food.'

'Well we cannot return now. There is no coach tonight!' He murmured trying to pacify me.

Suddenly a thought struck me. If Edmund had journeyed to Stoneleigh he would have had to be driven as we had taken the only daily coach.

'What happened to the carriage and the driver?' I asked excitedly

'What do you mean?' The lawyer said wearily.

'Well when we came to visit you in London, we came in Edmund's carriage. He left me at Whitefriars and said he was going to the Albany in the carriage.'

The lawyer nodded in agreement,

'Yes, you are right. Let us go out to the stables and see if the horse is there.'

We both headed down the corridor and out through the rear entrance and down the steps into the courtyard. The fountain in the courtyard was clogged with leaves and the water had long since stopped running. It had settled in a green slime at the bottom of the stone base.

As we looked around I heard a rustling in the bushes and making my way through the overgrown tangles came to a clearing. There before me was a horse, grazing under a tree, silently munching in the darkness. It had been untethered from the carriage, which was resting some yards away.

'He must be here!' I cried running into the undergrowth.

The lawyer caught me and chided,

'Do calm down Aphra. Perhaps he has gone to the village. We should make our way there. If you do not wish to stay at the house, we can see if we can stay at an inn. I feel the need for an excellent supper to make amends for the wasted journey we have had.' He sat on the edge of the moss stained fountain to catch his breath.

'He must be here. He wouldn't go to the village. I feel instinctively that he would stay at the house.'

'Well I can't imagine where he is.' The lawyer stood up and stretched himself. 'What is more, where is the driver? He would have wanted some food and a bed for the night.'

As he spoke I wandered over to the carriage and peering inside, saw the bundled up body of the driver. His coat was pulled around him, his collar was turned up against the chill air and his hat was covering his eyes. Calling out to the lawyer I shook the slumbering figure awake. The large man began to stir and then realising who was standing there, leapt from the carriage offering his apologies. As he did so a strong smell of alcohol permeated the night air

'Have you been drinking my man?' The elderly man reproached severely.

The driver looked embarrassed and clutching his hat replied meekly,

'Only a little guv, to keep out the chill. I've been waiting all day. The house is locked. The Major left hours ago and I ain't seen him since. He was acting strange like. He told me to put the horse in the stable and when I returned he'd disappeared. I wandered down to the village to see if he was there but 'e wasn't.'

'You found an inn though?' The lawyer said with disapproval.

The driver still apologizing muttered,

'I just popped in to warm me self. I didn't stay long, but it was blooming freezing waiting out 'ere.'

I nodded in agreement, it was cold and still raining and I sheltered under the canopy waiting for the lawyer, who went to investigate the exterior building. At last he reappeared from the other side, his arms held across his chest, banging his shoulders with his hands to try and warm himself.

'Well there is no sign of him. I think all we can do is return to London. I am cold and hungry. Now we have a driver and a carriage, there is no point in remaining. We can wrap up with some rugs and Fentham can take the horse and go to the village and fetch some provisions.' The driver seeing a way to redeem himself stood to attention and tipped his hat, and referring to himself in the third person said smartly,

'You just tell him what you want in the way of vittals and he shall get 'em.'

Ignoring him I still would not believe that Edmund wasn't there.

'He must be here. There is no where else to go and the driver has said that he hasn't seen him. We must look upstairs. We have only searched a few rooms downstairs haven't we?'

The lawyer sighed with irritation and headed back to the front of the building, having first instructed the driver to make the horse ready for the return journey. Once back inside we edged along the dark corridor until we reached the wall brackets and with some difficulty succeeded in lighting some candles. At least this now gave us some element of light.

'I will go. I think you should remain here.' He said and breathlessly began to climb the stairs, his bent figure now casting tall shadows along the stairway, making grotesque shapes on the walls. He lit several other candles along the staircase and made his way up. I stood at the base of the stairs anxiously looking at the flickering images that led to the landing. I heard a door slam above and my heart started to pound but I reassured myself that it was only Mr Stebbeds searching the rooms.

I felt cold and shivered with fear. I did not know whether I was afraid of what we might find or whether it was the memories of the forbidding house. I lost all sense of time as I sat in the cold, waiting, trembling at the slightest noise. The flickering shadows were disturbing and unsettling as horrific memories of the past came flooding back. I had to stop myself from running out of the house as I began to feel a great sense of unease and apprehension.

In the oppressive silence there was only the occasional sound of creaking floorboards as the lawyer walked around the upper part of the house. Finally, unable to wait any longer, I steeled myself to go to the study door which was closed. With a sinking heart I turned the door handle, hoping that it would be locked. However, to my surprise the door swung open and I tumbled into the study letting out a cry as I fell. As I did so there was a large fluttering of wings and something hit me in the face, flapping wildly. I managed to beat it off, screaming as I did so, until at last I realised that it was only a bird that had fallen down the chimney and was trying to find its way out. Chiding myself for being so foolish, I rallied and opened a window and shooed the bird out.

At first I could not see properly but as my eyes became adjusted to the dark, I lifted the candle and looked apprehensively around the room. There still seemed to be a smell of chloral hanging in the air and I convinced myself that it was only my imagination. I shuddered in the gloom almost expecting to find Roland still there; slumped over the desk. It was with relief that I found the room was empty but it was in total disarray. Books were strewn on the floor and the papers littered all around. I was surprised because I had understood that the house had been cleaned and the contents for the most part were in storage. I stooped and picked up some books but as I did so, I had the distinct impression that someone was standing behind me. I spun round but there was no one there. However, the door creaked slowly shut and anxiously I ran to it fearing that I was going to be locked in. It re-opened without any difficulty and I angrily told myself that I was imagining things.

I placed a book that I had picked up from the floor on the desk and as I glanced at the mess of papers my heart sank. There was no mistake; there were pages and pages of meaningless scribblings that I recognised only too well. The writing that filled the pages in thick black ink was signed with a flourish by Edmund. Shaken, I knew that he had sat at Roland's desk writing furiously just as he had done so often at Threshingham Park.

'Oh Edmund!' I whispered. 'What has happened to you?' I stared at the papers, unable to stop my eyes from blurring with tears. Then to my dismay my candle began to flicker its last light. I grabbed the papers and ran into the corridor as I heard the lawyer calling to me from the staircase. He had looked everywhere upstairs and no one was there. In fact he was certain that nobody had been upstairs since the dust covers had been placed over the furniture, as nothing had been disturbed on any of the upper levels.

As he made his way down the stairs slowly, breathing heavily I ran to him excitedly waving the papers.

'He has been here,' I cried. The old man didn't listen but kept on muttering,

'All this running around the country is too much for an old man like me. My bones are just used to sitting behind a desk. This place is so damp it seeps right through them.' As I gazed upward I suddenly spied the painting of Freya hanging on the landing wall and cried out with surprise.

'What's the matter?' Mr Stebbeds asked with annoyance.

'That painting. It is the one of Freya. Her portrait in the green dress. How did it get back there? It had been packed away during my stay at Stoneleigh. It was only by chance that I found it hidden behind a cupboard. I left it in my room. Who replaced it?'

'I expect the cleaners returned it.' He sighed rubbing the dust off his jacket and trousers.

'But that cannot be. Even if they found it, they would not know where it belonged?

'You'd be surprised what people do, once they have free reign in a place. Now don't start imagining things. I am more or less certain that Edmund has not been here. We have been on a wild goose chase.'

'No you are wrong,' I said quietly. 'He has been here. Look!' I waved the illegible papers at him again. 'These are full of the meaningless scrawl that he used to spend hours writing at Threshingham Park. They are all signed with his name.'

The lawyer peered at them through the gloom, taking his spectacles out of his pocket to look more closely. After a few minutes he commented,

'Well that is even more worrying. If he has been here, he is not here now.'

'He must be,' I shouted as I ran down the hallway. 'Something is dreadfully wrong, I feel it. Where could he be?' The lawyer swung a lamp that he had found upstairs but it only revealed the speckles of dust floating around in the light. The grotesque shapes on the walls becoming more threatening and disquieting. Finding the papers had upset and disturbed me and I ran along opening doors, but there was no one there.

The elderly man stood up stiffly and trailed behind me calling out,

'I think all we can do is to return to London. It is too late to go searching out places in the village.' Running back towards him, verging on hysteria I pleaded,

'We can't leave before we find Edmund.'

The lawyer looked dismayed.

'I am too tired to do much now. I need to rest for a while whilst we wait for the carriage to be ready.' He slowly walked into the drawing room and sat down on a nearby sofa, pulling a dust cover around him for warmth. I did not know what to do. Desperation was setting in. I could not bear to leave without finding Edmund. I followed him in and sat down on the sofa in despair and when I next looked his head was drooping with tiredness. I spoke to him and he jerked awake and patted my hand and within seconds the elderly man had drifted off to sleep whilst I sat in the lamp light, cold and miserable. Meanwhile the flickering shapes all around me seemed ominous and menacing.

After a few minutes I decided that I would remove the portrait and take it back to Threshingham Park. I could not think of leaving Freya on the wall in an empty mausoleum. Leaving the lawyer asleep I headed back to the staircase, bracing myself not to become disturbed by the dark and the shadows. However, I tiptoed up the stairs as if frightened to make a noise. The frame was heavy but I managed to free it from its holdings and tried to manoeuvre it with the least sound. Every creak made me look around apprehensively as if expecting to be caught out. I had a strange, anxious feeling that I had to do everything quietly. That if I made a noise it would shatter the silence and bring down disaster. Yet I knew I was being foolish.

It did not matter to anyone how much noise was made. However I could not rid myself of this feeling.

Struggling with the frame I awkwardly carried the picture down the staircase, trying not to trip myself up in the process. The lamp was placed on the landing to light my way, but I kept missing my step and several times nearly dropped it. However, at last I reached the bottom and stood back to get my breath. I then went back for the lamp and propped up the painting at the bottom of the stairs by the banister and returned to the sleeping lawyer.

Again I had the feeling that someone was there, and I lifted the lamp to light up the shadows, but I was alone. Suddenly, I heard a noise that startled me so much that I dropped the lamp. It flickered dangerously as I desperately retrieved it and to my relief it righted itself as heart pounding I looked around again. I called out Edmund's name but there was no reply. Then I heard the noise again and this time I knew what it was. It was the sound of a piano as if someone had struck the notes discordantly.

Shaken, in an instant I knew where Edmund was. He was in the music salon, the one place that we had not looked. I couldn't wait any longer and I ran down to the furthest part of the house. Not sure if I was afraid or relieved, unable to think about anything but finding him. As I arrived I found the door swinging open, creaking noisily. Holding up the lamp, I saw him. The dust covers had been pulled from the piano and he was sprawled out on the Chesterfield. The lean, muscular body that had become so thin was spread-eagled as if he just lay where he had fallen. His blonde head was hanging down over the edge, almost touching the carpet. His regimental jacket was hanging from one shoulder, the gold braid reflected in the moonlight. All kinds of feelings washed over me. The relief at finding him overwhelmed me, and fighting back the memories of this room, I called out for the lawyer and then ran to Edmund's side. He looked as if he was peacefully asleep, but he was lying in such an unnatural position that I was filled with dread. As I reached his side and could see him more clearly I noticed the rise and fall of his chest and overjoyed I touched his cold face with my lips. As I did so he opened his eyes and a faint smile played round his mouth. It was that gentle expression that I knew and loved as he whispered,

'My angel has returned! I have been waiting. Why did you take so long?' Shaking I put my arms around him, crying,

'We didn't know where you were. We have been looking for you.' As I touched him he felt so cold that I quickly tucked a dust cover around him to keep him warm. Meanwhile Edmund lay silently, his eyes closed. I urged him to sit up, all the time talking to him, reassuring him, but he did not reply. Suddenly he lifted himself and pushing me away, sat up. He leaned back against the hard leather chair as a pained tremor flickered over his face. I desperately searched his face trying to fathom what was wrong. Then he smiled and seemed to be lost somewhere in the inner recesses of his mind, as though he was remembering something and revelling in the experience. The look of pleasure on his face un-nerved me and I tried to urge him to stand so that we could go back and wake Mr Stebbeds, but as I went to leave he clasped my hand to restrain me.

'At last my love has come to me,' and pulling me towards him gently kissed my mouth. His lips were hard and cold as again I urged,

'Edmund we must leave. Why did you come to this place?'

He smiled a weary smile and sighed,

'I was searching for you. I looked and looked but you disappeared. I was in a long dark tunnel but you drifted away every time I reached you.'

I felt cold fear descend upon me. I recognised that tunnel all too well. I had too been there when I had been so ill. Desperately I tried to push away the maudlin thoughts and said gently,

'Oh my love, I was waiting for you at Whitefriars. You said you would return for me. If it hadn't been for your friend Lieutenant Paget we wouldn't have found you.' And I put my arms around him. Edmund was quiet for a moment and then asked,

'Where am I?'

'You came back to Stoneleigh.'

'No!' A puzzled look came over him and then he gasped and stiffened with pain. 'It is all a trick. You are not real. Any minute I will wake and find I am back in that stinking hovel surrounded by men rotting on their beds.'

'No my love it isn't a dream. You are at Stoneleigh. Let me help you. Mr Stebbeds is here and he is waiting for us to go back to London.'

Edmund shook his head as if he didn't understand what was happening and then said,

'Stay with me just a little bit longer. It is so dark and I am so tired. If I sleep will you promise to still be here when I wake?'

'You must come with me Edmund. You can sleep in the carriage. The driver is outside.' Not listening he continued,

'Promise you won't ever leave me.'

'I will always be with you,' I whispered as he shivered and closed his eyes still whispering,

'Stay with me. Hold me and tell me you love me.' As he did so he held me tightly as over and over I tried to make him stay awake and urged him to come with me.

'You can't sleep now my love. We must leave,' but he did not stir and I lay close to him trying to encourage him.

'It is so cold,' he shivered.

'That's why we must leave,' I said and pulled another dust cover around him to keep him warm. His face and hands were frozen and I placed my cheek against his and rubbed his hands to warm them. He murmured something but I did not catch what he said. I was at a loss. Edmund was so cold and tired and nothing I could do would persuade him to leave, yet I was concerned that should he fall asleep he might never wake. As I gently urged him I realised to my dismay, that he was asleep and nothing I did made him stir. In a panic I pulled another dirty, dust cover around him and ran to fetch the lawyer.

The old man was still sleeping and I desperately shook him awake, crying out that I had found Edmund and I needed his assistance. At first the elderly man had trouble moving, being so stiff with cold, but finally he pulled himself together and urgently accompanied me back to the salon. As we entered, to my dismay, I found that it was empty. Edmund had disappeared. The lawyer looked at me with a quizzical look and began to tell me that I must have imagined it. I protested vehemently and ran back along the passageway desperately calling out to Edmund.

Suddenly I heard an angry voice shouting,

'I don't know where it is. Someone must have moved it. It isn't my fault. I did as you asked.'

The lawyer who arrived at my side looked at me with amazement and gazing up we saw that Edmund was now standing on the first floor landing, staring at the blank space where Freya's picture had been. He appeared to be talking to someone, his voice becoming more agitated as he argued with this invisible presence. As we stood looking on he exclaimed,

'I will settle this once and for all. The last time I saw the thing I hung it on the wall.' The lawyer and I exchanged glances, at last we had an explanation for the replacement of the painting but it didn't explain why Edmund had done it. He turned and stared directly at us as we waited at the bottom of the stairs, but looked right through us. There was blankness about him and he appeared to be sleepwalking. I started to walk up the staircase, but the lawyer held my arm and whispered,

'Don't disturb him. The shock could kill him if he wakes.'

'But he is looking for the painting. I don't understand.' I replied, watching in dismay as he shouted violently.

'I didn't take it I told you. Why would I want it? Who did? Don't be ridiculous. I took her to London she isn't even here. If you say that again I will kill you. I am tired of listening to you going over and over. Do you hear me?'

Horror struck I realised that he was referring to me and that he thought I was in London, before I could stop myself I called out to him that the painting was by the stairs. The words escaped before I could stop myself and at the sound of my voice Edmund spun round and with a look of total confusion lost his footing, over balanced and fell. The lawyer and I ran up the stairs to try and prevent him from crashing down, but he was too heavy and we all tumbled in a tangle of arms and legs to the bottom. I screamed as Edmund banged his head with a sickening thud on the stone floor. The lawyer landed at the bottom but staggered to his feet unhurt, whilst I saved myself by clinging onto the banister but Edmund lay spread-eagled like an ungainly marionette with broken strings.

With a cry of anguish I rushed to his side and tried to hold the crumpled body. There was blood pouring from his nose and ear as I knelt by him helplessly trying to give him aid. The lawyer cried out to me that I should not try to move him as I could make things worse but I needed to hold him. Meanwhile he hobbled out to the driver to summon help.

As I lay my head against his chest, he opened his eyes and seemed to stare right through me, as broken hearted I tried to comfort him. I was in torment but then as I watched his expression softened and he became Edmund again. My Major! My love! He lifted his head painfully and whispered,

'Remember I love you!' Then with a sigh closed his eyes and fell back. How I recognised those words, they were engraved on my heart. They were what he had written secretly in his first letter. A sob rose in my throat as I shook my head unable to understand what was happening.

'Why was he arguing about the portrait? I am sure he knows I am here. Oh please help him. He seems to be unconscious.'

The lawyer now returning with the driver and still trying to catch his breath, lurched over to Edmund's battered body and with concern bent down to feel for a pulse.

'I am afraid he has gone my dear,' he said helping me to my feet. The words hit me just as if a bucket of freezing ice had been thrown into my face and I gasped with shock.

'No! That is not true. He can't be.' I screamed in despair and flung myself across his lifeless body, holding him close to me, desperately kissing him, willing him to be alive. The lawyer tried to restrain me until finally, immovable, I sat at Edmund's side with his head in my lap, the blood seeping onto my clothes as I sadly drank in the features of the handsome face that I loved and which now looked so young and peaceful. All the anger and rage had gone from him and he just appeared to be in a deep sleep. There was even a flicker of a smile playing on his lips, just like the one that always made my heart race, but now in my grief I could only sit by his broken body and repeat over and over how much I loved him.

I don't remember how we left that dreadful place or the funeral. I know that Edmund was buried at Threshingham Park, next to his mother. I collected my son, who had no name, but I called him Edmund and took him to live at Motts Clump. He doesn't remember his time at Blackfriars and is a happy, healthy child and laughs a lot. I have started my school and so far I have six pupils. My son does not know of his inheritance, I shall keep it from him. When I am alone I often think of the time before I went on that journey to Stoneleigh. How happy I was as a young girl, when my sister was alive and we both attended the grand balls and filled our dance cards. Just for a moment the memory makes me smile. However, my thoughts soon darken as I recall that dreadful place and its curse. Lieutenant Paget calls to see me sometimes, when he is home on leave from his regiment. Joel says he loves me and wants me for his wife but I have refused him. I shall never marry.